CRYPTID

CRYPTID

The Lost Legacy of Lewis & Clark

A Novel by Eric Penz

Micheal,

Thanks for your support. Enjoy the hunt.

Eric Penz

7/06

ANWA

iUniverse, Inc.

New York Lincoln Shanghai

Cryptid
The Lost Legacy of Lewis & Clark

iUniverse books may be ordered through booksellers or by contacting:

iUniverse
2021 Pine Lake Road, Suite 100
Lincoln, NE 68512
www.iuniverse.com
1-800-Authors (1-800-288-4677)

ISBN-13: 978-0-595-35974-5 (pbk)
ISBN-13: 978-0-595-67305-6 (cloth)
ISBN-13: 978-0-595-80424-5 (ebk)
ISBN-10: 0-595-35974-4 (pbk)
ISBN-10: 0-595-67305-8 (cloth)
ISBN-10: 0-595-80424-1 (ebk)

Printed in the United States of America

cryptid \ ˈkrip-tid\ *n: subject of Cryptozoological scrutiny; animals of unexplained form or size, or unexpected occurrence in time or space.*

In memory of Meriwether Lewis, William Clark, and Thomas Jefferson. May your souls be at peace now that your timeless story has finally come to a close.

Acknowledgments

Cryptid is the culmination of a project I began in a literary program years ago. Though the characters, places, and events exist exclusively within my imagination and between this book's covers, much of the story's premise is rooted in the world we all live in. *Gigantopithecus* is believed to have suffered the fate of extinction thousands of years ago, to have been a knuckle-walker, and to have been of less intelligence than the gorilla (though recent evidence, as stated in this book, suggests otherwise on all three counts). Meriwether Lewis probably did commit suicide (though there are those who would say he was murdered), and his field journals do have many unexplained gaps in their record (foul play being one of the possible explanations). And it is a felony to shoot and kill a Sasquatch in the Washington county of Skamania. As for the existence of a bipedal, intelligent ape in North America, well, the verdict is still out, and I'm afraid will continue to be until a flesh-and-bone body is offered in sacrifice to the scientific establishment.

To the team of instructors and fellow students all those years ago at the University of Washington, I want to thank you for the many hours of labor you all put into this project, especially Pamela Goodfellow, Richard Clement, and my critique group. To the many hands and minds at iUniverse, thank you for your care and attention in bringing my story to life. And to Diane Gedymin, originally my agent and now my mentor at iUniverse, I truly thank you for seeing our pet project to the end. I cannot thank you enough for your persistence and loyalty. Much success to the both of us. It is to my wife, however, that I owe the greatest appreciation. Chrisann, your invaluable support may never be known to the readers, be they many or few, but it is known to me. Thank you, dear.

And lastly, to you the reader, thank you for plunking down your hard-earned cash to spend a few hours with me and my imagination. I hope we can share many more adventures in the future.

—Eric Penz
mail@ericpenz.com

There is little hope of discovering new species.
—Baron Georges Cuvier

Nature provides exceptions to every rule.
—Margaret Fuller

Science has but one purpose, the discovery of truth.
—Jonathan Ostman

Monticello
October 28, 1809
8:52 AM

Jefferson watched the night shadows abandon the open spaces of his private study as morning sunlight worked its hand across the room. The withering darkness had nearly retreated to its usual refuge among the odd angled corners and crisscrossing rafters of the dome-shaped attic before the freshly oiled pull-down staircase came up flush with the polished floorboards at his feet. Then Clark's muffled footsteps below slowly faded into silence, finally leaving Jefferson alone with the leering shadows as he pondered the news of Meriwether Lewis's suicide.

At least that is how Lewis's death would be recorded by history. In truth, he was murdered. Shot twice, wrists sliced and butchered for effect, and left to die alone in a rural inn in Tennessee. William Clark's report had spared him no details, nor had he deserved any such decency. Lewis's recent bout of severe melancholy would certainly make the official report in the papers that much more believable, even to those who knew Lewis well. Jefferson's only solace was the knowledge that Clark had ended the life of the man who pulled the trigger just minutes after the fact.

Minutes. If only he had sent Clark out to retrieve Lewis those few minutes sooner, or at least had been more decisive in reacting to the rumors whispered from Washington. And what if he had? Could he, or even Clark, really have saved Lewis so long as they wanted him silenced? No, Jefferson supposed not. His actions, especially now, had no more effect on them than Clark's killing of a murderer who most likely was naïve to both his victim and employer.

The room slowly came back into focus around him as his distant stare softened. As too did the letter he realized he was still holding. Lewis's letter. Written the morning before his death and addressed to Pres. Jefferson, though Jefferson hadn't been president for months now. Clark had carried the letter with him back to Monticello, not even so much as removing it from its envelope along the way.

Turning his back to the shadows, Jefferson swiveled his chair around to face his writing desk and began once again to read the final words penned by his dear friend. But this time he could not. The words blurred on the page as another, and sharper, wave of guilt washed over him. As if his own hands had shed the innocent blood. It was, after all, he who had insisted Lewis was the only man who could be entrusted to lead the Corps of Discovery; he who had issued the orders, both written and unwritten; and he who had held Lewis to those orders upon his return. Had he traveled that far down the dark, seductive path that there was now so little difference between himself and them? Surely he had not. And yet it felt as such.

Then his mind cleared as it finally tripped over the words on the page, suddenly reading them with a fine clarity.

I canot think. Even now I wunder why I am writing to you, for I would never entrust these Words to the watchful eyes of the Post, not even in code. Only by the Omnipotent hand of Almighty God will this letter make it into your possession, for I know now with a certainty that it is not by my hand that it will be delivered. Monticelo might as well be the mouth of the mighty Columbia, & my grave those rocky Mountains. This I feel because I travel not alone these past few days, and who it is that keeps me Company shows not himself, like a lazy shadow. But he is there. Waiting for the oportune moment. He has been sent, of this I have no doubt, to keep me from my destination and my intention.

My dear Pres. Jefferson, I know your heart is right & your orders necesary, my loyalty is ever yours, but I can no longer endure. The wound in my soul since returning has drained me, I can not bare another day. I think of nothing else but the Nez Perc, the Mandans, the Clatsops, & how this Govrnment is quikly about the work I started, of clearing the way. The peaseful life as I knew theirs to be is already fading into history, as they too soon will. I think of the wide open spaces, the sea of Buffaloe, the deer, elk, Wolves, bear. An Eden still guarded by Cherubim. Most of all tho I am tortured by that fateful hunt at Fort Clatsop. Still I can see its eyes so clearly, staring into mine as Death finally gripped it. There was much fear in them. The fear of the innoscent who lack understanding, like that of a child. But I saw too the hatred, the malevolence. The shear want of its Soul to destroy mine. And that Single moment is what gives me pause, for before that day I knew no other creature with a soul but man, created in God's own image. Yet there is no mistaking what I saw in those eyes. A soul, no less than mine own. But how, souls are born of God, a divine gift with inalienable rights. Should this mean all of creation is equal to man, deserving of liberty and justisce, and a right to exist as all men possess? Is this why my conscunce is rent and I live with the guilt of having killed a man tho I have not? Am I the same as the man stalking me, the man preparing for my murder?

This is why I have finally come to be about the publikation of the journals. All of the journals. The publik must know, must come to Believe as I now do, that the souls of men are not alone on this Earth. And for this I beg your eternal forgiveness and to releace me from my oath to you, my Nation, and my God. I also beg your collaboration should this letter find its way to you and I should not. Please consider these words, please finish what I could not. Publish the journals. Let the citizens of this great Nation and empire that you have had so an instrumental influence in building learn the truth of why we went to the Pacific, & the truth of what we found there.

Jefferson looked up from the letter with intent, to the object lying concealed beneath the white linen on his desk, and then to the sheet of paper next to it. He picked up the one-page inventory of all items brought back by the expedition and slid it atop Lewis's letter. Holding them as one, he searched down the invoice until he found the single item noted near the bottom: One large & complete male prymate skul.

He had no answers for his friend, for he too doubted. Jefferson had been struck deeply by Lewis's account upon his return. The same evil mix of emotions whirled in his own soul. Staring into the skull's empty unseeing eyes was haunting enough, but to think of the animal alive and of peering into its soul would chill the heart of any man, make him question his deepest beliefs. The fleshless skull had been more than enough to cause Jefferson to do the same. And that was this new animal's power, its value to men. It forced them to see the world as it truly existed, not the lie men lived in their own minds. It shed light on the full evil of man's selfish corruption. It was the very motive behind the actions Jefferson was about to commit.

He surveyed his now-cluttered desktop: the veiled skull, the two small chests containing the journals, and the letter and invoice he set down next to them. In spite of assurances he would make to the contrary, this bit of evidence still existed, and that gave him heart. Perhaps he was not yet the same as them. Those with wealth, power, influence. Those who had not yet surrendered to the principles of the Revolution, who mortgaged public resources for private gains. But he also could not as yet honor Lewis's request to publish it all. No, he had to stay the course, for the sake of the Union, for the dream.

Patience and wisdom was what was needed. A time would come when the nation would be strong enough, and the hearts and minds of the people willing to hear the truth. For if the truth came out now it would not survive long enough to find its way into history and be preserved. Until then they would believe the truth destroyed, for that's what he would tell them when they asked, for certainly they would. He would simply lie—a thing any good president becomes skilled at.

He reached out and eased open the lids of the two chests containing the two sets of Lewis's field journals. The question then became, what *was* he to do? But as soon as he thought it, he already knew the answer, had indeed been planning it for months now. Only now he was not dealing in theory but in practice, and he found it much harder in the doing.

His fingers were on the leather-bound spines, walking along them as he took inventory, assuring himself they were all there. And they were. It was Clark, after all, who had retrieved them along with the letter. Nothing less would be expected.

Jefferson paused, fingers resting on the spine of the last volume in the chest, and waited for the resolve. These were not personal journals, though that would be ill-mannered enough. No, these were the property of the government of the United States of America, official military records, proprietary documents protected under the Constitution. And he was no common citizen ignorant to his actions. He was a founding brother of the Revolution, author of the Declaration of Independence, and third president of the Union. But then, this would not be his first unconstitutional act, and he was not, for that matter, any longer president. And so, he held a deep breath and gently lifted out the last volume in the chest. Confirming he had chosen correctly, he set it atop his desk and then selected another, and another, each being easier than the last, until there was a small stack in front of him.

Breathing freely now, he eyed the volumes still inside the chests. And then with a sigh he closed the two lids, locked them, and set both chests next to the stairs for Clark to pick up in the morning to take to Philadelphia for publication. From a bottom desk drawer he retrieved a lockbox, placed it on his desk, and opened it. Surveying what remained—the skull, letter, invoice, and journals—he felt shameful for not including more, for there was so much more he could. But it was all he could afford. Any more and the enemy would know of his actions. Besides, nothing more would fit in the box. Not that the skull fit, but that was a minor detail he would certainly resolve.

So this was it then. These were his crumbs of bread to be left along the trail for a generation yet unborn to follow, that is if they know their history. But where should he begin? The end, of course, where it would be most painful, the punishment most just. And with that he took out his ink and quill, opened a volume from the stack of journals, and on its few remaining blank pages began composing his confession.

Keep in mind, skeptics once claimed that fossils had been placed by God, giving earth a history as he gave Adam a navel.
—Paul Russell

All legends possess a grain of truth, for fiction is too easily forgotten.
—Philip Prescott

China
May 3, Present Day
9:58 AM

Each stroke of her curved dental pick threatened to resurrect the past from its grave. Time raced in reverse as a hundred and fifty thousand years of lime accretion fell to the cave floor in fine slivers. This was the moment Samantha Russell craved, like an addict chasing her next fix. The moment when the veil of time thinned.

Light from her lantern glinted off the steel tip of the pick. She lifted the last flake of limestone, and felt the flash, the jolt to her soul as the present touched the past. She leaned in close to blow away the loose grains, smelling the ages of damp decay stored in the stone. A Dragon Tooth, as the peasants mistakenly called them. Another fossilized molar. Now fully exposed and naked to her well-trained eyes. Large enough to indeed be the tooth of a giant lizard, but was actually from a giant of another sort.

With the patience of discipline, Sam continued to ignore the numbing bite of the cave floor on her knees while she worked the fossil free of its bed. Then she raised it, cradled between thumb and forefinger, into the blazing white glow of the lantern. *Gigantopithecus.* Giant ape.

A quick rush of blood filled her cheeks, and she was twelve again, at her father's side as he raised that first tooth in triumph before his crew. Despite her ignorance of what her father had discovered, excitement had coursed through her, down to her toes. Over the years she had come to recognize the feeling as simply the innocent joy of time spent with a father who always had somewhere else to be. She rolled the molar between her fingers. Today the rush was more of sadness than joy.

The icy finger of a single drop of water touched the back of her neck, sparking a shiver down her spine. She glanced quickly over her shoulder into the black throat of Cave III. The shiver was not born solely from the wet chill. Something unseen had stirred in the dark.

From an overhead stalactite, another drop fell onto the gas lantern with a hiss. Within the realm of the lamp's light, only the confining yellow walls and littered remnants of her dig were visible. Beyond the glow, she knew shadows could not exist, yet these past few days she could not banish the feeling that hers was stalking her, leering at her from behind a notch in the wall, through the trees of the rainforest, or through the tattered linens on the windows of their hotel room.

Nothing moved. Nothing was heard. She squinted into the darkness just the same. Something *was* there. But assuredly nothing more sinister than a few half-starved rice farmers from the valley sneaking around the caves for more Dragon Teeth. *Gigantopithecus* had been extinct for one hundred and twenty-five thousand years. If not for her father's discovery of its fossil record, Western science may never have known the once-great hominoid existed at all. With the rate at which the Hong Kong pharmacies sold the few fossilized teeth and jawbones that trickled out of the hills, all that might soon remain of the giant ape would be those fossils her father, and now she, had collected. And most of them were collecting dust in a museum.

Sam raised the tooth again into the light, studying its every nook and cranny as she debated whether she should chase the grave-robbing peasants from the caves. She had done so many times before, as had her father. But there seemed to be little point in doing so now, much like sweeping the porch before a fall windstorm. Let the Chinese have their archaic traditions. Let them grind the last remnants of a fellow primate species and all the secrets to its evolutionary mysteries into their all-curing herbal remedies. Let the truth be once again trodden underfoot by politics and greed.

She dropped the dental pick into her father's old dig bag in surrender.

The bastard Prescott, cutting her dig's funding without cause. Without warning.

She threw the rest of her tools into the bag one by one.

Leaving her whole crew stranded, at the mercy of the heartless Chinese government who hadn't wanted them here in the first place.

She pocketed the tooth, keeping this last one for herself.

Making her paranoid, turning the shadow of every undernourished, oppressed peasant into the lurking specter of a communist government agent.

She closed the bag and grabbed her lantern.

And Prescott would hear about it, too, sooner or later.

Another light pierced the gloom coming from the mouth of the cave; bouncing, dancing, throwing its beam from floor to ceiling and along the walls. The sputter of tripping boots and heavy breath brought Sam to her feet. The light caught her square in the eyes. She braced for the cocking of a firearm, the arresting broken English of a Chinese soldier. Instead, there was only the winded exclamation of her assistant's Midwestern accent.

"They're coming."

The half breath of relief stuck in Sam's throat. Days sooner than she had expected, they were coming. The Chinese.

Running, Sam in the lead. Their lights hitting floor then jagged ceiling, her father's dig bag clipping against her thigh. Panic swam through her mind. They were so early. "That bastard. What did he do? *What did he do?*"

"Left us to the wolves is what he did." Megan's voice was as ragged through her rushed breathing as Sam's.

The oval haze of the cave's mouth yawned in the dim beyond their lights. The trickled sound of frantic chaos leaked into the dark. What Prescott did was yank their funding, stranding them all at the mercy of a mountain of communistic red tape that was now free to rain down on their heads. But why? And why were the Chinese so quick to react?

They burst into a camp alive with frenzy and awash in green light raining down through the canopy. The desperate voices of her crew buzzed the air, the clatter of gear being snatched up rang from the four corners, and the ever-present beat of the rain thrummed. Sam ignored it all and dashed to her tent. She had to see how much time they had left.

Mud peppered her pant legs as she weaved through others on their own mad errands. Reaching her open tent, she tossed her lantern and dig bag inside. She noted the stack of shipping crates still crowding the entrance. Skinny drops of rain slipped down through the leaves, kissing her cheeks. Megan had barely kept pace at her shoulder. Sam threw an irritated and unwarranted glare at her assistant. "The crates. They're still here."

"I know. We had an unscheduled delivery earlier, but no pickup yet. And FedEx is giving me nothing but excuses."

Sam glanced at her wristwatch. 10:07. "Megan."

"I know."

She marched past Megan, slapping through puddles, to the edge of camp. The thin gap in the tight clutch of trees offered the only view of the valley below. Her breathing gathered into tiny clouds in the late morning chill. She took a slow step back, unsettled as always by the expanse and quick dive down to the brown waters of the Xun snaking its way through the patchwork of rice fields. Her heart fluttered in her chest like giant butterfly wings, a childish phobia that had stayed with her like a bad nickname.

A vintage courier van bounced up the road from Yishan. Their Federal Express pickup, running over an hour late. And lower down from the bobbing and weaving FedEx van, a gaining procession of late model sedans. The Chinese, running days early.

Minutes. They had only minutes.

"Samantha." Megan's voice carried that same nagging tone as her mother's. "It gets worse."

Sam turned from the view of their now impending fate thinking how in the world could it. Her assistant held out a single sheet of printer paper.

She accepted the printout with a searching glance into Megan's anxious stare, but found no comfort for a familiar dread welling up inside. It was a print of an e-mail from her mother, and the absence of her mother's usual curt hello was immediate confirmation of her dread.

Her father had relapsed. His second round of chemo hadn't taken. The doctors gave him weeks, months, certainly less than a year, and could only offer to ease the pain. The e-mail closed with a request for her to join the family back in Boulder as soon as her schedule would permit.

The faint echo of laboring car engines rose up the valley.

Sam stared at the neat text feeling next to nothing, and yet everything: the grating irritation of her mother's ability to invoke guilt by pretending to respect her career and demanding schedule; the hopeless anger of science, her own revered institution, not being able to unlock the secrets to cancer's cure; and the fresh wave of self-pity for standing here instead of at her father's bedside.

"We have no choice now, Samantha. We have to cooperate. Can't give them a reason to detain you. It's just not worth it."

Sam scanned the camp and the waves of frenzy still flowing through the compound for the slightest hint of a reason to stay, to fight, to refute her assistant's obvious wisdom. Instead, she saw her father in his bed, the family gathered around, her hand in his. She tried to remember his fat cheeks and full head of hair, but there was only the memory of the last time she'd seen him: cheeks sunken, scalp pink and bald, eyes dull and dark. There was nothing left here she could do. She had failed to add anything of substance to her father's work, and succeeded only in cowering from his slow death. In more ways than one, she was truly her father's daughter.

Yet there were still the crates, the specimens, all of which needed to get back to New York. And so did she.

Megan was still planning. "I could arrange a connecting flight to Denver. The layover in Seattle wouldn't be long. Hopefully not more than a—"

"Alright."

Megan's words choked to a stop.

Sam folded the e-mail with a sharp crease. "But I don't leave here until we get this shipment off to New York. And I'll need to call Emmet."

Megan nodded, then was sprinting again through the mud.

"And make that layover short." Sam hesitated a quick glance down the valley road at the ascending caravan of sedans. They had already fought the deep ruts to pass the FedEx van, leaving no time for convincing herself that she would once again be able to watch her father die.

*   *   *   *

She rounded the corner of the tent, the kick of the sedans' engines murmuring in the air. Her time was short, very short.

Yet she paused at the opened tent flap. Scanned the camp, the trees, peeked inside. No one. Though she felt someone, someone watching her. She swore at herself and ducked under the flap. There was no need to be paranoid any longer, she knew they were coming.

Sam wiped the rain from her face and sucked in the musty odor of the tent as she saw everything inside: the stacked crates of specimens to be sent to New York, her field notes cluttering the foldout table, weeks worth of work filling plastic file bins on the tent floor. What to save first, what to destroy? Would it even matter?

Prescott. The lying, backstabbing, greedy....

In truth, though, this was as much her own fault as Prescott's. She'd been so desperate to get back to Liucheng she had put up with his neurotic business practices and baseless pipe dreams. The notion that she might find bones—bones, not fossils, but bones—should have been clue enough of the mind she was dealing with. And now he'd canceled his check and left them at the whim of international politics.

Swearing the bastard's name with increasing tone, she pushed loose, wet strands of hair behind her ears and set to work. She went to her notes first, passing by the stack of crates. But one caught her eye. A single wooden crate atop the others. It was smaller, unfamiliar. She remembered Megan mentioning a delivery earlier this morning. She eased closer, inspecting the shipping label. The stubborn shadows inside the tent made for foggy reading, but it was addressed to her and apparently had originated out of Seattle.

Seattle.

Prescott's institute was in Seattle. She snatched a small crow bar from the table and slipped the tip under the lid. The nails screeched as the lid slowly gave way.

The squeal of brakes and splash of mud sounded outside. They were here.

Her fingers lost their coordination, nearly dropping the bar. But then the lid popped free, exposing a nest of shipping confetti topped by a single sheet of folded paper. A nub of white had pushed up through the confetti. She hastily grabbed the paper and unfolded it. It was a letter. Dated two weeks ago, April 18th, from a Dr. Jonathan Ostman. The name was weakly familiar, as if from reputation only.

Car doors closed. *Bam. Bam, bam.*

The letter slipped from her fingers. She caught it, held it back up, her eyes falling on a line toward the end.

...for they will come for the bones. And when they do you will no longer doubt, only then it would it be too late.

Bones. Sam glanced up at the crate and the nub of white, and realized then that four Chinese uniforms were standing inside her tent.

Megan shouldered through, pulling their interpreter on her hip. She and Sam shared a frantic look, and then all hell broke loose.

English and Chinese filled the air in a series of rushed dialogue, Megan doing the talking for Sam. The man with the most badges, medals, and glitter on his uniform barked demands at Megan. The two interpreters translated with the speed of court reporters. Sam was mute, standing in the center of the tent holding the letter, watching the foray in near shock. Behind them all, she saw a confused FedEx driver waiting his turn and holding up a clipboard to be signed.

The crates.

Bones?

The letter.

She looked at it in her hands, then at the opened crate. A chaotic panic swirled in her chest. Were the Chinese the *they* this Ostman referred to? Unknowing, unsure, but going with her gut, she slowly folded the letter, casually pulled from the crate the one visible artifact, which filled her palm, and then set the lid back on. She back-stepped toward her table, detaching from the others, watching the eyes of the Chinese. They watched her in return.

Sam understood enough from what Megan was saying to know that a sudden misunderstanding, a sudden misstep and she, her crew, and the crates would be going nowhere pleasant. So she didn't move, didn't blink, though she was dying to inspect the nugget in her hand and read the rest of the letter. All she could do was wait.

Thankfully, the tension in the room slowly dropped two notches. Megan passed her a glance of relief as she led the group outside to apparently confirm the FedEx pickup was legit and to deal with the waiting driver.

The tent cleared, except for a young armed soldier who kept watch at the entrance. Sam took the opportunity to turn her back and make a move for her lamp. She heard two other men come in and begin loading the crates in the van. The translated discourse continued outside. So far so good.

Sam flipped the lamp on and opened her fist within the stale yellow glow. And there in her sweaty palm sat a tooth. Her heart went cold. A molar, four times the size of a human's.

She dropped the letter to the table, yanked the Giganto tooth from her pocket and held them up together, keeping them shielded from watchful eyes. They were nearly identical in both size and shape, except for one aspect, the mere possibility of which caused her throat to constrict, turning her breathing into more of a wheezing.

There was a pounding behind her, begging for her attention, which could not be given because the teeth held her fixed in a trance.

Her tooth was rougher, darker gray in color. The other, from the crate, was smooth, a fresher white.

It had not yet fossilized. It was still the original bone.

And it was impossible.

She scrambled around for the fallen letter, for an explanation. Picking it from the mess of notes and journals, she held it right up to the humming light bulb, the teeth clutched, one in each hand. She read the first lines:

> It has been said that science is not about truth, but about what can be proved. Over the years I've come to fear that this may indeed be true. And so I must first urge you with all due sincerity to guard this crate as if your life depends upon it, which I regret it may.

Sam glanced up from the letter she held with an unsteady grip.

The crate from Seattle. All the crates. They were gone.

Then she heard the double slam of the rear doors on the FedEx van and the stuttered ignition of its engine.

She tore from the tent, past the alarmed and confused guard, out into the rain and muck. The rear of the van sat hunkered in the slop twenty feet away. Exhaust rose in choppy clouds from its tailpipe. Then the wheels began to turn.

It was pulling away.

Waving her arms and yelling as she ran, her boots sinking into the black earth with each step, she made maybe ten feet before the van's rear doors slipped behind the green curtain of rainforest and turned down toward the river. Her panic drove a hammering pulse through her temples as she came to a dejected standstill. The letter and teeth still held in the grip of her hands, she quickly remembered. Remembered the Chinese and the young, armed soldier as a hand grabbed her upper arm.

The bantering had stopped. She heard only the raising and cocking of rifles, and the falling of the rain. She turned, as if she had a choice, to see all eyes, American and Chinese, firmly planted on her.

5:48 PM

The collective glare of the headlights lit up the scarred ground of their camp, now as barren as when they'd arrived all those weeks ago. Long shadows stretched across the mud to the entrance of Cave III. Standing behind the open passenger-side door, Sam set a hand on the wet roof of their Toyota and met the impatient stares of the Chinese. They stood at attention alongside their own running vehicles, their drab, pressed uniforms possessing more warmth than their expressions. She swallowed back once again the flurry of purple language gathering on her tongue. At this point she had to count herself lucky. She still possessed the letter, the teeth, and her visa home. But their armed escorts were like wild animals: they could turn on you in a heartbeat for no greater sin than looking at them wrong. There was no choice but to leave, while they still could.

With a stronger than needed hand-slap to the roof, Sam dropped into the passenger seat and closed the door. "Let's go."

Megan shifted out of neutral, spun the rear tires until they caught, and slowly eased them onto the river road.

Sam lowered the vanity mirror and watched the others fall in line, followed immediately by the Chinese. With a grunt of frustration, she flipped the mirror back up and stared out at the muddy stretch of road visible within the headlight beams. A view that wouldn't change until they got back to Yishan. Taking advantage of this first opportunity, she pulled the teeth and letter from her pockets. Thankfully Megan was too involved with fighting the road to notice or even hesitate a glance.

The old Toyota's dome light switch was broken, which meant the light was on regardless. So Sam had at least a weak glow with which to decipher an explanation as to how it was that she held a tooth of bone from an animal gone extinct during the Pleistocene. She would start there at least, for a litany of other questions had been collecting since losing the crate.

Her eyes went immediately to where she'd left off.

> ...which I regret it may. Since the recovery of these specimens, one close associate of mine has already been killed, and I no longer posses the ignorance to believe it was an accident or that he has been the only one. But as the price of truth is never cheap and I lack the credibility to bring justice to the matter, all I can do is continue my crusade.
>
> If I sound paranoid and dramatic, I apologize. I take no pleasure in it, or in the fact that by sending you these bones I may have placed the innocent in harm's way. But I have no choice and do so for two reasons. Unfortunately our profession is not immune to the failures of human subjectivity. As such,

my reputation prevents me from bringing forth this evidence with any success. You, however, for reasons that should be obvious, will have no such challenge. In fact, I'm quite certain your and your father's names will soon be etched into scientific history. For you see, these bones, which I'm sure you've taken quick note of, exist contrary to nearly everything we believe we know about primate and human evolution. For starters, they're a mere two thousand years old. Of course, you'll want to date and examine them yourself. You'll find, though, that their age is just one of many surprises.

As for the second reason, it is with regard to my "partnership" with Philip Prescott. Of your relationship with him I know only what I've surmised, but rest assured he cannot be trusted. I had been deluded to think he would support my efforts in revealing my findings, only to learn such an event would only be in conflict with his greed. In short, if any misfortune should befall me while I'm in his company, these specimens would not be safe. Therefore, the enclosed report details all that you would require to document and publish this historic discovery.

However, once you learn the location of the site from which the specimens were recovered, you may be inclined to entirely disregard this letter and the accompanying crate, believing as the rest of the scientific community that my work is nothing but a hoax. But let me be clear. These bones are proof of more than a new species of primate. They are proof of a human conspiracy far more unbelievable than any mystery of nature. A conspiracy that exists not only within our own governments, but within our own minds. For this reason you must take me at my word, for they will come for the bones. And when they do, you will no longer doubt, only then it would be too late. Your only security is to both confide in no one and entrust the crate to no one.

We have much to discuss, especially if this project of Prescott's bears fruit, so I will make contact as soon as it is safe. Until then I pray my words relay the intended truth with which they were written.

Jon Ostman

A thick spray of mud hit the windshield as their Toyota bounced through another massive mud hole. The jolt brought Sam upright in her seat as she watched the wipers smear the grime across the glass, reducing visibility that much further. Megan was squinting, lost in her own struggle behind the wheel. Sam took another breath to calm her heart, and to think.

Jon Ostman. The name still plagued her, the association anchored too deep in her mind to be retrieved. All she could grasp was that she'd seen his name somewhere recently in print. That he was working with Prescott did little to boost her confidence in him, regardless of his proclaimed mutual distrust, and only made the urge to pay that lying snake a visit that much stronger.

Folding the letter, she tucked it in her shirt pocket, her heart refusing to slow its pace as it tapped against her fingertips. She scrutinized the tooth again under the frustratingly pale light. A tingle buzzed through her fingers and a flush swelled in her cheeks. A *Gigantopithecus* tooth dating as recently as two thousand years old: the suggestion was beyond ludicrous; it was simply mad. And yet, within some corner of her heart, she felt the energizing hand of hope. What if Prescott had another dig, that this tooth had come from another cave in China she'd not yet heard of, a remote location deeper within the jungle? What if this Ostman's dating was accurate, including his belief that the tooth came from an entirely new species? Much about primate evolution would indeed have to be rewritten. It would be historic beyond her dreams.

But then she smiled and tucked the tooth in her pocket, next to the letter. And what if her father woke in his bed in the morning, miraculously healed. No, even given his acknowledgment of such, this Jon Ostman was either attempting to mastermind a hoax more outrageous than even the Piltdown man or there was much he was not telling her.

If only she still had the crate and was back in the States at her lab. Simple carbon dating and DNA tests would reveal any fraud. The bigger question as to *why* would require much more. Anyone with the ability to create such an artifact should also be aware of how easily the deceit would be detected.

Her seat lurched and hopped as Megan did her best to ride the smoothest line down to the river. The rain was getting worse. Sam sank into the seatback, catching sight of the headlights in the rusted passenger-side mirror. The haunting flavor and words of the letter still swam in her head. *They.* Despite her logic she couldn't in all honesty deny being slightly infected by its paranoia. The tooth was too solid and real. And her own paranoia of recent was still too fresh. Yet, declarations of conspiracy were always the first clue that a given tale was more fiction than fact. To be safe, though, she would mention the crate to Emmet. If it showed up, he had best set it aside until she determined the authenticity of this Ostman's claims and the identity of *they.*

For now, her priority was getting out of the country. In the meantime, she would just have to endure the frustrating burn of not knowing the location of the site where the tooth was found. That one detail alone would reveal any veracity to the letter and the crate's contents. She would know simply by seeing where the X marked the map.

The Toyota dropped into another hole, nearly giving Sam whiplash. The random junk under her seat sloshed out and collected around her boots. Out of habit she leaned over to brush it back under. She froze in midmotion, the unyielding seatbelt pressing uncomfortably across her chest. Even so, she held the position, staring unbelievingly at a book lying upside down at the heel of her boot. The title was still hidden by the seat. The cover was faded, smudged with mud, and seriously dog-eared. It was the same book she'd been shoving back under her seat for weeks. The author's name was printed in small black type at the bottom of the cover: Jonathan M. Ostman.

The level of blatant coincidence struck Sam with a chill as she reached down and grasped the spine. "This yours?" She hoped her voice came out casually as she leaned back in her seat.

Megan barely glanced over. "No. I think one of the guys left it. I've been meaning to clean all this stuff out, but…well, it's kind of pointless now." She ground the gears as they finally turned east onto the valley road.

With the sudden hope of gaining insight into the tooth's origins, Sam held the book up to the light and eagerly read the title.

A Scientific Inquiry into North America's Oldest Legend

Remembering the crate's Seattle postage stamps, she dropped the book into her lap with disgust. "Oh, you've got to be kidding me."

A hoax sufficient to explain the facts
was even more unlikely than the animal itself.
—J. Napier

Ape Caves
April 16
11:21 PM

The instant they swept their lights over yet another mound of basaltic debris to pick their path or examine the upcoming bend, the cave reached out and reclaimed into its inky black depth what had previously been illuminated. The unnerving result was a visibility existing explicitly within the limited range of their headlamps. Coupled with a silence so profound that their footsteps echoed as if from inside a tomb sealed to the world centuries ago, Jon Ostman found himself believing more with each step that this cavern could hide any number of secrets, a rumored collection of skeletal remains among them.

For the second time, Xuan Li raised his gloved hand in a quick motion to bring the two of them to a stop.

Jon glanced about, hoping this time their arrest was due to having finally arrived at the fabled newly discovered passage. "What is it?"

"Shhhst." Xuan's young, narrow eyes were focused on the cave floor, his head cocked in strained listening. Beads of condensation glistened atop his short-cropped, black hair as Jon looked down at him.

He'd heard something again, or at least thought he had. Even for Jon, Xuan was proving surprisingly edgy. Sure, sneaking around inside an underground labyrinth with illegal intent was enough to tighten anyone's nerves. And as deep a recess as they were in, even those old forgotten childhood demons of the dark could be resurrected. But Xuan was reacting to a more specific and tangible angst. One that he'd already explained had recently developed since beginning his internship with the government. Jon couldn't fault him there. He'd been living with his own similar paranoia for decades now. Still, Xuan's hypertension was becoming far too contagious and jeopardized their ability to think clearly. Until they found this passage, the chance of failure was far greater than success, and Jon was not about to leave this cave empty handed. Not after thirty years of doing exactly that.

For a minute, maybe more, Xuan held the pose, the sharp creases of his uniform revealing only the slightest tremor of muscle movement beneath. Jon's heart slowly climbed up his throat as he succumbed to the inevitable tension. The only sounds to be heard, though, were the shallow rhythm of them breathing and the distant dripping of water.

Then Xuan relaxed, peering into the abyss behind them. His whisper came out with a white cloud of breath. "Sounded like boot steps coming down the metal entrance stairs. Except…we should be too far in."

Jon took a long inhale of the damp, stale dark, bringing his heart back to rest in his chest, and adjusted his weight atop the mound of rubble. "Xuan, look. I appreciate the risks you're taking here. I do. But perhaps you're a little overanxious. It's one in the morning. No one knows we're down here. I'm sure we're quite alone."

Xuan flashed a boyish smile, reminding Jon instantly that not so long ago this man standing before him had sat in his freshman History of Western Civilization course, young, struggling with a new language, and yet so eager to learn. It was unfortunate that time had brought them back together under such shady circumstances. Jon only prayed that his asking Xuan to guide him, and his insistence it be tonight, was not another decision he'd soon regret. These days, it seemed, the ends were all too often justifying the means. Of course, it had been Xuan who'd brought this all to his attention to begin with.

And then Xuan slid his thumbs under the shoulder straps of his backpack as his smile slipped away. "You're probably right, Professor. You're probably right." Xuan glanced up the corridor. "You hear things, though, working for this government. Even in the parks. Rumors about internal policing and censuring, people suddenly losing their jobs." His eyes shifted up to the many cracks and fissures splintering across the basalt ceiling. "And that this cave is scheduled to be closed, by managed collapse."

Jon patted Xuan's shoulder and then stepped past him to end the moment before their paranoias could feed off of each other, and to keep his own mind from dwelling on the obvious connection between the apparent house of cards above him and the tons of shattered rubble underfoot. "Rumors, Xuan, just rumors. Like you said."

Xuan's now nearly accent-free English echoed back at him. "You mean, like the rumor about a new passage being discovered that's littered with giant ape bones." He came up alongside Jon, his grin having returned.

Jon could only smile back. "Yeah, I guess so."

Once down the other side of the mound, Xuan picked up their pace as they enjoyed the change to level, solid ground. Unlike the previous sections, towering basalt walls now rose up over them into the dark like those of a massive subway tunnel. Occasional gaps in the ceiling revealed other channels running parallel overhead. All of which was soon explained as Xuan fell into the routine of his day job. They were not in a cave, really, but a lava *tube*. A network of tubes to be exact, all stacked and interwoven into a maze of corridors and chambers: the result of a series of lava flows cooling from the outside in. The end product was certainly awesome in structure and dimension, but lacked any effect of natural beauty. Void of color or life, the place left you feeling stranded inside an asteroid hurtling through the cold depths of space. That the air had never been touched by the warmth of the sun only aided the illusion.

What interested Jon most, though, was learning so many channels had not yet been fully mapped, and better yet, new passages were indeed discovered from time to time. So Xuan was confident this latest discovery was a reality, not just empty bragging by a fellow employee. Supposedly last week this employee had stumbled across a small, overlooked side passage that carried for some distance. He dropped down into another level within that and found himself inside a substantial chamber lined with a deep layer of sediment on the floor. Further examination revealed a number of skeletal remains, all of which he didn't recognize, other than that they appeared primate in origin. Aware of the strict government regulations regarding historical or scientific finds, he left them alone and reported them immediately. Apparently he'd been mysteriously reassigned the next day and before Xuan had a chance to talk to him. But from what Xuan had gathered from others, he had a strong guess as to the passage's location, and a description of a tooth.

"I've seen the few teeth my father kept from when he dug for the pharmacies as a boy, Dr. Ostman," Xuan had said when he'd called yesterday out of the blue. "And this tooth they're talking about…well, it's at least worth your time to find out. That is if you're still…searching."

Jon had needed little convincing, though, after hearing the magic words, "skeletal remains," which implied they were not fossils, but bones. And thirty-seven hours later, Jon was three stories underground, following a former student of his whom he hadn't seen or heard from in ten years toward what he hoped would finally be the end of his crusade.

Xuan slowed and moved to the right-hand wall. He ran his light up the rough, uneven rise of basalt, searching the shadows overhead. Jon's hands went clammy as he stood there watching, and praying. Xuan followed the wall for a few feet, then began climbing the vertical face with an ease that made Jon wonder if he could follow. Coming to a lip, Xuan glanced down at Jon once and then vanished overtop. A long, eternally long, moment passed with Jon standing alone in the black expanse, his heart in his throat again. His attention wandered down from the lip as he noticed a curious white mark at the base of the wall. It was too geometric to be natural. And he was about to have a closer look when Xuan's round face peered out over the lip with a grin and an outstretched hand holding a thumbs-up.

They'd found the passage.

Jon was so high on adrenaline and anticipation he didn't even realize he'd climbed the wall until he and Xuan were moving along the lip toward a narrow gap in the basalt. Once there, Xuan turned, his Asian features lost in the shadow cast by his light. "There's an old code of the cave: Leave nothing but footprints. Kill nothing but time. *Take* nothing but pictures."

"And all rules were meant to be broken, at least once," Jon responded as he reached up and tightened the beam of his light, which revealed that the gap came to a quick dead end. Concerned they were astray, he leaned in for a better look.

Xuan placed a light, but sober hand on his shoulder, regaining Jon's attention. "It's also illegal."

Jon could only stare at him, realizing Xuan hadn't just been spouting ranger rhetoric. Jon hadn't expected to need to explain that decades of venturing out into the back forty and coming out empty-handed every time was a trend he was more than ready to break, even if that meant breaking a few laws along the way. Xuan, of course, was always free to walk away, but then why had he called Jon in the first place. And he was about to say as much when he sensed, more than saw, Xuan smile.

"Just being sure, because this is the point of no return." And with that he stepped into the gap and vanished to the left.

Stunned that Xuan had seemingly walked through the wall of basalt, Jon took a breath to collect himself and then followed. Inside, though, he saw only the same dead end, that is until he angled his light just right and caught the shift of the back wall's shadow. There were two walls here, one set farther back from the other. A hidden entrance, and one deceptively easy to overlook.

He felt with his hands for the way, no longer trusting his sight, slipped between the walls and found Xuan crouched, studying the passage before them.

"Not hard to see once you know it's there, huh?"

Jon nodded at the unintended wisdom. "Unfortunate but true."

Xuan stood. "What is?"

"Oh, nothing, just me being old and cynical." Jon took in the confined corridor that wound out of sight to the left, ascending at a good pitch as it did. The air felt colder, if that was possible, and smelled certainly more ancient. It was the perfect place. The one place, if any, that could have hidden such a secret for so long, and the place he'd dreamed about for far longer than he could remember. They were on the verge of history. He felt it as deep and sure in his bones as he did the penetrating bite of the cold.

Xuan passed by, having to duck to keep his lamp from grinding the ceiling. "We're burning moonlight, Professor."

Bending more at the waist than Xuan had to, Jon fell in line, too excited for words. They followed this smaller and much tighter tube, or chute as Xuan called it, for a hundred yards or more, driven to their hands and knees at the end by the sloped ceiling. A hole, or circular gap, between the tube they were in and one running beneath them came into view at the edge of their lights. The air had become so thick with particulate matter that their beams cut the dark with an almost solid quality. They gathered around the hole, Xuan leaning over and shining his light in first. Nearly itching with impatience, Jon felt the urge to push him out of the way until he sat up, the broadest grin yet spread across his flushed face.

"We're here."

A squeeze of anticipation tightened Jon's chest as he leaned over and shined his light into the hole. Maybe ten feet beneath them lay a sandy, gray floor that stretched back out of sight in both directions. A fresh grouping of boot prints marred the sand directly below them. Xuan's coworker apparently hadn't taken more than three steps from where he'd landed before climbing back out. Beyond them, Jon searched the monotonous gray throat of the chamber for any ripple, notch, or bulge that would suggest the rest of the tale was just as true. And as he did, the sum total of what Xuan had told him and what he now saw stoked the coals of a smoldering hope from years past, warming him from the inside, even until the coals turned white with intensity.

Because at last he saw it. There, just off to the right. A smooth, pale knob peeking through the sediment, its curving shadow lengthening under the angle of his light.

The brow of a hominoid skull.

He'd studied too many to be mistaken, and enough to know this one wasn't human.

"Ready to dig?"

Xuan had unloaded a wrap of rope from his pack and was securing it to a hefty notch protruding from the wall. He tossed the slack down into the lower chamber, grabbed hold, and straddled the hole. The gleam in his dark, narrow eyes was that of man about to step into history. Yet he stepped aside, handing the rope to Jon with a smile and a shrug. "Respect for your elders and all that."

Jon took the rope with a nod. "I'm not *that* elder." He looked into the hole feeling the same moment of glory. "But I won't argue." His descent was so rushed it wasn't much more than a free fall. Landing heavily on his feet, he hustled right to the knob of bone. Xuan landed with a softer thud behind him.

Years of training beckoned him to first inspect the chamber, documenting and preserving the sight as they found it. Instead, he dropped to his knees and emptied his tools from his pack. He heard Xuan crouch nearby, then quickly shuffle over. He shoved his open hand toward Jon. A gray lump of bone rested in his palm. A tooth, a molar. The size of it made Xuan's already smallish hand look like that of a young boy. Jon reached with a shaky hand and raised the tooth to his eye like a gemologist would a ten-carat diamond. The bone weighed more for sure.

"My father would have called it a Dragon Tooth." Xuan's voice sang with an excitement that sparked through the air. "Just a rumor, huh?"

Jon studied every notch, every ridge of the tooth up close in the glare of his light. "If there's one thing I've learned, Xuan, call it legend or call it rumor, if you dig deep enough it's really just the truth in disguise."

Still, this was the first time for Jon that such a rumor had indisputably revealed the nugget of truth hidden beneath its layers of hearsay. And finally touching it with his own skin was nearly an out-of-body experience: seeing himself hunched down in the sand, molar held between his fingers, the shadows of the chamber bidding their time at the edge of the light. Yet the strength of his faith made strong by decades of use actually lessened the elation of the moment. There was no true surprise in what he held. It was what it could only be. "*Gigantopithecus blacki.*" And it was all bone. That fact in itself would rock the field right down to its foundational beliefs. Only it would just be the beginning, a beginning Jon had waited nearly half his life to start.

"Professor. Hell-loo?"

Jon blinked, and wondered how long Xuan had been kneeling beside him. "You say something?"

He tapped his watch face. "Tic tock."

The curve of bone still sat nestled in the sediment at his knees, begging to be released from the sand. No one had ever seen a Giganto skull. His blood thickened with impatience to do exactly that, yet the reality of coming face to face with his cryptid was nearly paralyzing. But Xuan was right, it was time. "Let's dig."

Blowing the loose sediment away from the bone, he gently started digging with his fingers. Minutes passed without either of them uttering a word, both hypnotized by the hollow face that began to peer back at them from the grave. First one eye socket, then the other, followed by the nasal cavity, all three black and empty. Naked teeth grinned up through the sand. And in place of a forehead, there was only a ridge of bone that ran from the top of the nose to the back of the skull. A sagittal crest. And where pockets for ears existed in humans and most other primates, thick arches of bone curved around the skull. Zygomatic arches. Robust, carnal, and clearly born from an age no human had ever known, yet it was a face Jon knew just the same, knew it in his heart if not in his head.

Xuan leaned low over the skull, his head dwarfed by the proximate comparison. "Hate to meet this thing in the flesh."

Jon swallowed to clear his throat, to peel his tongue from the roof of his mouth. The sour air inside the chamber made that of the rest of the cave taste almost fresh. He exhaled it in a whisper he barely heard himself. "Trust me, you couldn't even if you tried."

The skull was amazingly well-preserved and complete except for its lower jaw. And yet, only a complete skull would truly do, to either confirm or deny the most crucial aspects of his theory. So he gripped the skull by the Zygomatic arches and ever so gently pulled. Held fast by untold centuries of being entombed, the skull finally came free, grains of sand falling from its jawless mouth. The coolness of the bone touched his fingers, the reality of it touched his soul. Decades of failure and rejection and ridicule rose to the surface and instantly were purged by the solid truth in his firm grip. Even so, there was no denying the small stab of disappointment at the void where the lower jaw should have been. "See if you can find the jaw."

"Already on it." Xuan sifted through the sand.

As he waited, Jon flipped the skull, cradled it in his arms as he would a football helmet, and pulled from his coat a cast of a fossilized Giganto molar he'd brought along. *Gigantopithecus* was defined by science from only a small collection of teeth and jawbones, so identification was essentially limited to a dental comparison. He rolled the cast tooth in his fingers, then placed it alongside those imbedded in the skull's upper jaw. The match was immediately obvious and undeniable, but, as expected, it was not exact. The crowns were not nearly as worn down from mastication as was that of his cast. Other variances from the norm existed as well. The incisors held a fine cutting edge and the canines were remarkably long, chipped even in one case. Even so, Jon had no doubt the teeth were indeed *Gigantopithecus*. Only this ape had been a hunter, not a grazer. An invaluable distinction, though surely just one of many to come, that would go a long way toward proving his theory. All of which, including the obvious young age of these bones, would fly in the face of conventional wisdom.

But Jon had never prescribed to such wisdom, and so, for him, the hopeful discovery of such remains was not only possible but inevitable. Time and the odds had finally dealt a hand in his favor.

If only they could find the lower jaw.

He glanced over to see how Xuan was coming and found him staring up at the rope and the hole they'd descended through. Jon had no children, had never spent any time with them, yet to him Xuan's expression was exactly that of a child staring through the bedroom's gloom to the closet door and its handle that was sure to slowly begin to turn. "Xuan, hey. What is it?"

Blinking after several long seconds, almost in a delayed reaction, Xuan dropped his gaze from the hole. "I don't know, nothing I suppose." His face lightened then, as he extended a hand. "The heavens are smiling on us tonight."

In his hand lay a lower jawbone nearly as long as his forearm.

Jon took it gingerly in his own hand, rubbing a finger along the fully intact mandible and feeling like the old, weathered, and beaten prospector who finds that first nugget gleaming in the bottom of his pan.

"And that's just the tip of the iceberg, Professor." Xuan motioned to a small pile of teeth and jawbones at his knees. "This place is like a graveyard."

Jon looked from the collection of bones to the holes Xuan had dug but a few feet from the coiled excess of rope...and then back to Xuan. "What did you say?"

"That this place is littered with bones. It's a graveyard."

Jon aimed his light as far back as it would go, studying the lumpy surface of the sediment and the sharp angular objects protruding up at irregular intervals. Bones. Hundreds of them. How had he missed it? Xuan was right. This *was* a graveyard.

He came to his feet even as an old, unanswered question came clear and immediate to mind. A question that had plagued the best minds in the field for years, including the renowned father-daughter duo. All of the Giganto fossils ever recovered, most of which were teeth, had come from a handful of caves, all much like this cave. Outside of that, no remains had ever been found. Theories as to why had abounded, but until now the simple answer had never been suggested. "That's it. Sweet mother of Mary. They bury their dead."

"Who does? What are you talking about?"

Jon took in a slow breath, his thoughts suddenly ungrounded by his own words. "It should have been so obvious, so many skeletal remains in one location was not natural...." He stooped over, fingered through the bones Xuan had gathered—another lower jaw, a dozen teeth, give or take—and let the links of logic unfold in his mind. But before he could follow the chain to its conclusion, he plucked a much smaller molar from the pile, and suddenly had his thoughts unwind into a tangled mess of chaotic disbelief.

This tooth...this tooth was human.

And in the time it took Jon to grasp at the only explanation, the rope hanging loose between him and Xuan fell with a thwump into the sand, the complete length of it piled at their feet.

A sudden chill, germinated by years of his own paranoia, sprouted at the back of his neck as he saw again that mysterious band of the white spray paint in the main passage. X marked the spot. Realizing his error, his not seeing the paint as a location marker, he raised his mortified stare up to the empty black of the hole overhead. He dropped the bones back to the sand. "Lift me up."

Xuan made no move to obey. He was frozen in his own terror, his eyes locked on the hole.

"Xuan."

Startled, he met Jon's glare, then offered his open hands held at his knees. Relief in not being the one to stick his neck out of the hole was more than evident on his face.

Jon stepped onto Xuan's palms and slowly extended his reach into the hole, convincing himself as he stretched for the rim of basalt that the rope had simply come loose, that no one was up there, and that he and Xuan were letting the dark get to them. His hands eased over the ledge. His boots were at Xuan's shoulders. And his pulse thrummed inside his head as his view rose above the lip and into the upper passage.

But there was nothing to see. No motion, no sound, no light. No one.

Jon began an exhale of relief, only to choke it off as he panned his headlamp back to his left. Light. The faintest glow of it. Approaching from far down the passage in the direction of the main shaft. Or was it retreating in that direction?

The answer came an instant later when the light blinked out.

His body went stone rigid, except for the swaying effect of Xuan's waning strength. He didn't even breathe. Someone *had* followed them.

His headlamp scoured the dark from the low-hanging ceiling only five feet above the hole that was riddled with hairline cracks, revealing a sight that tingled the hairs on his neck. Two small lumps of drab green clay were attached to the basalt. A thin line of wire protruded from each and ran down along the floor out toward the exit. Explosives.

He hesitated to move, even speak, the world now seeming so fragile the slightest sound could bring it down around him. The image of it quickly crystallized in his mind, of the whole cave collapsing, filling with the same basaltic rubble they'd trudged up and over to get here.

A cold panic settled into his stomach.

He pushed off, landing in the sand face-to-face with Xuan. "We're leaving. Now." He grabbed his pack, unzipped it, and threw in the teeth and jawbones. The skull wouldn't fit.

"Is someone up there? What did you see?"

Jon shouldered his pack and handed the skull to Xuan. "Not anymore, but they left enough explosives to seal this graveyard with a thousand tons of basalt." Determining which end of the chamber sloped up, Jon grabbed Xuan by the arm and pulled them in that direction. "Congratulations. You're two for two tonight."

Their situation apparently having sunken in, Xuan clutched the skull like a fullback and met Jon stride for stride as they sprinted over the sand and bones. The smell of their own fear and sudden sweat sickened Jon.

"But I don't know where this leads." The intended meaning that death could be waiting for them this way just as easily was all too clear by the crack of Xuan's voice.

And Jon didn't know either, other than that it was taking them up. More importantly, though, was how long they had. He could almost hear the ticking of a clock chiming in time with his laboring lungs.

The sand deepened, slowing them. The walls grew tighter, the ceiling lower. Yet Jon ran on with every muscle on fire, Xuan's hot breath in his ears, and the expectation of being thrown face first into the ground any instant hanging over him like the impatient scythe of the grim reaper. And then the worst of all scenarios presented itself: a sudden rise in the floor to a dead end that offered them but one demented hope for escape. A hole barely the size of Jon's shoulders ascending up into oblivion.

There wasn't time for debate or consideration. Any delay would paralyze them in indecision and lack of nerve. Jon slid out of his pack. Xuan dropped his to the ground, holding only the skull. Jon stuffed his pack in first, gave a final glance at Xuan, who was staring behind them at the dark, then pulled himself in. Instant claustrophobia nearly drove him back out. Flat on his chest, he could only grip the rough basalt with his elbows and knees, inching himself into the wormhole. The scraping of clothes and grunting from behind was the only confirmation that Xuan had followed. There was no looking back, and Jon considered the very real possibility that the tube could constrict further, until there was no going forward or back.

And then, if he'd had any doubts that perhaps he'd overreacted, they all vanished in one heart-stopping boom that shook the basalt around him into a blur. Thunder raced up their backs, followed by the crash of collapse. Wind rushed into the pipe, spraying shards of basalt like shrapnel. Then only the lingering echoes of pops and cracks.

Jon opened his eyes, took a breath, and gagged on air now choked with debris. His heart thumped against his ribs and the rock beneath him. He was alive. A cough came over his shoulder. They were both alive. This graveyard hadn't become theirs, at least not yet. "Don't look back Xuan, just move and don't look back." His voice bounced around in the confined space, sounding as eerie as anything out of Hollywood.

More coughing came in response, and then, "We're going to die. Oh, God, we're going to die."

"No we're not, Xuan. You hear me? Just move." Helpless to do anything else and praying Xuan's nerve would hold, Jon committed himself with a deep inhale, as if he were plunging into an icy pool instead of a lava tube that fit tighter than a coffin, and began the tedious task of snaking his way. His clothes tore and caught against the basalt. The light from his headlamp illuminated only the first five or so murky feet in front of him, the way beyond an endless void. His breathing rang off the narrowing, circular walls and condensed in his light. His elbows screamed, his knees complained, but he couldn't slow. He was driven by the continuous chaos he heard behind them and the hope of seeing the sparkle of the night sky one last time.

At the edge of his vision, the curved walls suddenly shimmered as if they were no longer solid, and the rock beneath his chest lurched up into his ribcage. A second explosion.

It was the wrong thing to do, he knew, but his instincts took over and he came to a frozen stop. He lay there listening, holding his breath, hoping he'd just imagined it. And not until he failed to feel any more tremors and heard only the scrambling of Xuan behind did he begin breathing again, and wondering if he weren't stranded in some awful dream that ended in a cold sweat. That's when the first thin, black lines in the basalt snaked their way into view at the edge of his light, and when he no longer wondered. Dreams were never this hellish. He watched in breathless terror as the zigzagging cracks in the rock approached and then slowly and silently passed under him.

Panic unraveled in him like an errant spool of fishing line. He tore at the cave walls, clambering up the shaft in a mindless frenzy. All sound, pain, and thought were severed from his awareness. He saw only the blackness before him.

The walls around him creaked and groaned as another violent tremor rocked the tube. A flurry of more black lines splintered off at a dizzying pace, shooting over him and down the walls beside him. His stomach jumped up into his throat, and then he was falling.

A voice called out, "Professor, Professor…God help us."

It was Xuan's.

Pain stabbed through his head, shot down his legs, as he hit hard. He coughed down dust and his own dread as he picked himself up.

Trees. He saw short, scraggly pine trees. And through their branches, stars and a full moon perched above the distant white shoulders of Mount St. Helens. They were out.

"Xuan, we're…." Jon spun about, seeing only a mess of rock at his feet and a ten-foot high scar of basalt jutting from the ground. The lip from what was once a small opening in the lava was all that was left, it now being choked solid with debris. He sank to his knees, pressing his face up to the ugly wall. "Xuan. Can you hear me? Xuan. Xuan." But minutes of attempting to pry rocks free and calling until he was hoarse forced him to accept that the wall of broken basalt was as permanent as a headstone.

Wisps of clouds floated across the pale-faced moon and the few stars poking through the night's thick cloak. He'd slumped down to his butt, his body too numb and heavy to support any longer. The cold hand of Xuan's grave came through his clothes as he leaned against the basalt, wishing with every fiber of his soul that it could somehow be Xuan out here and him in there. Wiping his eyes, he saw his pack lying next to him, the top open. Pulling it onto his lap, he peered inside. The teeth and jawbones lay in a pile at the bottom. Hours ago, he'd believed he would fail again and suffer the pain of leaving empty-handed. Now as he came to his feet, holding his pack containing the evidence he'd coveted his entire career, Jon envied such pain. A lifetime of failure was far better than the guilt already eating at his insides and the wrenching shame that his remorse wasn't strictly of Xuan's death. For what stung his heart the deepest was instead a selfish regret over the contents of his pack…or rather regret over the lack of a crested skull.

The head of a flashlight beam lit up the branches off to his left and was moving quickly his way.

He clipped his pack shut, pulled it over his shoulder, and gave the pile of rubble one last look before he sprinted into the trees. Remembering his own light, he reached up to his forehead, flicked it off, and pushed through a wet curtain of pine needles.

The safety of the forest closed in around him and the glow of the encroaching light faded. Yet he plunged ahead with no break in stride and a deepening terror that sat like ice in his gut. If he did escape this night, to provide the world with the first credible evidence of an aboriginal North American primate, then *he* would become evidence of something far more unbelievable: a government that already knew of the animal's existence and that was quite willing to kill to maintain the delusion that the ape was just a legend.

11:58 PM

Mikel Locke glanced at his watch, the second hand sweeping around the illuminated face. His men were nearly finished installing the grate across the cave's mouth. Another five minutes and the operation would be complete, ten minutes ahead of schedule. A breeze whistled through the pine needles. Gray moonlight filtered down from the surrounding pine tops. The forest had become as still as when they had arrived. All in all, another successful mission.

He rubbed at his left ear with a gloved hand, the stub of cartilage made stiffer in the night's chill. He thought of the two men they'd just buried alive, and that their deaths in truth represented at least some level of failure. Casualties always did. Yet, as infrequent as they were, casualties were at times unavoidable. And, of course, so too were the occasional loose ends that had to be dealt with. He zipped his black flak jacket up to his chin. An operation was just so much cleaner without either of them.

From atop the basalt steps, Locke watched the progress of his men and the grate, under the glare of two floodlights. The rebar mesh bolted into the rock sealed the cave so tightly only a mouse could enter.

Inside his right ear, his good ear, his receiver crackled and hissed to life. Interference was common around so much rock. He tapped it, and Thatcher's voice came in clear.

"I repeat, we have an uninvited guest on the northeast perimeter. Advise, over."

Locke kept his hand over the receiver and turned to shield his collar mike from the clatter of his men's welding and drilling. "Understood. Is this guest civilian?"

"I believe so, yes. But sir, he came up out of nowhere."

Meaning, from the ground. A hole overlooked by his men. Damn, this place was like an anthill.

"Sir, he's advancing quickly out of range. Again advise, drop or release, over."

Locke tapped his earpiece in consideration. If one of them had indeed escaped, then he must assume this man wasn't leaving empty-handed. There was opportunity in every situation, and here was a chance to limit their casualties by eliminating the risk: the bones. They could easily be retrieved, leaving only a man with an outrageous story that would be buried as a small article in the local paper. Without the bones, he had nothing but a story. Locke gave the receiver one last tap. "Release and cover. I repeat, release and cover from a safe distance. I want him followed and identified, with special attention paid to any souvenirs he may have obtained. I'll take it from there."

"Roger that. Releasing now. Will follow and report at oh-six-hundred."

The floodlights went out. His men were coming up the steps, gear in tow, their jobs complete. Locke waited as they filed past, thinking his order to release now meant that his job was not done. That is, of course, only if this unknown survivor fleeing into the trees proved to be carrying a backpack laden with certain items which Locke had been sent here to destroy. Should that be the case, his order had just created more than extra legwork, it introduced the risk of others coming in contact with the stolen bones before they were recovered. A risk, however, that was acceptable, for surely he would have any souvenirs back in his possession by this time tomorrow. He tugged at his deaf ear, reminding himself how mercy had rewarded him in the past. And if not, if even so much as a single scrap of bone should escape him, then ironically his order would result in *more* casualties, not less. Life was a bitch that way.

Giving a two-fingered salute toward the darkened mouth of the cave and the man he'd buried within, Locke issued a final order to the last of his men coming up the stairs. "String the tape."

Stopping at the top step, his men strung yellow caution tape across the opening in the wooden barrier encircling the mouth of the cave, then hung a laminated sign from the tape declaring:

APE CAVES CLOSED INDEFINITELY
By order of the U.S. National Park Service

Washington State University
April 17
7:43 AM

The approach of measured footsteps out in the hall startled Jon Ostman awake, his eyes flashing open, his sleep-laden head snapping up from his desk. One after another, the tempered thud of soft-soled shoes filtered through his closed office door and across the cramped space, lit just enough to spawn the faintest of shadows. With breath held and heart racing, Jon watched the dull brass doorknob as the thuds grew louder and closer, only to then fade away to the right.

Inhaling with relief, he rubbed his swollen, dry eyes and shook himself alert. Holed up in his office since sunrise with next to no sleep in thirty-two hours, his icy edge of adrenaline was thawing. He'd let himself doze off. He rose from his desk and split the blinds hanging over the long window alongside his door. The hall was now bright with daylight and overhead lighting. It was also empty. He pulled his fingers from the blinds. Another lapse like that could get himself killed.

Coming back to his desk, he turned off the low chatter of the radio. He'd heard what he needed to. The collapse had already been reported—a planned collapse for *safety* purposes, much like an induced avalanche. Unfortunately, during the process a freak accident led to one parks' employee being killed, prompting the National Park Service to close the cave system down permanently to the general public. And just like that, Xuan's death had been swept under the carpet along with the truth. With Jon's reputation, anything he might offer contrary to the NPS would be dismissed as another outrageous and paranoid claim. Not only that, he'd make his and the bones' whereabouts known to *them*, something he had to delay as long as possible if he were to have any chance. He had no illusions. They would come for him, to clean up their mess.

And so they had silenced him before he could even open his mouth, leaving him with no choice but to bear the weight of Xuan's death with closed lips in sacrifice to revealing the *full* truth.

He eased back into his chair, the old thing creaking in protest, and beheld as if for the first time the line of bones across his desk. They had revealed so much to him over the past few hours, but unfortunately not an explanation for Xuan's death that he could live with. He was only sure of the root cause—greed and power, the seeds of all evil.

Years ago he'd put out of his mind any hope of obtaining his type specimen, the sure bet to proving his cryptid. Though more than possible to obtain in theory, he'd learned it was not so in practice. And so before him now sat the best evidence he might ever realistically possess. Several jawbones and a handful of teeth. Only a skull would be better, convincing skeptics merely by the returned stare of its hollow sockets and the intimidation of its protruding brows. He chewed an earpiece to his glasses as regret once again stung so deep it rivaled his guilt. Beggars never could be choosers.

He picked up one of the teeth from the lava tubes and then a cast of one of the Chinese teeth. Both were molars. Both were hominoid. But the first was a hundred fifty thousand years old and from a grazer. The second was two thousand years old and from a hunter, or at least an animal as omnivorous as the grizzly. He set the cast down and plucked up the small human tooth they'd found. And a hunter of more than its next meal. Jon may not have a skull and thus a measurement of its brain cavity, but he had more than good reason to estimate its intelligence and level of social capabilities as far greater than anyone thought possible for an ape. How else could they bury their dead, indeed, their victims as well?

He scanned the row of lower jawbones at the top of his desk, from oldest to youngest. Minor revisions obviously needed to be done, but he took more satisfaction than he'd ever known by being dead right about the core of his theory. The angle of the diverging rami and the width at the rear of the jaws increased in each case. They were snapshots through time. The five jaws from China, dating from seven hundred fifty to a hundred twenty-five thousand years ago, had always been suggestive, but the jaws from the lava tubes clinched it. This ape, like humans, walked erect.

And more than that, the jaws disproved the true myth of *Gigantopithecus*. It had not gone extinct. It evolved.

In fact, so much so that Jon now believed the bones spread before him proved the existence of not one species, but two. *G. blacki* and one he planned to name *G. americanus.*

He pushed off from his desk, stood, and began pacing through the gloom of his office, past the shades drawn over his window and a month's worth of journal-reading stacked precariously on his credenza. Proof. What a subjective term, as if the truth exists only after we acknowledge it, that the all-knowing human race had the last say as to what qualified and what didn't. Yet there was no denying the steel grip the scientific establishment held on the human monopoly of knowledge. As such, these bones lying plain as day on his desk might as well be lying under the basalt with Xuan and the skull. Anything he brought forward would be either ignored or discounted with an almost irrational fervor. More than any other profession, in science your reputation was everything. A fact most unfortunate for Jon.

He slowed as he paced along his shelves of texts and collection of plaster castes. The bottom shelf held a series of hominoid skulls, all staring out at him as he passed. The chimpanzee, the orangutan, the gorilla. At the end of the shelf, as he still had no skull for representation, sat a stone sculpted into the likeness of a head. It came to life with just a few simple, broad strokes, creating an uncanny likeness to that of the mountain gorilla. Uncanny for sure, as the sculpture had been carved ten thousand years ago by Native Americans on the British Columbia coast. Resting a hand on the cool stone, he felt the urgent ticking of his wall clock in his bones. He couldn't hide out in his office any longer. It would be one of the first places they searched. But he had nowhere else to go, and, worse, he had no one to turn to. Even if he did, the bones were simply not safe with him and would need to be documented by someone else, someone with just the right reputation.

He gave the stone head one last rub before turning back to his desk. And if she could be found and if she would consent, then he knew exactly the woman for the job.

The grating jingle of his cell phone split the room's protective silence. Jon spun around in startled reflex, then froze as he stared at the small black phone on the corner of his desk. It rang a second time. And a third. On the fourth he found the courage to pick it up and check the caller ID. The number was foreign to him, but from west of the mountains, near Seattle. The fifth and final ring before switching to voice mail hung in the air as he debated the risks and the chance they had learned his unlisted and rarely given-out number so soon. With a cringe, he pressed the answer button. "Hello."

His voice hid none of his anxiety.

"Is this Dr. Jon Ostman?"

He looked to the locked door, taking a wary step toward it. "Who wants to know? And how'd you get this number?"

An arrogant chuckle came through the phone. "This is Philip Prescott of the Prescott Institute, and I got your number off your grant application from two years ago."

Jon stood at the locked door, recalling the application he'd sent and the cold rejection he'd received in return. His nerves had gotten him worked up for nothing yet again this morning. He took in a breath and thought of the quickest way to end the conversation. He had no time now for grant discussions. Being rude usually worked like a charm. "So, what, you've changed your mind? I thought you had the world's diseases to cure, or have you already run out of patients?"

"I'm calling because I read your book, Jon."

Jon's chest went tight. The tone of Prescott's voice was too sober. Usually such a comment preceded a joke, but Jon didn't feel one coming. This call was not about his application. His only response was speechless indecision.

"You never said, though, why you suddenly switched fields back in the seventies. Did you get tired of the hunt?"

A single bead of sweat ran down the inside of his arm. This conversation was now well off the beaten path, and not seeing any destination on the horizon unsettled Jon more than the voices he suddenly heard out in the hall. "If you had indeed read my book, I'd hope the answer was clear. Closed minds open best a step at a time. Besides, I've learned this animal is much easier to find once it's dead and buried."

Another chuckle. "I guess I missed that."

The voices outside persisted. Jon ventured a peek through the blinds, Prescott's voice in his ear now nothing but the buzz of a mosquito. At the other end of the hallway, the department's secretary was talking to a man and pointing Jon's way. The stranger's hair was shaved close to his head and he wore loose-fitting, athletic attire. His left ear, even from this distance appeared seriously deformed. He was not from academia.

"…you might be interested in examining it…."

The stranger glanced down the hall and Jon yanked his fingers from the blinds. They'd found him.

His body tingling with adrenaline and dread, he scanned his office, seeing first the shaded window, then his soiled backpack from last night.

"So what do you think?"

Prescott. Damn. Jon held the tiny phone up to his ear with his shoulder as he threw the bones into his pack. "I'm sorry, think about what?"

"About driving out this weekend to the institute."

Light footsteps stopped right outside the door.

He glanced up at the doorknob, afraid Prescott wouldn't be the only one to hear his whisper. "Why wait for the weekend? I'll be there this evening." And find out then what it was he'd been invited to do.

Silencing Prescott's enthusiastic response with a press of the END button, Jon pocketed his phone, shouldered his pack, and heard the first jiggle of the doorknob.

$$* \quad * \quad * \quad *$$

Standing at the closed door to the corner office, Locke watched the narrow blinds for the slightest hint of movement, sure he had just seen them split by two fingers. If so, combined with the missing nameplate on the door, it meant his visit was expected. It also meant this loose end was unraveling fast.

He checked the knob. Locked. No surprise there.

He rapped a knuckle softly below the empty brass plate. "Dr. Ostman?"

Silence.

He rapped again. "Dr. Ostman?" More silence.

The halls to the left and behind him were still empty. He slipped a gloved hand inside his jacket and brought out his tool. A breath later he heard the satisfying click of the lock releasing.

Twisting the knob as he reached into his jacket for the grip of his taser, he savored the rush. His man was cornered. There was no avoiding the use of force.

In one motion he stepped inside, closed the door, and had his taser aimed. But there was no target, only a dim, cluttered office lit by a single desk lamp and a swath of sunlight pouring in through a hastily opened window. The shades lay torn on the floor.

He lowered the taser to his side, then tucked it safely home.

Bones sat spread atop the desk, giving him a sudden and false elation of easy success. But they were casts only, copies of fossils labeled as *Gigantopithecus* and with dates in the early seventies. He returned the one jawbone to the desktop. These were harmless, unlike the bones that were now halfway across campus.

He picked up a book sitting among the fossils.

A Scientific Inquiry into North America's Oldest Legend. By Jonathan M. Ostman.

The first chill he'd felt in years shimmied down his spine. He lowered the book and scanned the shelves. Ape skulls. An ape sculpture. Plaster castes of over a dozen clear tracks, all of them dusty and bearing signs of aging.

A fanatic.

He'd let a fanatic escape last night with bones. With bones. And a fanatic *scientist* at that.

He tucked the book inside his jacket and stared out the window at the lazy blue sky and crowds of students hustling to their first class of the day. His hand rose to touch his ear.

Loose ends. Loose ends and casualties. Inevitably one leads to the other.

The Olympic will surely be attacked again and again for its timber.
—John Muir

Olympic National Forest
April 19
9:37 AM

"I understand the business of two nights ago is still unresolved."

Mikel Locke shortened his stride to stay just shy of Director Frank Keyes's shoulder as they picked their way through the stumps and over the raw land that had been laid bare by the recent clear cut. The director's cheeks were flushed, but other than that he appeared as strong as he did before the bypass. His firm hand at the helm had been missed. And it was good to have him back in the field where, like all good leaders, he was most effective. "Loose ends only, sir. No damage has been done, and my men will have them tied off neatly very shortly."

"Good, because there are other concerns in Washington that need attention. Our new secretary is still playing by his own rules. Resolve this business with these bones and report to me at the superintendent's office in forty-eight hours."

Director Keyes had stopped, his white, bushy brows arched above eyes set intently on Locke's. Locke matched the stare as he clasped his hands behind his back. Two days wasn't much time, considering he had no idea where Ostman and the bones were. But he wasn't about to insult either the director or himself with excuses. Committing with a nod, Locke looked to the top of the barren ridge where Superintendent Tujillo and the timber exec were conferring. "Then you'll be staying for awhile?"

"Unfortunately." The director's gaze also shifted to the ridge top. "Those two seem to think they're the only ones cutting west of the Mississippi. I've got timber projects, mining, you name it, from the Everglades to Yellowstone that need managing. But...when the largest timber company in the world asks for a little handholding, you give it."

"I wouldn't know. I was never any good at that." Locke studied the clean lines of the Sutherland Timber Company helicopter bathing in the rare, crisp sunlight with a wall of eighty-foot tall spruce trunks standing in the background. Among many things, he still missed the high that came from jumping out of a chopper into the black of night with a handful of men who'd die for you without hesitation, and usually did. The rush was like none other. His hand went reflexively to his left ear. Fortunately for him, there were other ways to serve his country.

Director Keyes tapped Locke's arm as he trudged up the hill. "Which is just as well. This country has enough politicians, all of whom would be useless without men like you."

Locke smiled and nodded in agreement at the meaning between the lines. Politicians and the messes they made were job security for men like him.

At the top of the ridge, Locke held back, letting the director join the superintendent and the exec alone. He stood at ease just within earshot of the three men.

After the handshaking, the suit pointed his way. "Who's that? It was only supposed to be the three of us."

Without even the slightest glance Locke's way, Keyes replied, "That, Jack, is someone it would be best you did not know exists. Good enough?"

Jack, who Locke took to be Jack Sutherland Jr., gave a long skeptical look his way then turned a fleece-clad back to him. Locke returned the gesture and turned toward the newly exposed view of a distant Puget Sound.

He wasn't surprised to hear Sutherland's impatient voice first, immediately drilling the director with a litany of concerns and complaints. Corporations had grown fat and spoiled on the tit of America. Interesting to him, though, were the impassioned concerns regarding the newly appointed secretary of the interior and securing the upcoming cut. Locke, or at least those he commanded, would certainly be involved in both matters, and there was no doubt why the director had sent for him.

Savoring a deep breath of the long-awaited spring air, he gazed beyond the expanse of stumps and dirt, beyond the thick rainforest descending unbroken below the clear-cut. He followed the logging road he'd arrived on as it wound through the blanket of evergreen like a brown river, ending thirty miles down the valley at the new View Top development on the edge of the national forest—the only sign of civilization to be seen, other than the Seattle skyline flirting with the horizon across the sound.

The clarity of the infinite sky overhead was so pure the three sisters were even visible to the southeast: the broad, white shoulders of Rainier, Adams peaking over the Cascades, and the knob of St. Helens brooding near Oregon. Just two nights past he had been on the old volcano's slopes. As rare as it was, he could now admit, if only to himself, that he'd made the wrong decision that night. So much for the praises of mercy.

Sutherland's hot voice rose again over the director's, spurring Locke to turn around.

"I don't care if things are different than the last time we cut in the Olympics, these forests are still some of the most profitable in the world. And they're made even more so because most of our tree farms are useless for another decade, and South America is becoming a red-tape nightmare. No, we need guarantees these contracts will be honored, not more empty assurances."

"Jack, we both know the risks." Director Keyes offered a half-smile and pointed to a spot on the map held out by Superintendent Trujillo. "But I can guarantee you this: down the other side of this ridge lies the largest and most remote stretch of old-growth anywhere in the lower forty-eight. Over the past two decades we've slowly cut public access off to the entire valley, leaving your logging road here the only way in or out. It's all yours, Jack. Just stick to the contract, don't get greedy, and you won't have any troubles."

"And what of rumors that the secretary is revoking all contracts made by the NPS? We need to know—"

"Come on, Jack." The director put a hand on Sutherland's shoulder and started them toward the chopper. Locke fell in line several paces back, hoping this babysitting session would be over soon so he and the director could get down to real business. "You're not new to this game. Appointing Secretary Mason is simply the president's attempt at fulfilling his environmental campaign promises. And if the president and the secretary don't already know, they will soon learn two important facts about America: We didn't become a coast-to-coast empire and world power by hoarding and locking up our resources, and the Constitution ensures change occurs on the scale of generations, not presidential administrations. So don't worry, your contracts will be honored, and your mills will stay open."

They were only a few yards from the sharp row of spruce running laser-straight along the ridgeline. Every third or fourth trunk was marked by a large red X, designating the park boundary. Sutherland Timber Company hadn't cheated even an inch over the line. At least not yet.

At this distance, though, Locke noticed a measurable decrease in temperature, and not only from the shade cast by the spruce tops eight stories up. The trees were packed so tightly that nothing but darkness was visible within, yet they couldn't contain the sunless chill they harbored.

Glancing ahead, he realized they'd stopped. The superintendent and Sutherland were staring at a patch of ground, Sutherland's eyes wide with panic. Director Keyes was squatting on his heels, looking back and motioning for him with a calmness completely at odds with Sutherland's expression.

Locke kept his hands clasped at his lower back as he slowly strode over, considering the possibilities. There weren't many.

"Tell me that's not what it looks like, Frank." Sutherland finally found his voice. He took a step back, pointing at the dirt. "Tell me it's not."

Locke came up and dropped to a knee next to Director Keyes, whose lifted brows meant he wasn't as calm as he appeared. And with good reason. Sunken into the rich, black soil was the worst and most unexpected of possibilities—a single week-old track.

He traced a finger inside the lonely footprint. The ridges usually separating the five digits had worn away, leaving an expanded hourglass shape roughly sixteen inches long and two deep. An adult male. Judging from the old injury—evident by the deformed outer shank—and from the track being outside the park, the odds were it had been left by a rogue male prowling the perimeter, looking for his own territory. This created an especially nasty scenario, considering the homes going in just down the valley.

Aware of the weight of their eyes, Locke nodded at the director. "A week old, at least. Could be fifty miles from here by now." Ideally in the direction of the park's interior.

"A week old! Hell, what if one of my men saw this thing. Dammit." Sutherland started pacing like a nervous cat. "Since the seventies, you guys have been assuring us you wiped these things out, and now you're telling me they're traipsing through my cut."

The director rose, his patience clearly waning. He took a strong step forward, landing his boot exactly on the track and erasing it with a sweep of his heel. "Jack, take a breath and listen. There has always been the chance a few small populations survived. Have a good look around."

Locke kept an eye on Sutherland while searching the ground for more tracks. Somewhere out there a fanatic was running around with a handful of bones, and now he had the real deal popping up out of nowhere in the middle of a damn logging operation.

"Nothing but thick, virgin timber and mountain after mountain right down to the sound, Jack. Exterminating an entire species in such terrain isn't that easy, nor is definitively documenting your success. Trust me though, what few individuals remain are safely hidden within the most rugged of the national parks, like here in the Olympics. And when they do turn up, we track them down and eliminate them, just as we will with this one."

Locke caught the glance the director gave him, the same as written orders. Not that it was needed. He stopped at the edge of the trees, feeling that same foreboding presence that he did whenever he was in these forests. Hunting this male was a given, as much for business as for pleasure. It had been a few years since he'd had the opportunity. They may only be animals, but they were more of a challenge than any man he'd hunted. He pushed his hands into his pockets with a sigh. The trail was so cold though, he'd have a better chance of finding a needle in a haystack the size of Rainier.

Sutherland's pacing now took him in a circle. "And what if you don't? What if someone else gets to it first, someone not as discreet as you? Then you'll have no choice but to acknowledge their existence. They'll go on the endangered species list, and we won't be able to so much as look at another tree west of the Rockies, let alone touch it with a saw."

"Dammit, Jack, stop. Listen. Forget about the list. They can't go on it if they're already extinct. You have my word this track is the last sign you'll ever see, the last sign they ever existed."

Director Keyes brought Sutherland to a dead stop by stepping right into the stunned man's face.

The awkward silence was finally broken by the ring of Locke's satellite phone. Pulling it from his jacket, he moved back from the group. "This is Locke."

After the usual time delay, Thatcher's voice responded loud and clear. "Sir. Thatcher."

With the group having regained their voices, though with less fervor, Locke separated himself farther, stopping right at the trees. "Tell me you have good news."

"I have news, but it's not all that good. We pulled Ostman's cell phone records. There hasn't been an incoming or outgoing call since early the morning of the seventeenth, probably just before he disappeared. The call was incoming from a Philip Prescott, owner of a small research institute in North Bend. Specializes mostly in pharmaceutical R&D, and one of the few U.S. labs that provides animal testing."

Sutherland and the director shook hands, each man faking the same smiles they'd worn at their greeting, then Sutherland turned for the chopper, setting the clock ticking. Locke's phone conversation would be over as soon as those blades started turning. "Has surveillance been set up on the institute yet?"

"Yes, and it appears we've missed them both by a day. We have reason to believe they left the institute yesterday with three to five other men in two Suburbans heavily loaded with equipment. But here's the part you should be sitting down for. This Prescott turns out to be a bit of a dabbler in other interests. Specifically, he's been heavily involved in gorilla research in the Congo and chimpanzee work in Zaire. And the kicker is that he's the sole backer of several digs in China. Need I say more?"

The second chill in nearly as many days shot down to his feet. "Only if you were about to tell me where they were headed."

"Negative, sir. And no leads as yet."

"What about the possibility Ostman has already unloaded the bones on someone else?"

"We've drawn up a list of candidates and have men following up on them as we speak."

The whine of the rotors coming to life split the air.

Locke put a finger in his left ear and pressed the phone tight to his other. "Good, but I want you on the first name on the list."

"Already on my way to the airport. Plane leaves for China in four hours."

"China?"

"Yes, sir. A Dr. Samantha Russell, daughter of Dr. Paul Russell, the man who discovered and named *Gigantopithecus*. She's the project lead for one of Prescott's digs."

The finger in his ear started picking at the cartilage, pressing against it until he felt the pain. He was yelling into the phone. "Then your orders are simple. Confirm receipt of all the bones, then bury them with this Dr. Russell in China."

Heads ducked, the director and superintendent trotted through the swirling dirt as the blades finally bit the air and lifted the chopper. Any reply by Thatcher was lost in the roaring chatter of the rotors, but Locke had no doubt his man had responded unquestioningly in the affirmative.

That evolutionary changes have occurred is a fact,
how evolution actually works involves theories.
—Delta Willis

Insensibly, one begins to twist facts to suit theories
instead of theories to suit facts.
—Sherlock Holmes

China
May 4
9:21 AM

"Emmet, it's Sam. I haven't much time. My plane's already boarding." Sam dropped her carry-on onto the metal shelf beneath the public phone with a clunk, pushing up the tattered cover of Ostman's book from an outside pocket.

"Well, good evening to you, too, or should I say, good morning?"

She stood with her back against the phone to stay free of the hordes passing by while keeping an eye on the crowd. That she did so with an attention to detail she hadn't possessed twenty-four hours ago made her skin crawl with shame, as had spending all night reading Ostman's damn book and studying every angle of his tooth. The longer she carried both, the more she wondered if paranoia were contagious and could be transmitted through reading a letter. "I was going to leave a message, but I should have known you'd be at the museum this time of night."

"Oh, I'm just spending some quality time with George."

Emmet's voice added ten years to the man's already senior status. It also made Sam ripe with homesickness. But not for the home she was heading to. "How is he anyway?"

"Good. You won't believe how much he's grown." His voice was dead, even in tone, but she knew it was his best attempt at humor. "We weren't expecting you back so soon, though. Everything all right?"

"I know. Change of plans. The Chinese government suddenly decided we'd overstayed our welcome." She couldn't help the awkward acceleration in her voice. "And anyway…my father's apparently not doing well. Family's all coming out for one last…."

"Oh, Samantha. We always knew that…." Emmet was doing no better than her. "I mean, take your time. I'm knocking on the door myself, and what I wouldn't give for a daughter like you to say good-bye to."

Sam sniffed, stood up straight, and with several quick blinks wiped away images of her father in bed waiting for her even now. "Well, you should be getting all the specimens soon. They were sent yesterday. There's nothing new really, but just the same, I'll get to New York as soon as I can to help."

"Samantha, listen. Don't write this all off as a failure simply because that bastard Prescott yanked the rug from under us. You don't *know* what we'll learn from these new specimens until we examine them. We may not have the answers in time for your father to hear them, but we will have them."

Sam realized she'd slipped a hand into her pocket and around the tooth. The book was staring back at her from her carry-on. Mentioning either would do no good. She didn't believe them herself. "You're right, I know. It's just that I'm afraid what we've got is all we'll ever get."

She didn't catch Emmet's reply as an announcement came over the Wuzhou Airport PA system. If any of it were in English, it might as well have been Mandarin. All she understood was 'Flight 934', her flight. Most likely the last call for boarding. "Listen, gotta run, but one last thing. I need you to set aside one of the crates till I get there. All right?"

"Uh, sure. And I'll know which crate how?"

Sam squeezed the molar in her pocket, testing yet again that it was real. The solid resistance of the bone never got her quite all the way there, but close enough to need to be the one to open the crate and to feed that infectious seed planted in her mind by Ostman's choice words: *they will come for it.* Assuming it arrived, of course. "You'll know the one. It originated out of Seattle." She shouldered her carry-on, swinging its weight onto her back. "I'll check in when I can. See you soon."

As she hung up the phone, she saw the attendant at her gate take the ticket from the last person in line. Elbowing her way into the masses, Sam pushed for the open doorway and thought of Megan sitting alone at the window, itching with impatience. She rushed along the row of phones where the current moved best until she bumped into a man near the end. She turned and slowed just enough to apologize. He was looking over his shoulder, too, his face lit up as if he'd expected to see someone running off with his wallet, and then quickly turned back to his conversation.

Continuing her dash for the door, Sam's apology died on her lips, but the man's steel-blue eyes lingered in her mind. Why, she hadn't the time to fully consider, other than to note the obvious. He was the first American she'd seen outside of her crew in weeks, and attractive at that. And from what she overheard, his business here was unfinished, like hers. And then, of course, she thought of Ian, and his steel-blue eyes.

Holding out her ticket, she sprinted to the attendant as she was closing the door, then was striding down the ramp, stuffing her ticket stub in her carry-on.

She had no idea what the man's business was, but by his voice it was clear failure wasn't a word in his vocabulary. Was it in hers? At what point did she leave her father's business unfinished to pursue her own?

When she mustered the courage to face him and say good-bye, that's when.

Until then she had to keep his work alive, a commitment that became less rational by the day as evidenced by her temptation to give the tooth in her pocket and the book in her carry-on more credence than they deserved.

And what was her deal with blue eyes anyway? Was she cursed to think of Ian every time she crossed paths with a man with magnetic blue eyes?

Emmet hung up and stood at his desk a moment, staring at the phone. He rubbed a finger across his forehead then waved it through the air and turned for his workshop.

He truly hoped Sam did make it to her father's side, for both of their sakes. Dying was unnerving at best, especially a slow death of cancer. But doing so with things left unsaid was a life sentence for the survivor, and who knows what for the deceased. If Emmet were a betting man, though, he'd put all his retirement on seeing Sam before her father did, if her father ever did again. He rubbed a finger across his forehead. She was too good at justification. There was always something more urgent.

He passed through the dim shadows of his office into the well-lit adjoining workshop, the silence of the sleeping museum nearly as heavy in the air as the scent of yak hair and adhesive. Shaking the inevitable tragedy awaiting Sam from his mind, he stepped up to his workbench and studied his sketch, refocusing on the task at hand. Picking up his fine trimming shears, he turned from his bench and addressed George with a wide grin of satisfaction. "Now then, where were we?"

Filling an entire corner of the room, George stood on all fours, like the rest of his knuckle-walking relatives. His crested head was held high and powerful, his deep-set eyes peering back at Emmet. The simple expression on his face belied an intelligence equal to his smaller cousins, the gorilla and chimpanzee. Coarse golden hair flowed down his back, fading to an auburn cast on his broad, humped shoulders that were eight feet above the hydraulic platform supporting his massive bulk. A brass plate bore his Greek derived name: *Gigantopithecus.* Giant ape. No printed translation was given, for none was needed.

Unfortunately, George was more art than science, though, as his ancestors took nearly all their secrets to the grave with them. But Emmet beamed with pride just the same. Combined with the specimens Sam had sent, George was sure to steal the new exhibit. He and his cohorts, like the Siberian Mammoth, were going to demonstrate that gigantism did not die out with the dinosaurs, but lived on into the Ice Age and perhaps even longer.

Emmet leaned back against his bench, setting the shears down without a single snip. As senior physical paleontologist at the museum for thirty years he'd had a hand in bringing to life every individual on display upstairs, but none, not even big T-rex, had consumed him as George had. And none were as lifelike. It took no imagination at all to see George roaming the great bamboo forests of Pleistocene China, peacefully grazing on his haunches, conserving calories until he had to move his immense frame to the next stand.

And now there was nothing left to do. George was done. It was just such a shame Emmet could only portray life and not create it, as it was a shame nature felt compelled to exterminate so many magnificent species. For George would have been a most awesome beast to behold.

Philadelphia
8:38 PM

South Fifth Street stretched off into the dusk beyond the fresh glow of street lamps. Its evening peace was disturbed only by the idle of Secretary Mason's Lexus parked on the curb. He'd been sitting there, enduring another wrack of pain through his abdomen while staring at both the prescription bottle he held atop the wheel and the reflection in the rearview mirror of the dark sedan parked four cars back.

He gripped and twisted the soft leather of the wheel as the slicing pain intensified. Just two of the small capsules he held in his other hand would erase the pain, seducing him into believing he wasn't dying, that he was as healthy as he'd been only twenty-four months ago—before his diagnosis, before he'd been told relieving the pain was all that medical science could offer him. A handful would end his suffering for good, erase his pain forever.

He popped the cap, tapped two capsules into his palm, and swallowed them.

The same decision he faced every day. Pain or death. He slipped the bottle into his suit coat. For this day at least, like the seven hundred preceding, he chose pain.

He turned the engine off and glanced in the rearview mirror a last time, the pain already beginning to dull. What he could see of the sedan's windshield was only a reflection of the night. No movement stirred within, yet he was certain it still harbored passengers. These days he was never alone. And though he'd yet to identify his shadows and the agency for which they worked, he knew the same tax dollars that paid his salary paid theirs as well. It had only been eight months since his appointment, not nearly long enough to fully understand the mountain of bureaucracy that was the Department of Interior, but long enough to catch glimpses, hear whispers and murmurs of an agency that no longer existed on paper. An agency that had its birth in the ancient and long retired U.S. War Department. An agency that began as custodian of America's wealth of natural resources. An agency, like so many still found on paper, that no longer served the public's interests but rather the private interests of corporations.

Secretary Mason sat back into the leather of his seat and waited for a reaction, knowing none would come. They were too patient, too disciplined. Yet one day they would come for him, long before the disease or his own hand. And they'd come on a day and at a time of their choosing.

He wasn't naive enough to think he could attack the status quo, change long-standing policies that would cost corporations billions, and not make an enemy or two. Enemies that would have no remorse in ridding the people of one of their little-known servants. In the last few months, though, he must really have stirred the hornets' nest. Since he cancelled National Park Service oil and gas contracts in Yellowstone and logging contracts in the national forests surrounding the park the heat on him had increased tenfold. And then came the proposal in the Senate to remove the grizzly from the Endangered Species List, a clear attack on his agenda as the grizzly's listing was what gave him the political leverage and teeth to take action in Yellowstone. The Endangered Species Act was, in fact, his one ace, giving him his only real source of power and authority to wage his war against the corporate raping and pillaging of America's once endless bounty.

But even after his attack on Yellowstone the vigil of his shadows hadn't become so obvious until he had set his sights on logging contracts in parks out West, especially around the Olympics. *They* wanted him to know they were there, that his life was in their hands and that it was time he started playing ball their way.

Mason opened his door, slowly stepped onto the curb and gave a long, steady glare toward the sedan and his shadows within. He closed the door, locked it with a chirp-chirp, and walked down the sidewalk in the opposite direction without the slightest temptation to glance over his shoulder. He was already a dead man, the disease just hadn't finished the job yet. All they could do was the favor of putting him out of his misery, something he'd not yet had the courage to do. Until then, he'd play ball his way and only his way.

He passed the public entrance to the American Philosophical Society Library, now closed until tomorrow morning, and rounded the building toward the rear entrance.

Unfortunately, though, his game had an abbreviated clock. The doctors had made no bones about it—three months, six, maybe as much as a year to live, but certainly not longer than that. And so he had been forced to get aggressive in his tactics. He no longer had the luxury of patience, as he once had those many years ago when he had begun his crusade. Ever since his mother had taught him about his family's legacy of public service, dating back to Thomas Jefferson, he had known his calling in life. Because of that heritage he had been on the inside track—a good thing for him, he later realized, as Washington might as well post a sign declaring: For Insiders Only. He also had quickly learned that corruption had practically stolen the government from the people. It was as if the entire bureaucracy were a marionette whose strings were in the hands of a puppeteer hidden in the rafters. Even the strings were invisible, at least to the nearsighted public. He, on the other hand, like all the rest of the insiders, saw glimpses of the strings, felt their pull from time to time, even obeyed the whispered commands of the puppeteer. And so at some point, he couldn't remember exactly when, he began taking notes, recording those glimpses and whispers in hopes he would one day have a hand in illuminating the puppet master and his strings. So the people could enforce their authority and restore the integrity of their government to the same sacred character it held in the time of Jefferson and his founding brothers.

Coming to the rear door, he pulled his coat close against the dark alley's chill and knocked three times.

With this recent appointment, he was finally in a position to act, to reveal the truth of who really pulled the strings. He even had obtained the sympathetic ears of two influential senators, Senator Pratt on the Intelligence Committee and Senator Smith on Government Affairs. Given his brief window of time, though, he must act as if there were nothing to lose. The reason he and the other insiders hadn't already thrown back the curtain on the puppeteer was there was always too much to lose. Of course, there was in fact still something to lose. If he laid his cards on the table too soon and didn't come away with the pot, then they would have blown the cover for Pratt and Smith, the only allies he had, and he would most likely be dead, or at least have lost his leverage and might as well be so. And all would be for naught.

The problem was he didn't know who the puppet master was, or much of anything about him except for the shadows he cast. It was as if there were a gaping hole in the center of the web where the spider should be. And without his, or more likely, their identity, Mason could not act. His hands were tied, and they knew it.

And so he was spending yet another night in the library's after-hours solitude, immersing himself in the nation's history, where the solution to all of its and his problems lay. The questions of today were no different than those of yesterday, and neither were the answers. All one had to do was know their history. In the meantime he had to do daily battle with the enemy, which meant, for starters, keeping the grizzly on the list. The species had already lost ninety-nine percent of its habitat in the two hundred years since Lewis and Clark recorded in their journals their first encounters with the bear. Likewise, the grizzly's population had dropped to a tenuous one percent of then. And yet there had been essentially no reaction, no outrage, from the public, not even with this recent effort to effectively sponsor the species' extinction. He had so few weapons to fight with, and public apathy made them almost useless. The public needed a jolt, a dose of smelling salts. Otherwise, when they did finally wake, they'd find their great country's God-given resources pillaged and reduced to stubble. His hope was that Lewis and Clark could shed some light on the matter, or at least provide inspiration.

As he waited, he began bouncing slightly on his toes for warmth and distraction. The conservator was taking his sweet time tonight. He was about to knock again when he heard footsteps approaching slowly from inside. Then the door's lock clicked in release and the door swung open.

"Five nights straight, Secretary. Never seen anyone so taken by the journals."

Mason smiled and stepped inside, greeted by a warmth as comforting as the smile he received in return. "You don't know anything if you don't know history, or so they say."

"*They*, huh?" The library conservator closed the door.

"Okay, so *you* say."

The old, thin man, grayer than dust, smiled again, adding a touch more warmth to the narrow entryway. He extended a hand toward the light at the end of the hall, which revealed bookshelves packed tightly and rising out of sight. "All the volumes are on a cart at the corner table, as you prefer. Enjoy, and come wake me when you're through."

Mason patted the librarian's bony shoulder and headed for the shelves. "Thank-you. But it may be you who has to wake me. Lewis gets pretty dry at times."

"Not if you read between the lines."

Unsure if he'd heard right, the old man's voice not much more than a whisper, Mason glanced back, but the conservator was gone. Shrugging, Mason stepped into the expanse of books that towered three stories above him. Even if he had a full lifetime ahead of him, he'd never be able to read so many books. But he quickly dismissed the wonderment he felt every time he stood in the midst of such a collection of knowledge and wisdom, finding instead his corner table and cart. He had neither the stomach for the depressing yet awesome thought, nor the time.

He eased against the wooden back of the chair and scanned the lineup on the cart. Eighteen volumes, four-by-six inches, of the same type used by surveyors in the field. Thirteen were bound in red morocco leather, four covered in marbled paper, and one in brown leather. Lewis and Clark's journals. A full account of perhaps the greatest expedition in human history. Nearly two centuries old, the volumes recorded events from September 1803 to September 1806. A trip that today took two to three days by car, but then seemed like traveling into the unknown, to the end of the world and back.

Mason gingerly slipped the volume he'd been working on last night out from between the others—volume thirteen, Lewis's account of winter 1806 at Fort Clatsop on the Columbia. He set it before him on the table, marveling again at the tiny piece of history. To think of where this book had been, who had held it, what had been said or done in its presence. It boggled the mind.

Though he knew the conservators had done their work well, he couldn't help but fear the pages would disintegrate at his touch; they felt so thin and worn. The smell of age and earth filled his nostrils and he breathed it in. It was the closest he would ever get to such a wondrous adventure and a time when everything was not yet known.

As he read, the words came to life in his mind. He saw Lewis laboring at his desk late into the night, recording by candlelight the activities of the day, the recent flora and fauna he'd examined, sketching them on occasion. It was as if no time had passed at all, and he was there at Lewis's side in damp, cold Fort Clatsop, adding to history with each word skillfully etched in ink. Lewis was penning a lasting snapshot of a world that was to be utterly lost within less than one generation—an Eden known to exist only by the echoes it left behind, and only by those few who were listening.

He turned page after page, as enthralled as he'd been each night, yet also deeply saddened by the loss to his generation and those to follow. No one would ever see this country with the same beauty and majesty as had Lewis. All Mason could hope for was to preserve and re-create a glimpse of it, a reminder of the marvel that had been America. All he asked for was a little help from Lewis to instill the same desire in those who now held his legacy in their apathetic hands.

Then, he stumbled over a passage written in late January 1806. He read it twice, three times, and then half a dozen more. He had to be misinterpreting it. The many Lewis and Clark scholars would surely have caught it before him. No, it just couldn't be. So he read it again.

> …our skill as hunters afford us some Consolation, for if there is any game of any description in our neighbourhood we can track it up and kill it. with the afore mentioned exception of this December. They being so hard to die reather intimidates us all. Our wappetoe being nearly exhausted tho & our want for meat great…

It was the second and third lines of the passage that struck him. Given that the entire record had been written in hand and was essentially Lewis's personal diary, many of the pages were cluttered with notes in the margins, and often lines had been squeezed in between others. It was by no means a polished and publishable document. And yet these two lines did not fit. They truly appeared to Mason as afterthoughts, new text added at some later date. Not that he was any sort of expert, but the handwriting even seemed different, as if those two lines, and only those two lines, had been written by an author other than Lewis. But most significantly, the lines clearly referred to an entry that had been made in the prior month, December 1805. Yet, unlike Clark's complete account, there was a gap in Lewis's journal record from August 26, 1805 to January 1, 1806. One of many gaps.

Mason ran a finger along the other seventeen spines. The many gaps were a fact of history. He leaned back in his chair, searching the level upon level of books rising to the ceiling for answers, answers unfound by those who'd come before him. Sure there were rumors of lost journals, of stolen journals, even of journals destroyed. Mason had heard them all, as the finger of guilt so often had been pointed at his heritage and the one Founding Father who'd had exclusive access. But all the experts agreed in the end, the gaps were there because Lewis had simply stopped writing from time to time for any number of hypothetical and innocent reasons.

He closed his eyes, suddenly aware of the late hour. The passage was not ambiguous, though. An entry *had* been made in December. Lewis was far too congruent for such a slip up. What then had happened to it?

Mason's eyes shot open, and he was on the edge of the chair, staring at the open journal on the table, hearing again the odd comment from the old librarian.

Not if you read between the lines.

Reading between the lines...not metaphorically, but literally. The offhand comment could very well just be a coincidence, yet he felt in his bones it was not. The librarian was telling him something, drawing his attention to this passage. But why?

Mason thought back, drudging up memories of his mother and her passionate mini-lectures to the groups of tourists. Questions and answers began to spawn in his mind, slowly at first and then in a flood. Who had possessed the journals before donating them to the American Philosophical Society? Thomas Jefferson. And when was that? Between 1809 and 1812. And where was Jefferson residing at that time?

Monticello.

Then the ten letters of the final answer swirled in the dark of his mind, replaced by sketchy images of a pull-down attic staircase descending in slow motion, of boyish-size feet clad in tennis shoes ascending into the musty space above, and then the slam of the staircase locking him alone in the dark, his ears filled with panicked, innocent screams for help.

Mason could hardly draw a breath, and not because of the sudden surfacing of this nearly forgotten memory but because of where his unsacred thoughts were taking him. It couldn't be. It just couldn't. He forced down a deep breath, even as he was forcing himself to swallow the alternative—that contrary to current history and legend, it very well could be. Those two lines could indeed have been penned at a later date. If so who else might their author be but Thomas Jefferson, and why else other than to leave posterity a message, a clue to completing the gaps in Lewis's record of the Corps of Discovery. And if one knew their history, then the clue pointed them in but one direction: Monticello. Exactly where the fingers of guilt had been pointing all along.

Somewhere over the north Pacific
May 4
8:36 PM

Sam turned the page and glanced down the aisle for Megan. She was still in line at the restroom. A flight attendant walked by offering a refill on her Diet Coke. Sam waved her off with a, "No thanks." She had a good ten minutes before Megan returned. There was a connection to Prescott's canceling the dig and Ostman's letter. She'd stolen every minute of solitude in the past twenty-four hours searching for it in the only resource she had, Ostman's book. That Prescott was even casually associated with Ostman and the tooth riding in her pocket were proof enough for Sam that she wasn't wasting her time, even if she weren't yet ready to be caught reading such rubbish. Besides, it was for Megan's own safety she not know about any of it, at least until Sam got to the bottom of it all. The same went for Emmet.

Being sure to keep the book's cover flat against her lap, hidden from view, Sam adjusted the brightness of the overhead reading light and found her place at the top of the page.

> History or legend. Is there a difference? I think not. Legends are simply forgotten history. And in this case we don't have to look that far back to a time when history and legend were one and the same:
>
> 1792, Spanish naturalist, José Mariano Mozino recounts from his exploration of the British Columbian coast a warning from its native peoples: "[The Matlox], inhabitant of the mountainous country, of whom all have unspeakable terror. They figure it has a monstrous body, all covered with black animal hair; the head like a human; but the eyeteeth very sharp and strong, like those of the bear; the arms very large, and the toes and fingers armed with large curved nails. His howls fell to the ground those who hear them, and he smashes into a thousand pieces the unfortunate on whom a blow of his hand falls."
>
> 1856, George Gibbs refers to the Tsiatko, feared being of the Nisqually: "[their] body is covered with hair like that of a dog, only not so thick…They are said to live in the mountains, in holes in the ground, and to smell bad. They come down chiefly in the fishing season, at which time the Indians are excessively afraid of them…Their voices are like that of an owl, and they possess the power of charming, so that those hearing them become demented or fall down in [a] swoon."
>
> And I could go on. Accounts like these abound in the journals and retellings of early explorers and mountain men of the Northwest, even in Theodore Roosevelt's 1892 book, *Wilderness Hunter*. Lewis and Clark's journals would

be the single exception[1], for they are conspicuously silent on the matter, to the point of giving the impression the native peoples of the Northwest had no such traditions—which we know for a certainty was not the case. And what of these native traditions anyway? Do we discount the plethora of Native American accounts that date from prehistory to modern day all simply because they were not written down? Even a cursory glance at an abbreviated list of their many names for the legendary beast should give one reason to pause:

<u>A Legend of Many Names</u>

Bak'wis	Kwakiutl and Tsimshan dialects, refers to the devil
Bu'ks	Bella Coola villages on British Columbian coast
Ohmahah	Upper Skagit tribes
St'iyaha	"whistler," or people who sleep by day and go out at night
St'iyahama	Umatilla tribes, stick Indians
Sti'ya	Northern Molala of Oregon Cascades
Huppa	Northern California, Klamath Mountain
Cam'eqwas	Great tall animal like a man but shaggy like a bear
Tsadja'tko	Quinault tribes, mountain giants
Skuku'm	Chinook for strong and dangerous being
Matlox	Inhabitant of the British Columbian coast
Tsiatko	Nisqually tribe
Seskwa'c	Coast Salish term near Vancouver
Seeahtlk	Devil of ape canyon, also spelled See-alt, See-ualt, See-yat, and Se-at-tlh (curiously similar to Seattle)
Sesq'ec	Used by natives of Frazier River valley in British Columbia, anglicized to Sasquatch[*]

*   The most infamous and anglicized term, Bigfoot, has no reference to Native legends, and was first coined in a local California newspaper in 1958.

---

1. It's hard not to conjecture what would be considered legend and what history if we had the two explorers' complete record.

Contrary to conventional wisdom, I believe it extremely arrogant to suppose indigenous peoples know nothing of the land they've inhabited, that they speak only of fantasy and fiction. Europeans settled in the Pacific Northwest only two hundred years ago, yet for twelve thousand years previous the Pacific coast had been populated with humans. Surely, if my theory holds of an aboriginal great ape of North America, the Native Americans would know of it. And they do. So do a few of us latecomers. We just haven't lived here long enough for it to become common knowledge.

In fact, if one takes the time to connect the dots, a clear pattern emerges. And nowhere is it more visible than in an isolated corner of Washington State, a place called the Olympics. Or as John Meares referred to the jumbled mass of heavenly white mountains when he sailed through the Strait of Juan de Fuca in 1778: a dwelling place for the gods. His impression rang with such truth that the highest peak would later bear the same name as the Greek home of the gods—Mount Olympus. And in some respects, Meares wasn't that far off. At that time, the Olympic Peninsula was still virgin territory and the pristine slopes of its interior mountain range had yet to be scarred by the boots of man. And they would remain so for the next hundred years.

Lying midway between the equator and the North Pole on the western corner of the United States, the Olympic Peninsula is bound by the Strait of Juan de Fuca to the north, the Puget Sound to the east, and the Pacific on the west. The southern flank is nearly as guarded, with the deep Chehalis River Valley running from east to west. Covering some 6,500 square miles with a 60-mile-diameter central core consisting of the Olympic Mountains, the Peninsula is the definition of isolation. During the Pleistocene, it was even more so, an island jutting up from a frozen landscape dominated by glaciers a mile thick.

Adding to its isolation, the land is inhospitable to the extreme. Less than forty miles from the coast, the Olympics form an 8,000-foot wall of glacier-clad, sandstone and basalt teeth that tear open the bellies of charging storm fronts blowing in off the Pacific. The result is the highest yearly precipitation in the continental U.S.—Mount Olympus is hammered by over 200 inches a year, most of it falling as snow—and one of the severest rain shadows in the world. Even more astounding, the Olympics posses a year-round snowline of only 5,500 feet—compared to 8,000 feet in the Cascades and 10,000 in the Rockies. Here, glaciers form at some of the lowest elevations on the planet and descend farther down their valleys than anywhere in the lower forty-eight. Where the ice stops its relentless grind downhill, silt-laden rivers such as the Hoh, the Queets, and the Quinault continue the steady chiseling of the already three-thousand-foot deep valleys in their pursuit of the Pacific.

This topography funnels moist ocean air so well that these rivers can rise six feet in a day after a healthy downpour and are home to the world's richest old-growth forests, which produce more biomass per acre than any other eco-system on the planet. Sitka spruce, Douglas fir, and western red cedar support these forests with trunks nearly twenty feet in diameter and form a canopy three hundred feet above the fern- and moss-covered forest floor.

If ever there were a place on earth where a legend, a myth, could survive the onslaught of the modern Information Age, it is here in the dark Olympics.

Up until only a hundred years ago, government maps were blank in the interior of the Peninsula, labeling it merely as terra incognita. Seattle and Tacoma, cities so close their residents could look out on a clear day in awe and wonder at the snowy heights, had been established for decades and yet no one had set foot on the Olympics. Of course, western civilization and its appetite for natural resources couldn't be held back forever. The Peninsula is now a national park and has a well-traveled highway circling its perimeter.

Yet, as far as it is known, the Native Americans never settled beyond the Peninsula's coast, never even crossed the great Olympics to trade with villages on the other side. Instead, they remained on the shore, content to travel the long way around. This type of cultural behavior wasn't a regional oddity by any means. It seems that native peoples of the Northwest, from Alaska to Oregon, preferred the coastal areas to the rugged, mountainous terrain typically found inland in the Pacific Northwest. On the surface there is an obvious and simple explanation. The Native Americans—with a distinctly different philosophy, believing themselves to be an integrated element of the natural world—simply took what nature gave them, demanding no more. Everything they needed was on the coast, so why seek after what they didn't need? Culture kept them on the shore.

However, upon a closer look, neither cultural nor even geologic barriers completely explain why the Native Americans refused to enter the mountains. Surely in over twelve millennia they could have overcome the rugged landscape and severe weather if they'd wanted to. It only took the settlers a hundred years. And it is equally hard to swallow that cultural beliefs could restrain so many people for so long.

Perhaps, then, there is a third explanation, one they were happy to share with the first white settlers. They recorded that the Indians remained in their coastal villages and shunned the interior of the Northwest, especially when it came to the Peninsula, more out of fear than any challenge of terrain. If so, then is it possible they chose the beaches over the mountains not because of comfort or world view, but because there was something in the forests that they were avoiding, perhaps something left stranded after the ice melted at the end of the Pleistocene?

Of course, in order for them to know what it was they were avoiding, and to have stories to tell, they would at sometime had to have actually entered the Peninsula's interior. Assuming that was precisely what they did after first arriving, then it follows that whatever they found must have been so terrifying and deadly that even generations yet unborn would be haunted. A living nightmare.

Whatever it was, their lesson had been learned so well that twelve thousand years later it is still being followed to the letter. Even today, young Native Americans speak of the Bak'wis, the cannibal people, and describe anyone who disregards the warnings and ventures inland as an "eqwus," or fool. And if they are asked why, they simply respond that the animal you should fear most is the one you never see.

But how could there be any truth to their fears? Modern Americans have been crisscrossing the Peninsula for decades now. If there were anything to be found, surely we would have found it, and most likely killed it.

The only problem is that there are a growing number of eyewitnesses—usually loggers, trappers, outdoor enthusiasts, etc.—who will swear on whatever they believe to be holy that they've seen something, something that walks on two legs like a man but that clearly is not. For them, like for the Indians, the nightmare is very real.

Sam looked up from the page, needing a breath of fresh air. She was drowning in Ostman's rich fantasy world. Connect the dots? He was like some astrologist who could point to a random group of stars, tell you they formed the shape of a two-headed dragon, and then tell you it meant your parents had lied to you and you were adopted. None of his work had any connection to the scientific method, no connection to hard reality at all.

She shifted in her seat as she glanced down the aisle. The tooth pressed into her upper thigh, reminding her yet again why she entertained any of this man's ideas. But the question still remained, was the tooth connected?

Megan was first in line for the restroom. Sam had a few more minutes. She flipped through the next couple of chapters, which she had already skimmed and couldn't stomach reading again. Within them, Ostman spent about fifty pages attempting to ground his theory, his myth, in what he referred to as "evidence from the fossil record." Essentially he began by re-explaining what was accepted theory on *Gigantopithecus'* extinction. Theory holds that a hundred and twenty-five thousand years ago a widespread bamboo die-off swept through southern Asia just as *Homo erectus* migrated into the area. The newcomer essentially out-competed other species, such as the giant panda, orangutan, and the knuckle-walking and bamboo-grazing *Gigantopithecus*. Whereas the panda and orangutan survived by migrating north and south, Giganto could not and simply went extinct.

He then gave what was the core of his theory, and nothing more than polished imagination. He claimed Giganto didn't go extinct, but instead migrated north, as did the giant panda. It went so far north that the species crossed the Bering land bridge into North America, becoming the only aboriginal ape on that continent and the beast that spawned a thousand native legends that live on into today. The description of the beast of legend, he claimed, matched identically to what was believed about Giganto, except it walked erect. This wasn't a problem, as he proposed that *Gigantopithecus* adapted, evolving bipedal locomotion along the journey.

The fact that such an ability to adapt to rapidly changing conditions required near human intelligence didn't appear to occur to Ostman, along with a dozen other issues that rose to the tip of Sam's tongue every time she thought about it. So avoiding the frustration of not having anyone she could spit them at, Sam turned to the last chapter in the book, "Burden of Proof," hoping for any insight into Prescott's interest in the man.

> Extinction can be very difficult to prove, much more so than science acknowledges. The only proof they have to support Giganto's extinction is that they can't find any bones in China more recent than 125,000 years old. Of course, if the species as a whole migrated out of the area at that time, none more recent should be found there.

> But even more difficult to prove is existence. And the farther a species is outside our comfort zone the harder it is (a uniquely human phenomenon worthy of study in itself). Take the platypus for example, or even the colobus monkey. The first skins of each were initially rejected by the scientific community as fakes. As difficult as the burden of proof may be it is by no means impossible. New species are discovered and catalogued all the time, despite Baron Georges Cuvier's famous and premature declaration to the contrary. For support, I'll name just a few: the American tapir, 1819; giant panda (ironically was also believed extinct around the time of Giganto); snow leopard; okapi, 1901; pygmy hippopotamus, 1909; komodo dragon, 1912; kouprey, 1937; Andean wolf, 1926 (based on only a single hide); Chacoan peccary, 1975 (believed extinct 2 million years ago); and the coelacanth, 1938 (believed extinct for 60 million years, yet locals had been catching them for generations).

An even better case in point is the mountain gorilla, which wasn't "discovered" until 1902. Its story makes for a textbook myth, except after four hundred years of rumor, denial, and lack of any fossil record it turned out to be true. As with the platypus and colobus, it took a complete specimen to prove the mighty gorilla of the Dark Continent existed outside the tales of drunken sailors and ignorant pygmies. Even to this day no fossil remains have been found of the gorilla, or for the chimpanzee for that matter. The acidity of the ground and the moisture of the climate they inhabit make poor conditions for fossilization, which is also why no remains of Giganto have been found in the Northwest.

And so it must be with America's great ape. Despite all the evidence that exists—the legends, the eyewitness accounts, the fossil record, the Patterson footage of '67, the recorded history, the footprints—only a body will satisfy science and the rest of the world. There is simply nothing left to offer, nothing left to open millions of closed minds. And that surely means a dead body, a hunt. For the past few decades, myself and others have been engaged in just such an endeavor. During the '70s there was a flurry of activity and sightings, and many close calls to success. Since then the forests have been quiet, and we still have no body. Why, is a question I've pondered many hours on end. The easy answer is the pressures and crowding of urban culture have finally done the species in. There simply are none left, they've disappeared before they were ever known. That they lasted this long is a testament to their resilience, their almost magical ability to resist nature's call to the grave.

Like most easy answers, though, it is too easy. What of the persistent eyewitness reports that continue to come out of remote areas like the Olympics? And what of the tracks that are found from time to time?

No, after three decades of experience it is clear there is only one reason why a body has not been obtained. They simply do not wish to be found.

"Next time I fly, remind me to wear a skirt so I can pee in a cup."

Sam jerked her head up and slapped the book shut. Megan smiled and slid past Sam's knees into her seat. She grabbed her pillow and immediately curled up against the closed window.

"I'll be here dead asleep if you need me."

Sam stuffed the book into her carry-on as casually as she could and stretched back in her seat, preparing for the inevitable question. But none came, Megan's eyes were already closed and her breathing heavy. Relieved, yet watching to be sure for several moments, Sam slowly reached a finger into her pocket and pulled out the tooth. It caught the reading light and shone white in her hand. It was larger than most of the fossilized teeth found, its ridges were sharper too. Even so, there was no doubting the match. There was also no mistaking that this tooth hadn't come from a grazer. It was only the solid weight of it in her hand that prevented her from dismissing the possibility of its authenticity, which she wouldn't *fully* accept until she got it into the lab, and drove her to continue to swallow Ostman's laughable notions and high drama. In all honesty, though, he was right about at least one thing. Science knew very little about Giganto, and all that was known came from the hand of her father. They still didn't know where to place Giganto on the evolutionary tree, assuming for now that it was in its own family. They certainly had no explanation for why remains were only found in a handful of caves, and with such density. And then there was the mystery of the occasional *Homo erectus* bones found among them. It was extremely unlikely the two competitors shared the same caves. And what of Giganto's life span; it nearly doubled that of any other primate.

With so many gaps and so little data, and with her failure to accomplish anything more than expand their collection of teeth, the existence of this damn tooth demanded she keep an open mind, at least until she was back in New York with crate in hand. Then she could finally get to the truth.

She sensed someone walking by in the aisle and reflexively stuffed the tooth back in her pocket and looked up with a smile.

But it was only Mr. Blue Eyes, the man from the phones who'd boarded just after her. He returned her smile with an awkward one of his own, glanced away, and rushed past.

That she found the man attractive with all that was going on gave her a chuckle, and was a reminder of the time of month. Another few days and she'd be free of her hormonal Jekyll and Hyde episode. Of course, that was simply a convenient lie to herself, her attempt to ignore the truth that Ian was still never far from her thoughts, or her heart.

Megan's breathing degraded into a light snore, reminding Sam that she too could use a little sleep. She turned off the reading light, slumped her head back, and closed her eyes. They'd be in Seattle in a few hours, and then she'd be off to Denver and her dying father.

Her body slowly melded into the seat, and she soon heard her own breathing shift gears. She hovered there, just on the conscious side of sleep. Her mind conjured the image of a photograph she kept on her desk. She was sixteen. The family had gone skiing at Aspen, as they had every spring break. Her father's face was full, tan, and creased with a broad toothy grin. His eyes were hidden behind sunglasses, but she remembered their brilliance. He held her and her grandmother in a big bear hug. It was the last time she'd seen her grandmother alive, and the last photo of her family before the divorce. Now the same disease that claimed her grandmother had come for her father, having reduced him to a fragile, weak, husk of a man—just as it had her grandmother.

Everyone had lost someone to cancer, at least so it seemed, but for her it felt more like a destiny than a statistical risk, and the fear and inability to deal with it was her family legacy. The closer she got to her father's bedside, the stronger the urge to run became, and the more she knew she didn't have the courage.

That was the other reason why, for the past twenty-four hours, she'd been obsessed with the curious tooth and the mystery it kept secret. And why she now pondered yet again, in light of all that she'd read, the persistent and burning question of what Prescott and Ostman have been up to.

The only reasonable explanation is that it is all some sort of a mistake and the tracks don't really exist. There is just one serious weakness. The tracks *do* exist.
—John Green

Prescott Institute
April 17
3:02 PM

A steady rain fell from a gray sky that hung so low the jagged peaks of Mount Si were lost in it. And tufts of fog drifted up the mountain's forested slopes like spirits from the grave. The tranquil view held none of Jon's attention, though. His stare was focused through the wall-length, tinted window, dripping with thin channels of rain, to the winding dirt road leading to the Prescott Institute.

The road was empty for now, but Jon expected to see a short caravan of black sedans come speeding over it at any moment. He wasn't fooling them by hiding out here, only delaying their arrival, but he hoped the delay would grant him enough time to safely unload the bones. How much time was the big variable. He had no idea where Dr. Russell was working and no way to locate her.

"Dr. Ostman? Your pack—may I take it?"

Jon turned at Prescott's Texas drawl, pulling the pack's strap tighter over his shoulder. The weight of the bones pressed against his lower back. "No, thank-you. I'm fine with it, really."

Prescott came around his polished mahogany and paper-free desk with two glasses of ice water, offering one to Jon. The glint of his Rolex in the track lighting matched that of his eyes. Despite their sharpness, they revealed as little as those of a master poker player betting the pot on a pair of twos. His face was tight and tan, but not from hours of labor. Only the speckled gray of his hair alluded to his true age.

He cocked his head just slightly to the side. "You all right, Jon? You look like you've been ridden hard and put away wet."

Jon accepted the water, downed the biting cold glassful with a lingering want for more, and held it empty with as much casual flare as he could fake. He hadn't slept or showered in two days, his nerves were raw and spent, and he had no idea why he was here. What choice did he have but to lie and change the subject? "Just old age creeping up on me I suppose. I believe you have something to show me?"

A light smile touched Prescott's lips, revealing a straight line of teeth that reflected the light with as much sparkle as his watch and eyes. "Skip the small talk and details and get right to the meat. My sentiments exactly." He turned from his desk, pointing to a table in the corner draped with white linen. "For reasons we'll soon discuss, I need to know with absolute certainty that this is indeed authentic."

Prescott led him toward the table. "And in this particular field, Dr. Ostman, you are one of a kind. If nothing else—"

A side office door opened near the table. A man in his mid-thirties came in and softly closed the door behind him.

"Ah, Ian. Just in time."

He came forward with a big grin shining below his bulbous nose, his bright blue eyes fixed on Jon's, a tanned hand extended. Jon shook it, noting the rough, callused skin, as opposed to the soft, manicured grip of Prescott.

"Jon Ostman. Ian Rettig, gorilla hunter." Prescott stepped behind the table as he made the introductions, then sipped on his own glass.

Ian released his grip and slid his hands into the pockets of his khaki shorts. "Primatologist, actually."

Long, blond hair as unkempt as Jon's, wrinkled khaki shirt and shorts, black socks and worn boots, his appearance matched the Aussie accent to a T. Even without the thick legs and squat frame, Ian was the outback poster boy. The question of what a field man like this was doing with the slick, all-business Prescott sprang immediately to mind. Jon almost forgot his curiosity about what lay beneath the sheet. That is until Prescott pulled back the cloth, unveiling a square slab of concrete where he'd expected to see a table.

A deep, hourglass impression stretched across the center of the slab. Jon took a hesitant stride to the concrete as a cold lump formed in his chest, as it always did when he came across another footprint.

Prescott pulled the sheet off and let it fall to the floor. "Impressive isn't it? We were hoping you might help us identify it, or at least determine if it's authentic."

Jon studied the two men's faces for a crack in their masks of soberness. He found none. They were sincere, a fact Jon didn't know how to respond to, other than to reach out a hand and run his fingers through the sixteen-inch-long track. The lump in his chest became denser, his pulse faster. Regardless of how many he'd seen over the years, seeing one preserved in concrete was stunning, as if the cement gave the track a firmer grounding in reality.

The shank of the foot and the five toes had left perfect impressions. He'd never seen such a pristine track, nor had he seen one so fresh in years. He could feel the rough texture of the dermal ridges and sweat pores, a pattern as unique as his own fingerprints. He checked for a groove along the length of the shank. The lateral expansions—the effect of the sole's thick fatty pad compressing and expanding outward under the animal's full weight—were deep, hinting at this track being from a large male. The track's width and depth in the cement suggested as much as well. It also displayed the variations one would expect as the foot comes in contact with the ground. No two tracks are exactly alike. In fact, this right foot bore the effects of an old injury. Two bulges distorted the outside of the shank, the result of several broken bones healing out of alignment. He could never declare it impossible that a particular track had been faked, but this one had all the right details in all the right places. A hoax with this level of integrity was far more unlikely than the animal itself. No, this track was real, and he knew if by no other sense than the anxious tingle working its way through his body.

His reflex was to unleash a flurry of questions on Prescott about how the track came to be in cement, from where, when, and how many other prints were there. But he knew from experience a track was nothing but a tease, even if entombed in concrete. What he desperately wanted to ask, though, was what the rest of the phone conversation had been that he'd missed? He hadn't been invited out here simply to comment on a single footprint.

"Right, mate. We're obviously certain it's far too large for a man, perhaps then from a black bear?"

Jon glanced again at the Aussie. He'd had the same question posed to him so many times he'd become numb to the ignorance of it. Even so, it struck him as odd coming from a supposedly experienced field primatologist. "No, I think you'll see this track is clearly not from a bear." He lowered his eyes to the slab. "True, like bears and humans, this track is of a plantigrade foot, but, unlike bears, this foot lacks any claws and is far too long and narrow." He checked for reactions from the two men as he continued. They appeared as if they were hearing nothing new. Perhaps they were about to. "Most importantly, though, this creature is not a quadruped. It's a biped. A very large and very heavy biped."

Ian checked in with Prescott by a shift of his piercing blue eyes, then set his brows as if he were digging in his heels. "I don't know, mate. I've seen a lot of tracks in my day, and this one smells funny. Like a prank. Another Sasquatch hoax."

Jon couldn't have flinched harder in surprise if Ian had thrown a punch. Why the hell had they invited him out if they were only going to spit on his analysis? He was working on no sleep, his nerves were shot from running for his life, and he carried enough proof on his back to put these two to shame if he wanted to. He also had run out of patience.

"Sasquatch, Bak'wis, *Gigantopithecus*, call it what you will, but it is no hoax." He stepped right into Ian's face. "And what exactly would you know about it anyway, huh? Anything? Have you spent even a moment's time studying the matter? Well I have, every waking moment for the past thirty years." Jon pointed a shaking finger at the track. "Do you even know what you're looking at? Can you see that there is no instep, the double ball, the lack of a dominant toe? Can you see the fact that it walks pigeon-toed, that it walks completely opposite from humans? That this *hoax* of yours would have a four-foot stride, left a six-teen-by-eight-inch print over two inches deep in the ground, stood over eight feet and weighed in at a good eight hundred pounds.

"No, I suppose you cannot see that this footprint is nearly impossible to fake, arrogance is too blinding. And if it were fake, what would be the motivation? Fame? Fortune? Believe me, there is no money in it. Your problem is that you're so closed-minded you don't even realize that up until a century ago your gorilla was also nothing but a hoax. You don't realize that primates have been experimenting with bipedalism for the past six million years. While you and the rest of humanity find it convenient to suppose we won, that we hold the magic formula for walking on two legs, you never consider what if we don't, what if one of nature's other experiments survived."

Ian stepped back, his arms up in surrender and a smile spreading across his face. "All right, all right. Bloody tense aren't you." He turned to Prescott. "I like this old bloke. Still full of piss and vinegar."

Jon took in a breath, aware of his hot cheeks and spit on his lips. He was getting sick of this charade real fast. He eyed the door and nearly headed for it when Prescott moved in the way.

"Easy, Jon. We just had to be sure."

"Sure of what?"

"That there was more to you than your reputation, that you were the right man for the job."

Jon looked from Prescott, to Ian, to the footprint imbedded in cement. Then he backed up, set his pack on the polished hardwood floor, and dropped into a leather chair in front of Prescott's desk. "You've got five minutes."

Prescott nodded and walked behind the slab. "Fair enough, then." His voice shifted, as if he stood before his board of directors. "What would you guess is the life expectancy of most great apes?"

Jon held his answer a moment, thinking of where it might lead him, but he had no clue where Prescott was going with this. He scanned again the collection of artifacts lining shelves high on all three walls near the ceiling. There were items from all times and all places. Jon was most attracted to the group of primate skulls above Prescott, which rivaled his own display.

Impatient or knowing Jon's uncertainty, Prescott nodded to Mr. Rettig.

Hands held at his back, the Aussie obeyed without a pause. "Fifty years for the gorilla, fifty three for the chimp, and fifty nine for the orang."

"Thank-you, Ian. Now, Jon. Have you any idea what experts believe was the lifespan for *Gigantopithecus*?"

So now he was getting warmer, but still felt vulnerable, unsure whether to attack or defend, or just wait. "I've actually never read any such report. I'd guess much the same as the gorilla."

A sheepish grin appeared on Prescott's face, like a predator watching its prey make that one critical and fatal error. "Evidence from dental remains puts their average lifespan at near one hundred years. Twice that of any other non-human primate."

The significance still lost on Jon, he nevertheless felt the impact of Prescott's words as they hung in the air. Giganto withheld so many mysteries from man, and here was yet another, or perhaps just another symptom of their almost magical resilience. Jon shifted forward on the seat, the leather creaking under his weight. "Your time's running thin. Do you have a point, hopefully one related to this footprint?"

"Indeed I do. Primate life expectancy became an interest of mine some years back when I came across an interesting case of a man reportedly dying at age one hundred and twenty-one. No Methuselah by any means, but noteworthy just the same. What really got me thinking, though, was his cause of death. At that age you'd expect a man to die from disease or other body malfunction. No, Mr. Anderson simply fell down his stairs and broke his neck. Not much was made of his passing, nor did science find him that curious, except for one short report I found indicating he'd had an extremely high level of antioxidants in his cells."

Jon realized he'd eased back into the leather. He may not know where, but Prescott was now taking him somewhere.

"This was years before the antioxidant/aging mania. We still know very little, but it seems clear antioxidants are involved in the aging process, among other things." Prescott's eyes flickered for the briefest of time, giving Jon the sense there was something being left unsaid between the lines. "It's a shame Mr. Anderson's body wasn't thoroughly examined. I don't have to tell you what a breakthrough it would be to finally unlock the code to aging and dial a few extra years onto our life expectancy."

And what a *profit* such a breakthrough would provide for the Prescott Institute. Jon was catching up quick.

"Cases like Mr. Anderson aren't exactly common, so I had to expand my search, to other species. For years now I've been working with experts in Africa, like Mr. Rettig here, on understanding primate longevity. I've also been working in China, hoping to learn more about Giganto, and most importantly hoping to find bones. I need DNA, not rock, which is ultimately why we've made very little progress."

Prescott set his hands ceremoniously on the slab, straddling the print. "Then, almost by providence, I read two books. One was a collection of native legends translated into English. Of particular interest was the legend within a legend; a Northwest tale of the ominous man-beast of the forest, and the regular hunting of it with the belief that whoever ate its flesh would have eternal life. I was quickly reminded of the Chinese practice of pharmacies selling *Gigantopithecus* teeth to cure anything from headaches to sexual impotence…and even to promote a longer life."

Prescott had a flat, all-business expression, as if he were now selling his board on the institute's latest drug. But Jon wasn't buying. He'd heard enough, and stood. "You know, not everything in a legend is true."

Prescott almost laughed. "Ah, yes, but knowing which parts are true is always the trick. You of all people should know that."

"Right, because the other book you read was mine." Jon grabbed his pack and stepped for the door, glancing once at the footprint. He was almost like an alcoholic, addicted to chasing down every five-toed, foot-long track in the mud. But he didn't need to anymore. He had proof enough. Proof you could actually touch, and best of all, not deny. "And to think they call me a fanatic."

Surprisingly, no move was made to stop him from leaving. Prescott strode lightly over to his wall of glass and the wet view of Mount Si. Ian sat down in the chair Jon had just emptied, crossing one bare leg casually over the other.

Prescott spoke with his back to him. "I guess I was wrong. I thought you'd jump at a chance to have what you've always wanted, what we and so many other institutions denied you in the past. A blank check and a legitimate sponsor to obtain the one body of evidence that can prove your critics wrong—to prove that you're a scientist, not a fanatic."

Jon hesitated only feet from the door. And not because of what Prescott just said. A tooth in the hand was better than two type specimens in the forest. And that was assuming a type specimen could be found simply by throwing money at it. No, it was what Prescott had said moments earlier—his working in China, with experts. There weren't many, and the best was Dr. Russell.

Jon turned from the door. "And this footprint is to convince me you'll succeed where others, myself included, have failed."

Prescott turned as well, his face as smug as if he were a drinking buddy and had seduced Jon off the wagon again. "Would it help if you knew where the track came from?"

Jon stood, pack over his shoulder, waiting for the answer he needn't ask for.

"*If ever there was a place on earth where a legend, a myth, could survive the onslaught of the modern Information Age, it is in the Olympics.* How right you were Jon. How right you were. This track was made as we were renovating a World War II bunker well up the Hoh valley that had been built-out into a crude lab by the National Park Service in the '80s. We've been using it as a cover for years now, running a wolf reintroduction program out of it."

Jon's legs carried him to the center of the office, where he asked the question on his tongue but not on his mind. "Cover from whom? The random hiker?"

"The NPS. Custodianship of the world's richest resources is not taken lightly or done so without teeth."

Prescott didn't offer anymore, and Jon didn't request any further explanation. Each man knew the other understood.

Jon eased closer to the window, feeling a sudden need to see the dirt road. See that it was still empty. He was now sure of his decision to not mention the bones to Prescott. Besides not trusting him, Prescott wouldn't provide Jon a safe haven if he knew Jon was being hunted down like public enemy number one.

"All arrangements are finally complete, and we're ready to begin the hunt. I think it only fitting you lead it. You'd get sole authorship of documenting the specimen, full credit—of course, after all testing is complete. I only want its DNA."

The scientific method was designed to protect science from the scientist. Especially scientists like Prescott. Any mistrust Jon had of Prescott was confirmed by what he said after "of course." It identified where his loyalty lay, and the slim chance Jon would come away with anything, let alone a specimen. But as Jon gazed through the rain beading up on the glass and the muddy road winding through the trees, he rationalized his decision, justified it based on a growing dread that he'd soon see the dark shape of vehicles appear on the road where it rose over the horizon. In accepting the offer, there was nothing to lose and his life to preserve, because Prescott had no chance of success, unless he had a miracle up his sleeve. If the Olympics could hide his cryptid for twelve thousand years, the rainforest could certainly hide him until he got the bones to Russell, which brought him back to the question still on his mind. "Tell me, these experts in China you're working with—would I know any of them?"

Ian stood from his chair with an almost painful sigh, a pain deeper than physical. Prescott appeared to notice, but ignored it just the same, perhaps too focused on reeling in his catch. "A few maybe. Certainly Dr. Samantha Russell, daughter of Paul Russell."

"Yes, I know Samantha." A flutter of hope rippled through Jon as he lied. All he needed now was her exact location, something easy enough to be found here in the institute.

Ian had stepped to the door, almost waiting to be dismissed.

Prescott sunk into his high-back, black-leather chair, wearing a smile of victory as he assumed the sell. "We'll be leaving early in the morning. Everything you'll need is waiting in your room. It's a pleasure having you on board."

Glancing down again at the road, Jon wanted to respond, "Why wait for the morning?" but instead took advantage of the time. "Then I have some business to resolve before then. May I beg the service of your assistant?"

Prescott stood and extended his Rolex and manicure again. "I'll make sure she knows to provide you with anything you need—anything at all."

Jon shook Prescott's hand with a smile of victory of his own, that is until he glanced back at Ian and felt that now familiar chill of paranoia.

The office door was ajar and the Aussie was gone.

Olympic National Park
April 18
4:01 PM

The tour began on the main level, with a walk down a hall lined with taxidermy. *Canus lupis* held the spotlight with a center pose, its back arched and mouth agape in a snarl of warning. The wolf shared the hall with a dozen or more other species, from the small shrew to the prowling cougar. Due to the success of reintroduction projects, all were species found right outside the bunker's thick concrete walls.

From there Prescott was called away, leaving the guiding up to the Aussie. Jon hadn't given much thought to Prescott's little lab in the rainforest, being preoccupied with obtaining Dr. Russell's exact location without being obvious about it. What he now saw was not what he would have expected, especially from a structure the same age as himself, which had been originally constructed like a bomb shelter. That's not to say that the building's age wasn't evident, also as with him. Cracks splintered across the walls like the work of a giant spider. The air was damp and thick with mildew, perpetually cool like that of a cave. Power cords and cables snaked along the bare cement floor. Industrial lighting hung from the ceiling, swaying at the softest touch of a breeze, which shouldn't exist inside a bunker built into a mountainside. But beyond that, the place was much like a lab in any university. Clean. Organized. Stacked with equipment only a scientist could love.

Jon felt almost at home.

Even for him, though, the place was too quiet. Deserted to be exact.

As Ian led them from the sleeping quarters on the second level back down to the main level, Jon alluded to as much.

They had stopped at a locked door at the end of a long, narrow hall that felt ten degrees cooler than the rest of the lab. Three shades dimmer as well. The door was polished white, newer than all the others. It bore a sign that read in red lettering: Authorized Personnel Only.

"Now that this project's up and running, Prescott put the wolf reintroduction on hold a bit, sent that team home for some R and R. Our crew is the only one here. And we're small." Ian punched in a code on a keypad just right of the door. "You'll find that Prescott takes no chances. He believes the fewer mouths there are the less chance there is of a security breach."

And Jon thought he was paranoid.

The lock clicked and Ian turned the steel handle. Footsteps sounded at the other end of the hall. A short Hispanic woman was coming their way. Ian held the door closed and called to her. "Maria, I thought you left with the others this morning."

She stopped in an open doorway midway down the hall and looked sideways at them over her hunched shoulder. She was only five feet, five two at the most, yet Jon found himself cringing at her stare. It was the stare his ex-wife had given him when he'd come home from work three hours late without calling. "Someone has to clean up around here, and I know it ain't you." Her stare softened into the hint of a smile. "Besides, I needed to hang around for one last mail run."

"I'll let the blokes downstairs know. When you leaving?"

Her stare flared again, this time focused on the door Ian still held shut. "Soon, and I ain't waitin'. Horses won't travel after sunset."

Letting her stare linger, she stepped through the doorway and out of sight. Ian snickered as he opened the door. "Maria. Gonna miss the old girl round here." Glancing at Jon, he added, "We don't get resupplied until next week, so if you have any communication to make with the outside world you better get it to Maria. And don't mind her. Her bark's not quite as bad as her bite."

Jon hesitated a moment before following Ian through the door, still watching the empty doorway Maria had gone through since she had mentioned mail run. Regardless of bark or bite, she was his fairy godmother, his rabbit out of a hat. Mail? Yeah, he had mail. And all he had to do was slip the bones and the report he'd spent all night writing into Maria's care in a form that could travel to China, without attracting questions he didn't want to answer.

The door closed behind them, and Jon realized he stood atop a narrow set of concrete stairs that descended steeply beneath the lab. The landing was no larger than required to open the door. Concrete walls darkened in shadow crowded him, holding back the weight of a mountain he could feel suspended overhead. Only the barest light shone from three lamps hanging from the sloped ceiling. Ian's boot steps rang dull in the air cooler than anywhere yet as he tromped down the chipped and cracked steps. The false impressions of having stepped into the dungeons below a castle of the Middle Ages or any number of mystic subterranean abodes flittered though his mind, leaving an aftertaste that spawned goose bumps on his forearms and had him quickly descending to catch up with Ian.

When he was a step behind Ian and the aftertaste swallowed, Jon became far more concerned with the ache in his calves and thighs. The all-day, ten-mile trek into the lab through the rainforest had taken its toll. In truth, his days for such work had long since past, but as he was the safest he could possibly be, tucked away under tons of granite and concrete with no one but Prescott or Ian knowing his whereabouts, it was a truth he'd keep to himself. And now that he'd found a way to ship his bones, sending them as it turned out as far away as possible, it was time he started doing his job.

The stairwell turned right at a sharp angle. Ian's voice echoed in the silence. "This lower level used to be the storage bays for the anti-aircraft battery's artillery. This whole bunker was built right into the site of an old mine. We're probably thirty of more feet underground at this point."

Another sharp right. Dull light ascended the stairs.

"Prescott's been secretly working his primate research from here for years now. The wolf reintroduction team doesn't even know what goes on down here."

Another bare cement floor came into view. Jon came down alongside Ian. "And how long have you been involved?"

The Aussie stopped at the bottom of the steps, making eye contact with Jon. "Prescott lured me out from Zaire five months ago. And for the record, I only know what Prescott wants me to know."

Such a statement struck Jon as more than just odd; it was almost a plea for further questioning, an ear to unload on. If so, now wasn't the time, as Ian lifted his palm at the wide hallway before them.

"No brass fittings or modern comforts, but where it counts you'll find the latest and greatest technology money can provide."

His attention called to it, Jon recognized the hushed buzz and chatter of a working lab. The banter of debating voices, the rattle of pipettes and test tubes. The whoosh of fume hoods. Several white lab coats traveled the hall, crossing from room to room. Amid it all, a muffled sound, a chorus of calls, floated like whispers just within his awareness. It was so thin, so fleeting, Jon couldn't name the sensation, at least with nothing more specific than sadness.

Ian continued their march to a destination yet unknown to Jon.

The first room they passed was occupied by two men bent over microscopes. The next was empty and resembled the operating room of a veterinarian hospital. It even had the hoist and harness necessary for lifting horses or bovine. Unusual for a primate lab, but exactly what would be needed should they succeed. An event Jon still doubted very much, especially since he knew next to nothing of their plan. "Tell me again, Ian, what exactly is your focus? Certainly something more specific than 'gorilla hunter.'"

The Aussie casually waved at a tall woman in a lab coat as she passed them in the hall. "My research has generally been centered on the emotional capabilities of gorillas and chimps. Of late I've been mostly involved in work relating to violent behavior and its origins."

Jon thought of the human teeth he and Xuan found in the lava tubes and the *Homo erectus* teeth found in China. Perhaps Prescott knew more than Jon gave him credit for. "And what have you found?"

Ian glanced over his shoulder at Jon, his steel-blue eyes giving nothing away. "Nothing that we don't already see manifested every night on the news. The more intelligent and the more social a species is, the more prone it is to violence. Males of the species tend to be most susceptible, as expected, because they have to compete for females. It's also interesting that the most violent species are hunters, or at least occasional meat eaters. Thus we find violent behavior increasing in intensity as you climb the evolutionary tree, primates being the neighborhood bad boys, with chimps and then humans being the real nasty s.o.b.'s."

They turned a corner to the right and entered an open doorway. They were in a narrow but deep room lined with workbenches, cabinets, and storage lockers. Tools and equipment of every kind lay atop the benches and hung from the walls. Enough firearms to arm a small militia stood in open-air cabinets, many of large enough caliber to down a charging grizzly. Electronic tracking equipment cluttered an entire corner. Jon thought he recognized infrared and night-vision gear to his left. Were they going hunting or to war?

Ian pushed his hands into the pockets of his shorts. "Thought you might be interested in seeing our collection of toys."

The sound of a door opening nearby was quickly followed by a wretched wail of animal calls. Monkey calls. Howls and hoots and screams. They sent a reflexive shiver of pity through Jon. Then the door closed and the voices were silenced, or at least muffled again into whispers of sadness. And Jon knew it wasn't only he who perceived them that way, for Ian's eyes of crystal blue clarity clouded over with a dark shadow of his own helpless pity. He knew what was being done to them and could do nothing about it, or at least had not done anything yet.

A subject of inquiry for another day. Jon kept to his immediate concern. "Not to sound skeptical, but I'm curious about Prescott's plan, to down a type specimen that is."

At this, the Aussie's beaming smile returned. "Oh, we're not going to kill it." He stepped over to the gun rack and retrieved one of the long-barreled rifles. He held it out for Jon's inspection. "Just like I do with the largest male gorillas, silverbacks we call them, we're going to sedate it."

Jon accepted the rifle as Ian pulled a tagging dart from a form-fitted, cushioned case on the shelf. Jon had given up years ago on the idea of drugging a specimen, for fear of killing it anyway with a serum derived purely out of conjecture. Might as well protect your own skin in the process and skip right to the bullet.

"Me own special brew. Guaranteed to work in less than twenty seconds or your money back."

Jon handed the rifle back. "Or you're dead, you mean."

Ian grinned. "That too. But I've used this juice on mountain gorillas for years. And after a few adjustments for the increased weight and slower heart rate, I'm willing to bet my own life on this stuff."

And in the off chance they got lucky, that was exactly what Ian was about to do.

Ian returned the rifle to its cradle and the serum to its case, then pulled a tiny plastic bag from a leather pouch on the nearest workbench. He opened it and plucked out a pinky nail-sized microchip. Most likely a signal-emitting chip that is embedded in an animal's hide to track it over great distances. They have a far stronger signal than the old radio transponders. "The best circuitry money can buy, which was probably why Prescott resisted at first. But I've convinced him to place this one on our lucky bloke. No use letting our legend disappear again into the unknown."

Jon had always dreamt of applying such technology, and to even think of succeeding at doing so now stirred old wells of hope. But to keep from being washed away into a quickly materializing fantasy, he had to clear the air, had to hear his own voice declare their odds. "Actually, I wasn't referring to what we were going to *use* to bring an individual down. All the cutting-edge narcotics and tracking equipment in the world are useless if you never get a glimpse of your target. Remember, we're dealing with an animal that's been bred to hate and fear man since the Ice Age. I've spent thirty years combing remote forests just like those outside these walls, these very same woods in many cases, and never seen more than a snapped sapling."

"That's because you tried to re-create the wheel."

Both Jon and Ian turned in surprise at Prescott's drawl. And he wasn't alone.

At his side, a half step behind in deference, a tall, dark-skinned man stood with his arms held at his back. His shadow black hair was shaved tight around his ears and cropped on top. Specks of gray glinted in the light above his weathered temples. His eyes were even darker, bottomless like lumps of coal. The skin on his face was loose, aged like leather. He wore name-brand outdoor clothing: fleece vest, flannel shirt, khaki pants, boots. Yet despite the modern image, his presence was anything but. Old wisdom, soft temper, and humility exuded from his stance, the droop of his shoulders, and the clarity of his gaze. He was an Indian pure through down to his soul, as any Jon had ever met.

"This time, Jon, you will succeed, because we're going to do it the only way it's ever been done." Prescott's smile turned with his open hand in introduction to the man at his shoulder. "Dr. Ostman, I'd like to introduce Sixen, of the Quinault. Like his father, and his father before that, and for unknown generations preceding him, Sixen is going to show us how to use just the right bait."

5:32 PM

Stealth was difficult to achieve with the weight of the crate in his arms and the wide-open, well-lit hallways exposing his every movement. Jon made it to the main entrance doors unseen only because the place was deserted above ground. Just the same, he paused with one hand on the chrome crash bar on the right half of the double doors and scanned the other end of the hall and beyond. He hadn't fully committed himself. He could abort, but not once he stepped into the open courtyard in front of the lab. There was no turning back then, no place to stash the crate.

Easing pressure against the bar, the door cracked open. It was now or never.

He slipped through the door, softened its return on its hinges, and looked around for Maria. She was beyond the landing and field of grass, on the edge by the trees. She was adjusting the straps and ties on two horses—the last two here at the lab, so Jon understood. If he ever decided to leave, it now meant his only option was another all-day hike, which might as well be no option at all should things sour fast. It also meant no communication with the outside world, aside from the resupply every other week.

No one else was in the courtyard.

He straightened, encouraged by his good fortune thus far, and strode up to her, shifting the crate from one arm to the other. The bones adjusted inside. He should have packed them tighter.

She turned at his approach, her big brown eyes taking him and the crate in like a mother watching her child coming home covered in mud. She made him nervous, if he wasn't already.

There was no need for chitchat. She knew why he was here. The wind soughed a soft hum through the surrounding pine tops, covering his near whisper, to his relief. "Got room for one more?"

Maria sized up the crate, then took it, without a glance at the shipping address and began strapping it to the back of the horse she would pull behind. Jon's next breath came a little easier. He held out a hundred dollar bill. "I don't expect any change, only a hope this can stay between us."

At that she smiled and snatched the bill. "Change? What change? I call it a handling fee." Her smile must have been something when she was younger; it still shone like a pearl of joy. Jon was quickly understanding why she was going to be missed. "And don't worry about our little secret. We're very good at keeping them around here." Her voice lost the sweetness of her smile for an instant, revealing her sarcasm. "I'm sure whatever your reason, it must be just as valid as Prescott's."

She mounted the lead horse. "Be careful Dr. Ostiman."

"It's *Ost*man. And why do you say that?"

Holding the reins tight, Maria glanced about them at the rising wall of forest and darkening cloud cover. "Can't you feel it, that we're not alone?"

"How do you mean?" Jon had a guess, but needed to be sure.

"Something besides the harsh winter has been preying on our wolf pack, paying us visits at night. The horses sense it. I sense it." She lowered her eyes from her perch. "And so do you. If you're wise, you'll leave it be. Some secrets are best left unknown." She let slack in the reins and her horse stepped quickly into a trot.

Jon watched as Maria was carried into the drape of hanging moss and embrace of a thousand tree limbs until she and her two horses vanished into the rainforest. The last image he had was of his crate rising and falling with the labor of its ride's haunches. The bones were now out of his hands. The safest place they could be. He only hoped they made it to their destination. If so, any success he had here was gravy.

Turning from the trail, Jon dug a hand into his pocket and pulled out the one tooth he had kept for himself, a piece of truth he couldn't let slip through his fingers. A thick, gray cloudbank sat atop the steep ridge three thousand feet above the lab. Among the matt of evergreen, white husks of charred and dead spruce trunks pointed up from the hillside with twisted arms and withered fingers, many partially hidden behind a mist swirling up from the valley floor. Around him the forest sat silent and brooding, a veil so impenetrable anything could be just the other side of the nearest trees: a herd of elk, one of many lost airplanes that disappear each year…anything.

So yes, like Maria, he did feel *it*. He had felt it since he stepped foot into the rainforest this morning, felt it every time he entered a remote corner of Northwest wilderness. It was the eerie mixture of solitude and company, like standing alone in a dim, cavernous room with a two-way mirror. And no matter how many times the sensation poisoned his nerves, its sharp chill never dulled, was always as cutting to the bone as that first time thirty years ago on the other side of the Peninsula when he saw his first track. The deep gash in the mud with five toes and shank, complete with ball and heel like a man's. It had been so fresh, water still oozed out from the rich black soil, pooling in the bottom of it. Then the tree branches around him had come to life, swaying and rustling as something moved between them, something big. An odor, foul as death and strong as decay, rose up from the ferns and squeezed tight around him, ripening as the movement in the trees encroached. And then he was running, sprinting with his life in his throat and the crash of timber behind him.

He had never come any closer to one than that day, never had the burning knowledge of a visual witness as so many others had, yet he *knew* just the same, knew that despite the lab being a day from the nearest street lamp or any other comfort of humanity, they were not alone.

Striding through the unbroken field of grass, he took in again the exposed granite face of the hillside and the bunker jutting out from it. With no windows and only the one set of double doors, the fully concrete structure still retained its original menace and impregnable stance. He noted the freshly dried section of cement added to the landing and imagined the line of tracks that had scarred the original pouring.

Whether Maria knew, like Jon, or whether she merely felt she was not alone, the effect either way was enough to hasten her departure. Jon, on the other hand, eagerly made his way back to the lab doors, even slowing his step at the end, savoring that sharp chill. Despite the odds against them—the manhunt that surely had tracked him to Prescott's Institute by now, and the tooth he caressed between his fingers—Jon was eager to give the hunt one last shot. Maria was wrong about this secret. Truth was always worth the risk and never best left unknown.

April 30
5:24 PM

The book and the eight-by-ten photos lay untouched on the desk in front of Director Keyes. He gazed at them, speechless, unmoving. After a minute or more had passed in the heavy silence, Locke wondered if Keyes even breathed. Locke had expected a reaction for sure; even the director wasn't coolheaded enough to simply swallow unwelcome news such as this without a flinch. But as Locke stood there at attention with the soft ticking of the government-issue wall clock behind him counting the seconds, he had the unpleasant feeling there was some bit of intel escaping him, something the director knew and that he too should know. The longer the director held his tongue, stewing on whatever brewed in his head, the more solid and uncomfortable Locke's feeling became, until he came to doubt his decision to fully debrief the director on current events, as he had come to learn was good politics on certain occasions. The doubt, however, flittered away into oblivion where it belonged by the next tick of the long, red second hand.

Finally the director reached out a hand ever-so-slowly and fanned the pages of the book, which Locke had taken from Ostman's office, as casually as he might those of a novel he'd read twice before. In fact, along with the brief but sharp recoil of recognition that flashed across the director's face when Locke set the book atop the desk, Locke wouldn't now be surprised to learn a copy of the book was on a shelf in the director's own personal library.

From his lower position seated across the desk from where Locke stood, the director's eyes followed his hand and came up in address. "Mercy is a seductive weakness, my old friend. It convinces you the easy decision is also the right decision, then it compounds your error over time until it comes back for payment years later and shows you nothing but justice." Director Keyes' eyes glanced at the center photograph, then back at Locke. The photo showed Ostman and Prescott standing together outside the old bunker up the Hoh, consulting a topographical map of the valley. The resolution was so fine that the quadrant Ostman pointed at was discernable.

The director eased out of his wood-backed chair, stepping to the window. "Not that your orders ever include reporting the details of your assignments, even to me, but in this case had I known…well, I would not have allowed it to get this far, mercy be damned."

So the foul had not been Locke's. There was back-story here that was beyond his need to know. Learning that Ostman was already known to the director meant the news he'd given was beyond unwelcome, and the situation was approaching desperate, as evidenced by the photographs he'd taken: the shot of Prescott and Ostman, a photo of a team of armed men gathered about the bunker in full gear near dusk, the close-up of their Indian—the most threatening image of all. Nevertheless, Locke felt back on firm ground and free to continue his debriefing. "The man with Ostman is Philip Prescott. The NPS records show a contract had been issued to his firm three years ago for a wolf reintroduction program to be carried out right here in the park. We weren't watching him, because he apparently had friends in high places. But it's clear we should have been." Locke pointed at the third photograph, "They have had the luxury of time, are well-financed, possess state-of-the-art technology—infrared, fourth-generation night vision, GPS, as large as .375-caliber rifles—and they have an Indian on the team. They're going about it just as we do, as my team two valleys over is right now. If Dr. Ostman succeeds...."

At this, Director Keyes turned from his view of the rainforest. He said nothing, letting his eyes speak for him. It was time for Locke to listen. Then the director returned to gazing out the window at the view up Hoh valley from the park's headquarters. A low ceiling of black weather was passing overhead, charging up the valley to dump its load. The forest, gnarled, draped in green, and shrouded in a mist settling in as the day slowly lost its grip on the land, hid the horizon and everything in between. A double-edged sword. The trees had no loyalty, keeping secrets indiscriminately. And now the director was pondering the same frustrating realization with which Locke had been struggling. As vigilant as they were, as alert and poised, they had missed an entire operation being organized, outfitted, and executed right in their own backyard.

Director Keyes spoke softly, but with strength. "It is Philip Prescott we should fear the most, not Ostman. The greatest threat is always the one from within."

Locke blinked in surprise. Apparently Prescott was known to the director as well, and an insider at that. So then, he had been operating under inaccurate assumptions. Ostman wasn't the key man. It was Prescott.

The director's voice went softer still, as if in confession. "The wolf contract and a private location shielded from watchful eyes in exchange for royalties from his animal-testing research. Business as usual, only this time it wasn't. The bastard had been using our deal as cover."

Still facing the window, Director Keyes calmly brought his hands from his pant pockets and clasped them together at his lower back. "You ever play dominoes, Locke?"

"Yes, sir," Locke replied. "No better way to take the enlisted boys' hard-earned pay."

Director Keyes finally turned from the glass. "It's important that you under-stand, this is all much, much bigger than some newly discovered primate species being listed as endangered. We can, we have, dealt with such matters before, though this particular case would present some unique and costly problems to be sure. But no, this is bigger because it is about trust. Despite their cynicism, peo-ple trust government, they trust industry. They trust the government and indus-try to protect them, to care for them, to think for them. But what do you think would happen if the people learned that their government had a history of using any means necessary to acquire and protect the world's richest reserve of natural resources, even if it meant sponsoring mass extermination of whole races and spe-cies? That their nation exists today solely because of such actions, because of the promises their nation made behind closed doors to men like my grandfathers, and because of the current efforts of men like ourselves.

"We exist because the people trust we do not. But when one domino falls, no matter how small, they can all fall. And when that happens the blinding spell of trust is broken, the light is switched on, and the people's ignorance erased. And that, my friend, is the worst of all scenarios when you live in the shadows as we do.

"And so our job is keeping the dominoes standing, and if we can't, then we have them removed from the table before they can fall. It's just unfortunate for Ostman and Prescott that we have failed in our duties thus far with respect to this cryptid of theirs. For if we had not and the species had been hunted into extinc-tion as we once thought, then I would not have to consider removing them both from the table permanently."

Locke's stance became stiffer, almost out of defense. No finger was pointing at him, yet the unsaid was often sharper and harder to hear than the said. The stakes had just been spelled out to him in no uncertain terms and he needed no remind-ing that it was his actions that had brought them all to this point. Perhaps, though, the director was overreacting. The situation may not be as dire as the one Director Keyes had so eloquently painted. "Sir, if you will allow me. That may not be necessary, because I believe all may be in order. Should the stolen bones no longer be in Ostman's possession, my men are in position to recover them, with the prime targets in China and New York being watched around the clock. And my team here in the park will bring this rogue silverback down before Pres-cott and Ostman even get a whiff of its trail."

"Oh, I should certainly hope so, especially with Sutherland's saws scheduled to start cutting on Monday." Director Keyes shifted his profile just enough for Locke to note the tightness in his jaw and the pinch in his brow—signs the direc-tor's patience was quickly waning. Locke had seen the look many times before, but never with respect to himself. "However, the time for mercy and discretion has passed." The director scooped up the photos. "You see, Prescott maintains a position in the center of the table, as does our good friend Secretary Mason—a particularly dangerous location should either of their inside dominoes fall."

Director Keyes handed the photos, and then the book, back to Locke. "No, I think all the other dominoes would be that much safer if we removed these from the table."

Locke glanced again at the photos spread in his hands, at the faces of the men he had just been ordered to kill. He had the old urge to reach up and rub his left ear, to calm the warm rush that always came with such orders. But he resisted, letting its warmth turn cold at the edges with anticipation. "And what of the secretary?"

A pause hung briefly in the air, then Director Keyes motioned with a raised hand before turning his back on Locke to enjoy again the view of the trees.

As Locke stepped toward the door and the ever-ticking wall clock, he felt a renewed admiration for the director. As Locke well knew, restraining your hand in mercy often required far less strength than raising it in justice.

Every time man asserts his mastery over nature,
he gains something in knowledge but loses something in spirit.
—Edward Cronin

Monticello
May 4
10:15 AM

The Virginia sky stretched into oblivion, high and unblemished by haze or cloud. Mason slowed his pace as he made his way up to the main entrance at Monticello. Since his diagnosis, he'd learned to savor every moment of splendor that came his way. Surrounded by well-manicured grounds that were secluded by groves of trees rich in the lush currency of spring and refreshed by the light purity of open air, Mason was in the grip of splendor. There was the near-silent rustle of leaves caressed by an unfelt breeze, the sharp odor of freshly cut grass, the rare sense of solitude. Mason would die with a smile if this were his last memory.

He paused on the entrance steps under cover of the Roman-inspired, column-supported veranda, relishing the serenity as he gazed out over the courtyard. To know that all that he saw was crafted by the hand of an ancestor elicited a sense of pride that came of its own accord and carried with it no residual vanity. It was not pride in himself, but of what could be accomplished in one's life, and that in this case it had been his own blood that succeeded.

Just as every coin has two sides, so too did his thoughts. He was quickly reminded how little time he had left to be the architect of his legacy, and that in so doing he was here in search of items that would unavoidably reveal hidden smudges of shame on the greatest of the Founding Father's legacies. He felt like a grave robber, greedily disrespecting the dead for his own gain. The feeling rose nearly to the level of blasphemy. If America ever had a leader that ruled the nation by divine providence, it had been Jefferson.

Nothing, though, was more divine than truth, nor as freeing. If his memories proved correct…well, he'd just have to let the chips fall where they may. His job was to preserve the nation Jefferson built, even if it meant attacking that very hero, Mason's own flesh and blood.

Taking one last inhale of peace, Mason turned for the large, oak double doors. With each step he consoled himself that the odds were stacked in favor of him finding nothing, as so many had before him.

With his hand on the door handle and his back to the grounds, the illusion of solitude splintered as his periphery perception became aware of motion in the nearest grove of maple. Disobeying his instincts to turn and confirm the impression, Mason gripped the handle tighter and slowly opened the door, his back tensing as if he knew it were centered within a sniper's crosshairs. The presence of his shadows needed no confirmation, and he did not doubt their growing courage that they might venture out in the open under the light of day. All the more reason to believe Monticello still held a few secrets in its rafters.

He stepped inside, and the door closed quietly behind him with the softest hiss. Whatever the line was that he was not to cross, the threshold to the entrance hall was not it. The trick he had to learn, and quickly, was to see the line ahead of time so that he might dodge the bullet as he crossed.

Alone in the room, Mason stood at the doors, letting the scent of age and antiseptic awaken memories of playing in this very room as his mother chatted with visitors and guided them through Jefferson's own eclectic museum of natural history. He could hear her melodic voice, explaining to an elder couple that the great clock was designed by Jefferson himself. And he saw other guests milling about the room, pointing at Mandan Indian artifacts sent back by Lewis and Clark in 1805, especially the portrait of the white chief, Big White. Still others discussed the copy of the Declaration of Independence on the wall and busts of great men such as Hamilton and Voltaire. Light streamed in through tall paned windows, and a fire crackled in the hearth.

Today, though, he was the only visitor, and the fireplace was cold and black.

But that very same aura of light was streaming through the arched windows, filling the eighteen-foot-high room with a soft hue of morning. And everything else was exactly as he remembered—the striking green floorcloth, the ceiling pattern featuring a bald eagle and stars, the balcony leading up to the mezzanine, and the classic Roman décor, with frieze ornaments from the Temple of Antoninus and Faustina.

Yet, everything was not *exactly* the same. In fact everything was smaller, cramped. The ceiling lower, the walls crowding. The furniture shrunken, the artifacts miniaturized.

Of course, nothing had indeed changed but himself. He had returned to enough places of his childhood to recognize the discrepancy between memory and reality.

He strode across the bright green floor, his back muscles and paranoia relaxing within the security of nostalgia. The faint thud of his footfalls carried well over the room's acoustics. On the opposite wall hung a set of moose and elk antlers. They'd been his favorite when he was a boy. He knew their story better than his mother. They were two of many plant and animal specimens collected and sent to Jefferson during Lewis and Clark's expedition. Many had not survived the test of time and the carelessness of man through the years. Few specimens were known to exist today. The only complete zoological specimen was the Lewis woodpecker preserved at Harvard. These two sets of antlers were special, because they were the only items to survive out of twenty-five crates of artifacts that were lost when the ship transporting them from Washington to Richmond went down.

A few Lewis and Clark scholars believed the missing journal volumes also went down with that ship. Mason too had prescribed to that theory, as opposed to the others: that Lewis simply stopped writing for long periods of time, that they had been stolen or destroyed, or that they'd been lost on the return trip. But Mason was not so sure any longer.

He gazed up past the antlers to the eagle with its extended wingspan and the stars sprayed across the ceiling. If those supposed missing volumes existed, then they were hidden here, in Jefferson's own home. How he knew that, he wasn't sure. Something from his past, something his mother had said.

The bigger question that had been plaguing Mason since Philadelphia was why? Why would Jefferson feel the need to censor the journals? That fact alone meant they contained something of value, at least two hundred years ago. But what? And what was the significance of an animal that was "so hard to die" as discussed in the "afore mentioned" entry from December 1805? Jefferson would surely not insert a clue at random, if the added text was a clue at all. That possibility had crossed Mason's mind a dozen times, though each time the alternative won out. Exactly why he wasn't sure, something beyond logic was at work. Of course, even if he were right, and the missing volumes were found, the odds were they would offer nothing of value to Mason's crusade. Nevertheless, the hunt for truth was reason enough.

"Secretary Mason. Welcome back to Monticello."

Mason dropped his gaze from the eagle to the open doorway that led into the parlor. A tall, angular man wearing a suit that fit one size too big stood with a smile of greeting and an extended hand. Mason returned the gesture as he stepped forward. "And you must be—"

"Aidan Thwaite. Head curator at Monticello."

"Of course." Mason gave an approving scan of the room. "You've done a fine job. Not even the chairs have been moved."

"Freezing a moment in time isn't easy by any means, but we do our best." The curator looked Mason down from head to toe. His smile was a polite facade; the pity in his eyes was the truth. Everyone Mason met for the first time who knew of his disease and pending death wore the same mixed expression. Mason couldn't judge the man. He had worn the same expression himself before he'd become the walking equivalent of a Greek tragedy.

Mason was impressed, though, with the curator's ability to maintain composure as a tremor of pain rippled up from behind Mason's ribs to collect as a stone grimace on his face. The curator simply waited patiently as Mason reacted casually out of habit, pulling his bottle of painkillers from his windbreaker, popping the lid and downing two capsules in one swallow.

Feeling his face loosen and his breathing resume, Mason smiled back in gratitude. "The miracles of modern medicine." The sarcasm was intentionally subdued, but not omitted.

The curator wisely changed the subject. "You'll have to excuse me, and not that a family member is not welcome, but my assistant didn't mention exactly the reason for your visit."

Mason slipped the recently refilled bottle back into his jacket and swallowed down the residual bitter aftertaste. "Well, to be honest, and if it's not a distraction, I've come to do a little snooping."

A sincere grin finally graced the thin man's bony face. "Ah, I see. Well you're in luck. Today's schedule is light. Perhaps I could assist, narrow your search a bit?"

Mason couldn't be sure if the curator's pity had anything to do with his ease at granting him full access, and he didn't care. Any benefits that arose from his slow demise could never shift the balance of fairness, and thus ever elicit even the slightest twinge of guilt. In the end, he'd leave this life with fate deeply indebted to him. Expecting the curator's green light to change to yellow once he announced his intentions, Mason responded with an expression as sober and hard-set as was possible, given the pain hadn't been fully washed clean by the drugs spreading through his veins. "I'm looking for Lewis's missing journals."

The curator lost his grin in surprise, then quickly found it as he camouflaged another stare of pity, this time for the foolish. "Well, I can say you're not the first, though it has been some years. I would have bet that line of inquiry had been resolved by now."

Mason pushed both hands into the outer pockets of his jacket, standing comfortably and unphased by meeting with one who thought contrary to himself. It was nothing new. He just waited.

The silence forced the curator to play his hand first. "Then again, Jefferson was quite the collector. History is never a known quantity. New documents come to light all the time. Though, I'd be quite embarrassed should the journals prove to have been sitting right under my own nose this whole time."

Turning inside his suit, the curator started into the parlor. "I'll show you to the cellar, where we keep everything that has not yet been catalogued. There's not much, but it's all there is."

Mason followed but veered to the left, toward the polished hardwood stairs that led to the second floor and beyond. "Thank-you, but I've taken enough of your time already. Besides, I think I'll begin in the attic."

The man stopped in his lanky stride, confused. "The attic? There's nothing but junk up there."

And that was exactly the kind of thinking that could allow the journals to remain hidden all these years. Mason kept that grain of logic to himself. "You're probably right, but if nothing else I'll at least get a final walk down memory lane."

He was pushing the pity thing a bit far, but the curator simply shrugged his pointed shoulders. "Just don't make a mess." He chuckled at his own humor and returned to his trot across the parlor. "If you lose your way, I'll be in the library. The staircase doesn't exactly jump out at you. I'd have never known it was there if your mother hadn't pointed it out to me."

Mason placed one foot on the first gleaming step and a hand on the smooth, smudge-free banister as he watched the wiry frame of the curator pass out of sight into the dining room. Then, with a smug air of victory, he ascended the stairs, sliding his left hand along the banister as he had as a boy. With any luck, Mason would soon learn if his mother had known of other family secrets, ones she would have eventually revealed to her only son had she lived long enough.

After three wrong turns and nearly twenty minutes of searching, he found the pull-down staircase. The curator wasn't kidding. If he hadn't been guided by memory, he'd never have found the perfectly disguised trapdoor in the ceiling at the end of the hall that led to the back bedchambers.

The stairs came down with a drawn-out creak of neglect. Mason slowly took each step of the narrow ascent with a growing sense of eerie familiarity. By the top step, the memory of the last time doing so had gripped him like a bad dream. Panicked screams for help rang in his ears. He beat on the closed trap door, pounding despite the pain to his fists. Darkness blinded him, and whispers assaulted him from the corners and rafters. Then, mercifully, his mother's voice was soothing him, and her embrace rocking him. "It's all right, T.J. It's all right. Mommy's here…Mommy's here." Her fingers ran though his hair. "I guess I have to let you in on a little secret now, don't I. You found Thomas Jefferson's private study, a special room known only to our family. And when you're older I'll tell you what other secrets this room holds."

The *clap* of the trap door rising back into place even with the floor woke him from his childhood, leaving him once again alone in this hidden sanctuary of Jefferson's. His mother may not have lived long enough to fulfill her promise, but with a little aid from the Almighty she may yet have a second chance.

The same dimensional weirdness from the entrance hall made him feel two feet taller than he was. Attics not being all that large to begin with, this one seemed barely the size of a loft. Its general shape was that of being inside a dome, contouring to the design of the roof. Several small-paned windows invited in just enough light to define the chaos of boxes and debris littering the bare floor by varying shades of shadows rather than any definite lines. The beams of daylight had more definition as they cut into the dark, gaining substance from air thick with two lifetimes of confinement. The dust coated everything, dulling what details he could see with a dark shade of gray. And the stale, rank air immediately coated the inside of his nose and dried out his mouth.

He picked his way through the junk, which wasn't all that inaccurate, to the one naked and inverted lightbulb screwed to an angled rafter. He pulled the chain, and a weak haze of yellow challenged the shadows, most of which remained planted firmly in place, unthreatened. Mason stood there a moment, surveying the task ahead of him and inviting guidance from whoever might be watching from above.

He started with the first stack of boxes, found nothing but old black-and-white photos and holiday decorations, and moved to the next. And the next. And the next.

Time passed, he knew, by the shifting angle of the light coming in through the windows and his growing pangs of hunger, but he didn't document how much by a glance at his watch. Time had become meaningless to him. He'd never have enough, so why start counting.

He had opened every box, scoured every crate, made a general mess of the place—despite the curator's half-hearted request—and was standing in the center of the attic empty-handed. He could hear the mocking voice of doubt starting to whisper in his ear. But he'd been so sure. The journals had to be here somewhere, if they were anywhere. He turned in a slow methodic circle, searching, pleading for guidance, for a helping hand from his mother.

But he could see no X marking the spot. He had scrutinized every inch of the room, every shadowed corner—

Mason stopped in mid-circle, staring at the far end of the room. He had *not* checked every corner. He took a cautious step, then another, until he was picking his way across the floor. This one corner had seemed too bare, too void of any unique architectural flaw to allow for a hidden space in the walls or floor. He had passed it right by, making it the perfect place.

Coming to stand in the corner's shadowed veil, he surveyed the walls covered in tattered and shredding wallpaper, the rafters rising up over his head, and the floorboards at his feet. He lowered himself to his knees, feeling a sense of reverence and humility as he did, and sensing too the hand of his mother guiding his actions. This was it, somewhere here in the floor.

He bent low, his face inches from the floorboards, and sent the dust rising into the air as he blew clean the section of floor at his knees. He ran his hands along each four-inch-wide board of hand-cut pine, digging his fingernails into the cracks between them, searching for leverage, a sign he wasn't fooling himself. And then, one of the boards moved, jiggled in place. It was loose.

Scooting closer, he wedged his fingers around both sides of the board, which ran to the exact point of the corner. Pushing his fingers in, tilting the board, it popped free, coming up into his grasp, revealing a three-foot slender hole in the floor. Blacker than midnight within, he set the board down and reached a hand in up to his elbow. His pulse was a jackhammer in his ears, and his breathing non-existent. *Thank you, Mother, thank you.*

His fingers jammed against a cold, hard surface—a slender, square box of riveted metal. Grasping the box tightly, he lifted it out, playing it through the space left by the removed board, praying it fit. It just barely did, pinching his fingers something awful in the process.

As if it were the Holy Grail itself, Mason gently rested the box on the floor at his knees and took a deep breath. In the weak excuse for illumination, he tried to take in what his eyes were refusing to see. A lockbox, silver with riveted seams, held closed by a brass lock that hung unlatched, inviting admittance to the contents held secret within for two centuries. He removed the lock, holding it in his palm, thinking of the last man to do so. Thomas Jefferson. But why hadn't he locked it? Unless he had wanted the box's contents to be found.

Setting the lock next to the freed pine board, Mason proceeded to lift the lid. Its hinges resisted some, but could offer nothing more than a soft creak in protest. After that it only took a glance inside from Mason for the whispers of doubt to be banished. There, placed neatly one next to another, were four elk-skinned field journals of the same type and description as those in Philadelphia, their covers looking as preserved as if they had been stowed away just yesterday.

The connection came to him immediately, as easy as his own name. Four journals. And four gaps of time within Lewis's personal journal record: September 19 to November 11, 1803; May 14, 1804 to April 7, 1805; August 26, 1805 to January 1, 1806; and August 12 to September 26, 1806. He couldn't take too much credit, because the dated covers made the realization almost too easy. The dates of the gaps matched the dates on the journals to the day. He itched to pick one up, any one, to discover their secrets and the reason Jefferson had felt compelled to hide their existence. Then he remembered the clue that had brought him here. December 1805. Jefferson was not one to act without cause. He wanted someone to know what had happened in that month two centuries ago. So Mason took a breath, then two, and lifted out the corresponding volume.

Lewis and Clark Bodices
Index I.—Lewis
Journal
Aug. 26, 1805–Jan. 1, 1806
(complete)
folios 21 pages 186

The cover resisted opening, its binding having grown tight with two centuries of slumber. He skimmed through the pages, recognizing Lewis's long, flowing handwriting. Somewhere in his consciousness he remembered why he was here, to understand why the journals had been separated to begin with, but his overriding wonder at being the first to read these entries since Lewis, or even Jefferson, left him capable of little more than holding the journal steady in his hands.

Eventually he regained some semblance of self-control and flipped straight to the end of the volume. Believing at first he would have to read many entries from that month to find the one Jefferson was referring to, Mason was disappointed to find only one entry.

Wednesday December 18th 1805

Two evenings past Comowooll and six Clatsops came to trade. They being unusualy excited Capt. Clark & I incquired to know why. A hunt, they had come to invit us to hunt. our hungar for meat great we readily accepted, especially as they are known for their skill. And we soon learned this hunt is of apparent great value to their people. Comowooll spoke of length regarding the import and not in terms of Satisfying hunger. the beast we were to hunt they refer to as the Skuku'm, or beast of healing and Devil of the mountains. They hunt it for its medecinal powers & to gain its longevity. Each of the Indian nations we have thus encounterd has Spoken of such beasts, beasts of legend. they seem to esteem highly their stories, tho Capt. Clark & I believd Comowooll refered to only the Wappetoe or perhaps the white bear. In private, myself, I had reservations. Since leaving the Missouri many nights have been spent around the fire watching the trees for the sense of something being out there. Terrible screams and whistles have haunted us on many occasion. Tracks of unexplicable size and shape have been found around camp in the morning, along with certain items gone missing. Needless to say I awaited the hunt with much curiosity, especially as Comowooll had told us our rifles and even espontoons were of no uce.

the Clatsops had given us a very formidable account of the Strength and Ferocity of this beast, but we counted their descriptions for naught as they had only bows and arrows & spears. Tho it did give Capt. Clark and myself pause when we saw the Clatsops going thru the same rituals as when they go on a war party. But the Clatsops' hunt was one more of strategem. A local was selected based on markers they found in trees. The top branches of them had been snapped off, the Skuku'm being territorial it leaves signs of its presence. a deadfall was then constructed, of the size that would kill four horses, and then bait was laid out beneath it. The bait being a full live hamstrung Wappetoe with a most impresive set of antlirs. And then Comowooll warned us of the Skuku'm's ability to thro its voice and to not be fooled when it showed.

the trap set we lied in waiting in the brush until near sundown. As night fell upon us we learned we were not alone. a whistle almost a faint call came from in front of us by the deadfall, and then another behind us. I beheld a smell as never had I before that cut my nostrils and boiled my stomach. The Devil himself could indeed have come for us. Then screams of my men sounded from across the clearing and they ran out into the open with the bait, and they being pursued by fight and fury, a blur of monstrous terror. The strategem had failed. Panik broke thro us, bringing us to the defense of our men. And thus it turned and came at us opened mouthed screaming a terrible roar. Shots and arrows were fired from all around, myself had time for one shot. and as I loaded another ball it made for me. Erect! On two legs! I retreated, loading my ball, hearing shots from everywhere. It charged on as balls passed thro its lungs, broke its knee and hip. still it advanced. Nearly obliged to discard my rifle and flee I made the load and aimed and fired thro its head, killing it dead at my boots.

A most tremendous looking anamal lay before me with two espontoons in its back. the Clatsops were quick to butcher it, desiring to eat the heart while it still beat. I shook from the matter for several minutes and counted myself Lucky among men when we learned twelve balls had passed thro it and two of the Clatsop had fallen dead. to see the wounds it would bear before being put to death and its face lying in the mud made clear and resolved my curiosity. This anamal they call the Skuku'm is no bear or any other beast of my imagination, tho perhaps a creature of the pre history as Pres. Jefferson had believed still inhabited the Americas. Or even no beast at all. for in its eyes as it past from this world I beheld something much more than beast, something akin to man.

Mason turned to the next page and immediately his eyes fixed on the sketch covering it from top to bottom. A perfectly drafted, artistically scaled rendering of a skull. A primate skull.

Mason's breath caught in his lungs, causing him to gag and cough. The face, even though on paper and having traveled two hundred years through time to reach him, sparked a tingle that spread over the little hairs on his neck. His mind reflexively rejected what it saw, rejected that this sketch was of the animal Lewis had encountered while on the Pacific coast. There were no primates in North America, and never had been, especially one whose skull alone made the gorilla look like a tame, furry lemur.

Mason fought through the illogical conjecture with reason. Simply put, why would Lewis have made it up?

He skipped back to the beginning of the entry and reread slowly, catching every word, every meaning left unsaid, second guessing Lewis all the way.

By the time he reached the bare-boned face awaiting him, his palms were sweating and his mouth drier than the dust choking the air. Lewis's meticulous, riveting narrative had banished any skepticism Mason had left. What he'd read had actually happened. The skull had existed. They had hunted down and eaten the beating heart of a giant ape. An ape that had walked on two legs and had resisted a dozen lead balls before taking two men with it to the grave.

Mason shuddered.

His hands and the journal fell into his lap as he desperately tried to fit this new piece into the puzzle he had believed to be complete and accurate—the puzzle he'd become so accustomed to, the one he knew as the world around him.

Then he remembered the legends still being spoken of in the Northwest, the legends of Sasquatch and Bigfoot. He recalled all the frenzied hunting and searching that had been in the news back in the '60s and '70s.

Was it coincidence?

And like that, the piece slipped into the puzzle as if it had always been there. No, it was not coincidence. Neither were a great many other things that up until now seemed to be. Mason was beginning to grasp, at least in part, Jefferson's motives.

He picked the journal up again to study the sketch, and noticed handwriting on the page, the only other marks besides the sketch. The handwriting was small and in the left margin, and struck him as similar to that of the handwriting that had brought him here—Jefferson's, to be sure.

26/9/06

A date, no doubt. September 26th, 1806. One that also fell within the gaps of Lewis's personal record. And perhaps another clue. Mason had the sense he was being led down a path. Where to was still very much in question.

So Mason obeyed and closed the one journal and traded it for the fourth volume in the box. August 12 to September 26, 1806. Obviously, he was again looking for the final entry of the volume. He skipped too far at first, finding only blank pages, and fanned back until he had it.

Friday September 26 1806

I stare at this skul resting atop my desk and ponder what it means to have finally come to our Journey's end, and of the cause of liberty and the honour of America which have sustained our hearts. we set out more than two years past on a mission from the president of the U. States with a list of directives. In sum & in private our mission was simply that of empire building, the largest and most powerful the world has yet known as Pres. Jefferson rightly boasted, from ocean to ocean, coast to coast, provided the Government is able to avail themselves of these resources so liberally bestowed by God on this fair portion of the globe. Because much work is yet needed to tame this great wilderness and the many Indian nations that inhabit it. Much more so even than hard labor is required, for all the resources in the world are for naught if no one has the coureage to usurp them. Having been to the Pacific and back I am intimate with the knowledge of men's fragile fears and weak minds. I know the average man, who will be needed to settle the West and forge the bonds of this great empire, will never be induced to leave the comforts of hearth and home if he knows of the fears and the many dangers that await him and certainly not for nothing grander than to be in the service of his Country. For this reason we were ordered from the beginning to Secrecy with respect to this specific knowledge gained along the way, our men charged to edit their journals and myself to keep two sets. Even the Indians were to be misled as to our intentions, & all others we might encounter with respect to our enemy nations, France, England, Spain, & etc. And is why I now must select out and keep this skule separate from our other specimens in preperation to hand over in all faith and wisdom to our president with a strong warning that it would be best if in the publik's mind it never exhisted as well with the entirety of its kind. For we have discovered these past two years many obstacles in the path of an American empire; the lack of an all water route to the pacific, the nearly impenetrable mountain range at the headwaters of the Missouri, the unwillingness of the Indians to accept this new commerce, the many wild and dangerous animals. But in the minds of the public where the true barriers lie this skule and the beast it is proof of is worse than these all. Much worse.

Tho I must admit in truth even as this skul watches me with its empty unsee-ing eyes, chilling me with Memories of nine months past, I have come to doubt my shameful actions and those I must soon perform. For I am haunted even to this day by the eyes of this anamal in death. haunted by what I fear I have done and what the Corps of Discovery has set in motion. Never before in my long service to this Nation have I before been tempted to describe its acts as Evil. For isn't it Evil to shed innocent blood, that which sustains the life of those who posses a Soul?

Mason could barely believe what he was reading. He felt as if he'd pulled a loose thread on his shirt, only to have the entire article unravel. He was getting into something he had not bargained for nor expected. And the sense of remorse, of doing something wrong simply by reading these documents, was taking a real hold on his conscious. He wasn't just uncovering a darker side of Jefferson's leg-end, but of Lewis's as well. Questions and possibilities were now coming faster than he could consider them, creating a chaos in his mind as unwieldy as that which he'd created on the attic floor.

His first realization was that these four journals represented the second set Lewis had been ordered to keep. An entirely separate record from the rest. Unbe-lievable in the least. Lewis and the entire Corps of Discovery had been censored even before leaving St. Louis, and by none other than Thomas Jefferson, the author of the Declaration of Independence no less. Historians were going to drop dead when they learned how much rewriting was in their future. Especially when it came to the apparent errors relating to America's supposedly innocent settling of the west. Because if nothing else, Jefferson had already forced a rewrite of his-tory, and one that would finally shed some light on business as usual in Washing-ton. Unfortunately, though, it meant that private deals and secret plans had been made behind closed doors even then, during the nation's virgin birth. The news struck Mason as sadly as that of his parents' divorce. But this was exactly what he needed, the public needed. The cleansing light of the truth.

And that was the second thing he considered, combined with this possibly new species discovered by Lewis. He thought of the pressure he'd been getting of late by the timber interests in the Northwest, more of the same overbearing claim to the public's forests and national parks. It seemed clear enough, by the testi-mony of Lewis, if nothing else, that the timber interests knew about Lewis's ape, had known as soon as Lewis made a full report to Jefferson, and whoever else might have been privy—the ageless puppet master for sure. It wouldn't surprise Mason if they had been carrying out their own version of Lewis's hunt ever since, may have even succeeded decades ago and that was why nothing had been found thirty years ago during the frenzy. He knew industry and government had covertly cosponsored such action in the past, the near extermination of the wolf, grizzly, and buffalo being the most notable and tragic.

The mysterious line his shadows were waiting to see if he would cross shimmered on the horizon, coming ever-so-slowly into focus.

He couldn't help the smile that spread across his face. As blind luck, or divine intervention, would have it, he had found his much needed ace-in-the-hole within Lewis's journals after all. If this species of primate existed in 1805, who was to say it didn't exist today. He only needed to prove there was a *possibility* they still existed. A species as closely related to humans as this one appeared to be—Lewis's talk of it having a soul was as good as gold when played on the heartstrings of environmental lobbyists—would demand ten times the protection under the Endangered Species Act as the grizzly now received. Mason could, in effect, lock up every stand of old growth and roadless area for eternity by simply having such an animal placed on the list. His smile broadened. This was exactly their fear, among others—revelations of their prior and current discretions being their basest of phobias. Mason could hardly contain his excitement. When all else failed, fight bureaucracy with bureaucracy he always said.

First he had to convince Congress, and that would take more than a sketch and Lewis's testimony. He would need the skull, if not more. Senators and congressman wouldn't lift a pen without hard evidence. Hell, imagine how fast they would jump to if he had a living, or even dead, specimen. But he needn't get greedy. The skull was a damn good place to start.

So he put his thoughts on pause and returned to the journal he still held in his clammy palms, praying for another clue, one that would finally lead him to something tangible. Anything to tell him if the skull had accompanied the expedition back—he dared not think of the cruel fate if the skull had been lost with so many other precious artifacts in that unfortunate shipwreck on the Potomac. Surely it had made it into Jefferson's hands. And lo and behold, there in the margins jotted next to the line describing Lewis's "orders" was another date.

28/10/09.

October 28, 1809. But that date was well after Lewis's return to St. Louis, by over three years. Even a few weeks after his suicide, if Mason had his dates right. Either way, the date made no sense.

Thinking of nothing to do but admit defeat, Mason casually flipped through the rest of the blank pages in the volume. Until he saw handwriting. Pages of it. His thumb had caught on the first one, the opening of an entry dated on exactly that date. The 28th of October 1809.

I pen these words with a heavy heart and dark conscience, for on this day by way of Clark I have just learned of my dear and cherished friend Meriwether Lewis's murder....

Mason had only enough self-control to read the first line and establish the mystery author's identity as who else but Jefferson. Why not deface an American treasure with his own two cents? It was certainly stacking up to be the least of his crimes at this point. As eager as he was to read Jefferson's apparent confession, two lose sheets of parchment had fallen free of the journal. They were folded in thirds, faded brown, and had become round at the corners. Yet they had obviously been treated and prepared for their long journey through time as they unfolded with resilience and a semblance of integrity. The first was a letter written by Lewis and addressed to Pres. Jefferson the day before his suicide. More intriguing reading for later. But it was the other document that had stolen his attention. It was an invoice, a complete inventory of the specimens that had accompanied Lewis on his return trip. And after a quick scan of every misspelled, badly faded word, Mason confirmed it was pay dirt.

The list was long and specific, including everything from the remains of a male and female pronghorn to that of a white weasel. And near the bottom, on a line by itself, were the magical words: *One large & complete male prymate skul.*

They rang with a loud, solid tone of reality in his head.

By the time Mason heard the wrenching creak of the pull-down staircase's hinges and the soft echo of rising footsteps, he had no choice but to clumsily snatch up the parchments and the four journals and stuff them inside his jacket, zipping it up to his chin until he pinched his neck. The last word he had read from Jefferson's opening line had just registered. *Murder.* Not suicide, but murder. Lewis had been murdered. And if they had no qualms about silencing Jefferson's lifelong friend while Jefferson was yet alive, then Mason could no longer harbor any illusions about what they would do to Jefferson's long-lost heir. Apparently Jefferson had not only created a scandal to rival even today's Congressional dirty laundry, but had given birth, and then unleashed, a bloodthirsty watchdog that had long ago turned on its master.

The light steps of men's dress shoes came to a stop even as Mason came to his feet, turning just in time to see the bone-hardened features and sinewy neck of Curator Aidan Thwaite.

The curator stood at the top step wearing a casual smile, but Mason didn't trust it, wouldn't trust anything from here to his grave. Thwaite glanced about the attic, his eyes pausing here and there, seemingly for the longest at Mason's feet. His hands started to come free from the pockets of his black suit pants as he began to stride toward Mason. "I was coming back from a late lunch and noticed your car. I'd assumed you had left hours ago." His glance pointed again at the floor. "But it appears you've been well entertained."

As casually as Mason could, he slid his hands into the pockets of his jacket, pressing them outward to disguise the bulk of the journals. He offered Thwaite a smile as sincere as he could muster and rushed for the stairs. "Yes, and thank you for allowing me the chance to put this silly notion of mine to rest." He passed Thwaite and was already stepping onto the top step. "As you said, there's nothing up here but junk. Sorry for the mess, but I did lose track of time."

He was halfway down the stairs before he heard the curator call out to stop. He took the last steps as loud and fast as he could without risking a header. If he didn't make it, he could always excuse himself for not hearing over the rickety stairs. Once at the bottom, he kept up his pace, heading for the entrance hall.

By the time he was crossing the green floor of the hall, the half of his brain that wasn't watching his back had already begun to work out a plan to return for the skull. Surely Jefferson had left one last clue, one that led the way to the skull's resting place and was certainly scribbled somewhere on the invoice. The invoice that was tucked safely away inside his jacket. And step one was losing his ever-patient and omnipresent shadows, a task even today's burning sun had failed to do.

Wrapping his fingers around the oak door's handle, he stole a glance behind him and summoned the courage to open the door. The game had changed since arriving this morning. There was far more at stake now than the golden years of one old and diseased man. The truth. And the liberating power it gave to the people who deserved nothing less.

With a deep inhale and another prayer, Mason stepped out into the daylight and the possible waiting precision of a sniper's trigger finger, feeling for the first time that it was he who was as vulnerable as a shadow under the scrutiny of midday.

Thwaite watched the sheet of folded paper fall between the secretary's legs to the floor.

He called out for the secretary to stop as he retrieved the single page. But the man must not have heard and was soon out of sight down the stairs. Thwaite was about to give chase, sure this was something that would be missed; only the gritty texture and familiar discoloration of the paper stopped him with curiosity.

Offhand, he was inclined to think what he held was old, two hundred years or more. Fragile and tender like so many of the documents he'd archived over the years.

He scanned the attic space, noting with a finer-tuned eye the disarray, the opened lockbox also of curious description, and the slender hole in the floorboards.

With the deftness and skill of a man who'd done so a thousand times before, Thwaite unfolded the sheet of paper as he might attempt to disarm a ticking bomb.

It took only as long as the blink of his well-trained and eagle-sharp eyes to discern what he held, what the secretary had found—an invoice written by Meriwether Lewis detailing the contents of many crates. As he skimmed the list, retaining more than the average person would if they were memorizing the content for a final exam, he bumped on an item well down toward the bottom.

Scowling in confusion at first, then understanding, then confusion again, Thwaite looked from the invoice to the dusty old attic chockfull of boxes, crates, chests—all open and pilfered—and then back to the hole in the floor.

So there was more than just junk up here.

It's not evidence if nobody believes it.
And the only thing they'll believe is a body.
—Jonathan Ostman

Olympic National Park
11:50 PM

It had been a long Tuesday night. So long it was ten minutes to Wednesday. And this was only their first watch of many nights to come.

Jon couldn't handle the muscle-tightening strain of remaining hunched and motionless behind the blind another second. He extended up from his haunches as slow as his quivering thighs would allow and took a long drag of the wet night air. His exhale came out a white steam that dissolved in the conflicting breezes that teased at the pine needles and stirred the long blades of grass within the clearing. Not that he could see the waves of grass or swaying boughs, for he couldn't see much of anything.

The weather had come in so low and thick not a single twinkle lit the sky. Even the moon had been snuffed out by the suffocating blanket of clouds. The night couldn't be darker or more disorientating than if a burlap sack had been pulled over his head. Standing there with the ferns and grass rustling against his legs, the blind creaking against the light touch of the wind, he was at the mercy of his other four senses: the cool mint of night air on his tongue, the light kiss of it on his cheek, the dampness of the forest in his nostrils, and the near-silent hum of a thousand trees resisting the pull and push of the storm gliding by overhead, threatening to unload at any minute.

He brought the goggles down around his eyes and switched them on with their faint electric *click*. And just like that the burlap sack had been snatched from his head, revealing a world as lit as noonday, only washed in a faint pea-soup green. The clearing stretched in front of him, the knee-high grass and sporadic stand of ferns flirting with the unseen hand of the wind. A ring of spruce, cedar, and Douglas-fir stood tall and straight, crowding the open space like a mob of onlookers pressing against a circle of police tape. Within those boughs, as unseen as the wind, hid the rest of his team. Each man, armed with enough stopping power to drop a charging rhino, occupied a stand built with a specific angle to the expected approach. To his left, Ian held the stand with the open shot to anywhere in the clearing and was the only man armed with nothing more than a cocktail of liquid sandman that they hoped would preserve all their lives should this actually work.

There in the center of the grass and ferns lay the key to it all. Their bait. The bull elk's rack remained high and held in defense despite the poor beast having been hamstrung hours ago. Rendered lame and immobile, it had given up attempts to stand and flee. It's bawling had subsided after only an hour or so. Now it merely lay there, waiting for death in whatever form was dealt it.

The experience of those first few hours were still so fresh Jon couldn't look upon the mighty Roosevelt elk without cringing in guilt and remorse. He'd had just as much a hand in this as any of them, if only for his reluctance to protest or even walk away. But he didn't. He was drunk again with the lust for success, the final surge for a summit he'd been climbing for a lifetime. He'd gained too much respect for Sixen these past two weeks, and too much confidence, to doubt their chances. If he were to live to see a type specimen in the hands of science, it would be in these next few days.

And so he'd committed to watch this innocent animal die a slow death, to be left here until its stench of decay had the adverse effect. And then they'd bring in another. And another. Until they either succeeded or were forced out of the park.

The Indian's method, as arcane as it was, was not without merit. Jon felt foolish for never considering it himself. No one ever had, except apparently the Native Americans. Giganto, being the opportunistic hunter or eater of carrion that Jon theorized that it was, would fill a similar niche as the grizzly, and thus be lured by the same weaknesses. An easy meal. Unfortunately for the elk, Sixen maintained that no artificial restraining devices could be used, such as chains or rope, for it would chase off their prey before they even knew it was near. All that was required then was to find a frequented game trail, slice a few tendons on the bait, and wait. And wait. And wait.

The massive head of the elk swung in Jon's direction. Its two eyes shone fluorescent green. Without goggles, it saw Jon as clear as he saw it. It made him duck behind the blind in shame.

Consoling himself, or more honestly justifying this witnessed slaughter, he pulled out the tooth he kept in his pocket, the tooth of a hunter and not a grazer. That was why no one had considered using bait, himself included. Live bait wouldn't work on a grazer. Yet another example of the inherent human blind spot he'd been fighting all these years. He knew he'd been pursuing an animal that hunted on occasion, and yet he hadn't thought in those terms.

Sixen did though.

What Jon hadn't been able to accomplish in three decades, Sixen had done in two weeks. The Indian saw the forest with different eyes, heard it with different ears. To him, every movement within the trees left signs as easily read as those on the Vegas strip. It was as if the forest spoke to him in a language only he understood or even heard, telling him whatever he asked, an eyewitness that saw it all. Even here, Sixen claimed that a well-traveled game trail cut across this clearing, yet nothing was visible, not in the brightest of daylight. Jon saw only a field of grass and ferns that was as benign as a slab of blacktop. Sixen saw a beaten path frequented by the Tsadja'tko, as he referred to them, passing feet from where the elk now lay. And according to Sixen, the signs suggested the same individual who left the prints in Prescott's cement was in the area. How he knew, no one questioned, nor understood. He just did, and that was all you could say.

Setting at ease within the blind next to Jon, Sixen was as much a part of the rainforest as were the elk, the ferns, and the cedars. He appeared to sway in time with the leaves in the breeze. He wore no goggles, saw through the dark with his own eyes. The rest of the team were all dressed in camo; Sixen wore only jeans and a flannel shirt. Yet Jon could see him now only because he knew he was there. Surrounded by men with high-caliber rifles, an elk dying as he watched, and with a remnant of the Ice Age being lured in for the kill, Sixen would be sound asleep if he was anymore relaxed. All of which was why Jon and everyone else who had ever joined the hunt over the years failed. They were foreigners in the land and didn't speak the language. Sixen was not. He was at home. And Prescott had somehow convinced him to give them all a tour, to guide them to where they wanted to go.

It was now only a matter time. Lots of time.

But Jon minded not one bit. He was used to waiting. And so he did his best to mimic Sixen, to settle into the tight fit of the blind, to find the dense wall of brush at their backs as comfortable as the couch at home. He rubbed the tooth once for luck and stuffed it back into his pocket, then pushed the .357 on his hip a little to the left, adjusted the earpiece in his ear and the mike on his collar, and loosened the goggles' strap around his head. He could wait as long as Sixen, maybe longer. Enough adrenaline was running through him that he might not sleep for a month.

Taking slow and easy breaths, watching the resulting clouds disappear at the touch of the night, Jon thought what an honor it was to share the blind with Sixen. No one else was permitted. All the others were to remain in the trees. Sixen would see the whole operation through from the ground, where he could commune with the forest, sense the slightest disturbance. Or whatever. Jon wasn't sure, was merely grateful he got a front-row seat.

A light fog was rising up from the clearing, shrouding the elk and Jon's view. He started to shift to the right to see better when Sixen touched his knee with two fingers. The pressure was light, but carried more command than if the Indian had shouted in a bullhorn. Jon paused in mid-motion, his heart jumping out of time. Then he heard it too.

A soft, high-pitched whistle that came out of the night from across the clearing and well up the valley. It was a sound Jon had never heard before, yet knew just the same, knew by the many eyewitnesses he'd interviewed, knew by the sudden rigidity to Sixen's posture, knew by the rash of tingles breaking out down his back.

At first Jon was stunned in disbelief that they might score on their opening night, and in shock at being within earshot of the animal he'd pursued nearly all his life. Then his shoulders slumped down from his ears. So close and yet so far, this individual had to be miles up the valley.

Sixen was still sharp as an axe, poised for the kill, rising up from his squat on the ground.

And so was the elk.

The damn thing had come to its feet despite all tendons in its legs severed clean through. It wobbled, staggered in the grass, yet held its head high, alert in the direction of the whistle. Its muzzle sniffed the air as if something were right there in front of it.

Another whistle cut the night, this time closer but still from across the clearing.

Jon was on his feet, clutching the goggles tight to his face, straining to see through the wall of trees on the other side. A part of him became aware of the forest's sudden stillness, that not a branch swayed and not a blade of grass stirred, as if all the air in the valley had been sucked out, leaving a stale vacuum in its place.

The rest of him was aware of the tension tugging at the seams of the clearing, the breaths being held in the trees as rifles were aimed here and there, and the ridiculously thin barrier their blind offered to whatever was now on approach.

Then he saw it, or at least thought he did. Yes, there, directly across from them. Two short, stubby trees swayed unnaturally. Something besides the wind was moving them, moving between them.

Then nothing. They'd stopped dead cold, as if petrified.

He scanned the clearing, the surrounding trees, holding the goggles like binoculars. He noticed the elk had stopped its pitiful attempt to flee, was standing as solid ice, staring directly at him with nostrils flaring in and out. Jon's neck pricked at the oddity of it, because the elk appeared to not even see him but was staring right through him.

Behind him.

Jon felt the tickle of a cresting wave of panic as he looked over his shoulders, was aware of Sixen doing the same while raising his sidearm. A breathless word leaked from the Indian's lips.

"Tsadja'tko."

The devil himself.

Jon's breath turned heavy, sucking in air by the lungful, and noticed it no longer carried the fresh mint of an old-growth forest but the stench of death. Not the ripe odor of a fresh kill, but that of old, rotting decay.

It was the same foul odor that started him on this crusade all those years ago. His spine went solid and cold as a core of ice taken out of the heart of Antarctica.

Yet he saw nothing but the compact, twisted bramble of salal and bracken that made up the back of their blind, and the crowded stand of spruce behind that. It was like staring into a brick wall of leaves and moss.

He pressed a button on the goggles, switching to infrared—body heat—and nearly jumped out of his boots when a towering hulk of red appeared only feet in front of him within the sea of green and blue.

Feeling every bit the bait now, he wanted to scream into his mike for Ian to shoot, for anyone. He would have reached for his own weapon at his hip, but he was frozen in a memory of a black footprint, a chase, and the snapping of trees closing in behind him.

His finger on the goggles slipped on the infrared button, and the massive red body that had slipped in the back door vanished, replaced by the eerie green tint of night vision and two luminescent eyes that materialized out of the mist, needles, and moss.

Paralyzed in fear and indecision, he could only watch as Sixen stepped clear and whispered as calmly as discussing the weather into his mike for Ian to take the shot. Jon thought to do the same, but the report of Ian's air rifle had already cracked through the air.

On approach to Seattle-Tacoma International

Ten minutes to Wednesday. Sam's week from hell was almost half over. She'd lost the project she'd been working toward her entire career. Her father was dying. And her period was making sitting in the cramped space of economy class for the past day as relaxing as being folded up and stuffed into a cardboard box small enough to fit in the overhead storage. So unlike the rest of the passengers, she was awake when the captain quietly came over the plane's PA system announcing they were beginning the descent and would be landing in twenty-five minutes. The optimistic thought that the week could only get better from here consoled her just long enough for her to sit up and reach across the snoring Megan to raise the shade on the window. The deep ache in her abdomen quickly splashed cold water all over that. Who was she kidding? Between now and Sunday she still had several days of PMS to endure, her mother's guilt-inducing presence to avoid, and her father's hand to hold for perhaps the last time.

Gazing out on the bottomless darkness of midnight, feeling the plane begin its drop from the heavens, she knew the sour knot in her stomach was not only from PMS or the sudden loss of altitude, but the final acceptance of what lay ahead. She had a one-way ticket to her father's bedside with only the layover in Seattle to stall the inevitable that she had been running from since before her father had been diagnosed—since she'd held her grandmother's lifeless hand with only her mother present to offer her the coldest of shoulders to cry on. She offered up a silent prayer as the touch of clouds caressed the glass, a request for courage so she could be there for her father as he was unable to be for his mother.

The question of who would be there for her inevitably came with the next thought. She lived in denial most of the time, but she was no fool. Cancer was a beast that would not be satisfied with only her grandmother or father. It would keep eating down the family tree until it devoured the roots. And so somehow she had mustered enough courage to be tested (not that her doctor had given her the choice), but not enough courage to take the lab's call with the results. She'd let the voice messages collect on her cell phone. But her ignorant bliss would not last—they would surely have sent the results by mail. Thus came a vision of her mail stacked neatly on her desk waiting for her return.

Mercifully, though, she lived in denial most of the time. Her thoughts reflexively shifted to her work, and as they had for the past day, to the enigma of bone in her pocket.

Several thousand feet below her, the Washington coast rose out of the chill of the Pacific, quickly giving way to breathtaking valleys of primitive forest and the sharp white spires of the Olympic Mountains, none of which was visible at the moment, but she easily recalled the images of that flight weeks ago when they had left for China. She had stared out over the sleeping Megan as she did now, only then she was wired with the excitement of a dream come true and stirred by the awe of the beauty she beheld below. Pockets of civilization dotted the carpet of green that stretched as far she could see. And to the north, a white mass of peaks shone so bright in the rising sun that she had to squint in its glory, as if the land was so raw her eyes were the first to behold it.

The irony of it all was almost more than she could bear. She was returning from China having come no closer to finding the whole truth of Giganto than had her father, and yet, if Ostman by some miracle or magic was in any way correct, Giganto was alive and well right below her, hidden by an impenetrable cover of night and cloak of evergreen. She peered through the two panes of glass and into the dark as a child might peer at a wishing well while tossing in a penny. She let her imagination wander unrestrained, feeling what it would be like to come face-to-face with her giant ape, to share time and space with the majestic primate. The experience could only be unearthly, a moment of thrill and wonder. To be down there right now, in its presence, would be more than a wish come true, it would be a dream, certainly not the nightmare Ostman proposed in his book.

She sat back in her seat, her imagination returned to its leash. And a dream only, because reality was much too harsh to allow a beast such as Giganto to survive eons of evolution without becoming another casualty of the changing times. There was nothing down there but trees and rock. The tooth and the rest of the crate's contents would prove as much once they were held under the harsh light of the lab. To hold hope for anything else was as naive as the hope of a recovery for her father. She didn't have the strength to hold out for either.

Megan stirred and stretched, her blanket falling around her knees and her pillow to the floor. She opened one eye, then the other. Her voice came out choked with sleep and bad humor. "We there yet, Mommy?"

Sam didn't respond. The motion of the plane turned to the north and with a steeper descent. She stretched too, at least as much as the latest waves of cramps allowed, and bent down to secure her carry-on. Unlike Megan, Sam was not looking forward to seeing this trip come to an end.

"Ah, American food and hot showers here we come." Megan was staring out the window.

Sam leaned over, catching the distant glow of city lights through a thin veil of clouds. Seattle. From there Megan would hop on a quick connecting flight to Chicago while Sam had to wait until tomorrow afternoon for her flight to Denver.

Reading her mind as Megan always did, Megan glanced from the view to her. Megan's short brown bob was knotted into a wicked case of bed head. The sight allowed Sam to smile in spite of Megan's continued mother-henning. "I promised your mother you'd keep your cell phone on until you get to Boulder, just in case…Well, it's not a bad idea anyway, I might need to reach you, too."

Sam's habit of only turning her phone on when she made a call was a constant annoyance for her mother and Megan, which was why Sam did it, that and, of course, dodging her doctor's office. But now wasn't the time for games. Sam didn't need any prompting from Megan. The phone would remain on and at her side until she reached her father. That at least was something she had the strength to do. There was nothing to be done, though, to ease Sam's worry of the next seventeen hours. Between now and her connecting flight to Denver she had to find a way to fill the time with something other than more thoughts of where she was headed.

Seattle
May 5
7:10 AM

The sound of her shower, that of the thin streams of water hitting the glass door, the tiled walls and her body, tempted Thatcher nearly beyond his strength to resist. He'd been in her room five minutes, four longer than needed to complete the search. He had verified the one tooth he already knew she possessed was in fact bone and most certainly sent from Ostman, as he'd found a letter stating as much, and more. Ostman had recovered much more than a single tooth and had sent it all to Dr. Russell. None of the other bones were here, though. So Thatcher had no choice but to leave the tooth and letter where he found them. Until he learned what she had done with the rest, he would remain in the shadows, staying his hand.

And that was exactly his concern.

Standing in the open doorway of her bathroom with the warm steam swirling around him, his image in the mirror blurring to the point he could no longer see the blue of his eyes, he'd been trying to talk himself out of the room. But the silhouette of her naked curves on the smoked-glass shower door had him mesmerized, paralyzed in lust.

No one knew he was here, not even her. It was one of the perks of the job. The training. He'd slipped in unseen and unheard. He'd taken his time going through her luggage, especially her clothes. Her bras. Her panties. In thirty seconds he'd gained more intimate knowledge of Dr. Samantha Russell than most husbands possessed of their wives. He even knew which brand of tampon she used.

So what was stopping him from pulling open that shower door right now? Or even stalling long enough for the water to shut off, for her to step out in search of a towel and find him standing there, *forcing* him to act?

The seconds ticked by in time with the droning of the shower as he probed for a reason to leave. In the meantime, her shape moved on the glass, bending and arching as she exposed every inch of herself to the heat of the water cascading on her.

If only she had all the bones. If only he could have acted upon first arriving in China. Then he would have been able to maintain his focus, keep his mind on the job. But now he'd been following her so closely for so long, the job was losing its urgency, and she was becoming something more than a loose end that needed tying up.

He kept thinking of where his weakness had gotten him before—behind bars and a court-martial. That memory was as strong as a splash of ice water. It reminded him of his oath to Locke. Mikel Locke was the best CO he'd ever served under, and the only man willing to give him a second chance and a place to serve his country, even if it was a place the public need not know about.

Thatcher would rather die than break that oath.

And so he slowly forced himself back through the open doorway, praying as he did that the bones turned up soon. If they didn't, and he was forced to endure the titillating torture of watching her every movement day and night, he truly feared what he might do—oath or no oath.

Then, with one foot in the bathroom and one in the bedroom, Thatcher stopped cold at the sudden shift from the sound of the shower to that of the throaty, rapid draining of the shower stall.

She'd turned the water off.

Her silhouette changed from the curves of a side profile to the hourglass shape of a frontal view.

The magnetic click of the shower door being pushed open echoed off the tile and through the steam.

Thatcher swallowed with weakening resolve. He didn't know whether to retreat or advance.

The steam-laden air of the bathroom mixed with the morning bite of the rest of the poorly heated hotel room. Bumps rose along Sam's bare shoulders as she combed her fingers through her heavy wet hair and let the cold strips drop against her shoulder blades. Standing in the open doorway of the bathroom, she glanced toward the hotel room's door out of nervous compulsion, because she thought she had just heard it click shut. But it was closed and secure, as she had left it. She then glanced across the room to the alarm clock on the nightstand on the opposite side of the unmade bed. The large, red LED digits burned through the dim light seeping through the drapes and that leaking from the bathroom behind her.

7:13 AM.

She made a quick calculation as she greeted the new day with more than a renewed and fresh outlook. She embraced it with a plan.

Cradled in the curves and wrinkles of the white sheets sat Ostman's book, the tooth, and an unfolded map of Seattle Metro.

With peaceful resignation, Sam pulled a pair of her favorite worn jeans from her duffel bag, stepped into them, and danced the sticking denim up her damp legs to her hips.

She had a good eight hours to kill, and because she was in the neighborhood, it would be downright impolite not to pay Prescott a visit, and, with any luck, perhaps even his buddy Jon Ostman. At the least, she had to express her gratitude to Prescott for his mysterious and timely yanking of funding for her dig without warning, freeing up her calendar for a trip home.

Prescott Institute

8:07 AM

Sam adjusted, scooted closer to the bulky armrest, and tried to find comfort in the stiff leather couch. The thing was all form and no function, as was everything else she'd seen so far in the institute. She wasn't all that surprised. Prescott, himself, was all salesman and no scientist. He also was pushing her patience beyond what was wise. If he thought he could hide behind his glossy office door and his little miss corporate assistant after cutting her funding off at the knees with no cause, no explanation, he was sorely mistaken. She'd sit right here in his office lobby until his bladder swelled up into his throat, and he was forced out of his gold-plated hole in the ground. Even the most recluse of snakes had to surface at some point, and when he did, she'd be here to thump him on the head.

She glanced at her watch.

If he made her miss her flight, well, then he'd quickly be persuaded it was in his best interest to donate the use of his personal jet as a token of his condolences.

The perky blonde behind the half-wall of a workstation hung up the phone, peeked her big green eyes over the top of it and repeated herself for at least the fifth time. "Dr. Russell. Please believe me, Mr. Prescott is not in his office at this time. I'll let him know you stopped by, but there's nothing else I can do."

Sam uncrossed and recrossed her legs, pretending she was as comfortable as a kitten on a sunny windowsill. And she wished again that she'd worn something more demanding of respect than her faded jeans and button khaki shirt, something Little Miss Muffet would recognize as a sign of authority. "Thank-you, again, but I'm more than OK with waiting. I've got nothing better to do today."

Sam clasped her hands in her lap and began bouncing her one leather boot-clad foot that was off the floor in time to a tune she hummed just loud enough to be heard from the other side of the workstation. The effect was immediate and delicious. Little Miss picked up her receiver while keeping those two green gems pointed at her like daggers. Sam heard her address the same man she'd talked to on two others occasions—a Dr. Simonsen. Sam kept up the tune and foot bouncing as she perused again the gaudy wall art. She felt like she was sitting in a lobby on Wall Street. The only thing remotely related to science in the room was a shiny brass plaque above the end table. She read it a second time to keep her steam up. Hypocrisy had always been one of her hot buttons.

> Historically scientific progress has come about by the meticulous stringing together of one piece of knowledge to another until a useful breakthrough has been achieved. This is the *evolutionary* method; the method subscribed to by universities and large research laboratories. Here at the Prescott Institute we

subscribe whole-heartedly to the *revolutionary* method. It is the way of the inspired and the risk taker, the way of Newton, Copernicus, Edison, and Einstein. Like those great minds, we hope to avoid all the small steps in-between by acting on intuition and sheer will, thus arriving at discovery all at once. And so we too will be working against the accepted thinking of today, striving to carry civilization ahead into the next millennium in one daring step.

—*Philip Prescott, Founder of the Prescott Institute*

"Dr. Russell?"

Sam turned from the plaque in surprise at the male voice that squeaked with nasal constriction. Before her stood a man in thick, black-rimmed glasses and white lab coat. Three pen caps protruded from its pocket. His skin was oily and pale, nearly as off-white as the coat. Likewise, his black hair was nearly as jet black as the glasses. He pulled a hand from one of the coat pockets and extended it. The nails were longer than hers.

"I'm Dr. Simonsen, institute director. What is it that we can do for you today?"

Sam smiled and stood. She'd be decent, but she wouldn't be escorted out this easily. His hand was soft and cool. She wondered if he had a pulse. "To be honest, there's nothing *you* can do for me. I'm here to speak with Philip. Unless, that is, you can let me into his office."

He slid his hand back into his jacket like a wet snake slithering down a hole. "As long as we're being honest, Dr. Russell, I can guess why you're here. Unfortunately, Prescott is truly out of town. I'd be happy to have Michelle put you on his calendar for when he's back. You can give him a piece of your mind all you want then. But until then, there's nothing else I or anyone here can do."

Sam plucked her cell phone and wallet from the end table, tucking the wallet under her arm. "And when does he plan to return?"

The delay and shifting upward of his eyes meant he either didn't know the answer or was making one up. Sam couldn't buy that he didn't know. "His itinerary is open-ended at this time—it could be a few weeks. I am in contact with him, however, and could—"

"Well, now, that is convenient, because as it is I'm flying out of town myself in a few hours to go home and watch my father die. And then I'll have to bury him, yada yada, and won't be back out this way for a good five years. Do you think Michelle over there could put me down for say noon on June 22 of that year?"

Little Miss glanced up from her work, having been pretending not to hear, and Dr. Simonsen took a step back, unprepared for the sharp tongue of a woman who was still PMSing, had a head full of jet lag, and had lost all patience five days ago when she'd found out she was unemployed via telegram. Sam smiled at them both, like following a head shot with a sucker punch to the kidney. She came here to make some noise, and that was damn well what she was going to do. And if that wasn't clear before, it was now.

Director Simonsen raised a hand in surrender and motioned to the door. "Look, would you believe me if I showed you?"

She studied him and the door a second, figuring his angle. He wouldn't let her in if Prescott were indeed inside. Meaning he wasn't, and he could be anywhere. But if nothing else, there was information in there she might be able to use. It was worth a shot. "All right, I'll go quietly if in fact Prescott is not in his office."

Simonsen nodded with obvious relief. He eyed Little Miss, who pushed some button initiating a faint click in the door's lock. He stepped to it and turned the knob, pushing the door ajar.

Sam took a short, casual step herself, then as the opening was just wide enough she took a second, lightning fast stride past Simonsen and inside Prescott's office. A floor-to-ceiling window stretched across the other end of the room. Shelves of books and artifacts wrapped around the walls. As expected, the high-back leather chair behind the paper-free desk was empty.

Simonsen recovered from his shock and came in after her. "Dr. Russell, please, don't make me call security. You can see we've been telling you the truth."

She held her tongue at the word "truth" and kept moving over the hardwood floor, staying two arms' lengths away as she took mental snapshots of everything in view. A table covered by a cloth that had slipped off one corner revealing what appeared to be a slab of concrete. A topographical map tacked neatly onto a wall-mounted corkboard, complete with red and blue location markers pinned in a random pattern near the center. Its title read Olympic National Park.

Simonsen came around the desk, herding her toward the door. "Dr. Russell, please, now."

Sam kept moving, seeing everything, even reading the spines of the books spanning most of the wall space. Nothing of note, except...*except* for the one she also had in her hotel room. Ostman's book.

She angled back to the map, keeping a set of leather chairs between her and Simonsen.

"Dr. Russell."

One white pin, larger than the red and blue pins, was positioned in the center of the others and was stuck into a black square on the map labeled Hoh Battery.

Simonsen nearly had his hand on her arm when she moved to the right, heading slowly for the door in a mock retreat. His pursuit slowed as well, believing he'd succeeded. Only he'd done nothing of the sort.

Sam paused at the open door, glancing back at the map then to the spine of Ostman's book. Prescott, and presumably Ostman as well, were indeed not here, but she had a good guess now as to where he was.

She pressed a button on her cell phone, causing it to ring, and raised it to her ear. She needed a cover for her exit. "Hello, Mom. Can you hold for sec?" She covered the phone with her hand as she backed out through the door. "Sorry for wasting your time, Dr. Simonsen. I got a little impatient is all. But I've got to take this call, so I'll check in with you later about Prescott's availability. Thank-you."

As she turned, he was standing in the center of the office, the sunlight through the window casting an aura around his wiry frame, with his hands back in their pockets and a puzzled frown on his near invisible lips. But he wasn't about to interrupt her phone call or delay her leaving. Neither was Little Miss as Sam passed with a forced, gracious nod. Once out of earshot, she cut off her fake conversation and punched in 4-1-1 on her phone for the information operator.

If she was right and they were on the Peninsula, the question then was, what were they doing there? Surely not what Ostman's book implied. Surely not.

She glanced at her watch. Time was running thin if she were going to find the answer.

Olympic National Park

8:31 AM

The scene through the small rectangular viewing window made of thick Plexiglas matched that of any operating room in any hospital in the nation. Except for two unmistakable details. The patient. And the shotguns.

Three veterinary surgeons hand-picked by Prescott, in their white gowns, caps and masks, were an hour into their tests. Jon could tell by their awkward movements they weren't used to working around a table of the size usually only required for equine and bovine. These were primate specialists. The largest thing they'd worked on was a gorilla.

And they weren't all that sure about the restraining belts and harnesses. Every now and then Jon would see one flinch, hesitate, or step back as a muscle twitched or an eyelid fluttered on the patient. He didn't blame them. He flinched too, standing on the other side of a foot-thick cement wall peering through the hazy window. Last night was still all too fresh in his mind.

The patient, who Ian referred to as a silverback, borrowing the term for a male gorilla, lay on its back with its girth bulging and brooding beneath the head-to-toe sheets. Having probably only recently come into sexual maturity, he weighed eight hundred ninety-seven pounds and stood nine feet eight inches. A big boy with still some growing left in him, and not an inch of his body was uncovered or unrestrained.

A man dressed in the same ER gowns as the vets stood in each of the four corners of the room. Two carried shotguns with slugs not sold over the counter. And the other two held at the ready air rifles loaded with Ian's sedative. Four men. Wouldn't matter if there were ten. If the patient woke and the restraints failed…well, all the firearms in the world were useless if no one had the courage to pull the trigger. Jon hadn't the courage last night. He had not even been able to raise his voice above a whisper to order Ian to pull the trigger. Thank God for Sixen. Jon was still shaking on the inside from the experience, the dizzy mix of exhilaration and fear.

By the time he had regained control of himself, their quarry lay at his feet with two darts centered in its chest, twitching with the contractions of its slowing heart. He learned later it also carried four slugs from Sixen's revolver, all four doing no more damage than cutting into the first few layers of skin and muscle. Then it was a mad, frenzied effort to get the specimen back to the lab before the sedatives wore off. Luckily they had been on the valley floor and not far from the lab, because moving it took them the rest of the night. That was another stroke of brilliance in Prescott's plan. Contrary to standard practice, in this case it was far easier to bring the lab to the specimen than vice versa.

It wasn't until an hour ago when the testing began that Jon finally had a chance to breathe and comprehend what had happened. He'd come face to face with an ape, one that stood on its own two legs and stared back at him with humanlike intelligence and cunning.

An extinct giant. A legend. A myth.

Gigantopithecus. Sasquatch. Bigfoot.

He was still high on adrenaline and lack of sleep, and wondered if he would wake to find himself in his bed drenched in sweat.

But the scene before him was too gritty, too unreal to be a dream. His senses couldn't lie so convincingly. His nostrils still stung from the stench of its hair and its breath. His imagination was not rich enough to conjure such a foul odor, or the piercing whistle and wail that rang in his ears every time he closed his eyes. No, this was real, and far worse than any nightmare. He'd pined his life away in search of a type specimen, and the vindication it would bring. Now when he had both within reach, had the blood and hair of the beast on his clothes, he found himself shut out and relegated to spectator.

The minute they'd brought the silverback into the lab, Prescott took over and restricted access to everyone but essential staff, meaning only those needed to perform his testing. Even Ian and Sixen were left out in the cold. That's when the biting slap of reality woke him to the hell he'd gotten into. Prescott was a fanatic. No, worse than that. He was a greedy fanatic with the power to dictate his will upon others. Standing in front of this two-inch thick sheet of Plexiglas for the past hour had given Jon more than enough time to see the outcome of all this, and the time to stir his anger into a boiling pot of ill will and contempt.

Whatever Prescott was after, immortality or just another zero on the end of his net worth, he was not concerned in the least with presenting this specimen as a scientific find for study. Success or failure, Prescott would see to it that the body lying down on that operating table was never going to leave the bowels of this lab. Jon had seen it in Prescott's eyes when he'd shut himself in with the beast. The focused stare of greed, power, and bottomless hunger. Jon had expected as much from the man upon their first meeting, but had quickly become intoxicated with his own greed and lust for the Holy Grail. Now he was no closer, only infinitely more tortured as he had drunk from the bitter cup but could not swallow the life-giving water. His only consolation was his fortunate wisdom in sending the Ape Cave bones to Dr. Russell. The truth still had a chance, as did his redemption—even if he never made it out of the lab alive.

Jon's more intimately pressing concern was for his safety, and the safety of everyone else confined within these cement walls—all those who had become prisoners of Prescott's lust and power.

Throughout his career Jon had proposed taking a type specimen dead versus alive. He'd taken heat for it, too, from his few fellow hunters. They'd accused him of being a murderer and worse. But what they couldn't or wouldn't understand was that a living specimen would be impossible to handle. Injury or death to it and those around an animal of such size, strength, and intelligence was unavoidable. Regardless of the security measures taken, there was no safety as long as it was kept alive against its will. Killing it at the start, documenting it, and then setting in motion the protection of the species as a whole was the only effective plan for a truly safe resolution.

Jon had shared his theory on the matter once again to Prescott this morning, and quickly realized Prescott was not interested in a safe resolution. He wanted only to have his tests run as soon as possible, and apparently needed the specimen alive during the process.

That's when Jon had for the first time given Prescott's story about the old man, his longevity, and the unusually violent primates here in the lab any real consideration. Before that, they were merely an explanation for Prescott's almost illogical interest. Jon hadn't cared why Prescott was interested in his cryptid so long as he got to come along for the ride. A man who lived to the age of a hundred and twenty-one was nothing more than a fluke of nature, and the Indians' and even the Chinese's belief in Giganto's medicinal properties was just the fictional side effects of their legend telling. But now Jon had his doubts. Perhaps brushing anything off as 'just a legend' was leaving a rock unturned, a truth undiscovered. In any event, Prescott was hell-bent on extracting any such mystery from their specimen's body while it still lived, and Jon presumed by the same methods as had been used on the other primates held in tiny cages in the next room. He could hear their muffled screams and howls even now, screams that chilled his blood and that had increased in volume the second they'd brought in the silverback. They were the most violent monkeys he'd ever encountered. Unnaturally violent. And proof that Jon's concerns were valid.

Prescott may have this half-ton ape drugged to the verge of a coma now, but what happened when he awoke? No cage would hold him for long. And to expect him to react differently than the other primates to the testing, whatever hellish methods were being used, was being naive. If Prescott wouldn't listen to reason, then maybe Ian would. Jon had every reason to believe he would, as the Aussie had disagreed with Prescott many times over the past few days on the treatment of the monkeys. Unlike Prescott, Ian appeared to have a conscience.

The only question was did Ian also have the backbone for mutiny. Because Jon would be damned if he would sit here in the corner watching his life's work being stripped from him for no better reason than greed.

Jon pushed the sleeve back from his Casio. Any minute now and he'd have his answer. And either way, he was through sitting on his hands.

Right on cue, the door behind him squeaked open on its ancient hinges. Jon turned from the window to see Ian standing in the half-open doorway. He was glancing down the hall to the left, then to the right. Finally he stepped inside the bare, cramped room and closed the door with another ragged squeak.

He looked as tired and strung out as Jon felt, yet there was that spark of electricity in his blue eyes. The Aussie, too, was running on pure adrenaline. He pushed a hand through his locks. "So you want to talk, aye mate?" Despite the thick walls of concrete, he kept his voice barely more than a whisper.

Jon dug his hands into his pant pockets and nodded. He wanted to say more, but realized he needn't. Besides the electricity, there was a desperate resolve in Ian's eyes. He too was done sitting on the sidelines.

Ian came around Jon to stand next to the Plexiglas. He placed a hand on the wall and leaned close, then looked back at Jon. The resolve had pooled into a deeper sadness. "Prescott didn't tell you everything, mate. It's worse than you fear."

Jon doubted that, but was nevertheless curious. He opened his mouth to inquire, or at least to solidify their intent, when Ian pushed away from the wall and moved back to the door.

"We do need to talk, but not now. My absence will soon be noticed." He turned the knob. "Sixen and I already have a plan."

Jon blinked. "Sixen?"

Ian smiled at what he was about to say. "He's tired of working for free. He wants his payment."

"And how much is that?"

Ian's smile widened. "Tidbits really. Just the silverback's beating heart."

Jon felt unbalanced, that he'd been kept even further out of the loop than he'd thought. "Excuse me?"

Ian eased the door open and began to step through. "As I said, there's much you don't know. I'll get away as soon as I can. Until then, lie low," he paused over the threshold and looked past Jon to the window, "and keep an eye on that thing."

Then the door squeaked closed, and Jon was again alone with the view.

He moved to the glass, his head full of questions, and gazed down upon the patient. There was the quickest flash of eye shine under the operating lights, sending him back a step with a start.

Feeling the jolt from his chest to his head, he peered closer to be sure, but the eyes were closed, sunken deep under those bony, protruding brows.

He was getting skittish. But the fact still remained. It was only a matter of time until those large amber eyes opened for real.

Interstate 90

9:28 AM

The large green sign alongside the freeway continued the countdown as Sam drove back into the city. This one listed two possible destinations. The Seattle ferry docks, 10 miles. And exit five to Sea-Tac Airport—and her hotel—5 miles. She eased her boot down on the Jeep's accelerator, taking it up to seventy-five. The countdown couldn't drop fast enough. The day was quickly getting away from her. Already the sun was high at her back, fully risen over the Cascades. The morning mist had burned off, revealing the cramped sprawl of Bellevue as it straddled I-90. Wet patches streaking the pavement from the night's rains were drying quickly under the heat of the commute. The activities of the morning had eaten more time than she had, and now she was racing among the BMWs and Lexuses to get from A to B. Her urgency was deeper than a corporate time clock needing to be punched.

For the third time, a sea of red brake lights lit up in front of her as traffic ground to a halt. She hit the brakes, driving her chest into the seatbelt, and swerved into the carpool lane to cheat this bottleneck.

She checked the rearview mirror to see if she'd caught the attention of any lurking State Patrol. All clear. Except…

She glanced again at the mirror to be sure. She wasn't mistaken. A black Ford Explorer had made the same lane change behind her. She kept an eye on it as she sped by the stopped traffic to her right. It was three cars back, moving far less aggressively than she was. And yet it remained always just within view, keeping its distance as might a cat stalking a mouse.

She forced her eyes off the mirror and on the road ahead, chiding herself again for her ungrounded suspicions. Just as there were a thousand Hondas sharing the freeway with her this morning, there were also a thousand Ford Explorers, many of them black. It wouldn't be all that unlikely that she had noticed an Explorer behind her on the way out to the institute as she did now. There were far more disturbing coincidences in life than crossing paths with the same type of car within a few hours. What was most disturbing was her sudden affinity for paranoid thinking.

Like this morning in the shower. Despite the skin-reddening heat of the water, she'd had goose bumps. There had been someone out there, watching her, or so she imagined. Of course, there was no one there when she stepped out of the stall. Why should there be? The room's door had been closed and locked. Nothing had been taken. And yet she felt violated the entire time she was in the room getting ready.

It was Ostman's letter and that damn tooth that had her feverish with paranoia. The Explorer was simply another phantom of her rapidly growing imagination. All of which gave her more incentive to get to the bottom of Prescott and Ostman's secret project. It was the only way she'd be able to stop looking over her shoulder.

She checked the mirror. The Explorer was still there, four cars back now.

Paranoia, nothing but irrational paranoia.

Sam sunk her foot into the accelerator, putting distance between her and the innocent sap in the Ford. She *was* in a hurry after all.

The V-8 of her Grand Cherokee growled as the freeway turned up. At the crest of the rise she got the first peek of the view awaiting her. Like some great inland sea, a huge shimmering lake sparkled in the rising sun. A hillside rose from the opposite shore, studded with homes. Beyond that, the Seattle skyline jutted up into the thick blue sky. Even farther in the distance, though they appeared to be right behind the skyscrapers and Space Needle, towered a rugged line of snow-capped peaks that stood crystal clear in the sharp morning light.

The Olympics.

Naming them after the home of the gods only began to do justice to their heavenly beauty, especially under such flattering skies. As a backdrop, they made the city of Seattle a contender with any city on the planet for aesthetic appeal. And to think the Olympics had remained unexplored for nearly a century while Seattle residents gawked on sunny days at their splendor. They looked close enough to reach out and touch.

Terra incognita had never looked so inviting.

The traffic had opened up again. Sam clicked the right blinker and exited the carpool lane. The sign declaring that exit five was next flashed by on the shoulder.

The boys at the outfitter she'd called had clued her in to the map hanging in Prescott's office. The Hoh River ran through the center of those lofty peaks, at the bottom of a three-thousand-foot-deep valley. And the Hoh Battery was an old World War II anti-aircraft bunker that had been built into an even older mine. It was just off the river trail, took a good day's hike to get there, and was recently being used as a lab by the National Park Service. She had no doubt that Prescott and Ostman were in that lab right now. Doing *what* was the question stabbing at her mind. She had to know, had to resolve the loose ends: the crate of bones, the tooth, Ostman's letter, his book, Prescott's mad insistence she find bones in China, and now his secret absence. The answers were there in the Olympics, just beyond her reach.

The sign announcing exit five stood as a final warning before the right lane sprouted the off ramp that would take her south to Sea-Tac. That is, if she took it. Instead, she gripped the leather wheel tighter as she watched the off ramp approach and then pass her by as she continued on, straight for the ferry docks and the Olympics beyond.

Her luggage would be safe locked inside her hotel room for the next few days. There was always another flight. She glanced down at her cell phone resting inside the cradle of the center console. And she would only be a phone call away should her mother need her before then.

Her fingers relaxed their knuckle-whitening grip on the steering wheel as she pressed her boot down again on the gas pedal. Shutting out thoughts of her father lying in bed with the family gathered around him, she located via the rearview mirror the backpack in the rear seat she'd obtained from the outfitters. She ran through a mental checklist of the gear inside. Packed for speed, she had only the essentials and a map. All she would need and no more to ensure she arrived at the lab by sunset.

By the shortening shadows cast by the cars behind her, it was clear time was not on her side. Sunrise had come and gone.

Yet one shadow resisted the banishing touch of daylight with stubborn resilience, lurking five cars back behind a Dodge Caravan. Sam shifted her eyes from the rearview mirror to the road ahead in a continued attempt to convince herself the black Ford Explorer, like the disease that was sucking the life out of her father with every passing minute, was benign and not stalking her.

Olympic National Park
12:58 PM

"Cancer. This whole damn thing's about a cancer drug?" Jon paced the narrow space of the workshop, his hands fidgeting with his belt, each other, then coming to rest inside his pockets. His right hand formed a fist around the tooth that had taken up residency in there. "Then what was that whole bit about the old man dying at age one hundred twenty—a longer life and all that?"

Ian sat at ease on a metal stool at the long, chipped and battered workbench. He had a collection of chemicals lined up and was mixing them into a beaker. The room was so tight Jon brushed against Ian's meaty and hairy knees each time he passed. And with the door closed, Ian's concoctions were sharpening the air in a hurry, even with the mask Jon was wearing.

"Like I said, mate. Prescott didn't tell you everything." Ian worked with rubber gloves, a mask, and goggles as he meticulously measured, mixed, and measured again. "A longer lifespan was just a side effect, a tip-off for that twisted mind of Prescott's to latch on to. That poor old bloke died with no signs of cancerous cells in his entire body. The coroner had made a big stink about it, apparently. Prescott, of course, saw dollar signs and went combing the planet for answers to why. From me apes in the Congo to fossils in China. I didn't mind much to begin with. Research money doesn't usually come in the form of a blank check, aye mate." Ian turned from his work and looked over his mask at Jon as he slowed his pacing. "I even went along with this whole circus of his. With the tight lips around here, I had nothing to lose if it were all a bust. To be honest, the idea rather goosed me a little. Not every day a primatologist gets to discover a new great ape."

Ian went back to his brewing. "Anyway, the point is, an entire species cannot be immune to cancerous cell mutations, even a species as unorthodox as the one we have down the hall. That's why Prescott has found no evidence for his new miracle drug, and never will. But as long as Prescott *believes* he will, he won't let you near it, let alone document it to the outside world. He only needed you to help capture a specimen. And what he doesn't need he quickly discards, like the Sunday garbage."

There was a rare and noticeable crack of emotion in Ian's voice in that last statement. Jon pushed to clarify, editing his question at the last moment to come at it from the flank. "OK, so I can do the math. I'm going to be left out to dry. Sixen doesn't get paid so long as Prescott keeps the silverback alive. We've got obvious grievances, though Sixen's desire to eat the animal's raw flesh begs a few questions. But what about you? Why should you want to shut Prescott down?"

A second of silence stretched into ten, then thirty, until Jon lost count. He'd hit a nerve for sure. If Jon was going to trust this man and plan to bite the hand that fed them both, he needed to know his motives, his deepest motives.

Jon stood less than two feet away, which was about as far as he could get without moving to the other end of the room, and waited impatiently. Finally, Ian looked up. The usually sharp, penetrating blue of his eyes had dulled to the gray of a winter's afternoon.

"Just before you came on, I learned what Prescott did to an old mate of mine, how he left her flapping in the breeze. A fresh kill for the vultures to clean up. I haven't been able to sleep since, can't look in the mirror longer than it takes to splash water on me face."

A thin, wet line swelled under those winter clouds blowing across Ian's pupils. This mate of his had been more than an old chum.

Ian blinked the clouds away and straightened on the stool. "Believe me, if there was any hope of a cancer cure I'd be in that lab meself, milking it out of that big ape. But there's not—only torture for it and the rest of the test primates. And that's the reason this all has to end. Prescott has been warned many times, and by more than me."

Jon scanned the arsenal of weapons and equipment housed in this cramped, makeshift headquarters for their mutiny. He realized, even though Ian had yet to detail his plan, he had not rejected the idea and refused to participate. Regardless of all else, Jon did not doubt Ian's assessment that he would not be granted an opportunity to examine and document this type specimen. That fact alone kept Jon from walking out on Ian; that Jon had come to like the Aussie only made him comfortable with his decision. He was not, however, comfortable with the possibility that Ian's plan included shouldering one of those shotguns and becoming a white-collar terrorist.

Ian glanced at the closed door and its rusted knob. When he spoke again his voice was one notch lower, as if he'd remembered their need for secrecy. The mask nearly absorbed his words. "I'm convinced now he has no heart, not for anything less than his money. The more he doesn't find what he's looking for, the more he puts these poor boys through, especially the chimpanzees. The tests run the board. He even had two chained to a table, catheters surgically inserted into their gall bladders, milking bile for weeks until their little hearts stopped beating. Just like the bloody Chinese do to the American black bear. All in the name of science and under contract for the National Parks. Well I wash my hands of this. I didn't spend my career conserving what's left of the planet's primate populations to be party to their deaths."

The image of two frail chimp bodies strapped to operating tables, their limbs bent in awkward angles in the leather straps, stamped a permanent scar into Jon's conscience. Their two little faces stared up in death, their eyes wide and holding onto the confused anguish that had built up in them over the weeks. Deep in his throat, the space squeezed smaller, making it harder to breathe until he swallowed down the pity and anger. There never was any greater monster in nature than the human mind consumed with greed.

Ian was staring directly at Jon, pining for his full attention. "Aside from the issue of ethics, though, it's the practical concerns that demand we act. Even from their calls, you can tell Prescott's monkeys are more aggressive than most. The only thing keeping them from lashing out in blind violence is the bars of their cages. After studying it for two decades, I know a few things about primate violence. The specimens we have here are beyond help. They'll attack anyone any chance they get. Now imagine what state of mind the big fella down the hall is going to be in after a few days of Prescott's tender loving care. What's worse, this bloke's certainly a rogue. Without even considering the danger to ourselves and anyone else here, I can't stand by and let another animal be ruined, especially the greatest find of the century. And I know you feel the same."

Jon couldn't disagree with any of that, especially with the two chimps still plaguing his mind. "Rogue? What do you mean by that?"

Ian stood from the stool and picked up an empty rifle dart from the workbench. Its long silver needle glinted in the fluorescent light coming from two of the three bulbs still burning overhead. "Nowhere else in nature does violence occur with such consistency and conscious intent as within the primate family, especially within the apes. And the males are almost always the demons. You see, mate, us blokes have it tough. Being the alpha male is heaven, you have all the Sheilas you want and all you have to do is keep the competition in check. But there's only one of him, leaving the rest of us out in the cold. We're exiled to the fringe of the territory where we nearly starve while we roam looking for a weak alpha to overtake. Meanwhile our hormones are swimming in our veins. We've got this burning need to mate, almost like a raging fire that demands to be extinguished before destroying us from the inside out. It's like road rage—a stress-induced state of temporary insanity. And the more intelligent a species is and the more social, and thus emotionally aware, the more acute the aggression. Our silverback is clearly on par with the rest of the apes in this regard. He is also a rogue—too young and too alone to be otherwise. The only difference is…he weighs nearly half a ton, if you get me drift."

Ian began filling the syringed dart with the new mix from the beaker. He was using a great deal of care for just working with a sedative. Jon was half tempted to remove his mask, only he was too absorbed with the support Ian was giving for his belief that the only safe type specimen was a dead type specimen. Hope was again embracing his heart with a warm hug.

"Grievances aside, the right thing to do is shut Prescott down, document this new and surely fragile species, and keep us all here safe." Ian turned, held up the dart and flicked the head twice with a finger. "Unfortunately for our big rogue that means a quick and painless death."

Jon was taken back. He hadn't seen killing their specimen as an option Ian would consider. "Kill him? Then what's with the sedative?"

Ian eyed the dart a moment then placed it in a form-fitted box, snapped the lid shut and set it high on a shelf. "A little hi-tech rat poison actually. Literally kill him in a heartbeat. Safer than a bullet, for him and us."

Jon found himself now sitting on a stool, unsure what sort of mutiny he'd gotten himself signed on to. "Now wait a minute. Even if we do kill it, then what? We can't just walk out unseen with it draped over our shoulders."

Ian slipped the mask off his face and tugged his hands out of the gloves. White lines creased his tanned cheeks where the strings had been tied back behind his head. "Oh, we're going to steal it all right. But not out through the front door." An innocent, boyish grin formed beneath those white lines as Ian unveiled his plan, one that involved the lab's secret back door.

Just as Ian finished, the door to the workshop opened and Sixen stepped inside. The ever-present, dampened wails and howls of the caged monkeys and apes leaked into the room, then quickly faded as Sixen closed the door behind him. Jon was still digesting the complexities of Ian's plan when he noticed Sixen carried an electronic device resembling the original bulky GPS units. It even had the thick black antenna protruding from its top.

Ian turned to the Indian with an obvious eagerness.

Sixen handed the device to him. "Your chip works good. The mountain and walls restrict the range, but we should be able to relocate without trouble."

Ian pressed a button on the face of the device and a low pulse began to emit from it in regular intervals. A display appeared to give coordinates and north-south directions. He turned it off, and the pulse stopped. "Prescott will be sorry he ever gave in on that request of mine." He set the device aside. "What about the locks?"

Sixen shook his head. His black shaved hair seemed to have grown grayer these past few days. "It would take lab-wide power failure to break them. Best to stick with the original schedule."

"Which is exactly what again?" Things were moving way too fast for Jon to keep up.

Sixen backed toward the door, as if he had somewhere to be, or that he would be missed. "Dinner's at seven. Prescott's call is at seven fifteen."

Ian checked his watch. So did Jon. They had less than six hours before the point of no return, less than six hours before Jon was again face-to-face with his lifelong dream, and his nightmare.

Sixen put his hand on the rusty knob as a single voice shot through the walls. Shrill and piercing, the voice carried a scream that rose in pitch and volume until it became a whistle, then a scream again. Similar in tone to that of the other primate calls, this too was a voice born of inhuman lips, but it rode the air with such power and force not even cement cured over fifty years could contain it. For nearly a minute the cry held them frozen, their minds tortured by the wailing that grated on the eardrums like fingernails on a chalkboard. Then it faded, leaving a silent vacuum in its absence.

The three of them stared at each other, none able to speak the obvious. *It* was awake, and not at all happy about it. Jon's skin pricked from head to toe, his pulse tattooing in his chest.

Sixen eased the door open. Not a sound filled the hallway, not even the incessant cries of tortured guinea pigs.

The Indian spoke one word—"Tsadja'tko"—then left Ian and Jon alone with the echoes in their minds.

But Jon heard more than a demonic scream replaying in his head. He heard his own boots clipping through the underbrush, his panicked breathing, and the shattering of tree limbs and timber gaining on him.

Now he had a real image to go with those memories. The image of it standing in the trees only feet from him with nothing between it and Jon but his hope and prayer that Ian had a clear shot.

It was awake.

Tsadja'tko. The devil.

The devil was awake.

Monticello

7:45 PM

Aidan Thwaite sat up and rested from yet another fruitless search of the hole he'd created in the corner of the attic's floorboards. He arched his back in a stretch and flipped his flashlight off. Monticello was as quiet as he'd ever heard it, the staff having left hours earlier, finally offering him the opportunity for his much-anticipated treasure hunt.

The delicious high of curiosity burned in his veins. An archivist spent untold hours methodically and meticulously cataloguing, preserving, and studying the mundanity of past lives long lost to this world. Decades and even careers could pass without note or discovery. That is why he had not slept a wink last night and had been tortured by the arthritic ticking of the clock throughout all of today. Somewhere in this attic was history waiting to be rediscovered.

Pushing up the sleeves of his University of Virginia sweatshirt, Thwaite rose to his feet and studied the room once again through the musty haze cast by the single naked bulb hanging from an overhead beam.

He had already attacked the many boxes and crates choking the room's floor, just as Secretary Mason had, and had made a fine mess in the corner by ripping up floorboard after floorboard. Yet he'd found nothing.

He retrieved the invoice from where it rested atop a box to his left, having placed it there to keep it out of harm's way. The document Secretary Mason had dropped proved to be exactly what Thwaite had guessed it to be. A complete inventory of all artifacts brought back with the Corps of Discovery. He had assumed one had existed and had searched Monticello high and low for it. Evidently, his treasure-hunting skills were not on par with those of the secretary's. Clearly the secretary had found more than this one document—perhaps even the fabled lost journals. And it was that possibility that had burned a hole in Thwaite's mind until he could no longer stand it. Five minutes on the phone confirmed his suspicions but provided him with nothing else that he didn't already know. Secretary Mason was keeping the rest to himself, and judging by that fact alone the good secretary was withholding more than proof of Jefferson's eccentric taste in zoological artifacts.

Therein lay the seed of Thwaite's curiosity. For the life of him, he could not fathom how locating a misplaced primate skull could cause so much interest for the Secretary of the Interior. Sure, it was odd and noteworthy that Lewis had obtained such a skull, most likely that of a gorilla from a trade vessel on the mouth of the Columbia nearly a century before the recorded discovery of the species. But at best that meant nothing more than revising the species' date of discovery in the textbooks from 1902 to 1805. No. There was something else at play here that Thwaite did not know, and that's what had him so hot. Archivists had no patience for being left in the dark, especially regarding items that rightfully belonged under their watchful eye and control.

And so he sucked in another dusty-laden gulp of air and pondered again those few words scribbled in the margin next to the listing of the primate skull. The handwriting was Jefferson's, according to Secretary Mason, and Thwaite had to agree. He'd read his fair share of the eloquent author's penmanship. The words were supposedly intended as a clue to the skull's hidden location.

Thwaite whispered them to himself as he searched the room for inspiration. "Corners and rafters. Where shadows and secrets survive…corners and rafters, shadows and secrets." His studied gaze dropped to the hole in the corner at his feet and then rose to the rafters overhead. "Corners…and…rafters. Hmmm."

He switched his light on and aimed it into the rafters converging on the corner of the ceiling directly above where he stood. The well-anchored shadows were burned away under the scrutiny of his torch, revealing an odd bit of patched woodwork, the surface of which didn't quite match up with the rest of the ceiling. It seemed a slight bit lower, perhaps allowing for a hollow space behind. "Could it be that simple? I wonder…"

Too much safety leads to danger.
—Aldo Leopold

Olympic National Park
5:09 PM

A behemoth of concrete, the lab hunkered at the base of the granite face, secure in its invincibility, its unbreachable walls, its sole set of doors the only way in.

For those inside, the bunker might as well be their tomb. Only one way in also meant only one way out. And Mikel Locke was going to take every advantage of that weakness. He rubbed at his ear with anticipation as he continued to study the relic structure. Every advantage indeed.

His two-way radio still gripped in his gloved hand, he clicked it off and clipped it onto his jacket below his shoulder. He wouldn't want it squawking to life unexpectedly now.

A soft drizzle fell through the clearing around the lab, leaving a wet stain on the bunker's cracked concrete skin and a sheen on everything else green: the stretch of grass between the trees and the landing, the needles of spruce and cedar, the shaggy carpet of moss that dressed the forest from earth to sky. A few hours from now and a Pacific storm in all its fury would batter the lab like a sledge hammer in the hand of a god, which was why Locke had chosen tonight. Death was always best served up in the midst of chaos.

From his vantage atop a rise to the south of the lab, Locke adjusted his balance and weight to conform like putty to the contours of the granite and bark around him. Easing air in and out of his lungs, the must of cedar and forest decay coating his tongue and throat, he became as motionless as the spruce to his back. The chipmunk scavenging at his boots was as oblivious to his presence as were those inside. Nothing but the thickening mist moved in the ferns around him or down on the grass. He saw it all without having to move his head, and he felt the day fast giving way to night, felt it in the air's light touch on his cheek and chill in his lungs.

He allowed himself the faintest of smiles, imperceptible enough that not even the chipmunk with full cheeks could share his satisfaction. All couldn't be better if he'd planned it.

Due to the curious stopovers Secretary Mason had made in Philadelphia and Virginia, his men had not acted on Locke's orders immediately, choosing instead to obtain confirmation in light of the secretary's unusual behavior. Their instincts had been dead right, for this new information had intrigued the director, to say the least. For now they were in a holding pattern until they could ascertain the secretary's MO. That was just a matter of time.

As was the situation in New York. Should Ostman's bones show up there, he had a team in position and willing to act.

But Locke was growing more certain by the hour that his men's efforts wouldn't be needed in New York. Sometimes being lucky was better than being good. He couldn't have gotten much luckier today. Of all things, their primary suspect for receiving the bones was en route here, to the lab. As Thatcher had already confirmed, she possessed at least one of the stolen bones, and surely must have received them all. Where she had disposed of them was the question, and the sole reason she was still alive. Certainly she was rejoining Ostman out here where they believed themselves to be safe. Locke eyed the lab's double doors and the square patches of light escaping through the inset windows. If so, then Dr. Russell was in for a rude awakening.

Thatcher was going to lead her right into Locke's open arms. They'd have a little chat, he'd show off his handiwork with her friends, she'd willingly offer up the location of the bones in exchange for her life, and then she'd learn her last lesson in life. Never trust a man with blood on his hands. Lying was no injury to his conscience after he'd found the taste for killing.

The tone of Thatcher's voice on the two-way radio still rang in Locke's good ear. The seed of concern he'd had then had sprouted like a weed in his mind. There was, he supposed, the possibility that the good doctor would never make it this far, that she'd end up taking the secret of the bones' location with her. There had been an impatient eagerness laced in Thatcher's words, an almost desperate plea for orders to eliminate Dr. Russell even before interviewing her. Locke had been hesitant to allow Thatcher to shadow Russell, unsure if his past might raise its ugly head again at the most inopportune time. But he'd needed his best man to go to China where there were big players in the game around every corner. And Thatcher was his best man, despite his history, or maybe because of it.

Locke sipped another lung-full of mist to calm his pulse. If he'd made an error in judgment it was too late to alter the outcome. Now was not the time for nerves and second-guessing, but for a cool head and clear thinking. If he had misjudged Thatcher, the worst part would be replacing him. Today's military didn't make men like Thatcher anymore.

One way or the other, everything would tie up nice and neatly—even the issue in the next valley over, where the saws were already busy at work. The silverback that had left the tracks on the ridge had simply disappeared, a trick they were notorious for. And the colder the silverback's trail got, the less of a chance his men would have in bringing him down. But soon Locke would be able to take up the hunt himself, and he was looking forward to it. The species was more cunning and more of a challenge than even his fellow man. He didn't often get the opportunity to meet his match.

First, though, he had to see to Ostman and Prescott. As the director had put it, their dominoes needed to be removed from the table, permanently.

A sudden breeze stirred the drooping blades of grass, teased the fringe of cedar boughs. The doors and lab remained unchanged, as silent and motionless as a possum playing dead.

Aside from the encroaching storm, Locke had picked his day with attention to the finest of details. It was midweek. Only one couple, honeymooners, had registered for an overnight permit in the whole valley, and they were well upriver. The last thing he needed was more witnesses. If one wasn't careful, they could get out of control like a blaze through ponderosa in August. Unfortunately in this case, Locke had thrown the initial match by letting Ostman live.

He angled his wrist to catch the face of his watch and the two luminescent hands, then searched the gray stacking up overhead. Sunset and his storm were on their way.

His eyes went to the power box on the side of the lab and then to the doors. A hungry finger tapped gingerly against the barrel of his Glock, held firm and ready in his right hand. Patience. Patience.

Once dusk rose out of the shadows to fill the void left by the retreating sun, there would be no more time for patience. This lab had to be put out of service before they found the roaming silverback first.

Locke checked his watch. Patience. He only had to be patient, then he could do what he should have done weeks ago. Show no mercy.

His finger tapped again.

6:03 PM

Sam ignored the sharp spikes of pain that shot up her toes and shins with each landing of her boots on the trail. She ignored the slicing weight of her pack on her shoulders and clavicles. She ignored the sweat soaking through the back of her shirt, the wet strands of hair stuck to her forehead and cheeks, the swelling of her fingers. Even the remnant cramps that flared up in her lower abdomen now and then were pushed from her mind. She had enough to think about. Walk faster. The sun was setting. She was lost.

Or at least she *might* be lost.

She hadn't passed a trail marker in more than an hour, and there had been four Y's along the way since then. Now the dense canopy a hundred feet overhead was being consumed by the dark hand of dusk as it chased the sun across the heavens. So, too, the few shadows that had survived the day among the trees were rising from their hiding places and sweeping through the forest, riding up her back as she humped along with the longest strides and quickest pace she could summon.

An hour, maybe less, was all the daylight she had left. After that, she was at the mercies of the gods and the batteries in her flashlight. A crapshoot really.

That was why she couldn't slow down, take a break, or even smell the roses of this heavenly garden she'd been wandering through for the past six hours. She had to get to the lab today, which meant before dark. She had to confront Prescott and Ostman, had to convince herself that this detour was necessary, that delaying standing at her father's bedside was not another symptom of her fear, her weakness. Bottom line, she wasn't geared for a night in the rainforest, which was exactly what she'd get if she didn't get there soon.

Her breath sounded in and out in time with the falls of her boots on the packed, narrow trail cutting into the belly of the rainforest. Though it was true she hadn't savored the day's experience and beauty as she might under different circumstances, there was no way to avoid being moved by the forest. Not unless she'd had her five senses ripped from her being, leaving her as innate as a rock.

The first thing that grabbed her, that grabbed anyone who came here unless they were blind, was the scope and depth of the forest, which were greater even than the rainforests of southern China. Once inside, she literally could not see the forest for the trees, or the ferns, or the moss, lichen, salal, devil's club, and a thousand other species of plant for which she had no vocabulary. She wasn't a botanist, after all. She knew bones, not living, breathing masses of vegetation that grew atop itself so cannibalistically that there was no telling where one plant began and another ended. A tree wasn't simply a tree, but rather six trees growing alongside and atop each other, a hundred mosses draping and coating their trunks and limbs, an infestation of dozens of lesser species wriggling and protruding from notches and bends—a monument to life and the power of nature to break boundaries and rules, as casually as humans lie, cheat, and steal. Nowhere that she looked could she see farther than ten or twenty feet. Manhattan could have been on the other side of those trees there, or there, and she'd not know, not have a clue. It was overwhelming, humbling, mesmerizing, and bewitching. It was the Hoh rainforest. One of the richest biospheres on earth. And one of the planet's best-kept secrets.

The forest was so alive, so *present*, that most of the day she'd endured the disturbing sensation of being watched. More than that, of being followed.

And of course she felt so even now. The forest was watching her, following her every move. It had become her silent hiking partner, her guide, and sounding board.

But the forest had two faces. That of day, and that of night. At the moment she was caught in between, witnessing the transformation like watching someone die. She began to miss and long for the company she'd become so comfortable with these past hours while dreading and fearing the unknown that lay ahead.

The metamorphosis began with the ever-so-faint muting of forest chatter. The chirps and calls of chickadees, the thunkity-thunk-thunk of a woodpecker, the scattering feet of chipmunks, the whistle of wind playing the pine needles, and the general indistinguishable chorus of a million lives sharing the same space all slowly dulling into a silent hum that was now filled only by Sam's quickening dash for shelter. Then there was the cool mist that spontaneously rose from the ground with the same spectral effect as dry ice in a black-and-white werewolf movie, cooling the sweat held in her clothes that had been milked from her skin by the day's humidity and warmth. Next came the shadows and darkening of distant trees. The claustrophobia of night descending upon her like a black sack cloth. Finally, like a rotten cherry on top, came the rain.

A drizzle at first, then soft sheets of it. Sam knew it was only the beginning, could feel the weather changing, feel the thickening of the air and the pulse of increased energy coursing in the clouds stewing above the treetops.

The transformation nearly complete, all that was left was for that final sheath of light amid the trees to blink out, allowing the forest to welcome night and all its unseen phantoms with eager anticipation.

Sam knew, of course, that her imagination was wandering into fruitless and dangerous territory. Night was nothing more than the absence of daylight. Despite all her self-talk and reprimanding, the *place* had an effect, like the spell an enchanted forest cast on the foolish who trespassed into its dark interior. In the deepest, most primitive part of her, she was tempted to believe beasts as mythical as Ostman's cryptid were stalking through the trees, in the flesh and within sight, as limited as it was.

And there she went again. Wandering into thoughts that would do her no good other than to occupy her mind until she could get her damn boots off.

She dug her thumbs under the straps coming over her shoulders to release the pressure, blinked away the rain dripping into her eyes, and doubled her efforts.

Her reward was to come around a bend, around a wall of dirt and roots created by an uprooted cedar, and be frozen by yet another Y in the trail. Like the previous four, there was no sign, no markings whatsoever. Her initial reaction was to take the left trail, as she'd been doing under the hope it kept her alongside the river, but decided another search of the map couldn't hurt, as long as she kept it brief.

Digging into a side pocket of her pack, she pulled out the map, flipped it over and orientated herself. Damp decay from the opened earth filled her nostrils. Rain pitter-pattered on the waterproofed map and every leaf within earshot. She realized that her other hand had found the tooth and was mulling it over in her palm, as if it might reveal the way.

It didn't, of course. And so she looked up from the map in anxious frustration. The two trails appeared equal in width and usage. The trees down each were slipping quickly into the shroud of nightfall.

Then she saw the most curious thing. Something she hadn't seen all day.

Someone was coming down the right path toward her. A man. A park ranger by his uniform. And he was as wet and trail-weary as she was.

He smiled as he came up to her. She noticed two things immediately. He wore no name badge, yet wore dark sunglasses under his National Park Service baseball-style cap.

From those two details, and those two alone, she pegged him untrustworthy, a danger. But thankfully her brain began to work before she blew her best hope of getting help. It was Ostman's letter, his paranoia, that was telling her to distrust this man she'd never met. Sure, a lack of a name badge and sunglasses made him seem to be hiding something, but what would a park ranger have to hide from her? Nothing. She was tired and irrational.

Besides, his smile was as disarming as a child's. It even felt familiar in a way. And so did his butter-soft voice.

"Don't mean to imply anything, but can I help you?"

Her pack suddenly felt ten pounds lighter, her feet two hours fresher. "As a matter of fact, I could use a crash course in orienteering, but would settle for simple directions."

He smiled again, and she found herself returning the gesture. She also realized she wanted to see the rest of his face behind those glasses. She hadn't ever imagined Ranger Rick could look so good in a drab green uniform.

"Directions I can do. Other than a couple of honeymooners up the valley you're the only soul on the Hoh today. After a day or two you get pretty tired of hearing your own voice."

"Yeah, I know what you mean." Sam felt the same way when she spent hours on end on a dig, secluded in her own mind. "Your own jokes get old real fast, too."

He chuckled. "So where you headed?"

"I guess it's called the Hoh Battery. It's a lab now, or something, for the parks." She didn't know what else to say.

"Oh, no problem. I can get you there before you know it." He nodded at her hands. "Say, that's a hell of a tooth. What's it from, a dinosaur?"

It was Sam's turn for a polite chuckle. "No, not exactly." Again, she hesitated to say more but found herself wanting to, needing to. She realized how much she'd been needing to unload on someone. And who better than a total stranger. "Here, see for yourself."

She offered the tooth, slick with rain. As he accepted it, he smiled again, only this time there was a deeper satisfaction behind it. Something surely more than a coincidental interest in bones. She sure didn't expect his follow-up question. It left her searching for a good lie.

"Wow. It's bone even. Any more where this came from?"

6:36 PM

After returning across the old footbridge, Cotton and Cheryl Jones traveled the last stretch of trail hand-in-hand and lost in their own conversation—the type of conversation only newlyweds have. They chatted without pause about things that never came up in everyday life. They talked of their childhood: Cotton being born in the Northwest and raised, by his grandmother, on a farm in a place in the sticks called Orting, and Cheryl being born and raised with a silver spoon in San Francisco. Cotton grew up so poor that Cheryl teased that he was her own little street rat. They reminisced about their undergrad days at the University of Washington where they met, and whether it had been fate that they had both left that frat party early only to bump into each other on the front steps. They planned for the future—when they would have kids; how many; what their names would be; if she would work or stay home; if he would take that job offer with Microsoft or not.

It was the type of conversation that confirmed to Cheryl that they were meant for each other. Destiny had been their matchmaker. They had become the couple she'd dreamed of being a part of since she was six, only then her husband's name had been Francis, her kindergarten boyfriend.

She squeezed his hand in hers, loving the bite of her ring on her finger under the pressure, and gazed into those green-gray eyes of his. The dusk in the trees behind him made their sparkle that more lively, that more true. He was hers for life eternal.

She glanced down the trail, hoping to see their camp appear out of the ferns and moss. It was their first night, and she was counting the seconds to be in their tent alone with him. Just them, their love, and…

A lonely, drawn out moan came down from the ridgeline. Then another.

…and the wolves.

Fate. Destiny. And a serenade by wolves. What more could a bride ask for? Well, a five-star honeymoon suite on Maui for starters. Then room service. Long days in the sun doing nothing but lying half-naked next to her husband, drinking anything that sported an umbrella. Then again, he was her street rat. So, instead, she was on her first camping trip of her life, stranded without indoor plumbing, electricity, mirrors, TV, or a telephone. She gazed again into his eyes, watched his velvet-soft lips move as he went on about his plans for tomorrow and the rest of the week, soaked up the heat from his hand, inhaled his scent like an animal in heat. Like she said, what else could a new bride want?

To get him into that damn tent, that's what.

The howls had faded away in anonymity, but Cotton was searching the ridge through the dark drape of the forest canopy. All Cheryl saw through the nearest trunks was a black haze. His brows were curled, the way they always coiled when he was perplexed, in what was one of his cuter expressions. "What is it?"

He shrugged. "Oh, nothing really. I didn't know there were wolves in the park." He looked down at her, a wide grin stretching across his face. "Kind of romantic, though, huh? Ever made love with wolves cheering you on from the cheap seats?"

She quickened her pace toward camp. The drizzle continued to dance down on them. "No, but if you'd hurry up we'll give them their money's worth and then some."

His grin widened further, like a schoolboy panting for another scoop of ice cream. Her schoolboy.

And then they were running, laughing and dashing down the trail.

The rain turned into a sudden shower, washing down onto her until she tasted the cool water slipping in between her lips and felt her shirt stick to her chest, which was no matter, because she'd have it off before they were even in the tent.

Cotton had them nearly at a dead sprint when the trail finally turned right and opened into the long stretch of grass. Their camp and tent sat waiting against a row of short, squat trees on the other end.

Giggling and egging each other on, they lost their daypacks first, then their boots—stumbling like drunks getting them untied—followed by their shirts and pants. By the time Cotton yanked up on the tent's zipper, Cheryl had her bra off and was timing her dive inside.

The tent flap came up with Cotton's hand, and she pulled his other arm in with her.

His sudden resistance surprised her. Kneeling on their open sleeping bags, the rain's residue dripping down her bare chest, she pulled harder on his arm. She giggled. "I'll be gentle this time, I promise."

He was looking out on their camp, his brows coiled with confusion.

It was enough to sober her, if even for a second. "Dear?"

He continued to study their camp and the adjacent trees. "I think something's been in our camp. Our gear's all a mess. And…the tops of these two firs are snapped off."

Was that all? Cheryl couldn't care less about their gear. She put all her weight into pulling him inside.

"Cheryl!" He laughed as he gave in and collapsed on top of her. His body heat soaked into her from head to toe. His back was as wet as her front.

Rain was coming in the open tent flap. He reached a hand up, zipped it closed, and shut the world outside.

Left in near darkness, their giggles faded into the pinging of the rain on the tent as they now let their hands do all the talking.

7:13 PM

He slipped through the deer fern, the sound of the fronds rubbing against his legs, the sole evidence he passed this way. The occasional chickadee could be heard amid the drone of rain coming down ever harder through the pine needles and moss. The forest was quickly slipping into slumber, and the storm was brewing to the west. His timing was perfect as he made his way to the lee side of the lab. They'd never know what hit them.

Locke traveled the last fifty yards with his back to the granite face, his Glock held loose and ready. Rivulets of rain streamed down his face, through his stubble, and dripped from his chin. His black flak jacket and combat pants were soaked clean through from two hours hunkered in the bush, yet it wasn't all from the weather. Much of it was sweat—from the heat of adrenaline, the torturous anticipation, and the old want that was about to be satisfied.

Night was waiting just beyond the nearest trees, lurking within striking distance with the patience of a predator that hadn't eaten in days. Locke was just as patient as he eased, boot over boot, to the lab's exterior wall. There he stopped and listened. Seconds swept past on his watch face, and nothing but rain and chickadees disturbed the air. His gloved finger tapped the Glock's cold, wet barrel, itching to pull back on the trigger.

Patience. Patience.

Breathing easily through his nose to catch the scent of anything, human or otherwise, that couldn't be heard, he stole his eyes away from the far corner of the building and examined the power box attached to the concrete. The mighty behemoth's Achilles' heel. The meter whirled away as the bunker sucked more and more watts from the NPS. He opened a pocket in the thigh of his pants and retrieved a hefty set of cable cutters. With the calm resolution of a soldier carrying out the most mundane of orders, he opened the jaws of the cutters and clamped them around the inch-thick cable running up from the mud, along the wall and into the bottom of the metal box.

The cut was clean. And inside the chaos had begun.

Tony Williams entered the monkey room with as much dread as a day-care worker did each morning when facing the horde of snot-nosed, full-diapered, screaming children. Only the day-care worker didn't have to dodge monkey dung and worry about having his jugular ripped out by a pair of three-inch canines. At least Prescott paid a whole lot better than KinderCare.

He closed the door behind him and immediately was hit square in the chest by a load of crap. Rancid, runny, and green feces from Hannibal, the mean-ass chimp on the end row. "Shit."

Tony didn't bother wiping it off before it ran down his white lab coat. There was always more where that came from.

In this long rectangular room, with the same thick cement walls as the rest of the lab, the monkeys' howls and screams reached volumes that threatened the eardrums. Tony wore a pair of earplugs, but, even so, the hateful and vengeful cries seeped through the foam rubber right into his brain.

He hated this job, plain and simple. The only reason he hadn't quit was because he feared Prescott more than the monkeys. So he ignored the feces that flew his way and the angry voices that tormented him as he went to the far wall and collected his injection equipment. Every day, precisely at 7:15 PM, he issued the daily doses of serum on the target individuals. Today was not unlike any other. While everyone else was upstairs having dinner, he was down here next to hell injecting 30 cc of Prescott's special brew into the asses of the meanest and nastiest apes and monkeys this side of the Wicked Witch's castle.

Filling the syringes, he thought of the good old days at Berkeley when he had been more than an ass poker. He'd been in the think tank, theorizing and stewing with the best. Now, because he'd sold out to Prescott, he was a high-priced slave condemned to Hades. The animals he'd worked with then hadn't been red-eyed and vicious, and he hadn't been constrained to live for weeks at a time in a musty, old pillbox. If the monkeys didn't get him, or if he didn't start injecting 30 cc in his own veins every day to shorten his life as he was doing to their expensive guinea pigs, Tony vowed he'd never trade his conscience for money again. He lifted the tray of syringes from the cold, metal tabletop and glanced up at the chipped ceiling and naked fluorescent bulbs. "I promise."

With a grimace, he turned and faced the awaiting hordes.

Stacked like cages in a pet store, four aisles deep, floor to ceiling, the rein- forced metal pens held chimpanzees, marmosets, rhesus monkeys, baboons, gib- bons, spider monkeys, lemurs, and a few orangutans. The front row contained the big boys, the baboons and chimps. The old female orangutan, Suzy Q, was on the end next to Hannibal. They were all up on their hind legs, shaking their cage doors, baring their long canines, and howling as if being tortured to death, which Tony knew wasn't far from the truth. As of yet, all derivations of Prescott's serum had backfired, killing the animals in a slow death and inducing immensely aggressive behavior, which intensified with the increased dosages.

The smell of feces was powerfully ripe in the air, nearly gagging Tony.

As he approached the pens, he could see the rage and blood lust in their eyes. They'd kill him in a heartbeat if they got the chance. That was why they never left their cages unless sedated and why he used a six-foot rod to issue the injection. Small, round green LED lights glowed brightly from each cage, meaning the magnetic locks were functioning properly and receiving plenty of juice. He reminded himself the only danger was swallowing the next lump of green feces that came his way.

Yet even with electromagnetic locks, reinforced pens, six-foot injection rods…hell, even with a full suit of armor, he couldn't keep his nerves from fraying at the ends every time he got close enough to smell their breath, see the decaying matter stuck in their teeth, feel the pent-up violence wound in their muscles. He inhaled through his mouth to keep from retching and told himself for the hundredth time that the quicker his job was done, the quicker he could get out of their presence and get a hot dinner in his belly. Tonight especially he wanted to finish, because he was sure to be missing the buzz at dinner about the latest addition to their primate collection.

Mounting the first syringe on the rod, he stepped in front of Hannibal's pen. The three-foot chimp leaped to the top of the cage, slammed into the bars and crashed down with a howl and a stare to kill. He rammed his head twice into the bars, then a third time before baring his teeth and the nasty green feces smeared across them.

Tony raised the rod, took a step, and aimed through the bars. He always did Hannibal first. Hannibal was the leader, the big alpha male. He hated Tony, and the feeling was mutual. The look of betrayal and pain on Hannibal's black little face when the needle broke through the skin on his bare, red ass was almost payback for the crap he threw with dead aim. Tony's money was on Hannibal being the next to succumb to the treatment.

Tony eased closer and slid the syringe between the bars. A sudden spray of feces from three cages down peppered his face, burning his lips and tongue with the warm and sour taste.

Hannibal screamed and slammed into the bars.

The lights overhead flickered. Flickered again. Then went out.

Tony froze in shock as the room went black. Deep black like he had suddenly been transported to the far side of the moon, which would have given him no more of a surprise than he just received. The silence that fell across the room was no less deafening than that on the lunar surface.

Even as he thought first of the locks, of the glaring absence of rows of little green LED lights before him, the silence was broken by the realization of his worst nightmare.

Clickclickclickclickclickclickclickclickclickclickclickclickclickclickclickclick.

It was the sound of nearly a hundred cage doors coming unlocked and swinging slightly open on their hinges.

That meant the cage directly in front of him, Hannibal's cage, was now open too, leaving nothing between him and the eerily silent chimp but a few feet of darkness.

He didn't dare move. Didn't dare breathe. Just stood there and prayed they were all as night-blind as he was, though he knew most of them were nocturnal. In fact, he thought he could even see the faintest hints of luminescent green dots hovering in the black velvet that filled the room. Eye shine. Eye shine from dozens of beady, hungry, and opportunistic eyes.

His blood ran cold through his veins. His muscles went taught.

A hinge squeaked. Then another.

The sound of tiny, bare feet and knuckles slapping on cold cement.

He hesitated a step back.

Something brushed his calf.

Then his hand.

He swung the rod in a wide arch while moving for what he hoped was the door. He opened his mouth to scream, to scare them back, but his voice stuck in his throat.

Something landed on his shoulder, followed by a sting of pain behind his ear. Then it sprang off. A warm trickle ran down his neck.

His back collided with a wall or a door. He prayed it was the door. Stealing a hand from the rod, he felt behind him. Nothing but cool, hard concrete.

In front of him he saw with a certainty now the glint of eye shine, bobbing and weaving just above knee height. The devilish gleams gathered around him like children at story time, only they were in no mood to listen.

Jon stood outside the door to the primate pens, glanced both ways down the narrow hallway, and checked his watch.

7:15 PM.

The moment of truth. Once he opened that door there was no turning back, no explaining his actions. Total commitment to success or failure.

He removed the lens cover on the palm-sized digital video camera and placed a hand on the new alloy door handle. Cries and howls echoed through the door, the same tortured banter he'd heard every day for weeks. He pushed the red record button, aiming the camera's microphone at the door.

Take Prescott down. At least that was the plan. Somehow Jon had found himself on the tip of that sword, obtaining a piece of the evidence Ian would use to shut this project down. Meanwhile Ian and Sixen were at the other end of the lab stealing the evidence he'd been chasing his entire career.

He listened for a few seconds to the screams and hoots inside, the rattling of cage bars.

This wasn't how it was supposed to happen. He wasn't supposed to be playing espionage games and cutting down his opposition with razor-sharp red tape. But he'd also come too far to stop himself. It was one thing to merely believe in a theory, to hope for what he could not see, but another thing entirely to *know*, to have a visual witness of the truth. After that, there was no turning back, no denying, no obstacle too big. *Gigantopithecus* was as alive and real as the primates on the other side of this door. Its cries were as deafening, its odor as pungent, its eyes as penetrating. Science had a responsibility to know as Jon did—to study, to conserve, to learn. Even if Prescott was barking up the wrong tree for his miracle cure, there was much to be learned from an animal that had lived among us for ages without public acknowledgment. More than anything, the species was the canary in the coal mine. If we could delude ourselves all this time as to its existence, willingly refuse to connect the dots, then what else were we blind to? What else could we not see for the mote in our eye? For whatever it was, whatever truth was out there unseen, possessing the knowledge of it may ensure the future of our species, just as knowing the gas was building in the mines allowed the miners to escape with their lives.

Gigantopithecus was not just another great ape, not just the greatest discovery since the dinosaur. It was a hard stop in human thought, a true opportunity to reveal the conspiracy in our own minds. The chance for us all to see the greatest of human weaknesses. Arrogance. Arrogance so deep it blinded us to truth, in whatever form it took.

First Jon had to get the canary out into the light of day, and that meant shutting Prescott down. And so he took a breath, raised the camera near his eyes, and eased down on the door handle.

His pulse raced as the door cracked ever so slowly open. The screams inside leaked out, rising in volume as they escaped into the hall. Jon flinched in fear at them giving him away, but could do nothing but continue.

The first row of pens stacked to the ceiling came into view through the thin slit. Small monkey hands were wrapped around the cage bars, shaking them with all their might.

Jon nudged the door further, until he saw clearly the first six or eight pens.

And like clockwork, just as Ian had said, a lab technician, a Tony Wilson or Williamson, was brandishing a long rod capped with a four-inch syringe. He was aiming the end through the bars on a cage containing a very irate chimp.

Jon eased the camera lens into the gap between door and jamb, watching the terrible scene through the angled view screen.

The lights went out.

Jon snapped his head up from the camera, stunned, thinking at first he'd somehow been caught.

Inside the primate room, it was darker than night. Out in the hall wasn't much better. Periodic, red emergency lights on the ceiling had come on, bathing the hallway in a milky red shade of black that did nothing but tease the eye with a hope of sight, when in fact Jon could barely see the wall across the hall, which was less then six feet away.

Standing stupid and frozen in the gap of the open door, Jon realized something that made his skin crawl over his spine.

The monkeys had stopped their wailing.

The lab was as silent as the inside of a coffin.

Then a flurry of soft, faint noises thudded over the floor inside the room, like rough, bare skin rubbing over sandpaper—or in this case the cold cement floor.

The monkeys were loose.

And the door to their escape was open, if only a crack.

Jon nearly dropped the camera in his attempt to grab the door handle, and realized as his hand met nothing but empty red darkness that they'd already discovered their opportunity. The door had been swung fully open.

He was hit in the shin as something scampered past him. Then the other shin. He jumped out of the doorway and slapped his body against the wall. More rubbing of skin on sandpaper.

They were fleeing into the lab.

Then a curdling scream tore out from the primate pens. A human scream. A scream of death-looming terror and flesh-searing pain. It bled into many. Screams so horrid Jon couldn't help but fill in with his imagination what he couldn't see. The lab tech was being eaten alive, or at least torn to shreds by a horde of vengeful monkeys.

The thought to rescue his fellow man flashed into his panicked mind until, from above, he heard the dullest of rapid-fire reports. His immediate connection was with gunshots—lots of quickly delivered gunshots.

Ian Rettig loaded the hypo into the air rifle, closed the chamber, and signaled with a nod to Sixen standing at the door. It was time for a bit of mutiny.

Ian held position next to the massive gurney and pretended to wait for a hand from the Indian. Instead, Sixen moved from the room's outer door to come behind the two men assigned to escort the silverback to the awaiting Prescott and his teleconferencing board. Sixen jammed a syringe deep into the back of each man before they reacted to his odd movements. Their faces went wide with surprise and intended counterattack. But the sedative hit their veins too fast, and they slumped to the floor like wet towels.

Their shotguns clattered onto the concrete next to them. Sixen retrieved each and nodded back to Ian.

Ian couldn't help the smile that came. He was quickly finding this American Indian to be quite the bloke. The kind of mate one always needed in the bush to watch your back.

An ear-splitting scream erupted from behind the triple-reinforced steel door at the other end of the gurney. A devilish cry that made Ian cringe every time. It was an animal's voice for sure, but the tone carried too much heart and pain to not be confused with that of a human. A human in deep emotional pain.

Ian coiled his forearm into the rifle's strap and brought the weapon comfortably to his shoulder. Soon the big bloke would be pain free, slumbering away into eternity.

Sixen had finished sliding Frank and Thomas out of the way, leaving them resting peacefully in a far corner of the antechamber to the silverback's pen. He wore both shotguns on his shoulder and came over to assist with the gurney. If things went sour in a few minutes, Sixen shouldered enough firepower to drop a charging Kodiak twice over.

The keys to their success from here on out were speed and stealth. In less than ten minutes Prescott would be stewing with impatience, yelling for them to be found, for the prize to be delivered and displayed before his investors. By then, Sixen and he had better have the male down, its girth hoisted onto the gurney, and all of them hidden away safely behind the walls. After that it was a waiting game. Sixen had stored enough gear to last them through the coming winter, so time would be on their side. Jon would hike out in the morning with the film and other smuggled evidence of inhumane treatment of the primates. He'd present them to the authorities, and Prescott's gig would be unplugged within forty-eight hours. Then he and Jon could take their sweet time in delivering the body to science. From there it was all ice cream and cherries.

He was about to embark on perhaps the finest hour of his career, of any primatologist's career. Thinking of it in those terms made him wonder about Samantha, something he found himself doing with greater regularity after learning how Prescott had burned her. What he wouldn't give to share this moment with her—to share every moment of the rest of his life, for that matter. To see her eyes light up at the sight of the big, old silverback, for her to witness her and her father's work alive and in the flesh instead of a handful of bone fragments and teeth. To hold her face in his hands again, one more time, to feel her perfectly full lips on his, to smell her hair as it touched his cheek. Even to hear her voice, see her smile.

But she wasn't here and would never allow herself to be. For being here, now, required acting on more than empirical evidence, rock-hard theory, and conventional wisdom. It required a leap of faith, a willingness to take a risk, the self-permission to consider the impossible.

No, here was the last place on earth she'd ever be. Just as it had been with Africa. Life had intentions of its own, and sometimes those intentions kept no regard for love and happiness. Life was selfish that way at times. But Ian had accepted that truth years ago.

Nevertheless, it *would* be nice to have her company, even for this one moment.

A thump shuddered the steel door as Sixen moved into position to open the small, square hatch centered in it that would give Ian a window with which to fire his hypodermic needle. Then another thump, this one shaking the door on its hinges and leaving behind a raised welt.

Ian and Sixen shared a look of admiration for the animal's strength. It knew they were near, and didn't like it one iota. Ian didn't blame the bloke either, not after the welcome it had received today.

A third whump, and a second welt.

They cautiously stepped back.

Ian glanced at the green LED light that indicated the magnetic lock was functioning and secure. He nodded at the hatch, telling Sixen he was ready. Time was running short.

A flicker overhead from the fluorescent bulbs. Then they blinked out, dropping a hood of pitch black over the room.

Ian had a panicked rush spike through him, a daze of confusion until he understood the power had gone out. In fact, more than that, it had to have been cut. In that initial frozen second of time, when his body ceased to respond, when the room fell away from in front of him and there was nothing but black, empty space, he realized how valid Prescott's precautions had been, how real was the hidden threat that lurked behind the NPS. No agency or arm of the government was without its deadly guard dogs, not even the Department of the Interior or National Parks. They finally had called Prescott's bluff and had come to collect on the pot. They'd come and had no intentions of leaving any witnesses behind.

Such awareness woke him from his panic like ripe-smelling salt, and just in time to register the absence of the green light and click of the magnetic lock releasing.

Whump. Slam.

The rush of air from the steel door being thrown open and slamming into the wall carried a raw, sour stench of fresh feces, rotting meat, and decaying boiled eggs. Ian had the same gag reflex he had last night when he first stood over the silverback's sedated body lying in the ferns.

His gut went equally as sour as it dropped into his bowels with a sick twist of adrenaline. His weapon came back up to his shoulder, though he had no target and could as easily hit Sixen as the silverback if he pulled the trigger.

The echo of the door slamming faded into a mute, leaving only Ian's own breathing to be heard. There was no sound from Sixen, and no indication he was still in the room, though he had to be.

Ian stepped back. His boots scuffed against the floor.

A fleshy, heavy rub across the floor replied. The deep in and out of lungs far larger than Ian's mixed with his own breathing. Hot air settled on his face, as rancid and foul as anything he'd smelled in his life.

He thought to run. Thought to pull the trigger. Thought to stand there and wait the bloke out.

Then he thought of how well the thing saw in the dark, even probably in this black, formless soup. It surely saw him standing there, gun raised, barrel shaking from nerves too raw to control their associated muscles.

Another fleshy rub scraped over the floor. Closer this time. Within its reach for sure.

More hot breath licked his face.

He saw it. Or thought he did. A looming black silhouette, darker even than the abyss in the room. A presence that sprang from the dark itself, that was at home in it, and that was now free.

He spun toward the shadow within the dark, pressed his cheek to the rifle's stock and squeezed the trigger.

Whoosh. The dart cut the air with near silence.

But the shadow was gone, and the hypo exploded on the far wall.

Had he seen nothing at all, nothing but his own fear?

More fleshy scraping. More wheezy breathing.

Whump. Slam.

The outer door. The door to the hall and the defenseless lab.

The black gained a hazy red hue.

The devil was now not only free, but no one knew he was coming.

The board sat at Simonsen's back like a hungry band of vultures on withered tree branches waiting for the carrion to admit defeat and drop dead.

Simonsen stood at one end of the institute's conference room with his back to the twelve perfectly tailored and pressed black and navy suits to keep from making eye contact with any one of the silver-haired veterans of corporate guerrilla warfare. They sat at assigned, high-back, leather seats around the long, oval conference table that was so polished each man's face reflected off the dark cherry wood, doubling the number of vultures leering at Simonsen with growing impatience.

The largest of the executive chairs sat empty at Simonsen's end of the table, pushed in snug against the smudge-free polish. Prescott's seat.

Simonsen stood a few feet from it to the right, making sure not to obstruct the vultures' view of the near wall-sized video screen. He wanted all their attention focused on the stalling image of Prescott and not his own signs of weakness: the glistening of perspiration on his brow, his shifting of weight from leg to leg, and his constant fidgeting with a pen in his left hand.

Prescott had been rambling on for ten minutes now, essentially begging the board members to keep from standing and walking out of the room. Not only had the supposed specimen not shown up yet, but Lasiter, who was supposed to deliver the latest round of test results, was AWOL. Simonsen knew Lasiter well, had worked with him for decades, and if he were delayed, it was not due to a lapse in time management. Simonsen had that sour twist in his belly that told him something was not right at the lab. Something Prescott either didn't know about or that was so disastrous and sudden he had only one choice: cover and stall.

Prescott's face came through the miniature video camera mounted on the laptop on his end looking every bit as nervous as Simonsen felt. Simonsen had been reading Prescott's manicured features long enough to tell the anxiety wasn't from bluffing. Prescott had what he said he had. His angst was from the humiliation of declaring he had the greatest find in biochemical research history only to be caught empty-handed when the buyers came to window shop. He looked a little like the boy who cried wolf the one time he really had seen a wolf and no one believed him. In this case, however, it wasn't that he claimed to have seen a mere wolf, but more like a werewolf that danced, yodeled, and did bar mitzvahs. Needless to say, the board members were checking their gold, light-catching watches with increased regularity. They had been humoring Prescott on this project, going along for the ride based on his track record—a record that had bought many of them those gold watches. Only now their humor had run out. They needed proof. They wanted to see that damn werewolf stand up and do its best jig right in front of them, prancing around while they counted the dollar signs rolling off its back.

And that's what bothered Simonsen. He was the one here in the flesh, the one who would be left alone when the conference call was over to answer their surgically sharp questioning and accusations, the one they'd swoop down on from their perches to sink their beaks into when there was no dancing canine, or ape, or whatever Prescott claimed to have pulled out of his hat.

He was so desperate that for the past two minutes he'd been considering whether he should change the subject to inform Prescott of Dr. Russell's visit this morning. If nothing else, it would give Prescott an opportunity to discuss other successes the institute had of late, even if the work in China was nothing of note for the history books.

But he didn't. He couldn't open his mouth. As ashamed as he felt, he knew he was not the man to stick his neck out, even for Prescott. He'd rather suffer a blow to his personal integrity and watch Prescott squirm—which was exactly what he was doing.

"I assure you all, my time out here has not been a waste. Far from it. Our findings will place the Prescott Institute in a dominant position atop the pharmaceutical industry just as DOS did for Microsoft." Prescott let his professionally enhanced smile emphasize the coming joke. "As you can already see, though, wrestling the exact DNA sequence from our Alpha specimen will be far trickier and slow in coming than it was for Gates to *borrow* an overlooked collection of zeros and ones."

The board's reaction to the joke was as poor as the joke itself. Prescott was dying up there, his eyes glancing every other second behind him for someone, anyone, to come to the rescue.

Simonsen fidgeted with his pen, shifted his weight, and did nothing.

Huguez coughed. Busch leaned back and tapped the tabletop. Huguez coughed again.

Prescott smiled, the same glow appearing on his forehead, and snuck a glance over his shoulder. Then the screen went black. Black as Busch's suit.

A surprised murmur swept around the table. Simonsen stopped fidgeting, stopped shifting. His mouth was caught open.

The screen was black, but the connection had not been lost. Prescott's voice came through, confused, almost panicked—yelling for Lasiter, Rettig, and a list of other names Simonsen didn't recognize. Several four-letter words slipped in between.

At first, Simonsen assumed it was a gimmick by Prescott to release the tension, to claim technical difficulties. But the stress in his voice was too real, too raw. What they were hearing was real.

"Rettig? Damn it. You hear me. Lasiter?"

The crash of a chair falling back, slapping the floor.

"What happened to the power? Dammit, anyone out there?"

The scuffle of slick-soled cowboy boots on cement. The squeaking of rusty hinges resisting being spread apart.

The power had been cut. But how was the connection still up? Then Simonsen recalled that Prescott was transmitting over a wireless uplink, and his laptop was battery powered. His computer was independent of the lab's electrical system. Who would cut the power?

The instant the question came to him, Simonsen knew the answer. The very organization they'd been deceiving for this very reason. The NPS. Or at least the organization that infested the NPS and other federal departments. The organization that was so well hidden, black budget and all, that even Prescott's connections could not reveal its true identity.

Simonsen's weight sunk into his shoes, leaving him as planted to the floor as if he wore boots made of lead.

A dull, muted series of screams came over the room's speakers. Then the howl of a baboon. A screech of a chimpanzee.

Prescott's voice came next, heavy, breathy, and moving as if he were running toward the computer. "Rettig? Is that you? Damn it, answer me. Rettig?"

Another in-and-out hiss of breath filtered down from the surround-sound speakers. Deeper. Wheezier. Nasal. Animalistic.

"Sixen...Lasiter...Who is that? Answer me!"

A fleshy scrape against cement. Like sandpaper. Then a *whoosh*. *Crack*, like splintering bone. A thud. A crash.

The breathing went silent. The screen dead. The connection cut.

Simonsen's own breathing filled the speaker's void. He felt the board now very awake, on the edges of their seats. No longer impatient, but still vultures, hungrier than ever for their dinner.

Simonsen cleared his throat, selfishly hoping he wasn't the only man left stranded under the blazing heat of the sun, that Prescott's face would blink back onto the dull, blank screen. "Uh, hello. Are you there? Philip? Hello."

Her boots planted on the muddying trail, Sam watched the canopy above them grow ever darker, listened to the increasing chatter of the rain playing off the million leaves within earshot, felt the wet chill sink deeper into her bones. The one thing she did not do was watch the ranger standing on the metal grate or comply with his requests for her to join him. As with the tooth, he was oddly curious, almost demanding, if not for the innocent boyish manner in which his questions came across. She was quickly learning the best tactic was to be blunt, especially if she wanted to get them moving again and off his latest tour guide bit. "I have a thing."

"A thing for mine shafts?"

"No."

"A thing for heights?"

"Yeah."

"A childhood thing?"

"Sort of." She kept her eyes on the treetops as they turned darker shades of gray by the second.

"Fall out a window or something?"

"No. Like I said, it's just a thing." She heard the bite of impatience in her voice and hoped he did not. She was so grateful for his willingness to guide her to the lab and for his company, yet his inability to step out of uniform for a second and just get her from A to B without a blow-by-blow essay about the flora, fauna, geology, and history of the ground they walked on was eroding her good manners. She was cold and hungry, and her bones and muscles ached. She had no time for a tour guide. Instead she needed an all-business escort. The only thing of promise from this latest detour was that this grated mine shaft meant they were close to the bunker, which was built atop an old mining operation.

"I'll have to remember that."

"Remember what?" She reflexively glanced down and saw him kneeling atop the level grate on the ground suspending him over the black open maw of the mine shaft. Her stomach twitched up into her chest.

He studied his watch a second or two, then stood, still staring down into the yawning abyss beneath his boots. "Remember that you have a thing."

Despite the light-headedness besetting her from being less than three paces from the grate, her eyes were fixed on the ranger, and the almost perfect image that was not. He was nice, yes, polite, cordial, non-threatening in anyway. Clean-cut, clean-shaven, handsome even, filling out his spotless and pressed uniform in all the right places, leaving slack just the same. But then there was the matter of his sunglasses. They were still on below the brim of his cap, even though they were spotted with rain and there was far more of dusk between the trees than daylight. And his backpack appeared closer to military issue than parks issue, as did the silver-barreled rifle over his shoulder and the black-handled pistol on his hip. Too, there was his unusual interest in fossils and, in particular, her tooth. She'd had to nearly steal it back from him. The whole conversation left a suspicious taste in her mouth. In the end she'd told him nearly half the truth, deciding the truth was as good as a lie to him, though she'd omitted anything about the other bones, more due to the fact that she knew little more than he did than from any desire to withhold. He also had yet to offer his name. In fact, she knew nothing about him, left with only her assumptions. He knew more about her tooth than she did about him.

And now she couldn't help feeling that he was stalling, standing there on that grate looking down on nothing but the rising night and checking his watch. He seemed oblivious to the haste implied when hiking through withering daylight and a thickening rainstorm.

Then, like that, he stepped off the grate, gave her that perfect, endearing smile, and stepped back onto the trail. "Well, night waits for no one around here. Better get a move on."

Paranoid. That's what she was. Paranoid.

And all because of that damn letter of Ostman's.

For they will come for the bones. And when they do you will no longer doubt.

Oh, they had much to discuss all right, and she couldn't wait to see the surprise on his face.

Suspicious of a park ranger. She chided herself as she fell in line behind him. She couldn't be in better hands than if she were out here with Lewis and Clark themselves.

Her fluttering heart and cotton head subsided as the mine shaft slipped away into the whispering ferns and lurking shadows. She wished she could leave her entire phobia behind with it. After a lifetime of its haunting company, she doubted she would ever be so lucky. The trail led them away from the river at a gentle slope, but after eight hours of speed-hiking her quads and toes were having none of it. She had a hard time keeping his pace.

With her head clearing, she realized what had been nagging at her about the mine shaft, besides its gaping jaws. She doubled her stride to come up right behind his shoulder so he could hear her over the rain. Her toes screamed in defiance. "You know, I wasn't aware that mining was allowed on National Parks land."

He kept his head low, rain draining off his brim. "Typically that's true. But the NPS issues a few permits every now and then. And besides, this mine was tapped and barren long before the bunker was even built. In fact, the Hoh Battery sits right on top of the old mine's main shaft."

Heavy drops of rain beat on the trees. Sam was counting the seconds to be free of the unwelcome shower, to shed these soaked clothes, to bring warmth back into her skin.

She swiped a few drops clinging to her brow. "Thank-you again for your escort. I feel bad. It's so late, and you must have such a long hike back."

His head bobbed atop his smooth strides. "Not at all. We rangers keep a cabin that's only a short hump from here. Has all the comforts of home, minus electricity, indoor plumbing, heating; you know, all that unnecessary stuff."

"Sounds cozy." Sam was relieved to hear that he was not several hours from his bed, but her guilt lingered as she watched the night begin snuffing out the last remaining bastions of light.

"We should be at the lab in a few minutes. It's just over this rise."

She nodded at the welcome thought of being under a roof, any roof.

The trail widened, the fronds and devil's club were beaten well back. Hoofprints marred the slop under her boots. It was, or had been, a well-traveled section of the trail. Yet, even with that comforting knowledge, the woods around them had changed. It could have been the coming night, the darkness, the rain, her butt-dragging weariness that altered her perception, but the stand of cedars they were trotting through *felt* suddenly different. The fresh rash of bumps along her neck and arms testified that they had indeed left the 100 Acre Woods behind.

The rich orchestra of forest sounds that had accompanied the hiss of the rain was now deafeningly absent. Darkness had brought a chill to the air, but so had something else. She shivered. It could just be her imagination.

She elected to go with imagination, it being easier to deny.

The ranger led them off the trail onto a narrow spur, where the ferns and a host of other broad-leafed trailside residents crowded up to them like rabid fans, clutching and picking at their pants, boots, and hands. A short series of chipped concrete steps protruded from the mud, as if the rest of the structure had been washed away in the rains. They climbed them to the top of a level tier and followed the trail to the right.

Through the thinning trees she caught first sight of her objective—the Hoh Battery, and now NPS laboratory.

It stood in near-shadow across an open stretch of grass. The block of concrete came slowly into focus as they circled it within the trees, which had given way from cedars to slighter, shorter spruce and fir. At last they came to stand at the threshold between the trail and the thick, rain-beaten field of grass.

For some reason, the ranger stopped, one boot in the wet blades and the other in the muck of the trail. He stared out on the lab.

And so did Sam.

A low, chalky fog was creeping from the trees behind the lab, spilling out in front of it, edging their way. Rain and wind swirled and spun within the rare skylight in the canopy. A bough creaked. A metal hinge whistled from somewhere, lost in the folds of the night, which had hunkered down around the clearing and was filling in the gaps between the trees like black tar. Nothing moved but the antagonized blades of ripe green grass. No one was about, and no light burned from the inset windows on the lab's double doors.

Sam had been thinking about Prescott's and Ostman's reactions to her uninvited arrival. Up until a few minutes ago she hadn't considered the reality of such a moment. The awkwardness, the possible outcomes, the likeliness that she would not be allowed to stay. She had been entertaining the slightest notion that this had not been a well-thought-out plan. Now, standing at a stranger's side, in the deepest abode of wilderness in the country, confronted by a bomb shelter that was anything but inviting, she was pretty damn sure she could have considered this a little further before hopping in the car this morning.

Hindsight being twenty-twenty and all that, the bunker still had a roof. If nothing else, she'd be out this infernal rain.

The ranger straightened his posture, stuck a thumb under the strap of his rifle, and nodded to nobody as if he were committing himself to some somber course of action. He mumbled something, then grinned over his shoulder at her. "I take it you're not expected."

"No. Not exactly."

"Well, let's give a knock and see who's home."

This time it was Sam who nodded to nobody as she joined the ranger in a trek across the grass.

Rain fell harder in the open, beating into her scalp. The slick blades licked across her shins.

A blue jolt of light cut the sky overhead. Its forked fingers lit the clearing like the sun had suddenly doubled back on the night.

She saw what had been hidden in one panoramic snapshot. A hand-poured cement landing. The boxy, hulking lab jutting out from a granite wall. Short, hungry, and withered trees clinging and draping over its flat roof. Moss and tangled ivy shimmying down the front wall. The forested slope up to the ridgeline above. The white husks of dead and charred trees sprinkled among the carpet of evergreen—the first sign of death she'd seen all day.

Then the thunder hit like a sonic punch, rattling her nerves even though she knew it was coming.

Once again the veil was lowered, and she saw only the grass at her boots and the ghost of the bunker in the shadow of the granite.

They stepped up onto the landing. She noticed a fresher patch had been poured at its corner. Sharing a look, they slowly came up to the double doors. Above them, etched deeply with large letters, read: HOH BATTERY. Below that: April 21, 1944.

Neither of them spoke, which made the slowly passing moment that more unnerving. She felt as if they'd stepped up to an ancient shrine or tomb and that their voices would only anger and disturb the dead.

There went her imagination again.

Sam placed a hand on one of the cold metal handles and leaned in to the glass. As she already knew, the sickly glow of fluorescent bulbs had been extinguished inside. All she saw was a black shroud extending the length of a hall and into an oblivion that was tinted dark red by distant, pulsing emergency bulbs.

She leaned back and looked over at her guide. He stood by waiting, giving her the lead now. Unbelievably, his damn glasses still hid his eyes. The rest of his face, though shaded by shadow, had grown tight and uneasy. She took it to mean it may not just be her imagination. He sensed it too.

She squeezed her palm and fingers around the vertical door handle until the pain of it rose up to her elbow. She had to be sure it was reality that she had a hold of, because she felt as if she were about to open Pandora's box and step into the eerie glow of a nightmare.

When you have eliminated the impossible, whatever remains,
however improbable, must be the truth.
—Sherlock Holmes

The practice of science is like that of law.
Neither is interested in the truth, only what can be proven.
—Jon Ostman

7:28 PM

The door swung open, heavy on its hinges. Rain rushed in. Violet darkness and cold silence leaked out.

The empty, wide hallway that greeted them quickly vanished after a few feet, lost within the pulsing murk.

The silence. The darkness. The thick stillness. All whispers carried over the beating rain. Whispers of warning. Whispers of no trespass. Breathless cries for help.

Sam's imagination ran the gamut as she and the ranger pulled flashlights from their packs. None of the scenarios conjured in her mind boded well for those inside and those foolish enough to enter. Sometimes knowledge came from nowhere, or everywhere, like now. Sam *knew* all was not well inside. And her reasons for standing at the threshold to whatever ill lay hidden by the dark were fully decloaked, revealing their underlying petty and spiteful motives. In an instant, she wanted nothing more than to find Prescott and Ostman happily engaged in their work, whatever it may be. And above all else, alive.

Hell, maybe they were all holed up in a room watching videos or playing Trivial Pursuit.

Or maybe they weren't.

Sam took a breath, the first she was aware of since opening the door. They would never know which "maybe" was correct if they remained out in the rain.

The ranger read her mind and stepped forward, torch beaming a path through the gloom. "I better go first."

Sam wasn't about to argue, and followed him inside nearly in his hip pocket. The door whooshed closed and banged shut, locking the rain out and them in. The echo of it ran off into the unseen beyond their lights. Not a "hello," "who's there," "go away," or even a surprised peep answered in reply. They seemed as good as alone, yet she felt they most definitely were not.

Cabinets of taxidermy lining the two walls stared back at them with dozens of beady eyes glinting with eye shine as they passed. From field mice, to beavers, to timber wolves, the faces and muzzles behind glass gave her an initial scapegoat for her feeling of being watched. But the illusion was fleeting. She sensed movement in the dark and the almost imperceptible slap and scrape on the bare floor of very light footsteps.

Her damn imagination.

Nevertheless, she kept close enough to the thankfully well-armed ranger to smell his aftershave. It was pine scented, or was that just a perk of the job?

He unsnapped the holster strap, freeing the butt of his pistol, and panned his light in wider, quicker arcs.

His imagination must be as bad as hers.

A red bulb blinked on and off overhead. The taxidermy cabinets came to an end. And so did the hall. It "T'd," and they were forced with a choice. Left or right. None came any simpler or any harder to make.

A loose drop of rain escaped her bangs and ran down her jaw, leaving a cool trail on her skin. The Mini Maglite in her palm burned a hole through the dark, which was so thick she could almost believe she'd entered the very lair that the night retreated into after every sunrise.

Thus far, the lab was sparsely furnished, function taking precedence over form. A wooden chair lay on its back. A small table displayed a hastily discarded full house, two hands of nothing better than a pair of aces, and a dealer's deck that had mostly fallen to the floor. Cables ran along the corners of the hall, duct taped to the floor here and there. Everywhere else she panned, the light revealed barren cement baring the same wounds of time as did the exterior: chips, hairline cracks, mildew growth, rust stains, bullet holes…

Bullet holes?

Two pock marks on the wall opposite Sam scarred the cement much the same way she imagined bullets would. Not that she had any expertise. It was just the first thing that came to her. She wanted to point them out to the ranger, but he had already decided their fate and had chosen to take the hall to the left. He decided to break their silence.

"Hello? Anyone home? Park ranger here." He looked back at her, his dumb glasses reflecting their lights like bug eyes. "Anyone hurt, need assistance?"

He watched the darkness for a reply. None came.

Sam felt the tension ride up her spine like an eight-legged vampire, its tiny hairs tickling a rash of bumps in its wake. Something was about to happen, had to happen, or else she was going to burst like an over-cooked potato.

A clatter of dishes. The bang of a pot. Silence. More clatter. A faint, fleshy scuffle.

The ranger's hand flew to his pistol. Sam's heart stuck in her throat.

A shadow appeared in the open doorway just in front of them. They shot their lights on the black metal jamb in unison.

The shadow leaped back into the shelter of the room within.

The ranger slid his sidearm free, crossed his hands atop another, and aimed the light and weapon together with surprising deftness. "This is a ranger speaking. I'm armed. Please identify yourself and step into the light with your hands up."

He must have seen the bullet holes too. He had suddenly turned into Dirty Harry.

Sam eased a step back, her breathing coming in labored in-and-outs. Things were unwinding with tragic speed.

A second crept by. Then two.

A piece of silverware scraped the floor, and movement returned to the doorway. It came low to the ground and slow. The ranger dropped his aim and caught the blazing glow of eerie green eye shine. Animal eye shine.

It was a monkey. No. A long-muzzled, broad-shouldered, bony-browed baboon.

Sam wouldn't have been more surprised if it had been her father who stepped through that doorway. Or better yet, Ian. Or maybe her first-grade teacher. The stunning blow filtered down to her toes, numbing her as it went until she stood as solid as the wall, staring in awe at the baboon who was staring back at them. The ranger's surprise was expressed in just the opposite. He hopped back with a startled grunt. And although his aim remained on the animal, his stiff, defensive posture melted in apparent relief.

Perched on its knuckles and hind feet, the baboon peered up at them with black eyes that revealed internal wounds. Wounds that left no scar or scab. It was pitiful, standing there almost begging for a comforting hand.

Sam found her legs and came alongside the ranger with the speed of running sap. He glanced at her.

"What do you think?"

The baboon looked from the ranger, to her, and back again.

"Must be a test subject that got loose. They're used in some labs, though I had no idea this lab was one of them." Sam kept her voice calm, slow, and reassuring. Every second that passed seemed to carry her farther from reality and deeper into the surreal.

"Is it dangerous?"

The baboon shifted its weight from side to side, listening to them discussing it, or so it seemed. It was really rather cute. Its nose was wet and black like a dog's.

"Not likely. It's been raised in captivity. Probably as tame as a kitten."

The ranger lowered his weapon and handed his flashlight to her to hold. The rest of the lab was still as quiet as a morgue at midnight, and just as dark. She centered both beams at the animal's hands and feet, keeping the glare from its eyes. The eye shine gleamed back at her.

"I wonder how you got loose there, fella." The ranger eased down to its level and offered a hand for it to smell—the hand not holding his sidearm.

The baboon leaned back on its haunches at first, in expected distrust. Then, slowly, it moved toward the ranger's open hand, offering its muzzle in the same gesture. Its lips and the surrounding hair were darker than the rest of its face. Sam noticed how irregular the pattern was, as if it were random and not genetic, not the true color of pigment and hair.

Its muzzle was now inches from the ranger's hand.

"I bet you're hungry." The ranger's voice sang with a natural smoothness that calmed even Sam's nerves.

Until the light reflected off the bits of flesh stuck in the hair on the baboon's chin.

Its lips pulled back. Teeth, long canines, shot forward like from a spring-loaded steel trap. Their whiteness flashed in the lights.

Faster, and more amazing, were the ranger's reflexes. He snatched his hand back as he slammed the butt of his pistol into the monkey's face. *Crack*. It snarled and yelped in the same breath. Leapt at Sam. Teeth and clawed-hands aiming dead on. Eyes focused with insane rage.

Sam could only watch it come at her. Plow into the lights held in her hands. Its breath rushing up into her face.

The lights fell from her fingers.

Movement came from her left. She was pushed back.

The lights crashed to the floor, rolling and spinning away from them, sending spectral shadows running up the walls with mad abandonment.

She hit hard on her tailbone. Kept her momentum. Carried her weight over her shoulder. Came back to her feet.

Then she was holding her light, aiming it anywhere and everywhere, her mind spinning with desperate panic and confusion. And to her relief, the ranger stood in front of her, weapon trained down the hall at the baboon's hastily retreating red ass. He held his finger, and the baboon escaped around a corner.

He turned from the empty hallway and picked up his light. "Tame as a kitten, huh?" He was grinning and as collected as the moment she met him.

She, on the other hand, was anything but. Her heart thrummed in her head. She was breathing like an asthma victim who'd lost her inhaler. The beam cast by her light shimmered on the walls from the tremors shooting through her limbs. He'd saved her life, or at least kept her from a great deal of pain. She wanted to hug him in gratitude, but didn't, for she was also stunned at his performance. Ranger Rick never moved like that. Those were the moves of a trained soldier. Apparently the National Parks' recruiting pool now included the Special Forces.

She let go of the miniature flashlight with one hand and stood taller, faking a full recovery of her nerves. "I guess I owe you one."

He shone his light through the doorway from which the baboon had appeared and mumbled something about not tempting him.

"What's that?"

He shook his head. "Sorry. Nothing." His attention was now clearly on what he saw in the room.

Curious with dread, she came up next to him and whispered. "What do you think happened here, or is happening?"

"You're asking me?"

She caught his confusion. "Oh, no. I don't work here or anything. I was just coming out to...pay some friends a visit." Her lie sounded even shallower under the circumstances.

His voice suddenly carried an oddly calloused edge. "Then you might not want to go in there." He nodded at the doorway and room beyond.

Having not looked any farther than at the broken glass and food debris just inside the door, she finally threw her light in deep with the ranger's and gasped.

It was a kitchen, or better yet, a mess hall. Or was. Now it was a garbage heap. Tables were overturned. Chairs toppled. Food, dishware, and utensils lay splattered about the floor. One door of the doublewide, metallic refrigerator stood open. And in the room's center lay three bodies. Human bodies. Contorted in their poses of death.

Their blood painted the cabinets, the walls, even the ceiling with blots and dots in the same way an artist working with watercolors sprayed her canvas with a flick or two from a wet brush. Though Sam had no experience to call upon, no instincts to guide her, she knew the answer, at least in part, to what had happened. The unthinkable had become the unbelievable. Homicide. Murder by a hail of bullets.

Her body went cold, wicked east wind at night in the dead of winter cold. She twitched with shivers. The scent of the victims caught in her throat. She needed to look away but couldn't, and instead she stepped forward into the fray.

Her boots plowed through the litter as her eyes roamed the room. She knew on some level that shock was taking hold of her, but she could do nothing else until she stopped in the middle of the bodies. Then she realized why. She needed to see their faces, to ward off the debilitating paralysis of guilt while retaining hope—hope that the three faces were as foreign to her as the ranger's.

And they were. Neither Prescott nor Ostman had fallen here.

She breathed in, breathed out.

One was an older man, bald, heavy, and rosy cheeked. Another, short, frail, and sickly with greasy hair. The third was a woman, young, blessed with a model's face and body. They all wore lab coats. And all were marked with open, festering bullet holes: one at the throat, another at the temple, the third at the heart. Their killer had been a marksman.

9-1-1.

Her phone.

She yanked her shoulder straps off, threw her pack to the ground, and tore out her cell phone.

Holding it under her light, she jabbed at the buttons and held it to her ear.

Nothing.

She checked the number on the phone's display. It was correct. She hit END, then redialed, slapping it back to her ear.

Come on, come on.

No dial tone, no operator. Nothing.

She checked the display again. And saw the problem. Tears quivered at the corners of her eyes. What a fool she was.

Instead of a long, steady line of bars along the left of the display, the words NO SERVICE lined the top. Hundreds of miles from the nearest tower and inside a mountain of granite and concrete, there was not going to be any contact with the outside world. Nor with her mother. She couldn't help the dead or dying here, and wouldn't be there for her father when he joined these three at her feet.

What a fool. What a complete selfish, immature, ungrateful, naive fool. The worst daughter her father could ever have had.

She dropped into the rank filth on the floor as her failing nerves swept her feet out from under her. These three may be strangers to her, but death made them kin, for we all died and those left behind all likewise suffered the pain of loss. Her father could be dying right this instant, asking one last time to see her. Her mother holding his hand, telling him his daughter was there, lying to him to ease his pain, not telling him his daughter had not returned her calls. Then his eyes would glaze over and focus on some place far on the horizon, like this bald gentleman at her side whose open eyes stared up at the ceiling as if he were seeing into the heavens, if there were such a place. She hoped to God there was, and not just for the sake of these three.

A pair of tears trailed down her flushed cheeks.

"You all right? Uh…Samantha, Samantha, you all right?"

The ranger's voice sounded distant. It continued on in her ears. She paid it no mind, though she felt mild irritation that she'd told him her name and yet he'd not offered his. Now was not a moment to be spent among strangers.

The room ceased to exist beyond the beam cast by her light. She sat next to the deceased, mourning them, mourning the innocence and naiveté she'd had stolen from her. Death, it turned out, could be very sobering. She'd been running from her father's death and the claim cancer seemed to have on her family, and maybe even one day on her. And in one tick of the clock, reading two words on a piece of technology, she'd been forced to acknowledge the consequences of her denial. With no mode of communication, she was of no aid to these people, and, by being here, she had cut herself off from her father when a father needed his family the most. At the end.

Her body went numb with the pain of acceptance, of seeing the pain she'd caused in others.

The ranger's voice was distant in her ears. A salty drop rolled in between her lips. An image sketched on an open drawing pad lying at her side distracted her eyes. Beneath specks of drying blood, a half-finished ape-ish form came to life with the briefest of strokes at the hand of a skilled artist. An artist deeply disturbed, surely, for the ape was subhuman, erect, and possessed demon-like eyes that penetrated you even though they were nothing more than lead shavings on paper. Disturbed, definitely. She knew the feeling.

"Sam."

The name cut through her fog like the probing beam cast from atop a lighthouse. Sam. The name used only by her father, and at one time by Ian.

Only this voice was neither of theirs. She blinked. She was sitting on the cement floor, among uneaten portions of chili, corn bread, Caesar salad, and vanilla pudding. The bodies were only an arm's reach away.

The bodies.

Prescott and Ostman.

She looked up and back to the door. The ranger was there, peering inside the room at her and then out and down the hall.

"Sam. Samantha Russell. Snap out of it. We may not be safe here."

We may not be safe here. The words echoed, and revived her like ice water to the face.

"I think I hear something."

She was on her feet, light in hand. Her head was as clear as a summer day in the Rockies. Death was indeed sobering. Of course they were not safe, and wouldn't be until three questions were answered. Who pulled the trigger, why, and, more importantly, could he or they still be inside the lab?

Not knowing the answer to that last question spawned a sour chill deep in her belly and brought the dark around her to life, as if the darkness itself had killed these people and could cut her down just as easily and just as quickly without notice or warning. If the killer were indeed still inside, then her fear wasn't that far off the mark.

Stranger or not, she wanted to be at the ranger's side. When fighting the unseen, there was safety in numbers, or so the theory went. She closed the gap between them in a handful of rushed strides. He looked her up and down, then moved out into the hall, shining his weapon and light into the waiting nothingness.

"Stay close."

She silently complied and moved in behind him, whispering a prayer for the dead, the dying, and for the living as she left the room.

She knew it wasn't true, but the hall felt tighter, the dark darker, and the air the very breath of evil. Her imagination was on overload.

The ranger moved like a panther along the right-hand wall, his boots falling without a sound while hers thunked in a clumsy rhythm, his weight always in balance and ready for action while hers was shifting side-to-side in an awkward attempt at prowess. Special operations, Green Beret, Navy Seal, she didn't really care what his background was, but she was damn glad it wasn't the Boy Scouts or ROTC. Tucking in close at his back, she began to regain her nerve, began to believe whatever terrible thing had happened here had happen*ed* and was not still happen*ing*.

Their lights peeled the dark away from the wall and floor. Splintering cracks crisscrossed the cement from floor to ceiling. Cables ran in the corner at their feet. Nothing else was visible, not even the pockmark of a bullet hole. Her breathing came easier, lighter. The wisps of it hung longer in front of her. As they approached the corner, which was on their side of the hall, soft, whispering sounds leaked out of the dark, with the occasional crunch and crack. Her breathing accelerated. The wisps came faster, vanished quicker.

The ranger motioned her closer to the wall. He slowed his pace as the vertical edge of concrete crept toward them and the sounds of gibberish grew louder.

She had no idea who had pulled the trigger and for what reason, but she was quickly imagining a band of filthy, head-shaven, toothless white supremists hunkered around the corner slobbering over the remains of dinner. Their end-of-days and hate-crime weapons in their laps. Prescott and Ostman gagged, hog-tied, and naked on the ground wallowing in their own waste. Memories of such accounts playing over the news headlines from time to time emblazoned the image until she could barely bring herself to take another step.

Dragged along almost against her will by the ranger's apparent immunity to fear, she joined him as they peered around the corner, she on her toes to see over his shoulder.

The sight was worse than imagination could supply.

At the foot of a short flight of stairs, in an almost foyer-size space, three more bodies lay contorted on the cement. Only they weren't alone. As the two beams lit the room, four sets of eyes looked up from the bodies, eye shine as bright as diamonds. Blood stained the monkeys' faces. Shreds of flesh hung from their clamped jaws. Several chewed on as if they had not been interrupted. The large baboon was with them, standing on the chest of one of the deceased, his front paws sunk deep in between the man's ribs.

A rhesus monkey perched on the far body screeched and hissed, leaped forward, charged, then stopped, still hissing through lipless teeth.

"Stay back," the ranger whispered over his shoulder, then stepped out in the open, raised his gun and pulled the trigger. His aim was on the baboon.

The *CRACK* hit the walls like bottled thunder.

The baboon had time to rear back and bare its teeth, then was flung backward onto the bottom step. The rest of the devils leaped to their brother's defense, flinging themselves at the ranger, hissing and screeching.

CRACK, CRACK. Two more fell at his feet. He kept his stride, aiming as he went, as calm as an instructor showing the cadets through a firing gallery.

The last one got smart and turned tail, heading down another hall. The ranger took quick aim and dropped the rhesus in flight. The tiny body hit hard and slammed into the wall.

The ranger turned, the human and inhuman bodies at his feet, and holstered his pistol. "You OK?"

Sam didn't reply because in truth she wasn't. Instead, she joined him, casting only a superficial glance at anything below her knees. From here on out she would have to fake steady nerves. There'd be plenty of time for a breakdown later—assuming there was a later. "Never seen such aggression from test animals. Something's not right here."

He grinned again. "Whatever gave you that idea?"

Background or not, he was taking this a little too casually. He wasn't nearly as off balance as she was, or at least as he should be.

Sam pointed her light at the other end of the hall. A door was cracked open, revealing more darkness beyond. At the base of the door, another body lay sprawled on its back, a spread of pages littering the floor about its head. She eyed the ranger for his reaction, and he nodded in return.

"I think we have no choice but to sweep the place, confirm the gunmen are gone, or dead. We'd be no safer outside."

As much as she wanted to, she couldn't argue. At least the scene of the crime had walls and doors that locked. Besides, she wouldn't be able to sleep tonight, regardless of where, if she didn't find Prescott and Ostman. Hopefully alive rather than dead.

When they came to stand over the single body, she realized the door was open only because the dead man's foot was wedged between it and the jamb. A security keypad was on the wall, meaning the darkness behind the door was not coming from a coat closet.

The badge on the man's lab coat read like an epitaph, introducing them to J.M. Lasiter. An open manila file beyond his extended hand bore the label: Preliminary Results—Specimen Alpha. It held Sam's attention. Going against every cautious bone in her body that told her to keep moving, she dropped to her knees and gathered the upside down pages. Answers. She knew these pages would give them answers. She just wasn't sure to what questions.

The ranger stood over the body, keeping a protective eye down the hall and at the cracked open door. Sam shuffled the pages into a neat stack by tapping them on her knee and began to skim.

The text, single-spaced, ten-point and filling ten pages, was lab notes and test results. They were dated today, May 5. The opening summarized previous testing being done on various primate species, essentially acknowledging the long history of failures with a particular treatment.

Sam glanced up the hall at the small body lying crumpled like dirty laundry in the corner. The tiny little face of the rhesus still held on to the menacing grimace and tight-lipped snarl. Sad. Truly sad.

A twinge of guilt jabbed at her conscience for having ever worked with a man like Prescott, whose reputation regarding unethical animal testing proved to be all too accurate. Apparently he had been trying to extend their life span by subjecting them to intense antioxidant treatments. She was familiar with the theory. A gene from a cow had not so long ago been identified as coding for a natural antioxidant called superoxide dismutase. It had been inserted into the genome of a fruit fly and resulted in longer-living fruit flies. The implications for accomplishing the same result in humans caused quite a stir, but no action. That is until now. Prescott was the first to try the same experiment on higher life forms, going right for the top. Primates. He hadn't the patience for the science to slowly develop before he risked the lives of his test subjects. In fact, the notes clearly detailed as much. The animals grew more aggressive (more like insane with rage and blood lust), their immune systems broke down, and, in the end, their lifespans had been shortened, not lengthened. Yet he persisted. Sam sensed there must be something more to Prescott's motives, for the odds of succeeding were next to nil.

"We shouldn't stay here."

"I know. Just a second." Sam's eyes jumped down the page to a section of larger type separated from the rest of the body of text.

DNA HYBRIDIZATION:
SAMPLE A: SPECIMEN ALPHA
SAMPLE B: HUMAN
PERCENT SHARED NUCLEOTIDES: 97

She had to read it twice, doubting her weary eyes, but there it was. Specimen alpha shared 97 percent of its DNA with humans. That made it as closely related to humans as were the chimp and gorilla. She read up the page, prior to the hybrid results, searching for an identification of this specimen alpha. She had always understood chimps shared 98 percent of our DNA and gorillas 96. This individual didn't seem to fit either species. When she found the words buried in the fine text she nearly choked on her gasp.

Specimen alpha is of a previously unknown and as of yet unnamed primate species. By all indications, though, it is of the genus *Gigantopithecus*.

Gigantopithecus.

Ostman. His book. The tooth. His belief about the Olympic Peninsula. Pieces to a puzzle that now fit together all too well. Too well, as if they were manufactured. But what were they up to, what was their scam and why use Giganto? There was no money in it.

Curiosity burned through her veins like acid as she read on, mad for answers.

She flipped to the next page and got lost in the first paragraph. Literally ungrounded by the words, words she'd been yearning to read or hear for years, ever since her grandma died.

SKY and FISH analyses concur with MRI and MRS imaging. No presence of neoplasms, even within normal ranges, have been found. Manual inspection of soft-tissue samples reveal the same phenomenon. By all data to date, specimen alpha appears immune to abnormal cell growth, both benign and malignant.

Note: Extremely elevated levels of antioxidants found, but unfortunately no connection to such high counts and said lack of abnormal cell growth has been made.

The words stole her wind. She couldn't breath. Immune to abnormal cell growth, both benign and malignant.

Therefore immune to cancer.

Prescott was not after the genetic equivalent of the fountain of youth. He was after the cure to the deadliest disease in human history—cancer.

It was impossible, as impossible as specimen alpha being from a genus that had been wiped out millennia ago. Yet she didn't really doubt it. Research she'd done for her father when he was first diagnosed hinted that sharks might be immune, hording the cure in their cartilage. The idea wasn't new. Having hard evidence was.

She saw her father, propped up on pillows, his patchy black hair growing back after his last round of useless chemo. His lips chapped, eyes dark, breath sour and weak. His hand bony and cold in hers. But he was alive. And maybe…maybe he didn't have to die. Maybe…he only needed a miracle. Maybe that's why she was here. Divine providence. After all, God did work in mysterious ways.

Desperation like she'd never felt before lit her pulse like a fuse. Prescott and Ostman. She had to find them, and find them alive. Whatever their reason for feeling the need to incorporate myth into their science, for creating a phony specimen alpha instead of honestly declaring its true identity, whether chimp or gorilla, was forgivable, though unnecessary. She'd make them understand they didn't need to artificially resurrect an extinct ape to get the world's attention. Discovering the cure was enough. More than enough.

She thought of the bullet holes, both in the walls and in the bodies of the murdered scientists. She glanced down at J.M. Lasiter and his open, glazed eyes.

Perhaps not all of the world would embrace a cure with the same sentiment as Sam. As her family had quickly learned, an incurable cancer patient was worth a mint to the American medical and pharmaceutical industries—a very pretty penny indeed.

Unable to contain her thoughts any longer, needing to tell someone, anyone, she looked up at the ranger standing watch: his strong stance, rain-soaked uniform, firmly held flashlight. He was more than just anyone or someone. There was no room for strangers in the midst of death. She didn't know his name, where he was from, if the absence of a ring indeed meant he wasn't married, and if he was from a big family or was an only child. She knew nothing about him, except that he was here with her, and that meant she was as safe as she could be. He was like the younger brother she'd always wanted. And she would need his help to find Prescott and Ostman, and the true specimen alpha.

Before they took another step deeper into the labyrinth, he needed to know what she had found, and she needed to know his name. Still looking up, she waved him down. "You know, I never did catch your name."

Looking up at him with those big brown eyes of hers, so large they could swallow him whole, she waved him down. "You know, I never did catch your name."

He gave the dark sliver beyond the open door a quick check before easing down into a crouch across the body from her. Using the special tinted glasses to his advantage, which so far successfully disguised his face to her while sharpening his vision like amber lenses, he soaked up every inch of her. From the long, wet strands of hair framing her face, to the slight flush in her smooth, tanned cheeks, and the curves pressing through her shirt. Every second in her presence eroded his remembrance of his oath and duty, tempting him with habits he'd long since banished, or so he'd believed.

Finally, she'd asked his name. He opened his mouth to lie, then realized it made no difference. It was a name that meant nothing to her now, and by the time it did, it would be too late. He gave her a smile, one he knew she liked. "Stephen. Stephen Thatcher."

She returned his smile with a big, eye-twinkling one of her own. "Well, Stephen, I believe I know the *why* to what happened here."

He made his face go tight and long, as if she were truly going to enlighten him. She was so easy to play, and that made the temptation so much stronger, like hot lead jamming through his veins. How much longer did he have to resist the thoughts swirling in his mind, keeping them from being converted into action? And where in the hell was Locke?

She was explaining what she'd found, yammering a mile a minute, excited as a virgin on prom night. Something about cancer, and something about the monkeys. None of it he cared the least about.

"The race for the cure is big business, almost as big as keeping it off the shelves. Both are worth billions, and certainly worth the lives of a few scientists."

He only cared about the plan, which obviously hadn't gone *as* planned before their arrival. But he was still confident all was in order. He only had to keep his focus, and deliver Dr. Russell alive. If he could talk the location of the rest of the bones out of her, great. If not, then it was out of his hands. Either way she would give them what they wanted, including those notes she was waving through the air. Then she'd join the rest of the unlucky souls who had the misfortune of being inside this bunker today.

Her scent pushed through the stink of the freshly killed. It was intoxicating, sweet and musky from her day's exertions.

The hall was empty, silent, and dark. Nothing moved. Not the bodies collected on the floor. Not a door. Not a shadow. Her vulnerability and the hall's eerie privacy taunted him. He looked to the door propped open by the dead man's shoe, praying Locke would step through and relieve him of the burden of her, freeing him from the heat he could no longer stand. But his commanding officer did not appear, and Thatcher was half glad. His skin tingled from her scent, much like when an alcoholic who'd been on the wagon for months caught his first whiff of whiskey.

A terrible, muffled, inhuman scream came up almost through the floor. It was a scream he'd heard twice before. They had succeeded many years ago on his first hunt—it had been a female and her young they had killed then—but had failed on every attempt since.

It was a sound that drove through your flesh and bones, piercing your very soul, stirring primordial memories and emotions that came hidden within your genes. It was a sound he had hoped to never hear again, much like the whispering desires that had once made him victim to his cravings.

They had come too late. Prescott and Ostman had already succeeded. But they had actually done Locke and him a favor. With the good doctor in his safe care, custody, and control, and Prescott and Ostman no doubt below with the silverback, all the loose ends were about to be tied up once and for all.

Russell was on her feet, the flush in her cheeks draining into a pale mask of fear of the kind worn by those who knew not yet what they feared. They shared a look, a moment of decision, then he played her growing trust of him against her. He unholstered his Browning 9mm, exchanged the clip for a fresh one, and stepped to the door. He shined his light through the gap and down a flight of stairs. Without so much as a peep in question, she came to his side, lab notes in hand. She may be easily played, but she obviously had her own reasons for rushing blindly into the final moments of her life. He admired her strength, and as he nudged the door open with his shoulder, he wondered if he would be so brave.

They stood on a landing. Below, a narrow set of stairs descended deep beneath the lab. The same emergency lighting glowed weakly at intervals along the steeply sloped ceiling. Even so, the dark was thicker, more securely anchored at the bottom, some thirty or forty steps down.

Gunshots. The low, percussive blasts of shotgun rounds. The solid punch of heavy loaded slugs of the type best suited for blowing the skull out of a charging brown bear. Again and again. A flurry and frenzy of shots.

Thatcher smiled as he eagerly began their descent into the shadowy lair, where Locke was apparently still busy bringing the quieting hand of death to this lower level as he'd done with the two above.

Prescott Institute

7:43 PM

Simonsen watched his reflection in the floor-to-ceiling window in Prescott's office. His arms were crossed tightly as if fighting a chill. His eyes were dark, drawn. The telephone headset forced strands of his hair to stick up atop his head. The voice of Limpkin coming through it continued the list of bad news.

"We continue to get no response on the SAT phone. There's nothing there when we try to connect via the wireless modem. Cell phones get no service out there, but we've tried all the employees in the lab who we have numbers for anyway. There's just no use sugarcoating it. All ties have been severed. We're not going to get through over the air or network."

Translation: someone has to go out there in person.

Simonsen listened while Limpkin described the best plan for such a move and silently watched the night making itself at home beyond the glass.

Prescott's office was lit by a single desk lamp, providing barely enough light to keep Simonsen's distressed reflection alive. Like a shy child in the absence of its parent, the room kept its distance and withheld any of its warmth. Simonsen had long envied such a plush, executive suite, the quintessential symbol of success and acceptance in today's corporate fiefdoms. The more glass the room had the better, which was no doubt why Prescott only had three solid walls.

Tonight, however, standing alone in this office with the weight of its responsibility having been slapped on his shoulders by the departing board, Simonsen longed to be out of sight and out of mind in his tiny, sterile-white office while Prescott stood here and took on the world. Only that was the problem. Prescott wasn't here. And wouldn't be any time soon, if ever again. Things were *that* bad. Simonsen felt it in the tension between his shoulder blades and in the numb ache surrounding his chest, the ache of slowly forming dread. It was a feeling that had come to life the instant he had turned around to face the stunned circle of board members looking to him, and him alone, for answers. The muscles in his neck tightened even now as he remembered the vultures' stares.

A light tap of rain tinked off the glass. Raindrops appeared one at a time out of the dark, sticking to the window. The storm that meteorologists had been tracking in off the Pacific was already flirting with the Cascades, two hundred miles inland. Over the Olympics and the lab, the storm would be whipping itself into a frenzy. And by all accounts, it was a storm with stamina. Your standard North Pacific howler.

He couldn't request aid from the National Parks, as they either were already involved in the problem or would become so once they learned of the situation.

Contacting any other government agency would be as risky. Information flowed too quickly on the taxpayer's dime. That left sending out their own rescue/reconnaissance team. In a nutshell, that's what Limpkin was still blabbing about. Simonsen had no choice but to lead it. But he did have a choice as to when. After all, he was the one wearing Prescott's headset.

"No, no, no. Not tonight. Not in that storm. Have the team ready to leave at first light."

"And what if Prescott can't wait until first light? What if—"

"We can what-if ourselves to death, Limpkin. I'm not risking any more lives tonight. And that's final. Until then, keep up efforts to hail the lab. That's all we can do."

"But—"

"Enough. Check back with me in an hour." Simonsen snapped the headset off his ears and let it drop around his neck. Limpkin's voice leaked out in the air as he kept up the one-sided conversation. Any rush Simonsen might enjoy for succeeding at playing Prescott was doused by his reflection. The truth was that Prescott would have been on a chopper ten minutes ago, charging out into the heart of the storm, barking red-faced at the pilot to fly faster and lower. Simonsen instead was cowering behind excuses of preserving the lives of his employees, when in fact the only skin he was concerned about was his own.

The storm had been like pulling an ace from the top of the deck. It gave him a good eight hours to stall and hope—to hope Prescott was alive and would answer their calls.

But chance always had a flip side. Stalling damned Simonsen to eight guilt-laden hours of not knowing what the hell was going on out there.

Olympic National Park

The air grew cooler, the dark thicker, the red emergency lights duller. Descending the narrow flight of tiered steps, hugging the lifeless wall at Stephen Thatcher's heels, Sam had the eerie premonition it was the last mistake she'd ever make. Each step slowly came and went. She breathed in and out. A thin mist formed before her and glistened in their lights. After the carnage above, she knew more awaited them below. She only found the courage to keep Stephen's pace by the manila file of notes she held close to her chest. They were a plate of armor defending her against the suffocating and claustrophobic despair that grew stronger the deeper they went.

At the bottom, a long, lonely hall was all that awaited them. Nothing else but darkness, black, soupy-red, lung-coating darkness. Like breathing under water, Sam couldn't get enough oxygen no matter how hard she tried. She took hope, though, from the attack that didn't come, the bursts of gunfire that didn't split the dark. They were alone—for now. As she followed close behind Stephen, she realized, of course, how faulty her reasoning was. If indeed they had come to steal or prevent Prescott's work, they wouldn't leave a collection of notes lying on the floor detailing the very secret they either feared or coveted. And there certainly wasn't an unknown exit to the outside world buried this deep below the lab.

Stephen froze, dropping the aim of his light and weapon to a point on the floor in front of them. There in the beam of his light was what she reluctantly expected to find. Another victim, lying in a bloody heap in the corner of the wall and floor. A white lab coat, now a deep burgundy, draped the body like a sheet placed to honor the dead.

A sharp sting of bile rose into her mouth. Her stomach lurched as if she'd hit the peak on a roller coaster and was shooting down the back side. Only there was no pleasure in this sensation, just a simmering terror that threatened to overwhelm her, especially if she reached out to push the lab coat aside and saw the face of Prescott or Ostman. Her backbone at the moment was fully dependent on both of them surviving this nightmare.

Stephen acted before she could, kneeling next to the body and peeling back the coat. A wet, sucking sound hissed out as the cotton came away from the flesh.

Sam's hand flew to her mouth to muffle her gasp. It wasn't Prescott or Ostman. But the mangled face tested her wits just the same. The head was caved in. Smashed. Every bone in the skull and face crushed. The sick comparison to a watermelon falling from the back of a fruit truck and striking asphalt at sixty miles an hour came too easily to mind. The poor soul had been male. She could tell by the fit of his pants, but surely not by any feature above his shoulders.

Her stomach heaved again as the roller coaster threw her into another drop. She backed away until the wall stopped her, then turned and buried her face in the ice-cold cement. The cool slap was real, reminding her this was no dream, no twisted trip down into dementia.

But who could possibly feel the need to kill with such total disregard for the sanctity of life? The image of the mass of bone and flesh froze like a snapshot in her mind. Who could be so evil, so inhuman, and yet at the same time exist this side of the cover of the darkest of horror novels?

"You going to be all right?" came Stephen's whisper over her shoulder.

She let the chill of the cement seep through her cheek until her stomach settled. Then she eased away from the wall, breathing in deeply to swallow the bitter film on her tongue. "I'll be fine. Just as long as…"

Turning, she saw Stephen's face and noticed that it showed none of the concern he'd had in his voice, but rather a tense, jaw-tightening sense of alarm. His light was trained on the wall above her head. His mouth slightly open in awe.

Not exactly wanting to, but needing to, Sam brought her own light and gaze up the wall above her head. There, centered in both beams, was a bloody stain seven feet off the floor. Not any random stain. A print. A handprint. Complete with defined thenar pad, fingers, and opposable thumb.

There was no doubting this was an open hand. Probably thrown out to maintain balance, it had landed and left its guilty mark. The mark of a killer. Only this killer had a hand of the size any center in the NBA would covet, as well as the height. Spanning nearly a foot from thumb to pinky and resting well out of reach of even Stephen, the print was awesome indeed. Under the circumstances, its dimensions induced emotions far darker than awe. Including denial. Sam wanted with every ounce of her soul to deny what she was seeing, deny the feeling of doom that was growing in the deepest corners of her conscience. But she couldn't.

She'd been able to deny the cry of rage and scream of hate that had burned through the floor upstairs, been able to forget it in her rush of hope at finding the notes. And now the memory of it came fresh to mind, mixing with the image before her and the imagined voice of Ostman ranting on about walking giant apes and myths that wouldn't die. She saw the oddness of the print, the variations and angles in the fingers and thumb that were unlike any human hand. The weak thenar pad. The longness of it.

It was the hand of an ape, magnified two hundred percent.

The likeness was so exact she couldn't help the ridiculous thought that came. Perhaps this man's death appeared to be so inhuman and calloused because it had been issued not at the hand of another human being at all, but something very close. Something 97 percent human.

She sensed Stephen standing next to her. Hoping for reassurance and a voice of reason in her growing madness, she glanced his way. He was looking down the hall at the dark they'd yet to explore.

His stance had grown rigid, his shoulders and back high like a cat's hairs raised in defense. His handgun was in its holster. His rifle was in hand and raised, a white beam shining from a light mounted below the long, thick barrel. Seeing him from behind, oblivious to her, made her realize she'd been overlooking something, assuming too much. But the details of her impression passed like wind through attic rafters. Now she heard it too.

Sounds. Soft, fleshy sounds that shuffled here and there. Behind them even.

They were no longer alone.

No matter how stubbornly she denied the evidence, the company they kept was very likely not human.

Their backs were to the wall in a small alcove in a rear, forgotten corridor in the sublevel. Stuck in the middle.

By the grace of some unknown hand of fortune, Jon had rejoined Ian and Sixen at their point of rendezvous. They were now the only three left alive in the lab, except, of course, for the gunman stalking them.

Sixen was nearest the entrance to the mines, the secret back door Ian had alluded to in their brief planning sessions. Jon had noticed the boarded up and secured iron door before, but thought nothing of it. Now it was their only escape.

Before their coup, Sixen had unlocked and cleared the ancient iron door. Jon's responsibility was to resecure it, being the one to bring up the rear in their disappearing act. They hadn't considered it would be used by anyone else as an escape during the short time in between. But they also hadn't considered a hostile takeover of the lab or their silverback's subsequent escape, murderous rampage, and final disappearance into the mines, as if he'd been in on their plan the whole time. Certainly there was no way they could have guessed the rogue male would take Prescott's near lifeless body with him.

Saving Prescott, if indeed he were still alive, was on their minds, but quickly sliding down the priority list. Evading their pursuer while not having a surprise close encounter with the silverback in the mines was becoming paramount. Because Ian's little gadget, which tracked the signal of the silverback's implanted transmitter, was as silent as the mines themselves, they stood a great chance of doing just that if they entered the mines.

So they were standing their ground until a better option presented itself. Sixen covered the entrance to the mines while Ian watched the open approach from down the rear corridor and the nearby corner that led to the main hall and to the stairs. Jon lay low between them, wishing like hell that he'd had a chance to arm himself, with anything, even a skillet from the kitchen. As it was, Sixen's and Ian's shotguns—where they got them was a good question—were their only defense. The cache of gear stowed in the mines had enough firepower to arm a small war party. But that required entering the mines.

The scuffling of the monkeys came out of the dark. They were still a concern for sure. Jon had no illusions as to their intentions, not after hearing what they did to Tony. But they weren't lurking in the shadows brandishing semiautomatic weapons. *That* someone or some ones was sent by the government. As for why, Jon had only rough paranoid guesses, but Ian seemed convinced they were sent by the NPS to erase all they'd done. Wipe the lab clean like they'd never existed. Jon's ounce of wisdom in sending the bones to Dr. Russell was looking that much wiser by the minute. They may get to him, but not the bones. Not the truth.

Ian tensed, raised the shotgun. A faint footstep sounded beyond the corner in the main hall.

Their stalker was getting brave, and closer.

Jon eased back toward the mines, sensing Sixen behind him, standing his ground like the last warrior to fall in battle.

Another footfall.

A pinpoint of red light appeared on the wall opposite the corner. A laser sight. He would have night vision goggles too, for sure.

Jon watched with dread as the bright red dot shimmied and rose up the wall.

Ian slowly began moving back, herding Jon and Sixen into the mines. They had no choice, and only the hope that the tracking device would alert them to a surprise attack from the rear.

The dot stopped its movement along the wall, then retreated. A footstep sounded, this one farther away. The mystery guest was backing off, though Jon knew better than to assume it was for good.

Instead, he was only more perplexed and unsettled. They were sitting ducks. Their assailant had no cause to retreat. Unless, that is, another variable had been introduced. A newcomer to the game, perhaps? But were they friend or foe? And if friend, were they aware of the death trap they were walking into?

*   *   *   *

A hinge spoke with a rusty voice behind them, somewhere out of reach of their lights. They had passed no one or no thing on their anxious trek down the long corridor. Yet, they must have, for a door was being worked at their backs. Sam assumed by human hands, but her grip on reality was waning under such prolonged exposure to the milky red darkness. Perhaps other phantoms of the lab could work the handles. Her prayer was that the hand at work was not the same that had left its mark on the wall.

A "T" in the hall came into view within Stephen's rifle-mounted light. The hall was about to dead end. Again, they had to decide, left or right.

Stephen had them shinnying down the left-side wall, their backs pressed flat to the cement. Sam felt she'd been air-dropped into boot camp, except her weapon was nothing more than a strong pair of lungs, while everyone else was playing with live ammo. Twice in one night she was force-fed a dose of reality that made her realize how foolish she was. It was beginning to crack her confidence.

This adjacent corridor was narrower and, by the condition of the floor and walls, much less traveled. Grime and mildew hugged the corners. Cracks in the cement were thicker and deeper. The bulbs in the emergency beacons were, for the most part, out. The air even tasted staler, cooler.

Stephen brought them right to the edge of the corner at the pace of a lame snail. He did his best to disguise their presence by holding his light down at her feet.

A whisper of voices played the air. Human voices that she couldn't understand. A shuffle. A scrape.

Then Stephen ducked low, pivoted on one knee and came around the corner, rifle and light aimed as surely as if he'd done so a million times before.

Sam stood alone on the wall, watching, feeling naked and useless.

Stephen was yelling out that he was a park ranger, that their weapons should be dropped. Other voices were yelling back in chaos, fear, and confusion for him to do the same. A voice with a familiar accent rose above them all, begging Sam out of the shadows. Prescott? No. Ostman? She'd never even heard him speak. Then who?

Before she knew what she was doing, she stepped from the security of the wall and out into the corridor at Stephen's side.

The scene froze her like a cresting wave of liquid nitrogen. The corridor ended less than twenty feet from the junction. An ancient, iron door had been ripped from its hinges and laid half against the door frame and half on the floor. An infinite, yawning abyss stretched beyond the open door, like the very residence of midnight itself. Three men stood like deer ensnared in Stephen's light. A dark-skinned man at the door, shotgun at his shoulder, was the only one not ranting at the top of his lungs. A tall, lanky man with luminescent white hair, who resembled the photo on Ostman's book, was waving his arms in defense. Ostman.

And the third man…

The third man…

It couldn't be. But it was.

Ian. Ian Rettig. She knew by the long, wispy locks of sun-bleached brown hair, the bulbous nose, the twinkle of light in those blue, magnetic eyes, and most of all by the heavy weight that dropped from her chest into her boots.

She stood mute in the sea of chaos, staring back and forth at Ian and Ostman. The two of them together. Here. Now. In the middle of all this. She was feeling cheated, lied to, deceived. And yet tingling with a warmth she hadn't tasted since he'd left for Africa, since the last time they had been together. Since the last time life had swept her away in a rush that was as intoxicating as any narcotic, and far more severe in its waves of soul-rending withdrawal. He was here. Alive. Back in her life.

The old addiction rose from the depths of her heart where she'd banished it, filling her like hot water in a vase. She wanted to touch him. Hold him. Especially now with her nerves raw and spent. Then the moment sunk in. The frantic calls to disarm falling silent like a distant clap of thunder. The relaxing of weapons. The stunned look on Ostman's face. And the look worth a million dollars on Ian's. His chest had dropped into his boots too.

He was talking to her.

"Sam?"

His voice. Her name and his voice. A melody she missed more than she knew.

Strong. She had to be strong. Relaxing now, melting into his arms like she so desperately wanted to do, would put too much at stake. Their lives, for starters. And any hope of getting to the bottom of this supposed cancer immunity. She had to be strong until this was over, then she could melt.

When she came to, was back in the flow of time, the scene had changed to one of relieved confusion.

The Indian was still at the open door, shotgun barrel over his shoulder. Stephen stood confused next to her. And Ian and Ostman, standing side by side, were talking in tandem, nearly in stereo.

"Samantha. But how…are you all right? Are you hurt?"

"Samantha…Samantha Russell? But…you're in China, with my bones…"

And then in unison, "And who's this guy?"

She took some solace in her presence having unnerved Ian and Jon as much as theirs had her. Then she took a breath, glad to start with the easy questions first. "Stephen Thatcher. National Parks ranger. Where's Prescott?"

The stamina in her knees, the ability to stay on her feet, depended on focusing on her original goal and not getting off on the tangents and detours that were sprouting like weeds in her mind. Ostman and particularly Ian were staring at her as if she'd spoken in a foreign language. Ian's eyes were fixed on Stephen standing behind her, and she noticed for the first time the shotgun in his hands, held more at the ready than she felt necessary.

Ostman finally answered. "We think Prescott's in there." He pointed a thumb over his shoulder at the open door and darkness within.

"Is he alive?"

The Indian with the short-cropped black and gray hair replied with a thick aboriginal accent. "The devil shows no mercy. Certainly not for a man such as Prescott."

The devil? Did she hear him right?

But before she could follow with a request for clarification, Ian touched her arm and was easing himself between her and Stephen.

"Do you know this bloke?" He was speaking low in her ear. "I mean, *really* know him?" He was guiding her back toward the open doorway, keeping himself in front of her like a shield.

She reflexively resisted, staring at him like he was the one with a foreign tongue. Then Ostman was pulling at her.

"Tell me you got my bones. That's why you're here, isn't it?"

Ian let go of her, looking even more confused.

The bones. They were indeed the whole reason she was here. She pulled the one tooth from her pocket and held it up. "Yeah, I got them."

Relief washed over Jon's face like he'd just heard his only-born son had survived surgery. The relief was but a flash, though, as if he were slow to hear the part about his son being left paralyzed from the neck down. "What are you doing with that? You didn't bring them here with you? You didn't bring them all the way back here!"

"Uh…" The bones were still highly suspect, and so was Ostman, but standing in front of him, having to confess to losing them, she felt sheepish. His presence was far more intimidating than she'd imagined. "Well, no. I didn't bring them with me. I mean, except for this one. The rest…I don't know, I mean…I'm not sure where they are. They should be on their way to New York, to the Museum of Natural History with the rest of my—"

His eyes went as big as golf balls. He glanced at Stephen, then Ian, then back to her. "Oh damn. It was *you*, Sam. You brought *them* with you. Ian. Ian, run now."

Ian had Sam by the elbow, dragging her backward, raising his shotgun one-handed. "Right bit too well-armed for a ranger, don't you think, Sam?"

For the life of her, she couldn't figure out what they were talking about. Didn't rangers carry rifles? But in the instant she heard Stephen's voice, the butter having melted away to reveal the harsh burnt toast underneath, she knew they did not. Once again she'd been a fool.

"One. This is two."

As she was being pulled back toward the doorway, she turned to see Stephen talking into the two-way radio strapped to his shoulder while aiming his unholstered pistol at Ian's forehead. A grin she'd not seen before stretched across Stephen's lips.

"Cat's out of the bag."

An older, deeper voice replied over the radio. "Understood. Already in position."

A shadow moved at the corner behind Stephen. A red string of light flickered, then a bright red laser point appeared on Ian's neck.

Ian saw it too. Everyone did. No one moved. Ian's hand went still on her arm. Warm and nervous, it twitched at the fingertips.

Stephen was raising his free hand to his stupid sunglasses, removing them, smiling bigger than ever. And with a sparkle in the crisscrossing lights, she recognized his baby blues. They were as piercing as Ian's, only sharper. They were the eyes of the man at the airport, the man who had taken the flight with her. The man who must have been stalking her since China, since Ostman's crates arrived. She couldn't have been more wrong, or more blind to the truth.

They will come for the bones. And when they do you will no longer doubt, only then it would be too late.

Doubt. She was too full on fear for doubt. With the laser sight pegged on Ian's Adam's apple and Stephen's aim having moved behind her to the Indian, she certainly had no doubt that it was definitely too late. Too late for regrets. And too late for what-ifs.

She grabbed Ian's hand, pressed her palm deep into his and squeezed. He squeezed back.

The *plunk* of the accidentally dropped tooth hitting the floor left a faint echo to fill the silence.

The shadow moved out from the corner, revealing a man clad in black from head to toe. A short, snub-nosed rifle was cradled tightly against his cheek, which was hidden behind a black mask that covered his head with the exception of his mouth and his dark, focused eyes. The red tinsel of his weapon's laser flickered through the dust in the motionless air.

Seconds ticked by with agonizing stealth, taunting her with enough time to recognize these as the final seconds of her life but not offering a single tick more to do anything else except stand there and breathe.

Then to her surprise, a flash of motion and wail of hate erupted over the shoulder of the man in black.

Fur and teeth latched onto his neck and head, bringing his weapon's aim up to the ceiling. Two shots escaped the barrel, showering chips of cement from above.

Stephen turned, braced for an attack at his flank. And that's what he got.

A troop of chimps leaped from the dark, screeching and howling as they came. Their fists pounded the floor as they ran. A few swung shards of furniture like billy clubs.

Stephen dropped two chimps with solid *cracks* from his handgun. The man in black slammed his attacker into the wall with a sick crunch of bones followed by a soft, breathless whimper.

Stunned, shocked, bewildered, and detached from her body, Sam didn't realize she was moving until her elbow banged hard against the iron door lying half on the floor. The shooting tingle of pain woke her from her graveside trance.

Ian was dragging her through the doorway into the abyss.

A flurry of gunshots lit the dark.

Bullets whizzed through the doorway after them, spraying bits of rock as they hit the granite wall. A *boom* from Ian's shotgun shook her insides and dropped a cloth of silence over the air as her eardrums went deaf.

She saw rusted pipes descending out of the dark above, running along the chiseled walls. A rotting beam overhead caught her bouncing light. She was aware of the bite from the rolled up notes she'd hidden inside her shirt, and the absence of the tooth in her hand. Most of all, she was aware of the air. Still. Old. With the softest touch of something foul.

Ian nearly threw Sam down the corridor after Sixen and Jon. "Move, Sam. Move."

He cocked the 12-gauge, pointed it at the dimming light coming through the doorway and pulled the trigger. The recoil drove the butt into his chest, deep into his ribs.

No time to confirm if his aim had been lucky, he was sprinting after Sam and feeling the whiz of air at his back as bullets peppered the wall next to him. He had no light now, so he followed Sam's shadowy silhouette and prayed he didn't miss a hole in the floor and that Sixen knew where he was leading them.

The mineshaft was narrower than he'd imagined. Ancient, encircling them like a tomb. Blacker than the backside of the moon. And far too fragile. The beams overhead were splintered and buckling in their centers.

The place was also not as abandoned as it appeared. Their silverback was in here. Somewhere. Cornered with its back to the wall.

And Sam was racing toward it, unarmed and unprepared. She was as naive to the danger ahead as she had been when she'd opened the lab's double doors.

Thwack, thwack, thwack, thwack.

Ian guessed and ducked left. Hot lead chewed up the wall to his right.

The shaft curved, covering his back for the moment. Ahead, he saw Sixen waving them down a branch to the left. Jon took it first.

Sixen cocked his 12-gauge, expelling the spent shells, and raised it to his shoulder, aiming the barrel straight past Ian.

Ian bent low, hugged the wall and ran his boots off.

Boom. Boom.

The blasts tore past him, throwing him into the granite. Sam hit the ground hard in front of him. He had her by the hand, pulling her to her feet and down the shaft.

Her wide eyes looked up pleading into his, begging for comfort and an easy way out of this.

Wet hair plastered to her face and neck, clothes stained and hanging loose on her, dirt and fear darkening her innocent, girlish expression. The sight of her cut through to his heart, dead straight into his soul. She didn't belong here, didn't even understand why she was seconds from the end of her young life. Every muscle, fiber, and desire in his body screamed out for this all to stop, for them to put down their weapons so he could pick her up in his arms and walk her out to safety. Then they could talk. Hold each other. And erase the mistake they'd made years ago by walking toward their careers instead of each other.

Her grip on his hand squeezed his knuckles like a vice, reminding him a cease-fire wasn't likely. They ran together, hand in hand.

He would get her out of this. If it took his last breath.

*   *   *   *

Ian's hand held hers so tightly she felt the pain of its strength up to her elbow. But she wouldn't let go, not as long as she had breath in her lungs.

Ahead of them, Jon had stopped.

He'd *stopped.*

He was hunched over, his hands busy with something hidden behind a stout, vertical wall beam.

Ian brought them to a jarring halt next to him, letting go of her hand and shouldering his shotgun.

Filling an alcove in the wall was a bundle of equipment. A militia's dream cache.

Crates of food. Boxes of ammo. Duffel bags of things for which she didn't have the technical vocabulary but had seen on those military and police-force documentaries. And of course weapons.

Several rifles neatly leaned against the wall and a few handguns were in an open crate.

Jon, wearing a funky, space-age set of goggles strapped over his forehead, was loading a revolver, dropping more bullets than he slid home into the six chambers. "Put these on, but not over your eyes yet."

She stared at the rubbery mess of goggles Ian had slapped into her hands. "What are they?"

He was strapping his own on. "Night vision. Infrared."

He grabbed a rifle, two small boxes of ammo, and another revolver from the crate. He jammed it open, filled the chambers, slapped it closed, and stuck it in her hands. "It's a .357. Has a kick. So aim low."

She had time only to feel the cold, unfamiliar touch of the gun's black metal before the Indian sprinted up. He snatched a handgun, ammo, and a curious palm-sized device.

To Ian, he motioned down the shaft, to where it formed a "Y," and held the device into their lights. "Five seconds and counting."

Ian's eyes went wide, gleaming crystal blue in the eerie glow. His hand grabbed hers and began to pull. "Oh, damn, Sixen." He pushed Jon. "Run, mate. Run."

Her shoulder was nearly yanked from its socket before she could accelerate to match pace with Ian and Jon. She stumbled, was pulled up. The pages tucked under her shirt gouged into her armpit. The revolver weighed awkwardly in her other hand. She was tempted to drop it but didn't have the courage to do that either. The goggles began to slip down her forehead, risking blinding her, because she had no clue how to turn them on or what they did.

Jon and his towering shadow were angling into the left branch of the "Y." Still in the dark as to what Sixen had planned, Sam stole a glance over her shoulder before Ian raced her around the corner. Images came to her in bouncy clips, like she was watching a home movie shot from an old handheld video camera:

Sixen. Standing tall, slowly backing down the shaft. Device held at his waist in one hand, torch in the other, blazing the dark away in the opposite direction, toward their pursuers.

Stealthily advancing shadows appeared on either wall farther down the shaft. Stephen Thatcher. And the man in black.

The shadows slowed alongside the cache. Their weapons came up to take aim.

Sixen stopped, posing as perfectly patient bait.

Ian pulled hard to the left.

DUWHOOOMP.

The granite floor leapt up through her boots, throwing her like a limp rag doll headlong into sudden darkness. Ian's hand vanished with the light.

Her head hit hard against a rock.

Dust filled her lungs when she gasped in pain.

The clatter and tinkling of falling rock.

Then silence.

Blinding, suffocating, and oppressive darkness. And silence.

Then a pop and crack sounded above his head. Jon threw his hand about, desperately hoping to land it on his flashlight. Damn Sixen. What was he thinking, to bury them all alive?

Smooth, cool metal in the form of a narrow cylinder rolled into his frantically grasping palm. Thank God.

Jon spun it in his hand until his thumb found the ON button. He clicked it and aimed the beam straight up as the popping settled into the surrounding silence. Except for a soft beeping sound he hadn't noticed before. It seemed so out of place he hardly registered it.

The air was full of fine particles and bits of rock. His light had an almost solid quality as he scanned the cedar beam imbedded in the granite spanning the shaft overhead. It was intact, only complaining under its burden and sudden stress.

Feeling safe that he wasn't going to be buried alive, Jon angled the light down at the ground so he could stand and check himself for injuries.

Coming up off his knees while pushing with his left hand from the floor, he was hit by a sudden throat-tightening rush of déjà vu. His hand frozen to the granite beneath him like a schoolboy's tongue to an icy rail, he stared in amazed terror at the faint impression that encircled it. A footprint. Not a boot print, but a *foot*print. A raw, naked footprint far wider and three times longer than his hand.

A torch cut the dark to her left. It was Jon's. He was picking himself off the floor. She saw Ian already on his feet, slapping the dust off him and coughing.

They were alive. They were all alive.

She pushed herself up, feeling a sick, warm trickle down her temple. Her brain ached like she had a hangover. But she was alive. She doubted the same was true for their pursuers.

A soft beeping came from the dark, confusing her, but she was sure it was just a ringing inside her head from having her bell rung. She coughed, aggravating the hangover.

Sixen appeared out of the shaft's black throat like an apparition. He was covered in a fine dust, his hair and face glistening with thousands of tiny sparkles as he walked through Jon's light. He moved like the gunmen had: shotgun raised tight to his shoulder, sweeping the barrel left to right. But where was the threat? Surely not the two gunmen he'd just buried. Prescott, then? He was still unaccounted for and reportedly inside the mines. But why would he be a threat to them? He was the only one holding all the answers, especially with regard to the lab notes.

Ian gave her a nod and a big toothy smile as he began picking up his gear. He saw Sixen come between them. "Ay, mate? What's with the explosives?"

Sixen kept moving and sweeping his shotgun, his eyes didn't even flicker over to Ian as he whispered his reply. "Plan B. In case Ostman had not been able to secure our exit." Then he added in the softest of a hiss. "Check yourself, Rettig. Remember. We are not alone in here."

A quizzical look crossed Ian's smudged face, then he cocked his head. His expression went pale, even among the shadows of Jon's light. He slapped a pocket stitched into the thigh of his pants, dug his hand inside it.

Jon's anxious and taught voice entered the fray. "Uh, guys…"

Sam squeezed away the pain by pressing her fingertips to her forehead as she watched Ian pull a digital device from his pocket. To her, it resembled a hand-held Global Positioning System unit.

Freed from the smothering embrace of Ian's pocket, the device chirped like a Geiger counter in the midst of an atomic ghost town. The beeping hadn't been coming from inside her head. From Ian's hooded expression, it was clear the electric pulses were announcing the approach of more bad news traveling under the cloak of darkness.

Beep. Beep. Beepbeep. Beepbeepbeep…

8:09 PM

Cheryl came up for air first.

She pushed the sleeping bag off their sweaty bodies, rolled over on to her chest, and reached for a Nalgene water bottle. Propped up on her elbows, she tipped the bottle back and let dribbles of the water carelessly roll down her neck and disappear beneath her. He was watching her, and she hoped it had the same effect as the rain. If she had any say, they would be sleeping very little tonight.

Outside, the storm played the trees and the tent like Moroccan drums, like the southern Pacific waves pounded the sands. The backdrop was as far from tropical as she could imagine but was surprisingly just as carnal and seductive. And it was far more isolated. Their inhibitions had been checked at the trailhead, and she wasn't missing them one bit.

Cotton grinned with renewed hunger in his eyes as he leaned over her and unzipped the tent flap, inviting a rain-sweetened breeze. His chest brushed her lower back, teasing her with his warmth while the forest air sent a delicious chill, fueled by her body's sheen of perspiration, from her naked feet to her neck.

Another serenading howl challenged the weather.

She tightened the lid on the bottle, wiped her lips with the back of her hand, and looked at her husband through strands of hair, kinked and coiled by their love.

He pulled her on top of him as he rolled to his back, his hands nesting at the arch of her back. "You must be good. Our fans are requesting an encore."

She opened her mouth and kissed his upper lip. "Oh, I am good. But they'll have to wait. The encore's not for several more hours yet."

The night couldn't hide the twinkle in his eyes.

With only the rain and the wolf pack as company within this green bit of heaven on earth, she was pregnant with anticipation at the long night ahead. No distractions. No interruptions. Just them and the forest.

The rest of the world, with all its ugliness and pain, was far away on the other side of sunrise where it couldn't touch them. Until then, she would savor every minute spent engaged in her new favorite activity. And when tomorrow did come, it would be the beginning of their lifetime together—a long, beautiful life spent proving the world wrong with their love. *Till death do us part.*

Beepbeepbeep…

The electric pulses came faster, quickening Sam's heart rate in turn. Something was happening, but she had no idea what. That made her muscles tighten with dread.

The actions of the others told her enough to know they had jumped from the pot into the fire.

Jon was at her side, revolver and torch aimed ahead.

Sixen kept up a forward sweep with his shotgun, inching farther down the shaft.

Ian gave up on finding his light and instead unslung his shotgun, holding it and the chirping device. He motioned her behind him. He whispered, "Aim low. If anything moves that ain't one of us, shoot it."

"But what will I be shooting at?" she whispered back, unsure who it was they were afraid would hear.

"Later. Just shoot."

Left at the rear, exposed to the menacing darkness creeping up behind her every time she turned her back on it, Sam shivered from a chill that came from within. Her heart couldn't take much more of this. But she sure as hell wasn't pulling a trigger until she knew who her enemy was. Even then there were no guarantees. The handgun was really nothing more than dead weight in her hand, as useful as a rock.

Their crisscrossing beams illuminated an expansion of the mineshaft. The granite ceiling and walls ballooned out to form a cavernous space, one honeycombed with alcoves, nooks, crannies, and every other space the unknown could use to its advantage. A new odor rode the air, fermented in the ripest of animal feces…and something worse. Sixen stopped after only a stride taken within the chamber, his shotgun planted to his shoulder. They fanned out behind him, Sam the farthest to the left where a tickle of a breeze touched her neck. The shaft floor crunched beneath their boots, the sound carrying like it came from surrounding speakers, amplifying their lack of stealth.

Then Ian's device went mute.

A ripple of tension washed through the four of them. Sam felt it like a gust of November wind. The absence of the pulses somehow was more ominous than the pulses themselves. Why, she again had no idea, but the others' body language spoke volumes.

Then she began to see details of the cavern in their panning lights. Naked bone shone dull white, protruding from a pile of fur in one corner. Other bones filled cavities in the walls. Animal bones. A fresh wolf carcass here. Clumps of old and fresh feces littered a far section of the cavern over there, smeared on the granite. A stunning set of elk antlers rested against one wall. And in that instant she came to know true fear. Fear that gripped her soul, shattered the false, glass walls society had built around her, and left her breathless. More than standing in the sights of the two mercenaries, this moment showed her the harsh, unskinned reality of her mortal existence. She could die, would die. And now might be when.

Standing like Christians on unholy ground, none of them moved an inch, afraid to send even the faintest sonic ripple through the web of hanging air that would further pronounce their presence to whatever ill awaited the innocent.

They were in the lair of something. Something she couldn't name.

A scrape. A shuffle. A shadow moved to her right.

The others saw it too, their weapons spun after it, tracking it into the ether. She couldn't swallow. Her heart had lodged in her throat, yet she felt its pulse thumping in her hollow chest.

Motion blurred through their lights dead ahead. Ian's device chirped to life. A screech sprang from the walls.

Shots rang out, turning the still air into swirling chaos.

The dark came to life in front of her, coming at her with speed and feline agility. Ian's shout sang with terror. "Sam. Shoot."

She couldn't. Her arm had turned to lead. And so she watched with out-of-body distance.

Watched the night take on form and substance. Massive, towering, it came on two legs. Came straight at her.

Shots rocked the chamber, lit the night-in-motion. Eye shine raged back at her. Exposed teeth glinted.

Its voice tore through her like a thousand razors.

Her senses were hit all at once. The foulest animal stench to her nostrils. Coarse, long hair to her hand. Strength like a charging bull to her shoulder.

Then she was falling and landing with a crack to her head and a pop to her neck.

Feet rushed past her as she fought to keep the dark at bay. A hand took hers.

"Sam. Samantha, can you hear me?"

Ian. It was Ian.

She tried to speak but could only nod.

More stomping of boots. Flashes of light. She saw Ian's face inches from hers. Ostman and the Indian appeared standing above him.

"There's an exit from the mines to the forest. Tsadja'tko is gone."

The Indian sounded disappointed. The beeping of Ian's device began to fade.

"What on God's earth was that?" The tremor in her voice sounded foreign, unnerving, like hearing it played back from a cheap recorder.

Ian eased her slowly up from the floor. "That, me love, is a question I'll leave for Dr. Ostman to answer."

The truth is like a lizard's tail. You might seize it in your hand;
meanwhile, the lizard moves on, creating a whole new tail.
—wisdom from the African tribe of Kikuyu

I wouldn't have seen it if I hadn't believed it.
—old geologist's saying

8:16 PM

While Sam regained her breath and massaged the pain from her head and neck, the Indian had gone off alone down the new shaft with Ian's device. They both made her uncomfortable, so she didn't question his actions. She was too distracted with trying to get her feet back under her since coming around that corner and finding Ian Rettig standing side-by-side with Jon Ostman.

The foul must in the air. The overbearing darkness cut by their dancing beams. The bones and signs of death. Ian close enough to her she couldn't get a handle on her pulse. And Ostman standing in the middle of it all with a posture far too confident for a man who'd made a career of passing fiction off as fact. There didn't appear to be any chance of getting her feet under her, not tonight anyway.

And to think she'd come all this way to catch Prescott and Ostman in their hoax, or whatever game they were playing. Instead, Jon had the nerve to stand in her face, white hair aglow, and claim the thing that had plowed through her was her old friend *Gigantopithecus*. Up close and personal, in the flesh.

In other words, Sasquatch. Bigfoot. The boogeyman in a fur suit.

She watched Ian glance at her as he drifted to the chamber's perimeter, his eyes steely in the angled glow, his hair sticking to his face from sweat. The magnetic pull that had been there years ago tugged at her even now. He felt the draw too, she knew, and yet his movements were intended to distance himself in more ways than one, leaving only Ostman there to deal with her. He went through the motions of examining the debris littered about, but she knew his ploy. He was letting Ostman speak for him, an objective third party. Ian never had been able to stand up to her.

She had no energy for this, and no time. She hadn't been attacked by *Gigantopithecus* reincarnate. The thing that came at her, came on two legs. Giganto was a knuckle walker. She would cut to the heart of this whole facade. "I'm not having this conversation, Ostman. I want the truth, no more lies. I'm not the ignorant public you're talking to here. If your theories had even an ounce of merit to them, we'd all already know about Sasquatch, or whatever you choose to name it. Just like we know the gorilla. There'd be no mystery." Her words dripped with venom, as intended. People were dead. They didn't have time for games any longer.

Ostman didn't so much as blink. If anything his face hardened in resolve, as if her words had flipped a switch inside him, the final straw. "You're telling me you never heard of Sasquatch before today?"

"Well of course I have. I meant—"

He waved his hand through the dark. "What you meant is science, the Almighty God, keeper of all knowledge, has yet to stamp its seal of approval on it. Therefore it couldn't exist."

Wait a minute, he was twisting her words. How could he stand there and defend his ludicrous notions? "Of course not, but—"

"But nothing, Samantha. As you said, people are dead, and time is short this night. I may have debated you on this in my younger years, back when I didn't really know, only believed. Not now. Not after spending the past twenty-four hours in its presence. I know. Ian knows." Ian didn't glance up, just kept sifting. "And all those people upstairs, lying in their murdered blood, knew. So don't stand here in front of me and disrespect them with your closed mind and disbelief, especially with that tooth in your pocket. It was a long shot sending them to you, but I had believed you would know the truth when you saw it, that you'd be able to connect the facts."

Her tooth. She slapped her pockets, remembering as she did that she had dropped it in the lab. Dammit. The irony, of course, in debating Ostman while mourning the loss of the tooth was only a fleeting revelation.

His eyes glimmered in her light with passion and pent-up frustration. "And now you say you want the truth, but do you? Badly enough to believe it, badly enough to believe your own eyes? You're a smart girl, Samantha. Think about it. What's more likely? That we're all part of some elaborate hoax that's been in motion for centuries, planting false footprints from B.C. to California, inspiring hundreds of eyewitness testimonies, a hoax that has now been focused fully for your benefit. That we lured you down here, killing half a dozen innocent people in the process, just to scare you with a man in a monkey suit."

Mentally, Sam was reeling on her heels, stunned by the attack, surprised at being thrown on the defensive. She was speechless. Powerless to do anything but listen. She was even a little intrigued, mesmerized.

"Or perhaps, just perhaps, this is all true. Why else would I be here? Prescott may not be the most moral man, but he is no fool, not one to be swayed by impulsive curiosities ungrounded in potential profit. And why would he hire Ian, for that matter, an expert on the living, not the dead, like you or I? Maybe the truth is that Prescott had been funding your work in China because of his secret interest in finding *Gigantopithecus* bones. Maybe the truth is that those gunmen Sixen buried weren't here to put a stop to Prescott's illegal animal testing practices but to stop his attempt at capturing a live specimen. Maybe the only conspiracy here is the covert sponsorship of the government to liquidate the public's natural resources for private corporate gain, exterminating whole races, entire species, and anyone else who might threaten their agenda. And if you doubt, you need only think back to the fate of the American Indian, the buffalo, and a litany of other decimated species. If nothing else, let your imagination ponder the consequences to *them* should this particular species end up on the Endangered Species List."

He took a breath. Hers stuck in her throat. "Maybe, Samantha, the bones I sent you, the bones you claim you lost, are in fact bones. And maybe *Gigantopithecus* didn't go extinct exactly when *you* say it did."

The cavern and its unseen depths squeezed in around her, hampering her thoughts. And the smell...the smell was more toxic than a cramped hen house on a midsummer day without a breeze.

Her mind was a blur as she searched for a defense, a way to hold on to her reality. "Now wait a minute. If what you say is true, why wouldn't Prescott, or whoever *they* are, just go public. Think of what a living specimen, a living representative of our own species' heritage, would demand on the open market."

Jon shook his head in disappointment. "A few million at best, Samantha. Peanuts. Come on, now. We're talking *billions* in natural resources, and more than that. Power. Control. And in Prescott's case, a once-in-a-lifetime chance at a monopoly of the cancer drug industry."

"But..." She wasn't ready to give up so easily, but now that she had to defend her position, she was having a hard time mustering any ammunition. "Where are all the bodies, Jon? All the remains? A species always at least leaves their bones behind."

Ian had crouched next to a mound of rubble and pine boughs. He began picking through it, playing deaf to their escalating words. That he was letting Jon do his talking sparked beads of anger along her spine.

Jon smiled at her like he would a silly child asking yet another naive question such as why is the sky blue and the grass green. "What do you think your father found, that you've found, and that I sent you?" He worked a tooth, a large molar like hers, from the pocket on the chest of his shirt with one finger, rolled it against his thumb in the light. "What do you suppose this is?" He inspected it for a moment, then stuffed it back home. "But here's a better question. Why don't we find more?"

The *clack* and *plunk* of Ian lifting and resetting stones from the mound echoed around her like a swirling desert wind.

"They're survivors, Samantha. They learned quickly how to coexist alongside *Homo*, the greatest exterminator of species in earth's history. Out of sight, out of mind. So among other things, *Gigantopithecus* learned to bury their dead."

Clack. Plunk.

Images of her father first digging in the caves, of the buckets of teeth that came out, flashed like black-and-white still frames on a white backdrop. Mass graves. The idea rang truer than she was ready to hear. She wanted to object at the absurdity of it, but couldn't get past the images of her father and the buckets.

Ian's clatter split Jon's attention as well. He passed his light over the mound under dismantling with a growing scrutiny. "And not just that. Think about the *Homo erectus* teeth found in your caves among the other Giganto fossils. Isn't it interesting that I also found a human tooth alongside this one?" He padded the pocket hiding his molar as he slowly picked his way closer to Ian. *Clack.* Sam couldn't help but follow. "Ever wonder why, Samantha, that so many people are reported missing in the backwoods of the Northwest every year?"

Plunk.

The end of the mound nearest Sam fell apart as Ian jumped to his feet at the other. A pair of expensive snakeskin cowboy boots protruded from the grave. And though she couldn't see it from her angle, she knew at his end Ian had exposed a face.

Ian and Jon shared a glance and softly shook their heads, and then Jon, with all the respect of a priest giving last rights, answered his own question. "Because they bury their victims, too."

The tooth sat on the cement floor, the spots of red on it glinting in his light like tiny gems imbedded in the white enamel. He stopped with his boot inches from the tooth and stooped to snatch it up from the swath of blood painting the dull, gray floor and walls. Through the eyeholes in his mask, he examined the molar, confirming it was one of the stolen bones. Based on size alone there was little doubt. One down, and the rest he could now confidently leave to his men in New York.

The bodies of the chimps, ground up by dozens of rounds in each, lay about the hall. The damn things had been Ostman and company's get-out-of-jail free card. Locke kicked the head of the nearest chimp, sure it was dead but needing to hit something. Shooting something would've been even better.

The lab hissed with the silence of a massacre, except for the soft bumps and scrapes of the chimp's surviving cohorts milling about in the dark.

Locke tossed the tooth to Thatcher standing at ease next to him. Thatcher grabbed it from the air and slipped it inside a small pocket in his uniform. Like Locke, Thatcher was covered from head to boots with the fallout of the cave-in. His eyes shone sharp and blue, though, and his nerves appeared solid. There was no defeat in his features, only the set jaw and stare of a patient and determined man. He'd taken to the training well. And most importantly, he had not let his personal weaknesses detour him from his mission. Despite the delay, Locke had no reservations. By the night's end, the two of them would finish this business for good.

He brought his semiautomatic Krinkov up from his waist, cocked it, and tipped his head down the hall. "We've got work to do. You take the main level. Meet you at the entrance in thirty."

Thatcher cocked his own 9mm. "Yes, sir."

Locke watched him move like a cat toward the junction with the main hallway. Ostman and company had bought themselves a few hours, that was all. There was now only one loose end for Locke to deal with, and it was stranded in some of the thickest wilderness on the planet.

He held the Krinkov comfortably with one hand, pointed at the ceiling, and followed Thatcher's quickly retreating figure. A tingle of adrenaline teased his pulse. A little night hunt might be nice. An opportunity for Thatcher and himself to keep their skills sharp.

The face.

Poking through shards of rock, exposed by Ian's digging, Sam almost didn't recognize it. The man's facial structure was nearly crushed, masked in severe hemorrhaging. But the peppered hair and strong jawline were unmistakably Prescott's.

He had died by the same hand as the man in the hall in the lab's sublevel. A bare hand that needed no weapon to be lethal.

The encrusted eyes stared back at her from below the sunken brows. Closer together than they should be, they shared the same side of the face.

Unable to meet their gaze another instant, Sam had to turn, to bury her face in her hands. She breathed in and out through her fingers, smelling the tepid air and the day's mark on her skin. Tears came too easily, faster than she could swallow them back. The nightmare had taken more than she had to give. She was ready to wake, to see the sun through her lavender drapes.

Clack. Plunk.

They were putting the rocks back. Returning the dead to its peaceful slumber.

A hand touched her lowered head, caressed her hair, pressed her buried face into a warm, musky chest. Ian's barrel chest. She stiffened at first, only to give way and sink into his scent, his heartbeat. The beat brought memories of lying in the dark, the windows open, feeling the kiss of the breeze on her skin as she nuzzled into his chest and fell asleep to his solid pulse in her ear.

Tears came faster.

She shook, shook hard against him. He wrapped himself around her tighter, his warmth suffocating and intoxicating.

Clack.

In the darkness of her closed eyes, other images came: the bloody handprint, Jon holding his tooth, the Chinese in their uniforms ushering her out, their peasants digging up her fossils for their pharmacies, the flash of teeth in the dark and touch of course hair to her hand, the lab notes spread across the floor.

The lab notes.

Prescott's work. Cancer. *Gigantopithecus.* Cancer.

Her father.

A tiny spot of tingling warmth started to grow deep beneath her tiredness, her sore muscles, and general blah of menstruation. The warmth grew and swelled from head to toe, filling her to the point that it became true, as true as anything she'd ever known.

Plunk.

The miracle, the cure she'd lost hope for had been right there in front of her, hidden in the very fossils she sought. And if Prescott were right, if Specimen A were immune, and it shared 97 percent of its DNA with us, then the odds were we possessed the immunity too. We just had to find a way to turn it on.

The notes. In her shirt.

Sam pushed her hands against Ian, harder than she thought. He stumbled back.

"Easy, mate."

Her fingers were fumbling with her shirt buttons. "Ian. Jon. Listen." The buttons wouldn't let go. The roll of paper rubbed raw against her skin. "I found these notes. If you guys are right, then Prescott…" The damn buttons were sticking. The hell with it. She snapped the top two off, reached in and grabbed the bent roll of notes. Like a trophy, she held them up in the only light now shining, Jon's. "Then Prescott may have found a way to fight cancer."

Silence. The shock stunned her speechless. Ian's expression dropped, as if she had announced her own diagnosis. Jon came around, tiptoeing as if he'd come upon two squabbling spouses.

Finally Ian reached out to her, his eyes cool puddles of unwarranted sympathy. "Oh, Sam. I know it's tempting. But your father…your father is dying, Sam. Neither Prescott nor anyone else is going to change that, regardless of what those notes say."

She couldn't believe her ears. They didn't understand, must not know what Prescott had found. She waved the notes at them to wake them from their ignorant trances. "No. You don't understand. Specimen A. Prescott found…"

Jon stepped closer. Ian grabbed her free hand, squeezed it in both of his. "Prescott was high on the Big Deal and desperate in his failures, Sam. He'd had those notes written to sell ice to the Eskimos. The sad bit was he didn't need to. He'd already made the greatest discovery in history, but was too greedy to share it with the world."

Sam stared at Ian with narrowing eyes and ripped her hand free of his. The shadowed sympathy in Jon's face aggravated her more than Ian's touch. She couldn't believe this. She was saying she believed them, that she might have been wrong, and now they were calling her the fool. "What is this, Ian? Why are you doing this?"

He let his hands drop and looked to Jon for help.

Jon lowered his light to her feet, his face nearly disappearing into the cavern. "Earlier I said you had two choices of conspiracies to subscribe to. That's not entirely true, Sam. There's only one. And it's not a government conspiracy. For them it is only business as usual. Nor do I believe it strictly an American conspiracy; all governments have their own legends to slay. No, I speak of a human conspiracy. A conspiracy in our own minds to not accept the truth if it threatens our world view, our own self-interests. This delusion, this spell, is only broken when the pain of denying reality outweighs the pain of accepting it. For you, you're at the point you'll believe anything to save your father, even the truth." He reached out and took the notes from her strengthless grip. "But this, this is not the truth. This is only one man's perception of it."

Sam watched the roll of notes be swallowed by the dark as Jon pulled his hand back to his side. They were her one link to reality, the one justification for enduring all that she had, all that they had. The fog in her head let only the essence of Jon's words come through, but she heard them enough to want to turn them back on him and Ian. If a giant ape had been brought back from the dead, or more accurately had never died to begin with, then who's to say there wasn't a genetic code hidden within primate genes that could ward off the self-destructive onslaught of cancer. One was as impossible as the other.

The fog, however, held her tongue. She stood there instead, feeling her anger, frustration, and helplessness. Feeling every last nerve end stressed to its limit. Feeling too tired for this, feeling like walking out on these two self-righteous men right now. Except…except they were her only way out. She had no idea where *here* was.

Crunch, crunch.

A cone of light cut across Ian's back. The three of them turned at it in unison, Sam realizing that she no longer held her pistol.

Sixen. It was only the Indian.

He held their dusty goggles in one hand, Ian's device in the other. It was silent, for the moment.

"Time to go. Our Tsadja'tko is moving up the valley fast."

Ian nodded and turned back to Sam. "Sorry. We'll have to finish this later." His eyes drifted below her face. "Uh, Sam…" His eyes came up, then back down.

Sam glanced down. Her shirt was spread open at the top, revealing a teasing amount of rain- and sweat-slicked skin. The top two buttons. She remembered snapping them off. She tucked the shirt closed at her neck, having no permanent means of repair, and walked past Ian. She lightly let a few words go for his benefit. "Hope you got a good look. It's all you're gonna get."

She caught the quick flash of a smile and shine of his eyes as her torch lit his face. She kept walking by.

Coming up to Sixen, he handed her the goggles she'd dropped. She accepted them with as much trepidation as before, and noticed her revolver tucked behind his belt. Better there than in her hands.

Then Ian was next to her, reaching around her for his goggles as he called back for Jon. "Ostman. Mate. We're leaving."

"Hold on. This is amazing. A bed. A bed of twigs and needles. Just like one I heard about in an ice cave in the North Cascades." His voice was muffled. He had wandered into a corner somewhere. "Kind of ironic, though, all the effort we put into tracking a specimen down, and all we had to do was open the back door and invite him in. Should have known they'd been using this mine as a lair."

Ian strapped his rifle over one shoulder and across to the opposite hip. "Now, Ostman!"

There was grumbling and then reluctant footsteps coming up behind them until Jon appeared out of the gloom. "All right, all right already. Let the hunt continue."

As they traveled again within the narrow throat of the mine shaft, Sam re-experienced the sudden flash of teeth, the smell, the coarse, long hairs against her skin. In the void where a visual memory should be, her imagination borrowed from an image of her own George. Except she edited, making George erect, no longer a knuckle walker. She saw him in all his savagery, raging through the lab above, slaughtering the biologists and then slipping underground to his lair with Prescott's dead body under his arm.

Tiny needles danced down her neck as she braced for those lofty set of eyes to shine back at them from up ahead. And slowly she began to *feel* the reality of what she'd stumbled into, the raw, larger-than-life paradigm shift that was required to wrap her mind around it all. Prescott's Specimen A had tested negative on all counts for cancerous cells, both benign and malignant. *Gigantopithecus*. Specimen A. One and the same? If so, then the insane thing wasn't its supposed immunity, but that the four of them were damn fool enough to charge after it into the pitch black like it was a lost kitten.

The dark in front of her thinned, shimmering with the hint of gray. Then she stepped free into a light mist and full, face-on breeze. Both felt better than she could have hoped for. But the refreshment would soon wear off, she knew. The night was well entrenched, and the storm only taking a breather, gathering its strength. Once her adrenaline leaked out of her veins, she'd be shivering wet, coatless, and miserable. She'd be the lost kitten, wet and desperately homesick. Flannel sheets and hot cocoa never sounded so good, and neither did the old boring routine of being a college professor trapped on campus.

Ian came around in front of her, whispering. "We go without lights from here."

He helped her strap on her goggles, bringing them over her eyes. The world went darker than in the mine. She panicked behind the sticky rubber blindfold until he flipped a switch and it was like the sun suddenly rose to its zenith. A sun hidden behind a thick, sour-green lens.

"It has infrared capability too, but you need not bother with that."

Ian stood clear as day in front of her, his face masked by his own mammoth set of goggles. Jon was masked as well, and all lights had been doused. A fine mist hung in the air, air that tasted sweeter than honey compared to that awful den. The forest, ripe in its freshness, sat rooted around them, thicker than any rainforest China could offer. And above her head, beams rotting, joist angles leaning too far to the right, thick with moss, was an old entrance to the mines. So narrow was the opening in the hillside that only two of them could stand side by side under the arch. Sam quickly stepped clear of it and into this new green-tinted world.

Looking back at the entrance, tucked snuggly within this fold of the forest, she would never have noticed it if she hadn't just stepped through it. If she glanced away, she almost doubted she could find it again.

Sixen was pointing to a few short saplings near the mouth of the mine. The tops of them had been snapped off, the tiny branches dangling amid the lower ones. The young firs, though, were still a good twelve feet tall. Then he motioned their attention to a leafy shrub at his side and whispered.

"A good measure of blood here, and more down this game trail."

Jon whispered a little louder, and with real concern. "How many bullets can this thing take?"

Ian mumbled something about regretting the loss of a hypodermic syringe. Sixen turned on the tracking device and held it out, arching his arm slowly from left to right. A low beep joined the hushed voice of the mist falling through the forest. The silence between beeps steadily grew longer, and the chirps softer. The tiny needles returned to dancing along her neck.

Beep…beep…

The grainy image of the rainforest had a surreal, almost mythic feel. That a giant ape from millennia past was racing through it on two legs in mad retreat was neither surreal nor mythical; it was damn near unimaginable. Yet she couldn't help but be sucked into this new reality, with all its possibilities and terrors.

"There's nothing more dangerous than a wounded animal that feels cornered." Ian was following the sweep of Sixen's hand.

Beep…

"Except a rogue that has blood on its hands," Sixen countered. "Once they get a taste for it, they can't stop."

"Which is why we have to bring it down tonight." Ian checked the magazine from his handgun, slapped it back in, and cocked it. Jon did the same with his revolver.

Beep…

"Aye, hold on there, mate. Where do you think you're going?"

"I still don't have my type specimen."

"No, mate. You're taking Sam with you back to the lab."

The two of them looked at her, or at least their bug-eyed goggles turned in her direction. She scanned the green forest beyond them. If any part of Jon's theory was true, then all of it could be true. And so could the immunity. An icy prick stuck her heart. Then so too could Jon's belief that *Gigantopithecus* was now on the edge of extinction.

Beep…

And they were going to kill this one. The only specimen they might ever locate. The entire species, and any cure could be gone before anyone knew they existed.

Sam stepped up strong alongside Jon, standing as tall as her muscles allowed. "I don't think so, *mate*. Dr. Ostman and I aren't going anywhere, not unless you plan on stepping over our dead bodies."

Jon smiled beneath his goggles and stood closer to her. Ian chuckled with that back-of-the-outback voice of his that drew her to him like a moth to a flame. "Criky, she's feisty ain't she?" He stepped to her and took her hand in his, and spoke with a tender voice meant only for her. "All right, Sam. But you stay at my side. And I mean right by it, you hear. Because tomorrow we start making up for all those lost years."

The lingering chill in her heart from tonight and from those many years past melted away under the strength of his touch. Before she caught herself, she was on her toes, whispering in his ear. "Why wait for tomorrow?" Then, thinking of no reason to not, she let her lips touch ever-so-lightly against his stubbled cheek before dropping back to her heels.

As soon as she did, Sixen came near and poured cold water all over their moment by pulling the .357 from his belt and handing it to her. The only one without goggles, his eyes were that much more unnerving as he seemed to see her as well as she did him. "These forests are no place to be unarmed, especially at night."

The chilled metal dropped into her palm, awkward as a lug wrench. At least, though, she was armed. She couldn't help but think of the innocent people camped out in this night who were not.

Washington, D.C.

11:31 PM

The dark of his office thickened around his desk lamp and the glow from his laptop. The empty building deadened the constant hum of the city on the other side of the blinds, yet D.C.'s omnipresence seeped in and flickered red and white through gaps in the wall-length blinds. Thomas Jefferson Mason couldn't escape the city and all its bureaucracy any more than he could the disease. But for once, he took hope in the unwieldy American legislative machine. He tingled at the thought of using it as intended, to the benefit of its people, not the benefit of its legislators.

He paused in his typing, feeling the pull of a building wave of pain within his abdomen. He checked his watch. Time had gotten away from him. It had been too long since his last dose.

Retrieving the prescription bottle from his coat pocket hanging on the back of his swivel chair, he popped the cap and poured two into his palm. A third gel cap escaped as he raised the bottle. He stared at the three two-tone capsules as the pain sharpened beyond the warning dull ache. The temptation to not stop there, to fill his palm and end the pain for good came and went as it always did. But he didn't put the third one back in the bottle. He dry-swallowed it with the other two. He was going to be up a while, so a little overdose would do him some good.

The Indian cure-all Lewis wrote about came to Mason's mind as he returned the bottle to his coat. How truly wonderful it would be to partake and be cured, instead of simply having the pain eased.

He scanned back to the beginning of the ordinance he'd finished copying into the body of his draft. Not a word could be out of order or a typo left uncorrected.

ORDINANCE NO. 69-01

Be it hereby ordained by the Board of County Commissioners of Skamania County:

WHEREAS, there is evidence to indicate the possible existence in Skamania County of a nocturnal primate mammal variously described as an ape-like creature or a sub-species of Homo Sapiens, and

WHEREAS, both legend and purported recent sightings and spoor support this possibility, and

WHEREAS, this creature is generally and commonly known as a "Sasquatch," "Yeti," "Bigfoot," or "Giant Hairy Ape," and

WHEREAS, publicity attendant upon such real or imagined sightings has resulted in an influx of scientific investigations as well as casual hunters, many armed with lethal weapons, and

WHEREAS, the absence of specific laws covering the taking of specimens encourages laxity in the use of firearms and other deadly devices and poses a clear and present threat to the safety and well-being of persons living or traveling within the boundaries of Skamania County as well as to the creatures themselves,

THEREFORE BE IT RESOLVED that any premeditated, willful and wanton slaying of any such creature shall be deemed a felony punishable by a fine not to exceed Ten Thousand Dollars ($10,000) and/or imprisonment in the county jail for a period not to exceed Five (5) years,

BE IT FURTHER RESOLVED that the situation existing constitutes an emergency and as such this ordinance is effective immediately.

ADOPTED this 1st day of April, 1969.

Board of Commissioners of Skamania County. By: CONRAD LUNDY JR., Chairman.

Approved: ROBERT K. LEICK, Skamania County Prosecuting Attorney. Publ. April 4, 1969.

The date, April 1st, April Fool's, still caught his attention. But joke or no joke, the ordinance was binding and represented legal precedence. The intent was obvious. During the '60s, interest in the legend had reached a climax. Public officials felt they needed to ensure the public's safety while covering their bets should the amateur hunters actually bring back a body.

But Skamania County also had given Mason that extra bit of fuel to get a comprehensive law on the books, a federal law with teeth, specifically the mighty jaws of the Endangered Species Act. Since coming back from Monticello, he'd spent the past two days locked in his office researching and planning. Doing his homework.

His search of public records had given him the legal foothold he needed. His plan also required an expert, someone to give him credibility, someone who could stand before Congress and convince them that Lewis's ape existed and was indeed threatened. In short, a scientist with a very specific resume. The Museum of Natural History in New York had more scientists under one roof than any institution in the world. So he'd started there. Lo and behold, he'd found two who fit the bill as if custom tailored. A Dr. Samantha Russell and a Dr. Emmet Strauss. Judging by their resumes, Russell was the better choice, but no one seemed to know quite where she was—in the field, at her university in Chicago, or on her way home to deal with an illness in the family. Strauss, however, was in-house and available first thing in the morning.

The real challenge had been getting on Senator Pratt's and Smith's calendars with such short notice. But he'd piqued their interest. They'd be there, and more importantly they'd see the golden opportunity. They had been hunting the puppet master as long as Mason had.

Trusting Thwaite to come through was another matter. He was the one unknown, the one crucial variable. The curator had to deliver to make this all work. The recovered journals, Lewis's letter, and the testimony of a scientific expert were nothing without physical evidence. Mason had panicked when he realized he'd lost the invoice, the clue to the skull's location. But then, as if by providence, Thwaite had called inquiring about the invoice Mason had apparently dropped. After a lengthy conversation Mason had decided not to drive back to Monticello, accepting Thwaite's assistance instead. Mason had reminded himself he couldn't succeed on his own. He had to trust someone. Even so, he was betting the whole farm on the integrity of a man he'd known for less than forty-eight hours.

Finally he'd typed the last word. Satisfied his draft was more than it needed to be, he clicked the print icon. The printer behind him sputtered to life, chattering so loudly Mason feared the whole world could hear.

As his printer spit out sheet after sheet, he pulled them from the tray. This was no routine proposal. It had to be perfect. He again read every word of his proposal for the listing of a new endangered species. As he did, he couldn't help the ironic pang of loss that came. The draft was nearly a carbon copy of that for the grizzly bear written decades earlier, which he'd coauthored. As intended, the Endangered Species Act had brought the grizzly back from the grave, and worked so well that today greedy special interests were demanding the mighty bruin be taken off. Listing a keystone predator enacted such widespread conservation legislation targeted at preserving its habitat that industry had been locked out of some prime real estate for years. Having mined, tapped, and paved everywhere else, they were now drooling over the grizzly's forbidden lands. Legislators were of course caving to the dollars being slipped their way in the constant handshaking in the halls of Congress. And it was that greed that saddened Mason the most, fueled a fire that he knew was solely responsible for his living beyond the doctor's predictions. With all the success from being a listed species, the grizzly numbered at best only 1,100 individuals in the Lower 48, just 1 percent of the population at the time Lewis and Clark came West. And their habitat amounted to less than 2 percent of what it was then. How greedy were we? How much was enough? Do we need that last 2 percent? Do we need to squeeze every last species off the planet to make room for our own lavish lifestyles? He had saved the grizzly once, and now they wanted to kill it again.

But not as long as Mason had breath in his lungs. The grizzly would remain on the list, and soon it would be joined by an ape. Lewis's ape. America's one and only indigenous primate and great ape. It would do for the Olympics and the Northwest what the grizzly did for Yellowstone—stop industry dead in its tracks, and maybe even turn the tide within the department, tip the scales in favor of conservation instead of resource management.

His eyes drifted from the last lines of his draft to the open volume of Lewis's journals. That had been Jefferson's hope as well. A shift from a national policy of resource exploitation to that of conservation and preservation. The words of Jefferson's confession commanded his attention once again.

> I pen these words with a heavy heart and dark Conscience, for on this day by way of Clark I have just learned of my dear and cherished friend Meriwether Lewis's murder. History will record that he suffered death at his own hand, but history is only as honest as the men who write it. And as I have had a considerable influence upon how the future will remember this time in our great nation's history I can speak with authority. The truth too often is short lived, not surviving even long enough to see tomorrow let alone generations yet unborn.

> And for that reason as well as for the guilt I suffer from knowing Lewis's blood stains my hands as well as his murderer, I must preserve these few pieces of true history so that one day when the American Empire we have strived so hard to create is mature God will bring them to light. For unfortunately in our infancy we have had to make many concessions to the principles of the Revolution which we hold so dear. As we learned from the deals made to keep slavery off the Senate floor until such time as our sins could be redeemed, we also have allowed our government to follow the evil precedent of our European parents. There the corrupt abuse of public assets for private gain was inevitable so long as the deals of men were allowed to be made behind closed doors. Our nation is equally guilty, and my worst fear is that it may always be so. Unless an insider finally opens the door and invites the People in, empowering them to shine their light and banish the shadows of corruption forever from the halls of Government. And this is my solemn prayer, that one day when the nation is ready to stand on its own, independent of private interests, this small bit of history will be found providing the impetus for such brave action.

> In so doing I have detailed below all the ill that I have had a hand in, as well I have described the modus operandi of those genealogies whose legacy of abuse is nearly timeless. I wish I could offer more of substance, but current pressures prevent me from doing so. I can only offer up these journals of Lewis's and his final testimony as addressed to me as another witness. Be it known tho Lewis was only in the service of his Country, for it was I who issued his Orders. His-

tory must be revised as to his record, as well as to the founding of this Empire. It was not as innocent an endeavor as we have allowed you to believe. Trust me tho in knowing we did what we thought best and right. For it is difficult indeed to live up to the principles set down by God. May the future citizens of this nation be blessed with Strength where we have been so weak. And may they too take serious this precious skull that I leave as evidence of Lewis's account. I believe fully in what Lewis encountered at the Pacific, in an animal so like ourselves it must surely have a soul. It is a symbol from God that we must not grow arrogant, thinking ourselves above and separate from the world He so graciously blessed us with. And if this animal can have a soul, then nature too must be divine as we even are. Preserve this relative of ours, if for no other reason then to force us to our knees in humility. And if these words reach the future too late and this skull is all that remains of this great and unique animal, then I can only hope the Almighty will have mercy on all of our souls.

Mason couldn't have said it any better, and so he wouldn't. He'd let Jefferson speak to the two senators, and then through them to the nation at large. For what Jefferson had done was help Mason connect the dots to form an identity of who had been pulling the government's strings these past two centuries. At last he had a fix on the puppeteer, or more accurately on the names of the few privileged families who were the ones standing high in the rafters dancing the marionette to their favorite tunes. And one of those family names in particular seemed to have preferred status even among those few elect. Keyes. A name that adorned an office just down the hall from Mason's. The office of Frank H. Keyes, director of the National Park Service.

He straightened the printed draft of his proposal with a single tap on his thigh, stapled the pages neatly in the left corner, and set it down on his desk. Fanned out on the desk along with his proposal were the journals, Lewis's letter, and two empty FedEx packages. All the pieces now in hand, his plan was complete.

Even so, he thought through his plan again, of what he was risking. Because once he began down this new path it was clear his shadows would not let him travel very far. Lewis's letter testified to that. He couldn't risk all of his eggs by placing them in the same basket. If history repeated itself, he would ensure that his plan and Jefferson's final wishes lived on to see success, or at least he'd make sure the two senators had reason to pay Dr. Russell a visit. After that it was in the hands of the people. Mason could only wake the audience from the puppeteer's illusion by shining the light on the strings and those many busy hands at work in the rafters. It was up to those who had paid the price of admission to exercise their full authority and cut the strings.

Checking his watch to stay on task, Mason began enclosing the precious pieces to his master plan inside the two FedEx packages. He may not be able to outrun his shadows for long, but he was damn well going to get a head start. And that meant giving them the slip. He wasn't ready to be taken out of the game just yet, but he also knew with a certainty that those stalking him shared the same master with Jefferson's ancient watchdog agency. A beast that long ago had devoured and consumed nearly any evidence that Lewis's ape ever existed, including Lewis himself, and that was now salivating for the opportunity to unleash its hunger on anyone who came looking for the crumbs.

Olympic National Park
9:19 PM

Flames licked the dark within the inset windows of the lab's outer doors. Satisfied the laboratory would be ashes and concrete by morning, Locke turned his back on their labor and pulled his goggles down over his eyes. The forest lit up around him, though the mist and trees were still nearly as blinding as the night. Their work here done—nothing but unanswered questions would be found—time was now their enemy. The forest could swallow a trail faster than the morning sun burned off the dew. And at night in the midst of a rainstorm, the forest worked even faster.

Thatcher was at his shoulder, as was his place, his own goggles on, his weapons at the ready. He was the perfect soldier, despite his dossier. Stephen Thatcher was eager to serve and eager to die. He feared nothing and no one, certainly not death. Like a windup toy, once set in motion he would not stop. And on a night like this, with the weather about to break wide open and miles of unbroken forest ahead of them, a mindless machine was exactly what the situation demanded.

Head start or no, Ostman and company had better enjoy this night, because Locke was going to make sure it was their last.

Without a word, they nodded and double-timed it single file down to the river trail. From there they took the trail up valley to the first junction. At the "Y" Thatcher came alongside, shoulder-to-shoulder. His voice was steady and calm despite their cadence.

"Happy hunting, sir. See you at the rendezvous."

Locke peeled off, continuing down the Hoh River trail. "Remember, Thatcher. Clean kills. Keep it professional."

Thatcher nodded with his goggles. "Yes, sir."

Then he was gone up the trail to the Olympus Ranger Station.

Locke humped along in silence, listening to the forest and the growing strength of the storm. A favorite tune played in his head as he read the map from memory, plotting Ostman's most likely course and that of their prey, their escaped silverback. His Krinkov comfortably balanced in his hands, his legs begging to be let loose, Locke was more at home than most men on the couch with the remote in their grip. The tune even leaked off his lips, joining with the light drum of raindrops.

If his intercept were on, and if he made good time, then tonight would be payday. A sunny Sunday for a used-car salesman with a lot full of cherry-looking lemons.

10:09 PM

Running.

She was running from him. Through waist-high grass, orange sunlight painting the meadow in a brilliant wash of late-afternoon glitter. Her giggles danced amid the chasing butterflies.

He stumbled, laughing at himself, desperate to catch her, to hold her.

A faint whistle. *Waahhiit.*

Grass tickled his bare chest as he got up, running again. After her, chasing her giggles with the monarchs. She glanced back, her hair alight on the flower-sweetened breeze. She slowed, teasing him with the smile in her eyes and on her lips.

Motion flirted with the edge of the meadow.

He ran faster, encouraged by the sight of her tan back disappearing into the waves of swaying grass. His naked feet cut through the dew-softened blades. He reached out for her, nearly having her. Then she was beyond his grasp, moving away.

Waahhiit.

The whistle clashed with the breeze. Unwelcome.

She raced on, giggling and throwing her arms in the air.

He slowed, his own laughter fading. The meadow stretched in all directions as he turned in a circle, searching.

She kept running, running away from him, away from his protection.

He stopped his turning, seeing beyond her. Movement split the grass, came at her with violent fury.

She didn't see it.

She was laughing.

He was running, yelling. "Cheryl! Cheryl!"

The fury was nearly upon her. She turned forward. Stopped. And screamed.

His breath rushed out of his lungs. Cotton was up on his forearms, chest down to the inside of his sleeping bag, listening. And hearing only the soft in-and-out of his wife's peaceful breathing. Night had claimed the small space between him and the tent wall, and beyond that forest was quiet. Even the rain had been hushed.

But something *had* woken him, woken him from a dream that had escaped his thoughts the instant his eyes opened. Yet his heart remembered, for his pulse throbbed between his temples.

Cheryl was lying on her stomach at his side, arms encircling her head nestled against her Therm-a-rest. Her hair flowed down and across her neck and bare shoulders, fanning over the sleeping bag that had slid down her back. Her shoulder blades rose and fell in time with her lungs.

The smell of their lovemaking was like perfume in the air, sharpening his senses, washing the sleep from his head. Allowing him to hear clearly this time.

Waahhiit.

It was the awful sound from his dream.

Waahhiit.

And then it came again…from his left. No. His right.

He sat up higher—his forgotten dream now not so forgotten—wide awake and breathing like he'd completed a five-mile run. The sound was almost a whistle, only not any whistle he'd ever heard. Faint, high-pitched, and not from any forest voice he recognized.

He thought he heard it again, from much farther away.

The tent blinded him in every direction, and he hoped it hid them from the forest.

Cheryl stirred.

Waahhiit.

He jumped. This time it sounded almost right outside the tent door. He thought of the branches he'd seen snapped off in the trees at the edge of the clearing.

He stopped breathing and was staring at the tent door still half unzipped. Cheryl's eyes opened, looked up, saw him on his knees. She was about to move, to rise up too, her face blank with confusion.

His whole body tingled with something very close to fear. All he could think to do was stop her from moving, from making a sound.

He set his hand on hers, met her eyes like it was the last time, and silently mouthed to her, "Something's out there."

Chicago
May 6
1:10 AM

Megan tossed and turned under her heavy comforter and flannel sheets. Twenty-four hours. Twenty-four hours without any word from Dr. Russell. Something was wrong.

She flung the covers off and sat up. The bedside clock read 1:10 AM.

Dr. Russell had not checked out of her hotel, had not landed with her flight in Denver. There was no answer in her hotel room or on her cell phone. She hadn't checked in with either her office here at Northwestern or with Dr. Strauss in New York, and she was not responding to e-mail. At this point Megan could only say she had disappeared. But she was not prepared to use those words with anyone yet, which was why she had yet to return Dr. Strauss' calls. She had no answer to give to his inevitable question: *where was Dr. Russell?* She had even lied to Mrs. Russell, telling Dr. Russell's mother that the flight from Seattle had been over-booked, and that her daughter was stuck on standby. Megan had no good lies, though, when Mrs. Russell had later inquired about Samantha not answering her cell phone. Megan couldn't dodge the questions forever. She had to find Dr. Russell. Someone must know where she is.

The cool of the carpet seeped into her bare feet as she moved to the window, peeking through the blinds at the lights and empty streets below. Perhaps someone at the Prescott Institute could shed light on her whereabouts. It wouldn't be *un*like Samantha to drop in on them unannounced, being in the neighborhood and all with a bone to pick. Megan had nothing to lose. It was her last option before going to the authorities, a dreaded thing that would bring only more pain and stress to the Russells.

She slipped her fingers from the blinds, which came back together with a clink, and eyed her laptop sitting open on her desk. She wasn't getting any sleep, so she might as well rattle some cages at the institute, send a few e-mails that could be read first thing in the morning.

Flipping on the floor lamp and plopping into her chair, she ran a hand through her hair and rubbed a finger across the mouse pad to wake the computer. She yawned, leaned back, and set her fingers on the keys as the screen went from black to the image of her desktop. She cut her yawn short as the phone on her desk rang to life. Thinking it had to be Dr. Russell, she snatched the receiver up. "Samantha?"

Silent pause. A choked sniffle.

"Megan, it's Chris Russell, Samantha's mother." The voice was taut, strained, on the verge of cracking, and yet there was strength, more than Megan could ever hope to possess.

Megan felt like curling up in a dark corner, hanging up the phone, or anything besides continuing this conversation after the foolish way she'd opened it. She slowly closed her laptop with a click. "Oh, Mrs. Russell. I'm sorry...I thought...I..."

"Megan, it's all right. I guess that means though that you haven't heard from her either." The strength was winning out over the strain.

Megan brought her feet up onto the seat of the chair and tucked her heels in close against her. She clutched the receiver with both hands down by her mouth. Her warm breath condensed on her fingers in the chill of the room. "No. No, Mrs. Russell I haven't. And I have no idea when I will." The truth was all she had to offer, and the least that Mrs. Russell deserved. Even so, uttering the words left a mark on her soul, a stain of empathy and pity that would not fade anytime soon.

The strength Megan admired so deeply in Dr. Russell's mother suddenly came crashing down like a rickety fence in the wind. Several choking sobs, a sniff, then a barely controlled voice spoke through audible tears. "I apologize, Megan, for waking you at this hour. There's just no one else I can call, no one left to call. She's still not answering her cell phone or at the hotel." The tears drowned out the words for an instant, then a pause. "Her father's not doing well, Megan. I fear..." A long trembling sniffle. "I fear..."

"She'll get there, Chris. She'll be there in time." Megan had no idea how, but she was going to make it happen. She'd find Samantha if she had to call the police, the fire department, FBI, or the damn search and rescue. "She will."

Olympic National Park
1:15 AM

Today the forest had been alive. Covered in a layer of thick green moss and soothed by soft rays filtering through the clouds and mist, the rainforest had welcomed her into its lush folds, much as her Aunt Jean had into her kitchen with a breath-stealing hug. She had been serenaded by constant chatter from chickadees high atop the forest canopy, had startled several deer, and had spotted the retreating end of a red fox. The Olympic rainforest had indeed been Eden resurrected, justifying in full its divine namesake: home of the gods.

Tonight the forest was a far different place. Completely unholy. The dark hand of night reclaimed its realm, unleashing its spectral minions among the giant trunks of red cedar and fir. Even with the illuminating powers of Sam's goggles, shadows persisted, haunting her periphery, slipping out of sight each time she turned back to catch a bit of movement here or flash of motion there.

The air, crisp and morbid, chilled her throat and lungs with each inhale. A wet, heavy fog born of the previous hours of rain filled the gaps between the shoulder-to-shoulder stands of hairy cedar trunks and pillar-straight Sitka spruce. The once-graceful drapes of moss had become a deadly cloak, masking any attack while blinding them to the flight of their prey. Other than the clumsy sounds of them picking through the understory, the trees were unnervingly silent. The forest had become a surreal dream world, a place no longer welcoming guests. They were walking through a ghost town, all the doors and shutters closed until the evil had passed.

She plunked down on a log nearly rotten through, catching another mouthful of spiderweb and instantly gagging and spitting as she pulled the silky strands from her lips and tongue. She set her revolver beside her, happy to temporarily be free of its burden. The adrenaline high of hours past had waned, but there was enough of the intoxicating drug simmering in her veins to leave her concerned with unloading her revolver on a passing chipmunk for no worse of a crime than issuing a startling squeak.

She inhaled more of the frosty air and adjusted her goggles. Their weight was pinching off the blood supply to her nose and cheeks. Supposedly Ian had been leading them along a game trail, although Sam saw only an unbroken stretch of ferns and devil's club. Ian claimed to have tracked troops of gorilla through the Congo in worse conditions. How was a mystery to her, for this place absorbed any sign of you the second you took a step. If she sat too long on this log, she feared she too might be absorbed.

This rare reprieve from their steady march had only been granted because Sixen apparently shared her same doubts. As the signal from what she had learned was an implanted chip in the specimen proved intermittent at best, Sixen and Ian had become increasingly opposed in their assessment of the situation. Ian maintained that they were on the specimen's trail and closing. Sixen insisted they weren't, that it had doubled back and flanked them. So the two of them had left Jon and her here while they backtracked in an attempt to reestablish the signal, covering their asses in case Sixen's primitive intuition proved correct.

Her body had been begging for this moment for hours, a chance to sit and do nothing except breath. The shivers came on quickly, but she didn't mind. Having the weight off her feet was worth it, as was having the moment to think, to put it all together.

The greatest temptation and most common weakness as a scientist was the tendency to use one piece of newfound knowledge like a broad paintbrush, explaining all scientific mysteries with it in one fell swoop. Ironically, the tendency was known as being Darwinistic. If anyone had underestimated the scope of their discoveries it was Darwin. It turned out he knew much more than he'd thought he knew.

She glanced over at Jon, the pressure of the goggles ever-present against her face. In the milky green haze, he stood ahead on the game trail, peering off into the tangled nest of moss and tree limbs. Then his head of white hair drooped, and he began fumbling a hand inside a pant pocket.

The misuse of Darwin's name was not completely unjust, however, as evolution had proven to be one of the most fundamental principles within biology, pervading every field of study. So the temptation for her to deny Jon's and Ian's proposed North American great ape strictly based on evolutionary theory was hard for Sam to resist, and certainly not the only defense available to her.

Natural selection. Descent with modification. It was perhaps the single most powerful force of creation on earth. But it was slow in acting, taking millennia to enact drastic changes. *Gigantopithecus* as she knew it, as the rest of the scientific world knew it to be, was a knuckle-walker, an ape like any other the world has seen, only larger. It was also strictly herbivorous, as well as a specialist, a bamboo specialist. The odds were just too slim that it could have survived the massive bamboo die-off a hundred thousand years ago. The loss of their primary food source occurred too rapidly for the species to adjust and learn a new one, especially a mixed diet of red meat as Jon maintained. And certainly there was insufficient time for it to evolve bipedal locomotion. It took the *Homo* family nearly six million years. Even if you broke with the long-standing belief in gradualism, the slow, tedious process Darwin subscribed to, and assumed punctuated equilibrium was a more accurate depiction of the speciation mechanism, the margin of time was still too thin. Punk eek, as her students used to refer to the controversial theory, proposed the notion that evolution may not be gradual, but rather changes occurred suddenly after long periods of none at all. Gradualism was certainly not supported by the fossil record. New species burst onto the scene as opposed to transforming before your eyes, especially in the case of primates. But on the scale of eons, a hundred thousand years was the blink of an eye. There simply wasn't time for the species found in China to evolve into the one that Jon stated now inhabited North America.

Jon had retrieved whatever had been in his pocket and was studying it with what seemed a heavy heart. Soaked, chilled, aching from toenail to hair tip, Sam had the clarity of pain to see him for what he was. A man. Not the flake on the fringe, not the charlatan out for publicity, but an intelligent man who stood by what he believed. He was her equal, a colleague. Possibly even a pioneer.

Though the world did not see what Jon saw, he saw it clear as day. Everyone could see the same facts, the same dots, but it was viewing them from his perspective that the picture became quite different. Over the past few hours of debating with Jon she'd had a glimpse of it, and despite the laws of evolution, the picture was growing on her, even the explanation for why others were blind to it, including herself.

In her case, as Jon saw it, her blindfold was her belief that the next level of evolutionary theory would involve the search for the intelligence behind evolution. The prevailing theory in favor of randomness—that the perfectly harmonious and yet infinitely complex order of the universe was simply the result of the flip of the coin—as the creative force of nature had never set well with her. Jon had explained that what she really believed, deep under her lab coat, was that humans were created with a purpose, with intentional uniqueness. She, like all evolutionists, was in essence arguing the same point as were the creationists. Humans were separate from, and the culmination of, the animal kingdom. In either ideology the universe still revolved around us. And the discovery of another bipedal hominid would instead show us to be nothing more than another piece of nature's puzzle.

This blind spot, as it had throughout history with so many closely held beliefs later proved false, was what kept science and nonscience from seeing the facts objectively, from connecting the dots hidden in plain sight. The conspiracy in our own minds, as Jon put it. He claimed that if she were not still under the influence of this self-instilled delusion she would see clearly the true picture of

Gigantopithecus. She would then understand, for example, that the lack of a fossil record for Giganto in America was merely a simple side effect of the region it lived in. As in southeastern China, northwestern U.S. was a region of high soil acidity. No bones of any species ever survived to fossilize, a fact that should be obvious enough by examining the soils in the Congo and understanding why to date no fossil record of either the chimp or the gorilla existed. So it would not be surprising that when bones were to be found, they would come from locations isolated from the soil's corrosive effects, locations possessing attributes not all that different from a cave. However, the bones would not be from a knuckle-walking herbivore, but a bipedal omnivore. An omnivore, like the grizzly bear, with an affinity for the hunt.

As ludicrous as that sounded, Jon had reminded her that for millions of years primates had experimented with bipedalism, creating almost an explosion of new species as a result. *Homo sapiens* had always been believed to be the sole bipedal species to survive, the victor in the game of natural selection. But there really was no evidence ruling out the alternative, that another of nature's experiments also survived, one of the original experiments. *Gigantopithecus blacki.* A close inspection of the fossilized lower jaws would show this to be the case. The width of the jaws found by her father and those by Jon suggested they had diverged to make room for an upright spine. To Jon, this meant Giganto had *always* been a biped, as had humans. A thing she nor her father, or any paleoanthropologist, had ever thought to hypothesize. Likewise, no one had ever come to the same conclusion as Jon regarding the bones being found in such large numbers, clumped together like from a mass grave. Jon maintained it was proof of exactly that. No interpretation was needed. They buried their dead, right along with their prey, as evidenced by the *Homo erectus* teeth found among them.

This they did to survive alongside the greatest hunter and slayer of species the earth had yet known. Giganto had been bred to both fear and kill *Homo.* The ultimate recluse, *Gigantopithecus* left no trace behind, not even its dead.

In fact, they were such the survivor that when the bamboo die-off occurred, devastating the region, reducing all food sources not just the bamboo, they didn't give up the ghost as believed. Instead they migrated to greener pastures, as had the giant panda and orangutan. They traveled as far north as the Bering Sea. From there they simply walked across the frozen Strait onto the continent of North America on two legs, like *Homo* who followed. *Gigantopithecus americanus* was born.

Logically, of course, Sam could argue with great success that Jon's picture was full of holes not dots, but emotionally she had not a leg to stand on. There was no denying what she saw in the mines, no denying the touch of warm flesh and blood to her hand. Something had killed and then buried Prescott. Something had been tested and labeled Specimen A. Something was out in the night with them, eluding their best efforts to track it.

Jon and Ian claimed with all soberness that they saw it, had shared the lab with it for twenty-four hours. So for now that's what she'd have to hang her faith on, until she no longer had to rely on it, until she had her own perfect knowledge, undiluted by human bias. Until she saw *Gigantopithecus americanus* in the flesh and walking erect. She had no choice but to acknowledge that the truth may be contrary to popular belief, just as she could not deny what she had read in those lab notes. For her father's sake, for others soon to follow him, and for her own sake, she had to believe, had to follow this nightmare to its end. If the world could be wrong about Giganto, then Ian and Jon could be wrong about Specimen A.

From a certain perspective, it sure appeared to be the case. What else explained the Chinese's pharmaceutical consumption of the fossils, the Indian's similar beliefs, and Giganto's well-accepted long lifespan? And if Giganto did possess a genetic defense to cancer, then the odds were humans did as well, or at least did in their past, perhaps even living Biblical-length life spans. Like Sasquatch, Methuselah may be more fact than myth.

Jon had finished his moment of solitary thought and was ambling back through the ferns. They swished against his wet pant legs. As he got closer, she recognized what he still held in his hands. A tooth. Another tooth identical to the one she'd lost in the lab, the regret of which still ate at her conscience and nagged at her in those random pauses between thoughts.

She patted the soggy, moss-upholstered log next to her. "Take a load off before our mighty hunters return."

A weary grin appeared beneath his rain-spotted goggles. How she missed direct eye contact. Seeing despite the veil of night was probably worth it, but she wouldn't miss the mechanized bug eyes the instant they were off.

He accepted her invitation and plopped down with an unforced sigh. He rolled the tooth across his fingers, held it out quickly for her to see, then snuck it away in its pocket. She wondered if he'd hidden the lab notes on him somewhere too. Hoping one confession might lead to another, she offered hers first. "I lost mine back in the lab. And I probably lost all the others too."

He gave her a measured sympathetic expression, then shrugged. "Ah, without a type specimen they're probably of no use anyway. And that's what we should be lamenting, letting this one slip through our fingers. Because the more years that come and go, the more I see the '60s and '70s as the boom before the bust. I fear Specimen A may be one of the few surviving members of the species." He turned his goggles toward the forest, seemingly seeing right through the matt of moss and pine needles. His voice trailed off into the night, soft as a whisper of smoke. "To think is to feel, Samantha. An intelligent species cannot separate one from the other. Isn't that why we're out here, fear and revenge, hunting it down for its atrocities? I wonder, though, if our behavior tonight is exclusively human.

"I believe Ian and Sixen to be correct in their assessment that Specimen A is a sub-adult, a rogue male, the most stressed and potentially violent member of the primate social order. Their struggle to be alpha male, the one place they do not have to grovel, consumes their days. They're a dam just waiting for the floodgates to open. Fear and revenge may be powerful emotions, but when combined with intense, prolonged stress they become deadly weapons." Jon brought his goggles back to bear on her. The scrutiny of his eyes was not diluted by the luminescent lenses. "When tonight is over we may be regretting more than the loss of a few bones."

Sam looked past Jon into the haunting shroud of rainforest as rain began beating the trees with greater fervor. She shivered, and not from the wet and cold. Since finding the lab notes, she'd been so driven, blinded even, by the possibility of losing Specimen A and all the hope and knowledge that accompanied it that she had not fully considered the extent of what else might be lost—further human life. She scanned the infinite breadth of trees, looking for the impossible confirmation that they were empty of the innocent camper or hiker. Fearing the trees were not, she offered yet another silent prayer this night, though torn in her request. If even one aspect of Jon's theories were true, then all of it was true: *Gigantopithecus americanus*, its cancer immunity, the very tooth in Jon's pocket—the tooth of a hunter, one that perhaps rivaled humans in its lust and skill for the kill.

Nothing had been outside their tent, nothing except the sleeping forest.

Cotton had checked twice to be sure. And now, hours later, he even questioned his memory of the unknown voice. His sudden insomnia was all the proof he had that the whistles had been real and not lingering echoes from his dream.

He and Cheryl had dressed and talked in hushed whispers; he mostly reassuring her that he'd overreacted, that he'd had a bad dream and that there was nothing threatening in these forests. He had succeeded in getting them back in their bags, but failed in putting their nerves to rest. Despite her efforts at feigning sleep, they were both wide awake, she on her side with her back to him and he flat on his back staring at the shrouded shadows of the tent's ceiling. Wide awake and feeling the slow ticking of the clock.

Never had he experienced a sleepless night in the woods. Never. It disturbed him. His body was telling him something, something he could not yet express to his wife. He was afraid. Not the sudden, uncomfortable anxiety he usually felt when placed in situations that he doubted his ability to handle. No, he was *afraid*. Three hours after hearing it, after confirming nothing had approached their tent, he was still tense with raw anticipation, still mortally concerned for his and his wife's well-being. There was no beast in these forests that he knew of that was a threat to them. Not a single one. There was also no animal that could vocalize the sounds he'd heard. Not the wolves, not anything outside of Hollywood. And yet he had heard the whistles, of that he was sure. No effort to deny what he'd heard had convinced him otherwise. Therein lay the source of his fear. Something must then inhabit these forests that he was not familiar with, something new, something unknown.

Even if that were the case, there was no reason to believe they were in any danger. Nature had not created many animals bold enough to confront a human, and those that were had long since been exterminated or severely reduced in number. The remaining wilderness had been well-sterilized of any real threat.

Yet he lay on his back, staring up at the night, slowing his breathing so that he might hear the faintest of sounds from outside the tent walls. But all there was to hear was the occasional *plunk* of a fat raindrop hitting the rain fly stretched over their dome tent. The storm was catching a second wind.

"You still awake?"

Well-hidden by her usual confidence, the concern was nevertheless thick in her voice. The sound of it cut straight to his heart, because it was his doing that brought her out here, out where the nearest source of assistance was a strong day's hike away. They were out here alone. He was the only protection she had, the only means by which she could get back home. Such a realization was like having a fifty-pound weight on his chest.

"Yeah, Cher, I'm awake."

"You wanna talk?"

"About what?"

"Anything. Maybe it'll help us—"

"Shhht." His hand rose to touch her thigh before he knew what he was doing, before he could think about not upsetting her. But he had heard something, a rustle, a swish of branches.

Silence.

Then softly, she continued. "There really is something out there, isn't there?"

"I don't know, maybe."

She rolled onto her back, taking his hand in hers. Her skin was like the touch of ice. They listened together.

A *whish*, then a *crisht*.

Her hand tightened around his, and all he wanted to do was whisk her away to her tropical island dream honeymoon, away from this night. She wasn't ready for this. He wasn't ready for this, whatever *this* was that was happening to them, or about to happen.

Together they lay hand-in-hand in their sleeping bags for what seemed like forever until his breathing grew heavy again, and he wondered if sleep might yet transport them straight to the first tickling rays of sunrise.

A witching scream tore through the tent, through his subconscious.

He sat bolt straight in his sleeping bag, Cheryl did the same next to him, their hands still clenched. They stared into each other's wide eyes as the wail swirled about them, rising in pitch and volume until it verged on deafening, beyond hearing.

A scream, a wail, a moan, all three in one. And carried by a voice that sang with tragic emotion, emotion too clearly communicated to be anything but human, and yet the strength and depth of the sound was as inhuman as any on earth.

Then it was gone, the echoes of it trailing off into the occasional *plunks* of raindrops.

Cheryl's face was clearly pale even in the murk within the tent, her eyes big with ungrounded terror as they gazed straight into his pleading urgently for him to act, for him to wrap his arms around her like a warm, soft coat of armor.

His breathing beat with panicked rhythm in the eerie silent void. He glanced at the fully zipped tent door, testing his nerve for what action he was capable of. Doubt had left him the instant he heard its voice again. They were not nearly as alone as he had supposed. Something human, and yet not, called these forests home. And they were not welcome.

Ian and Sixen finally came trudging up the game trail, both expressing their failure with slumped, weary shoulders and hanging heads. At Ian's side, his tracking device swung back and forth in his hand, silent and useless.

"I had the bloke, I know it," Ian was saying. "Never once did I lose a trail in the Congo, not once. There's always a sign left behind. Always. Not this bloke, he just up and stops leaving signs, like he walked right off the face of the earth."

A raindrop splattered on the lens of Sam's goggles, dripping down out of sight. Another left a cool stain on her neck.

Apparently they'd truly lost the needle in the haystack they had been hunting. If it was neither ahead of them nor behind them, then where was it? She glanced about the trees as Ian and Sixen came up to Jon's and her log. If it weren't for the silence of Ian's GPS device, Sam could easily believe their prey was standing within earshot of them, watching them fumble about in its backyard, making fools of themselves. The thought brought on more shivers and images of the dead from the lab, so she looked down at her mud-splattered, rain-soaked, toe-squeezing boots. Never one to take to the sidelines, she was nevertheless forced to sit there on that log, her butt numb from the cold and wet, and wait for those who knew better than she to offer up a plan B.

Ian came to stand next to her while Sixen stayed off in the ferns. The Indian's eyes were as alert as a hunted rabbit's, darting left to right. His nose was held up just a touch. His ears even seemed to stretch out from his shaved head. Radar. He was human radar, seeing through the dark with a sixth sense. He moved through the night as freely as Sam had in the daylight this afternoon. Without him along, she knew she'd be a taut ball of nerves ready to unravel on itself into a mess of panic and distress.

"Do not give up so easy, Mr. Rettig. Tsadja'tko is out there. And closer than you think." The Indian's voice was like liquid sound, caressing the air softer than a midsummer breeze.

Jon slapped his knee, handed the revolver next to him back to Sam, and stood with an eager lift. His revolver was nestled tight in his right hand. "Not that I doubt you, Sixen, but why is Ian not getting a signal?"

Ian's hand drifted down onto her shoulder. His fingers worked a light rub up to her neck. Her skin tingled with desire for him to visit every sore muscle from her calves to that one spot at the top of her spine. But it wasn't happening tonight, and that was yet another reason she yearned to see the light of day and these forsaken woods in her rearview mirror.

Ian gave her one last fingertip-squeeze and stepped out by Jon.

Sixen glanced at all of them from over his shoulder. "Do not be so dependent on your technology. Nature rules here, not man."

In immediate response, the forest broke its vow of silence with a heartrending wail that lit through the trees like flames through gasoline.

It was the voice from the lab, the very same scream. Only here it was free of granite and concrete. Free to pierce the ear, to cut the night, to stop the heart.

Then, just as quickly, it was gone, echoing away down the valley.

No one moved or spoke. Sam's pulse skipped to life with an awakening dose of adrenaline.

Beep. Beep. Beep, beep...

Ian held up his palm-held tracking device like it was made of gold. A grin thinned his lips, the same grin he wore every time he thought himself to be right. "There." His whisper rose with his opposite hand, extending a finger in the direction they had originally been heading. "And close."

And then they were off, back on the hunt.

Sam struggled to keep the rear, her feet swollen inside her boots and her thighs not much more than jelly. But there was no chance of her falling behind. Doing so could be the last mistake she ever made.

The four of them moved single file, Ian leading the way. Their weapons carried a wet sheen of rain. They looked more like a band of mercenaries than a group of scientists.

Ian angled them through the ferns, first to their left, then quickly back to their right. All the while, the beeps gained strength and cadence.

The hours of slow, methodical picking through the trees and rotting logs for signs and listening for a signal had dulled her awareness of their true intent. Their dead sprint among the ferns was a quick reminder. They were out here to kill it. To find it and kill it.

She was so much better in dealing with the world of theory, not practice. The worst that could happen if you made a mistake in the lab was you could be wrong. There was far more than that at stake tonight.

Drops of rain hit her face, her hands, her goggles. Her body was tight with lactic acid, her mind awash with indecision. Her right hand gripped the revolver with white knuckles, but her finger was nowhere near the trigger.

The ferns parted. They'd crossed a well-traveled hiking trail that stretched off in two directions. Ian waved the device left and right, and back right. "This way." As they ran, the signal sang louder, calling them in, leading them like lost sheep to the shepherd—or to the slaughter. And then as the trail made a bend to the left, around a rising mound rooted with ancient spruce, a new sound filtered in. A dull, faint hum, like the distant rush of water.

So lost in the action and the unknown that she was charging headlong into, she didn't see it until Ian was halfway across.

A bridge. A narrow, plank footbridge well past its prime.

Then she saw the gaping chasm it spanned, the granite cliffs on both sides harboring gnarly, twisted, anorexic pines that glistened with fresh mist as they clung for dear life to the weathered rock. The hum had grown to a distant roar, rising from below on billows of river steam.

Her boots planted themselves to the trail, becoming as rooted as the foolish pines. Her heart and mind raced on out of sync. The goggles penetrated only so far below the bridge, the depth was beyond even their reach. Her mouth went dry, tongue-to-the-roof-of-her-mouth dry.

Ian had stopped midspan, his goggles turned back on her. He'd remembered, remembered her thing with heights. He was calling to her, waving her on. Slowly, ever slowly, his words worked their way through her phobia-induced paralysis.

But she didn't want to listen. She didn't want to listen to the pulsing signal, to Ian, or to her own conscience. The only call she wanted to answer was that of her fear whispering in her ear to turn back. And to turn her back on the tiny grain of hope germinating in her soul.

Cotton reached past Cheryl for the zipper.

"What are you doing?" Clearly, her want for him to take action had not included him leaving the tent. She wanted comforting and reassurance, not abandonment.

His adrenalized fingers fumbled with the zipper's tail in the murk. He resisted a glance back to her as he crouched at the tent's door. What he couldn't tell her, couldn't trust himself to say without cracking in front of her, was that comfort would do neither of them any good, regardless of how badly they both yearned for it, yearned to cuddle up against each other in sleep and wake to find this all a sour dream. Only this was no dream. The texture of the world was too rough, too fine, too ordered. The *plunking* of the rain on the tent. The humidity of the air inside. The slick rubbing of the sleeping bag on the tops of his feet. The look in his new bride's face that no husband could dream up in his most wicked nightmare. There was no waking from this, no denying what was out there. In nature's realm, the victim was the one sitting waiting for the attack to pass them by. If something indeed was out there, their best defense was a good offense. But he had no strength to make her understand, to pause even for a moment. All the courage he had was busy keeping his fingers on the zipper and his mind committed to stepping through and out into the night.

"I'm only going to take a quick look around, give whatever's out there a good scare." His fingers found the zipper, the metal cool in their grasp. The sound of the tiny black teeth being pulled apart complained against the oppressive silence like the muffled crack of bone. He cringed as he eased the tail around to the other end of the zipper. The flap of nylon fell away, revealing the black wall awaiting him. A raindrop or two landed inside. The air was so inert and totally void of presence that only its temperature touched his face. He saw nothing, literally nothing, not even the trees he knew were rooted no more than fifteen feet away.

Flashlight.

He reached an open hand out to Cheryl without making eye contact. "Hand me the flashlight. In the pack. In the corner." The lack of volume in his voice unnerved him, and Cheryl too, he knew, but he couldn't help it. He no longer enjoyed the false security provided by the tent's ultrathin, ultra-insulating skin. They might as well be sitting naked out on the grass.

There was hesitation on her part, and then a ruffling of nylon, a clank of tin cooking pots. She set the metal cylinder of the flashlight in his hand—also tainted by the night's temperature—but didn't let go. At this he couldn't keep from looking at her, as she'd intended. Her eyes were big as ever, the whites of them visible even in the meager light. An unsettled concern, an unspoken plea for him to stay passed from her eyes to his, communicating her heart as clearly as a thousand words.

His instinct was to smile and cut the moment with sarcasm. "Don't worry. This isn't the movies. I'll pass the light around, make a little noise, mark my territory with a good whiz, and be back before my sleeping bag cools."

She didn't blink. Her eyes weren't fooled. She released the flashlight anyway. "My mom always said I was marrying a dog."

"Woof." He blew her a kiss, clicked the light on, and rose up and out through the tent door.

His bare feet came down on the dew-softened blades of grass as he flashed his beam quickly in every direction, even back and behind their tent. He saw only mist flirting amid the tight hedge of trees, their unlit campfire, and the surrounding clearing of rain-trodden river grass littered with their packs and clothing from earlier. Years of experience and many nights spent under the stars had taught Cotton that in real life, unlike in the movies, when things went bump in the night there was always more of your own imagination at work than any bug-eyed specter. Tonight would prove no different. This was his source of courage, his shield of armor. He was not dreaming, this was true experience, and so no matter how rapid his heart beat or how reluctant his legs became, he would find nothing more sinister than a startled opossum or grazing black tail.

Repeating this to himself like a broken record, he managed his first step out toward the trees. His torch lit a clear path across the grass. He felt the gap he'd created between himself and the tent, between him and Cheryl. He thought to look back, but didn't. Doing so would only make what he had to do harder. He'd be back in her arms soon enough. This was real, remember. It wasn't like his next step was the first in a series that would ultimately lead to their eternal separation.

The first step came and went, as did the second, third…until he'd come to stand at the wall of firs encircling their camp. Raindrops fell against his head and face with increased regularity. The wet chill from his naked feet had risen up his spine, setting off a rash of goose pimples. Every second he stood there unassaulted, he grew more confident in his theory. His pulse went slack, but not steady. His legs moved freer, more willing to obey. He panned his light across the campsite, catching a glimpse of Cheryl sitting in the doorway watching him. Nothing but the expected shone back at him. He was about to declare this spot of forest exorcized when he glanced up at the two trees next to him.

The same two he'd noticed this evening.

Maybe ten feet tall, twelve at the tallest, the sapling firs had been decapitated. The thin trunk had been snapped clean in half at a point below the top few branches, and now the mess dangled amid the lower branches still attached. Cotton studied the firs in his raised light a moment, deciding how the act could have been performed, by whose hands, and for what reason. Ultimately he concluded the tops of the firs were out of reach of any animal from the ground, so they must have been topped by some random act of nature. Like the bewitching screams, the tree-topping appeared to be nothing more than another one of the forest's many close-guarded secrets.

Taking a long drag of midnight air, Cotton gave the trees one last moment of scrutiny and began his turn for the tent, his awaiting bride, and an expected hero's welcome.

Except…

The crisp air suddenly tasted sour, soiled. Like he had inhaled the escaping scent of an open grave.

He stopped in midturn. Listening. Probing for movement. Tasting and retasting the breeze teasing the pine needles about him.

A *whish* of rubbing needles.

He threw his light to his left, seeing no more than inches through the trees.

A faint snapping of a wet branch.

He threw it to his right. More trees. More impenetrable darkness.

The night was blinding and flat, reflecting his light back in his eyes. He squinted and leaned between the two firs, parting the branches as he willed his sight to penetrate deeply enough to reach the sounds whispering beyond the reach of his flashlight.

He tasted musty cedars. And something worse. Far worse.

Then the forest unleashed on him, breaking loose in a chaotic burst of motion. Violent motion that came straight between the trees and dead-set for him.

Fear scrambled his mind into a puddle of panicked frenzy.

Running.

He was running. Through the grass, yellow beam of torchlight flashing up and down, painting the campsite in sporadic splashes of midnight gloom. His labored grunts were chased by the splintering of timber and thudding of horrific weight in acceleration.

He stumbled, desperate to get to her, to protect her.

A faint in-and-out of massive lungs at his back. *In and out.*

Grass cut between his toes. Running again, toward her, racing for the tent. *In and out.* Light hit the tent door. Cheryl. She was waving, mouth moving, nothing coming out. Her eyes ripe in terror, her lips quivering between each silent exclamation, urged him on. Faster. Faster.

Motion came over his back, dark and heavy. He reached out for her, nearly there. Then pain, terrible biting pain, and she was beyond his grasp, rushing away from him.

In and out. Close, in his ear.

Her voice too. "Cotton! Oh, God, no."

The world spun to his right, going dark in a blur. His lungs sucked but no air came. They sucked again and again. Pain danced over his body, inside out, bone to flesh. His head took a sudden blow, feeling as if it had been ripped from his shoulders. And still no air came.

Then the pain was gone. Everything was gone. He was afloat in the dark.

He opened the only eye that would open to a low, angular light casting long shadows over the grass.

Within that light, he saw the tent collapse and be tossed like a leaf, saw a final parting glimpse of his wife, of her hair and then her face tortured with fear. The night was upon her, a darkness within the dark that had both shape and form. He reached for her, but his hand would not move. A scream cut his heart. Her scream. And then there was only the dark.

Her father lay alone in his bed, facing death with each new breath, fending it off by sheer will. Fear of the end, of the pain, of leaving them all behind had long become as much a part of his day as the incessant ticking of the wall clock.

Inhale…exhale.

And here Sam stood, frozen like a schoolgirl, paralyzed by a childish fear she never outgrew.

"Run, Sam. You have to run, break through the fear, girl. You can do it." Ian was striding slowly back to her, his hand beckoning. *Beep. Beep.* The device sang in his other.

Tiny hairs tickled the back of her neck, calling her attention to what she couldn't see behind her. She ignored them. Fear was playing tricks with her, distracting her. She was winning the battle, the guilt was thawing her legs. She could do this.

The rhythm of the rain. The ascending voice of the river playing off the walls. The thud of Sixen's and Jon's boots as they neared the other side. And something else.

She cocked her head, but lost it.

Ian stopped. He'd heard it too, and was turning toward the other side of the gorge.

There it was again. A cry. No. A scream. A *human* scream. Muffled by fog and trees. The piercing, bleeding scream of a female voice.

The fear melted under the heat of the pleading cry. Her legs shot her forward. Her boots beat across the planks like sticks on a drum. Her prayers had not been answered. There were others in the forest. Innocent others. Ignorant to what might be sharing the night with them.

Ian sprinted ahead, glancing back only once. His rifle came off his shoulder. His device was slipped away into a pocket. The signal cried on, taunting them, daring them to arrive in time. Promising them they would not.

The soaring depths beneath her tapped at the soles of her boots and tempted her eyes for a quick glance down, reminding her she was not brave enough. She ran on anyway staring straight ahead at Ian's back, telling herself she was. She had to be. Each thud of her boots encouraged her on, faster. The other side grew closer. Closer.

She was across.

Her soles pressed into the soft stability of the muddy trail even as the stuttered female scream went mute. Silenced, and yet the signal chirped on. She wanted to smash the wicked device onto a rock or toss it over the bridge. They needed time. A little more time. Hold on.

Weapons were at the ready. Boots splashed through puddles. Her own finger flirted with the trigger guard. They ran beyond themselves, beyond their strength, lifted by a very human need to save their own. To rescue the endangered. To save the most fragile and delicate of nature's creations. Human life.

The trail swung them up and to the left. Trees, ferns, bracken, sped past in a green blur. Her lungs burned empty. The goggles bounced against the bridge of her nose.

The trail widened. The trees parted up ahead. The pulsing signal chatted away as frantically as it had in the mines. In its lair.

Rifles came up to shoulders. Ian barked orders. They spread like a SWAT team entering a crack house, with Sam in the rear. The moment had come, and she had no clue what to do.

Their boots landed in deep, lush river grass.

A bra. Shorts. Two packs. A collapsed tent. A cold fire pit. And not a soul in sight, dead or alive.

Beep, beep, beep, beepbeepbeepbeep…

But they were not alone.

Ian took a step into the center of the clearing, rifle raised, his leading hand holding the barrel and the tracking unit. He swept them both in full circle, coming to rest pointing at the trees at the far end. "There. The signal's straight ahead, twelve o'clock. And moving away at a good pace."

His voice somehow managed an echo in the open night air, or else it lingered too long in Sam's ears. Everything was moving slowly, time nearly having frozen, progressing at the pace of a sleepy glacier.

Ian cautiously advanced through the grass, Sixen five paces to his right, Jon in tow. She couldn't muster a step, her legs mired in the icy flow of time. Her eyes were drawn to the tent, lying flat and wrinkled. Dark splotches peppered the nylon. The goggles colored them, like everything, in green, but she knew in the light of day their true color would be red. Dark, iron-rich red. They were too late. While she'd been cowardly stalling on the other side of the bridge, lives were being lost right here. Where she stood. A sliver of time between them. Innocent lives snatched from the night like a candle snuffed by the cold.

Beep. Beep.

The signal had grown distant and then steady. Ian and Sixen were nearly at the other end. Jon stood in the center, next to the slain tent, seemingly stalled in his own puzzlement.

Ian stared at the device like he would a crystal ball. "It's maintaining position a hundred fifty meters to the north. Just standing there—"

"Waiting." Jon scanned the trees in all directions.

Ian glanced back at him and spoke Sam's mind, as her tongue was as useless as her legs. "Waiting? For what?"

Sixen maneuvered next to Ian, standing an arm's length from the trees and all that might be unseen behind them. "Not waiting, savoring. Now is our moment, when the devil is drunk on its kill."

Mist thickened in the air, as did her blood in her veins from a morbid chill that ran deeper than she could feel. Death was knocking on the door, and the damn Indian couldn't wait to open it. Standing in the ankle-deep grass, breathing air that had just witnessed what lay on the other side of that door, Sam was quickly falling prey to fear-induced amnesia. The cold weight of the revolver in her palm, the awareness that the moment had come that would demand its use, and the threatening surrounding position of the forest eroded her resolve to find the truth at any cost. Hope and dread mixed into a conflicting cocktail of emotion. Her heart trembled with the need to bolt, to run until her legs collapsed beneath her. But she couldn't. Live or die, she had not the strength to leave Ian's side, or even Jon's or Sixen's. She'd rather follow them off a cliff than spend a minute alone in these woods.

She forced a step closer to them, then another, all too aware of the naked exposure to the trees at her back.

Jon was staring at the tent, his mind a whirl behind his goggles.

"On the move." Ian tracked the device to the left, than back right. "Keeping its distance. Hundred forty-eight meters."

Jon looked up from the tent. "They were the elk."

He spoke to no one, the words issued so lightly Sam nearly missed them through the pounding of her heart. But Ian and Sixen heard, and turned. Elk meant nothing to her, but there was a vague connect for them as evidenced in their sudden willingness to take their attention off the buttress of firs.

"Jon. What are you thinking, mate? Be clear."

Jon seemed to come back from where his mind had taken him, staring right through the firs.

Beep. Beep.

A thunderous, ear-splitting crash shot through the air like sonic shrapnel. The echo roared up the valley. Sam jumped halfway around, nearly losing more than her grip on the revolver.

Everyone spun toward the trail they'd come in on and the lingering sound of all hell breaking loose. There was something ordinary and expected in the sound, but she couldn't put her mind on it as her thoughts had been set free of their mooring and thrown into the eye of a storm. Until Ian's voice came over the silent wash of rain.

"A tree. Only a falling tree."

The splintering, cracking, popping, crashing, scream had been more than a simple tree. Nothing in a nightmare was what it seemed, but arguing was fruitless. Blind hope helped her swallow it anyway. Anything other than a tree falling was nothing but evil quickly coming their way.

The rain and the signal of Specimen A filled the air as they waited for confirmation that Ian might be wrong. And when it came, it came low and soft as the wind. *Waahiit.* But the whistle carried more punch to her heart than the sound of a thousand falling trees. For it was the voice of the night, the voice of the flash of teeth and eye shine in the mine. The voice of the devil himself.

Beep, Beep.

"Hundred forty meters." The change in signal's tone needed no interpretation from Ian. Specimen A was on the move and closing.

Jon turned suddenly animated, beckoning first to her then to everyone. "Move back from the trees. Move back now."

Stunned, then driven into motion by his urgency, Sam slowly complied. Sixen and Ian remained at the clearing's perimeter.

"Mate. Be specific. What are you thinking, 'cause I've got its location pinned down. It can't surprise us."

Another whistle…from the other end of the clearing. It was in two places at once. Sam turned again toward the trail, tingling from angst.

"What the…" Ian shook his device.

Sixen was first to turn his attention back toward the increasingly rapid chirping from Ian's hand. "The devil can throw its voice. Be not fooled." He raised his shotgun tight on his shoulder, bracing for battle as he selected the prime position within the clearing.

Ian stepped away from the trees, raising his rifle again too, aiming at the approaching electronic pulse. "Hundred meters. Ninety meters." He glanced back at her, his face solid as a rock. "Sam. Do as Jon says. And don't leave his side."

Jon was the only one still looking at the other end of the clearing, toward the ghost of the second whistle. His weapon trembled in his hands. First he whispered, "Get behind me. Stay between us no matter what." Then he spoke for Ian and Sixen to hear without doubt. "The elk, Ian. We used it as bait. Just as these campers were used. A trap. Ian. A trap. It's using the signal against us."

Sam stopped midstride, nearly at the tent. The word trap rang in her mind, sending off alarms like Fourth of July fireworks. A trap implied intelligence. And a trap they'd fallen into implied intelligence superior to theirs, at least while playing in its backyard.

"Fifty meters." Ian maintained his backward momentum. "You better tell me more than that, mate. You know something. What is it, now?"

"It flanked us by surprise before, the first time when we trapped it. It's doing the same now. It's not a ventriloquist. It hunts in pairs, Ian. Coordinated pairs."

That even got Sixen's attention. He looked back at Jon. They all did. Then at the trees surrounding them.

Two of them. There were two of them. And only one was wearing a transmitting GPS chip.

"Sweet Mary." Ian hustled backward at a sprint. "Thirty meters. Bloody hell. Sam. Everyone in the center. Now. IR. Switch your goggles to infrared."

He never taught her how. She leapt the final steps, fumbling with her goggles for a switch, a button, anything. Trying to keep the revolver in her hands as she did. They were converging on Jon, their backs to each other. Ian yelled out the signal's diminishing distance.

"Twenty meters. Fifteen. Nine. Six."

The rattling of tree branches, the snapping of weak limbs.

They were nearly together, back to back at the tent. Her boot caught on a backpack, something. She was falling, her arms leading her. She hit, her goggles burying into the wet mat of grass. She rolled over and came up...to a world of varying shades of blue and yellow with three solid figures of red amid it all. Infrared. She was seeing the forest, and Ian, and Sixen, and Jon for their temperature. The sound of the rain faded into the mist, and the touch of it dancing down on her blended into her panic. Yet blue sheets of it fell all around. Then she saw the fourth figure. Darker red than the others. Looming and motionless to Jon's left. Towering among the trees that had harbored and masked its presence. A whiff of decay came her way. Staring in shock, she wanted to cry out, to warn the others. But its girth, its mass, entranced her. It was huge. And yet it had navigated the hairline gaps between the trees without a whisper.

"Six. It's holding at six meters."

They couldn't see it! They were still focused on the signal!

But even as her voice came to her, it was too late. The dormant red shape sprang to life, a blur with speed and sure in its target. Jon had no chance.

The infrared was little more helpful than a blindfold. From her lame position on her butt in the grass, she witnessed a frenzy of red, one shape merging with another, forming amoebas that flailed like withering banshees. She lost track of which shape was who or what.

Cries of pain and rage swam about her. Shots rocked the clearing. Inhuman wails and screams joined that of her companions'.

At one point she was sure the red on the ground was Jon, motionless. A monstrous shape raged over him. More shots sang out in rapid succession, a litany of lead cutting the air. More screams. Then a shape leapt onto the other, hacking motions jamming up and down. More flailing. Screams. Wails. Shots.

Sam was crazed with fear, terror, revenge, hate, anger. She was awash with emotion burning through her veins. Her hand was up, aiming her weapon, finger depressing the trigger.

But she was blind. All she saw was red.

A heart-stopping wail rose above it all. The mammoth hulk arched, struck out at the air, stumbled. And fell like a tree.

Instantly, a moment of calm flooded the clearing. She felt nothing.

Not a single figure stood. Red painted the ground.

Sam dropped the revolver, clawed at her goggles with both hands to either free herself of them or summon back her night vision. There was a click, a whirl, then a grainy haze of green lit the space about her, like a bedroom shudder had been thrown, inviting the rising sun.

The carnage lay about her, stealing her breath.

Jon lay on his chest, his limbs bent at odd angles, his face and white head of hair pressed deep into the grass. Sixen was on his hands and knees, a wet knife clutched in one hand, coughing up a mix of blood and phlegm. And Ian…he was crawling over to her. Alive.

He came up alongside her, adjusted his goggles into place over his eyes and touched a button above his temple. Hearing through tight wads of cotton, she was nearly deaf to his long, heavy gasps and to him asking, "You all right?"

She felt guilty to say that she was, that she was the only one untouched. She didn't even know who or what happened, didn't know who needed her more. She touched Ian's hand as she nodded, then rose to her knees and scrambled over to Jon. She bent low, lifting his head and shoulders. He groaned.

He too was alive—for now. She rested his head on her knee and tried to see his injuries through the green haze. Then it caught her eye. Beyond Sixen, lying on the ground and protruding from the trees were two legs and feet. The legs were long like a man's, yet stout, muscle-knotted, fur-coated like a bear. The huge fleshy feet were also humanlike and yet not, ape and yet not, with calloused soles thicker than leather and five toes each curled into the grass.

The rest of the body had fallen into the nest of firs and forest thatch.

Sixen had risen to one knee, still hacking. Ian had joined her alongside Jon. He wasn't holding the GPS device, but she heard it. The signal was strong and in motion, approaching. Then it stopped. Sixen brought his head up, staring into the trees that had swallowed the fallen beast. Ian placed his body in front of Jon's and hers.

She couldn't believe her eyes. The forest shimmered where it met the upper thighs of the disembodied legs. Then the legs began to move. But not of their own will. They were being consumed by the trees, slowly, like a snake ingesting a rat. They all watched helpless, stunned and in awe until the raw, ugly soles disappeared last.

Despite appearances, it was not the curtain of evergreens at work. Sam had come to know the signal of Specimen A too well this night, knew that the sudden diminishing of the pulse meant it was now moving off at a steady pace, taking its fallen brother with it.

Then the signal went silent.

They were alone.

The balls of cotton in her ears thickened, she could hardly hear the thump of her own heart. The clearing disappeared from in front of her, and she saw only the spot in the trees where the beast had lay.

Gigantopithecus. Like doubting Thomas, she had to see it with her own eyes, in the flesh. She believed now. No. She knew. Her body tingled with the new knowledge, her heart danced. Her entire career and her father's career, both spent in the study of bones, fossils, crumbs left behind by a species eons ago, had not prepared her for the real thing. It had moved with such stealth, speed, agility. It was more a cat than a lumbering, knuckle-walking grazer. A terrible and beautiful work of art crafted by the loving, miraculous hands of Mother Nature. She couldn't have been more ignorant, more wrong about the species, nor about her dream of being in its presence. It was no dream. It was a nightmare. One which seduced her with hope, pulling her in deeper until she would not escape, until the promise of morning, of a new life, was left shattered and broken by a beast that was bent on teaching her a lesson it had learned ages past at the hands of her own ancestors: how to survive.

The movements of Sixen and Ian flirted with her senses, calling her attention like a nagging premonition. It took a groan from Jon to cut the fog in which she was adrift, pulling her back to the clearing. She was afraid to touch him. His injuries were extensive, more than she could possibly diagnose. More than one bone appeared broken. Blood matted his hair, dripped into his face. But he was breathing and alive. And mercifully unconscious.

Helpless but needing to comfort, she stroked a hand through his hair, feeling the blood stain her fingers.

She'd been wrong about him too. As she looked into his wise, sleeping face and felt the white strands caress her fingers, she experienced every moment of humiliation, of ridicule, of loneliness Jon had known and suffered because of his beliefs. She'd thrown her own fair share of stones, if only as a member of the crowd of onlookers, and felt now the icy slivers of shame for each one. She would see he made it back home alive, to take credit, to have the respect and redemption he deserved. She owed him this and much more. She owed him for the hope and courage she now possessed for seeing her father, in whatever condition fate now held him. She tried to imagine her father here with her, sharing in this moment of tragedy and discovery, but the image didn't hold and instead she saw him in a bed, the corrosive disease eating him from within. Her throat swelled, her eyes blurred. How different things might be now if she and her father had been like Jon, humble students of truth and searching for Giganto not among the dead but the living. Perhaps her father might not be caught in between the two. Perhaps a cure could have been found by now. She stifled a sniff as she pulled her fingers from Jon's hair. It was never too late.

Ian was next to her, talking to her, had been for several moments.

"Samantha. Sam, we have to go. It's not safe here. We have to get Jon back to the lab." His hand was on her arm, his goggles nearly touching hers.

Then he and Sixen were lifting Jon's limp body as gingerly as they would a doll made of tinsel sticks. Jon groaned, blood drooled from his lips. She wanted to cry, but the well was empty. She was too raw.

They were some distance back down the trail toward the bridge when she realized just how dazed she'd been. She seemed to wake from sleepwalking. The rain droned once again in her ears, tap-danced on her shoulders. Ian and Sixen were shuttling Jon with a crude stretcher of branches. She had no memory of them constructing it. In fact she remembered only the attack and the inhuman pair of legs that had been stolen back into the forest.

She carried a larger share of the gear now, including the rifles and the GPS device. For the moment the absence of a signal was a relief, a blessing. Yet half her heart prayed it would not be lost to them forever, that they hadn't blown their one shot at the beast and its impossible miracle.

She became aware too for the first time how rattled Ian and Sixen were. They watched the forest and shadows like spooked deer. They argued about the course of action: should they stay together or split up, one taking Jon back while the other continued the hunt. Hearing them even considering the idea of splitting up struck Sam cold with tragic humor. Their conversation was the same played out so many times in those novels or movies where the foolish actors go in separate directions and end up being picked off one by one. She wasn't so sure any more that they hadn't stepped from reality into the realm of fiction, but in either case they were not splitting up. Jon was the priority. She was not going to make the same mistake she made with her father—putting the selfish priorities of the living over that needs of the dying.

Yet she was unable to express her opinion, the words catching in her throat as they came around the last bend before the bridge. There was no bridge any longer, only the naked, exposed cliffs on both sides spanned by nothing more solid than billowing clouds of river mist.

There was a moment of hesitation, of questioning if they were in the right place, had taken a wrong turn. But the splintered ends of the bridge were still clinging to the granite lips. Most of all, the uprooted cedar dangling over the edge, its wall of roots still anchored into the rock, was solid evidence they were right where they thought they were.

She remembered the crash right before the attack, the thundering sound of a falling tree. Could it be?

Shaken from their path, Ian and Sixen eased Jon to the ground, remaining crouched as they stared at the open chasm and bundle of spider-leg roots.

"Have a go at this."

The rest, Ian left unsaid. The possibility that the tree had not fallen on its own accord, but by powerful apish hands set against the tree's bark with intent to take out the bridge, cutting them off from their escape. Trapping them.

Her head maintained it was a coincidence. Her heart knew better. A good scientist never took the easy way out. Everything was connected: cause and effect. Sharp icy tingles sprouted through her limbs as she put two and two together. Unless this was that one-in-a-million case of coincidence—the sick humor of the universe playing them for entertainment—then the only other valid assumption was they were dealing with an entity possessing unthinkable strength and calculating intelligence. It meant they were not the only ones out this night with the capability to think, to reason, to plot. And it meant they were in it deep and black.

Sam joined them at Jon's side, afraid to embrace the tiny sense of relief at not having to cross the bridge again. It only promised even worse was yet to come. Crouched on the trail, she got her first clear look at Ian and Sixen, and it struck her like a cold, wet towel to bare skin. Blood, whose she couldn't tell, was splattered about their clothes and face. A deep gash cut across Sixen's cheek and jaw. Ian guarded his left arm. It sat awkwardly in its socket. Mud and grass clung to them from boot to head. They had been to hell and back, and she'd been too lost in her shock to notice. Yet their injuries told only half the story. The rest was in their eyes, the mad shadow on their pupils of one who had stared straight into the depths of death and not blinked, in their speech, the rapid, frantic communication between those who no longer had time for the shackles of social etiquette, and in their body language, the rushed gestures and stiff posture that came from knowing the worse-case scenario could happen and was happening. Jon might die. They all might die.

She reached out a hand to Ian's, hoping he understood her gratitude and relief. She was alive only because they had stood between her and the grave. Hers and Jon's.

But Sixen was talking fast, explaining and planning, distracting Ian. "There is a bridge well downstream. Older and narrower than this one." His eyes flashed in her direction. "We would not make it across. Not Dr. Ostman especially. The only other crossing is several miles upstream, a decrepit hand-operated gondola. Tricky to use even in the day. Between here and there, there is a ranger cabin. And hope of a radio. I'll take you three there."

Ian followed Sixen's plan with his goggles, throwing glances up and down the river valley. "Aye, now hold on a minute, mate. *Us three*? You're not going after it alone."

The Indian's face wore the blood like war paint. His expression was as much that of a warrior's as any could be. "This is not over, Mr. Rettig. The sun has not yet risen."

Jon stirred. He was coming out of it and into the pain. She touched a hand to his forehead as she looked up into the dark ceiling of night that cloaked even the weather brewing above. She feared Sixen had more time than he knew. She feared that, like a watched teakettle that never boils, the sun would refuse to rise and chase the night's minions from the sky, giving them all one more day.

Fear wasn't exactly right though. More a dread laced with the hope of a miracle. The strange tonic sparked her heart more than fear ever could.

Beep…beep…

She glanced down at the receiver collecting raindrops on its digital display. They all three glanced at it with the same conflicted high. Jon moaned.

According to the readout, Specimen A was well in the distance and not moving in their direction. Sam's lungs tightened all the same. The implanted chip could only foretell the location of the beast not its intent. The destroyed bridge was better evidence of that. There was no longer any room for debate with regards to the mind of the beast. The once fleeing needle amidst the hay had secured all its dead and was now searching them out, coming to finish the job.

New York
5:42 AM

The slam of Emmet shutting the door of his Ford Taurus rang through the empty stalls of the museum's parking garage Level A. His quick, hollow footsteps followed him, nearly as closely as his shadow. Collar turned up on his overcoat, hands dug deeply into its pockets, he strode past the only other vehicle in the lot—a dark, four-door sedan with tinted windows that reflected the overhead lighting and obscured any view inside. If anyone was indeed sitting in the vehicle, he wondered what they thought of his disheveled appearance. Having been torn from bed by Ms. Kingston's frantic call, he was sure to look every bit the eccentric scientist his reputation claimed he was.

After a career dedicated to the museum and its mission of educating not only Manhattan but the rest of the world, this was the thanks he got. Ms. Kingston surely did not need any of this. It was her last day before retirement, and they had the nerve to order her in before the janitors had even finished their work. And what was he going to tell Samantha, whenever she showed up? The recognition and exposure George and this exhibit would bring to her work had meant the world to her.

Emmet rubbed a finger against his forehead then waved it through the sharp morning air. The bastard museum director was at it again, mucking up what he knew nothing about. And after all the work Emmet had put into George. He grabbed for the door handle on the entrance to the stairwell. A shame, a true shame, especially since Samantha's crates had finally arrived late last night.

He passed not a soul on his way upstairs to his office. The only light burning was that coming from his workshop.

He came through the open door, coat in hand, anger on his tongue. Ms. Kingston didn't deserve any of his venom, though, so he swallowed it before wishing her good morning.

"Good?" Her plump, weary frame dressed in a shaggy skirt suit and imitation pearl necklace stood hunched over a stack of opened crates. She looked at all of them, then at him. Beneath her nest of hair, her still-young eyes danced with menace. He was truly going to miss the old bat. "You call having your butt forced out of bed before the sun on the last day of your career a *good* morning?" She glanced back at the crate in front of her, poked a long, unpainted fingernail into her hair and scratched. "That's because *you're* not the one lugging all these teeth down three flights."

Emmet nodded to George, silently standing on his knuckles in the corner, as he hung his coat. "And neither are you." He walked toward his office through the maze of Samantha's crates courtesy of Federal Express. The elevators worked just fine, but they weren't nearly as fun to complain about.

She scratched again. "Humph."

As he passed her, he pulled a small gift-wrapped package from his pocket and set it atop the nearest crate. She noticed it, but didn't mention it. He smiled. Things were going to be different around here starting tomorrow. Perhaps she had it right. He could certainly retire if he wanted to, and Lord knows this stunt of pulling *Gigantopithecus* from the exhibit at the last minute for no reason to be replaced by something more *marketable* gave him one less reason to stay. Samantha was about all the reason he had left.

He glanced again at George. What could be more marketable than an eight-foot, prehistoric ape?

Coming into his office, he was welcomed by the stale must in the air and the chaos of polished bones, fossils, and animal skins clinging to shelves, hiding in corners and peeking from drawers. Continuing around to his desk, he noted the single crate in its center amid the mess of papers and journals. It was smaller than the others, different make of wood, and the shipping labels were different. This one originated in Seattle.

The sounds of Ms. Kingston making Samantha's specimens ready to be archived in the basement muffled her insincere complaints. Then the rustling and grumbling paused. "That one is addressed to Dr. Russell. Seems odd. Let me know if you want me to take care of it." She was a mind reader too.

He dropped into his chair, the metal wheels complaining nearly as loudly as his assistant. Curiosity tickled his fingers as he glanced about for a pry bar. Of course it would be in the other room with Ms. Kingston. Not wishing to add to her burdens, he got up and moved around his desk for the doorway, his eyes lingering on the crate from Seattle. The odd thing about it wasn't that it was addressed to Samantha, but that the sender's label added by FedEx also had Samantha's name.

He rubbed his finger to his forehead as something he had forgotten came so close to the surface it sent ripples through his thoughts. He wanted to think it was about Samantha, something she had said, but it sunk again into the depths before he got a good glimpse. Dismissing the lost memory, as happened more often these days, he left the crate on his desk and went in search of a pry bar.

Olympic National Park

Locke dipped a finger into the muddy five-toed impression. Fresh, less than an hour old. He traced the track's outline, noting the bulges on the outer edge of the shank. A cripple, the same rogue from on the ridge no less. He wiped the sludge on his pants, slipped his hand back in its glove, and stared at the footprint in the grainy night vision. Centered in the hiking trail, sunk deep into the earth, it had been placed with care, bold and brazen for all to see.

The uprooted cedar was to his right, the destroyed bridge in front of him, mist creeping over the granite lip. Tracks to them were a second language, like human body language. The placement of their tracks spoke volumes. And to leave one out in the open was a sign of aggression, a calling card, like their breaking of branches. *This is my turf. No trespassing.*

Locke let a smile grace his lips. Prescott had netted the rogue from the ridge and now it was bent on revenge. Arrogant scientists, they had no clue what they were dealing with. It had destroyed their escape route, left them stranded up here to be dealt with on its own terms. His and Thatcher's strategy had been the same. Take out all three bridges, then circle in for the kill. All good predators thought alike it would seem.

He stood. And judging by the three sets of boot prints trailing off upriver, the rogue either already had decreased the party by one or else they were carrying their injured. Locke guessed the latter, as two of the three sets of the prints were half as deep as the silverback's. He hoped such was the case. The rogue beating him to the punch on the bridge was one thing, but having it beat him to the kill would be unacceptable. He needed visual confirmation of each body. There was no way he was letting an animal do his job for him.

He rubbed the numb absence of his left ear, picked up the camper's bloody gear he'd collected and tossed it over the edge into the river well below. He was also not cleaning up another of its messes.

Slipping his Krinkov from his shoulder, he took a step into the ferns alongside the footprints of Ostman and company. Two bridges down, one to go, or maybe none if Thatcher had made good time. There was no escape. But the clock was ticking. Sunrise would come soon enough, and now he had competition. He was gaining on them, of that there could be no doubt, yet there was a real and present risk of arriving too late. Locke had to move.

He was at a stealthy trot in two strides. Mercy would not see Ostman through this night, his last. Justice would prevail. Though Locke was going to have to hump it to be the first in line to execute the punishment, if it weren't already too late.

New York

Emmet came back into his office, pry bar in hand, the sounds of Ms. Kingston rolling the first load of bones to the elevator echoing in the empty wing. "Now then, let's see what big mystery this crate has in store."

He nudged the tip of the bar in under the edge of the lid and began applying pressure. The nails creaked and groaned in vain resistance as the lid slowly gave way. Lifting it off and setting it and the pry bar on his desk, he studied the nest of packing confetti. A sheaf of notebook paper peeked through on one side. He slid the notes free. At first glance they were quite detailed and lengthy, authored by a Dr. Jonathan Ostman. He set them aside and spread the confetti. His fingers gently pushed a white lump to the surface. The impression of a tooth came to mind first.

The scuff of slick-soled shoes came from his workshop.

The lump slipped back into the confetti as he pulled his hands free. Ms. Kingston wore rubber-soled nurse's shoes. Someone else was in the other room.

Mason's eyes were dry from lack of sleep. Three hours had hardly been enough, especially these days. He rubbed at them with a chilly knuckle. But if he were to have any success in separating himself from his shadows he had to be unpredictable, do the unthinkable, such as hopping in the car and driving to New York at four in the morning. He smiled to himself, thinking of the black sedan that was surely still parked on the street in front of his apartment in Washington. So far so good. If the sight before him were any indication of his fortune, then all would continue to go according to plan and better. The room was an eclectic workshop, well-loved over the years. Tools of unknown use to him hung from the walls, shelves were overrun with bones and tiny animal skulls, and opened crates stuffed with packing material crowded the floor. The sour odor of animal hair and glue tinted the air. In the corner, rising well over Mason's head, was an intimidating and awesome replication of a giant ape. His instincts had guided him with eerie accuracy again. He had indeed come to the right place.

A throat cleared, followed by a scratchy, elderly voice. "May I help you?"

A man in his late sixties stood in an open doorway, reading glasses angled down to the tip of his nose, wispy gray hairs waving up from his blotchy scalp. Mason leaned back on his heels, pushed his hands into his pant pockets. "Never seen anything like it, so majestic and powerful. Imagine if conservationists waved a rally flag with this guy on it instead of an inanimate stand of old growth." He glanced at the man in the doorway, judging for a sign that he possessed any information of use. "What species of primate is it?"

Hesitation came first as the man scrutinized Mason with a long hard look, then he nodded down at the beast's fisted hands. "*Gigantopithecus.*" A brass plate read the same Latin name. The animal's genus. The man must have had some pride in the replication, because he continued, much to Mason's satisfaction. "It means giant ape. The species inhabited the bamboo forests of southeastern Asia before dying out in the Pleistocene. So I don't think George here would do conservationists any good. There's nothing left of his species to preserve except a few thousand teeth and bits of bone."

It wasn't the most encouraging bit of information, but the fact that this man referred to this stuffed beast by name implied he would also know the two individuals Mason sought. He reached out and stroked the wiry, coarse fur. "Southeastern Asia, huh. Any chance an animal like George here ever inhabited North America, perhaps even to this day, hiding out in pockets of remote wilderness?" Mason glanced at the man for a reaction.

And he got one. The man blinked hard in surprise, then studied Mason for an instant, as if realizing this conversation were going somewhere. "*Gigantopithecus* in North America? I don't mean to be rude, but…no. Not a chance. There are no indigenous primate species of any kind here, and certainly not Giganto.

"I'm sorry, but what was your name again and what is it I can do for you?"

Mason stepped forward and extended a hand. "Thomas Jefferson Mason. And I'm looking for doctors Samantha Russell and Emmet Strauss."

The wispy-haired man shook but pulled his hand back quickly.

"*Thomas Jefferson* Mason, is it? Well, Dr. Russell's not available at the moment. But I'm Emmet Strauss. Do you mind telling me what this is all about?"

Hit the target on the first try. He was better than good. "Oh, well, then. Dr. Strauss, it's a pleasure. Actually, though, I was hoping you might tell me." Mason retrieved a folded sheet of paper from his coat. He unfolded the enlarged photocopy of Lewis's sketch and handed it to Dr. Strauss. "What do you make of this?"

Dr. Strauss accepted the sheet with caution, hesitating before lowering his eyes to the page. Seconds slipped by as he scrutinized the sketch, tilting the image in his hands, glancing up at the massive head of the ape he called George. The intimacy and connection with the handcrafted animal present in his gray eyes revealed as clear as day that the beast was a product of his own hands. Mason had not only come to the right place, but was talking to the right man.

Through squinted eyes, Dr. Strauss returned his scrutiny to Mason. "Where did you get this?"

Curiosity. No better hook when fishing for the inquisitive man. And no better bait than an unanswered question. Mason withheld his smile. Instead, he handed Strauss a business card. "I need an expert, the finest reputation at work in the field of paleoanthropology. I came here for Dr. Russell and yourself. I'm putting together a task force to present a case for a new listing to the Endangered Species List. Talk it over with Dr. Russell. On the back is a date, time, and place to meet if you're interested."

First a closed mind had to be opened before it could be filled with a new worldview, and it always worked best when done so upon invitation. Mason turned for the door, savoring a last glimpse of mighty George standing tall and proud on all fours. Mason's work here was done, for now.

He knew the hook had been set hard and deep when Dr. Strauss' voice called after him.

"Aren't you even going to tell me where you got this?"

Mason lingered at the door. "Like I said, talk it over with Dr. Russell. Then you can see the original sketch for yourself." He couldn't withhold the smile any longer. "And better yet, if you decide to attend our little meeting you'll get to see the skull that inspired it."

Olympic National Park

The hours since Sam had stood alongside a man she naively took to be a park ranger and opened those lab doors were like a millstone around the neck. The weight nearly suffocated her in the rare moments as this when her body was forced to stop, because the mind and soul did not. Instead they reflected, absorbed, relived. The classic delayed response—when the action paused, there was no longer any distraction from the trauma left unfelt and unexperienced. It all came up raw and immediate, overpowering. Half of her couldn't take it, wanted desperately to rise to her feet and get back into motion. The other half was powerless to do anything but survive and endure. Aches pierced every tissue and muscle. Her limbs were useless sacks of cement, her head stubborn in its refusal to focus. Wet. Cold. Inhumanly tired. All made worse by the curse of the calendar. Any other week of the month and she'd have taken this night like a man, oblivious to the pain that could be suffered when the world chose to rain down on your head at the same time your body decided to bleed every ounce of energy from you a drop at a time.

Ian and Sixen, they didn't know how good they had it.

Sam took Jon's cool, limp hand in hers and began rubbing in her own meager warmth. His face free of his goggles that had been lost back at the camp site, she could see the inner torture he was experiencing come and go beneath the skin like the ebb and flow of the tides. Unconsciousness was the only drug he would be granted for longer than Sam cared to acknowledge.

Tired but alive, she too had it better than she knew.

Worse than the tiredness and pain, though, was the lonely despair the forest and night so cunningly beset upon her. The unending, unyielding presence of them both wore her down, eroded her sanity, tested her fortitude. Most of all, the harsh reality of their isolation had been made abundantly clear of the past hours. There would be no cavalry, no hope of rescue, no chance she'd soon be awakened by the irritating buzz of her bedside alarm. No matter how much she willed the opposite to be true, there was no easy escape from the forest's embrace. If they were going to make it through this night, it would be done on their own. And if not, she could better swallow that fate if she at least knew their deaths would not be in vain, that someone knew of their plight, knew what walked these forests at night and was busy gathering the troops, mustering the resources, and executing a plan to bring the truth to light. And maybe even explain to her mother why she never showed to say good-bye to her father. But there was no one, no one but those suffering with her, who had any idea where she was and what they were up against this night.

From behind her, Ian's and Sixen's whispered plans were nearly all that could be heard, except for the occasional shock of thunder from well down the valley. For the moment, this far up the valley was granted a reprieve from the storm. There was even enough moonlight cascading down through the cut in the canopy above to cast soft, gray shadows. It was a thing of beauty compared to the stubborn banter of the rain. With her goggles pushed up onto her forehead, she savored every ray of natural light, and even the shroud of night that colored everything in gloom.

"How's our patient doing?" Ian's hushed voice fell on the back of her neck in time with the touch of his hand to her shoulder.

She reached up and set her hand atop his, taking comfort in its strength. Jon lay on his stretcher of twisted, gnarled tree branches. Fronds from crowding ferns draped over his legs and stomach. His chest barely moved as his lungs struggled to work air in and out. The contusion to his head was obvious from this angle. His left arm was broken below the shoulder joint, his right knee had swollen tight against his pants, his face was bruised a deep purple. There was more, but she'd been afraid to see it. She gave Ian's fingers a squeeze to hold back the tears. "Thank God he's unconscious again." She swallowed, her dried-up tongue sticking to her mouth. "Tell me we'll get him out of here, tell me we'll get him out before it's too late."

He returned the squeeze to her shoulder and came down next to her. "Sixen says we're close to the cabin, but the terrain ahead is a bit ugly." His goggles were riding his forehead too. His eyes never looked so inviting, more alive. Everything was so much sharper, the moss, the ferns, the pine needles. Her mortality feeling as thin as an onionskin, the world around her had suddenly blossomed, dazzling her with its fragility. "The weather's giving us a break. We haven't picked up a signal in over an hour. There won't be a better moment to rest than now."

She didn't say anything, was sitting there torn between her own pain and Jon's tenuous hold on life. She didn't want to rest but knew there was good logic in doing so. All four of their lives may be depending on it.

Ian slipped her goggles off, then his, and set them beside Jon. "We'll just close our eyes for fifteen minutes, then we'll be on our way." His words messaged her stubborn will like a hypnotist's. He moved to a rotting, mossed-over log at Jon's feet and leaned back against it, waving her over.

Sixen stood off by the trees, watching them, weapon in hand. She nodded at him. "What about Sixen?"

"He's a machine. Says he'll stand watch." Ian tapped the ground next to him.

Sighing for her lack of will power, she crawled over, scooting in close. He was as wet and muddy as she was, but his body heat felt nearly as good as a steaming shower. Hesitating at first, then falling into old habits, she laid her head on his shoulder. He winced. She backed away, confused.

"No, no. It's good. Just my bad side is all." He smiled through the pain.

She blushed her apology. Leaning against his partially dislocated shoulder probably didn't feel so hot. "Sorry."

He pulled her back in anyway, forcing her head onto the shoulder. "It's worth the pain."

Her heart warmed ten degrees. She had really missed him and was only now beginning to realize how much. She kept her spine straight and tall, taking all the weight of her head and body off him, yet keeping the contact. Her eyes closed on their own, the last image being that of Sixen alone with his thoughts. Fifteen minutes. She'd just close her eyes for fifteen minutes.

Voices.

Soft, warm voices pulled him from the dark and into the pain. Jon resisted, afraid of where the voices would take him.

Light. The dark had parted. He saw blackened treetops. A feathery hand of a frond. Moonlight. And Samantha, Ian down by his boots. He wasn't alone, his prayer had been answered. He wasn't going to die all alone.

A shadow fell over him, down his chest. He strained to look up, to move, to speak, anything. All that responded were his eyes.

The shadow grew darker, nearer. He strained harder, ignoring the waves of crashing pain. He wanted to cry out, to stop it. He wasn't ready. He wasn't ready to go.

Her eyes snapped open, the fear she'd fallen asleep slapping her like ice water to the face. But the night hadn't changed, the moonlight had not shifted. Ian was still at her side. And Jon…

A man was crouched at his side, dressed in black, handgun to his temple. Jon's pleading eyes were open. He was awake, his lips moving in silent murmur.

She was on her knees, reaching for Ian. He had already risen to his feet, his revolver taking aim.

The man in black tapped the long, square barrel against Jon's head. "Easy now. You don't want to be the reason I pull the trigger."

Jon's eyes flashed back and forth, searching for a ledge to hold onto.

They were all dead if they complied, yet there was too much truth in his words. They had no choice but to stand down. Ian dropped his weapon. Sam glanced at the man's boots for their goggles. They were gone.

She had the feeling the man was smiling in self-satisfaction beneath his mask. The same mask the gunman in the lab's sub level had worn. She couldn't believe it was the same man, not without losing all grasp on her sanity. If he had survived the collapse, then she was dead. This time there was no last minute miracle hiding up their sleeves.

His eyes shifted directly on Ian. "Where's the Indian?"

Ian glanced about, as did Sam. The tiny space among the cedars was empty. Sixen had abandoned them.

Her heart sank into her ribs. The damn Indian had left them to dig their own graves.

When they didn't answer, the gunman stood, pointing the pistol at Jon's chest. His voice was harder, with an edge. "You've got three seconds to find your tongues. One..."

She and Ian began talking at once, their voices overlapping, pleading ignorance. They did not know where Sixen was.

"Two..." His finger began to move against the trigger.

Jon's eyes were trained on the weapon above his head. She realized he was calling out too, begging along with them.

"Three."

CRACK.

Jon's chest jumped.

The madman raised the gun on them. On her. "One..." He had no mercy.

Her hands were out in front of her, her head lost in panic.

"Two..."

Ian blurred into motion beside her, rushing the mad gunman.

A shadow moved behind the assassin.

"Three—"

A flash of silver at the gunman's neck. He collapsed into his boots, his gun falling with a thud to the forest floor.

Sixen's silhouette stepped from the night, wet blade in hand.

Ian's frantic voice came first through the dead in her ears. Then Sixen's answered, only more subdued. "A second shot would have given away our location."

Sam stumbled past Ian to Jon's side. She cursed the dark for hiding his wound from her. She felt for it, touching a warm gush in his abdomen. She pressed her palm into it hard, cringing at how he might be feeling the pressure, or worse, not at all.

His skin was warm. She checked for a pulse with two bloody fingers, but felt only her own terror. "Jon. Can you hear me?"

A raindrop landed on his calm, pale face, suddenly resembling her father's. Another drop fell from her cheeks, and she realized she was crying. Her body wanted desperately to run, to flee from the anguish of this moment, but she wouldn't. She wouldn't run any more. She would stay until the end.

She hit his chest with a tightening fist. "Don't you die on me, not now. Not now."

His life continued to escape through her fingers. There was no stopping it. All she could do was hold him tight and cry. His eyes were closed. And she thought to open them, to see once again their sharp green radiance, but she didn't have the courage. Instead, she lowered her lips, wet with tears, and moved to kiss his thinning, gray brows.

His eyelids opened into slits, the weak green within searching blindly.

She gasped and jerked back. "Jon. Jon, it's Samantha." Hope's warmth rushed through her, and she realized she was shaking him.

His eyes found hers, holding her gaze with such sadness they ripped a hole in the very fabric of her soul. Then his dry, cracked lips moved.

He spoke, she was sure, but she couldn't hear anything except a wet gurgle. She leaned her ear next to his mouth. His cool breath touched her cheek and she smelled the death that was taking him. "Your heart…knows…the truth."

She sat bolt upright, staring as if she'd heard the dead speak. He blinked twice, and then his eyelids closed, and his lips fell silent.

She felt his hand in hers and gave it a squeeze. His fingers came open, and in his cold palm sat his tooth. She gently plucked it up, rubbing it between her fingers as he had. The bone was smooth and warm. She noticed his other hand gripped a roll of wet, stained papers he'd worked free from between his shirt buttons. The notes he had taken from her. Prescott's test results. *Your heart knows the truth*. His final words had been to tell her to not give up.

Tears came freer, burning down her cheeks as she hugged his body in her lap, cradling it back and forth. "No. Dammit, no." She buried her face in his chest and cried. Cried for him, for her father, for all those who had died tonight, and for those that yet might.

When she finally lifted her head off his still chest, it was to listen to the night. And not to the faint rumble in the distance that echoed off the granite hillsides, hinting at things to come. But to the faint *beep, beep* that meant their time was up. Specimen A had found them.

New York

Emmet watched the man leave through the door, hands buried in his pockets, stride slow and short, and then glanced down at the business card in his hand.

THOMAS JEFFERSON MASON

SECRETARY OF THE INTERIOR

He flipped it over, and in neat handwriting there was indeed a time and place.

May 7th/9:00 AM/Monticello

He studied the copied sketch again, amazed at the resemblance to the skull structure he had created for George, the intricate detail and consistency with primate anatomy. He looked up at the ape's crested head. Amazing.

Emmet turned back into his office and ambled through the clutter to his desk. Secretary of the Interior? Endangered species? *Gigantopithecus* in North America? He shook his head as he set the card and sketch next to the opened crate. He had lived enough years to know this was one of those experiences that would make no sense regardless of how hard he tried. The Secretary of the Interior, a politician, needing help from an old bone digger like himself. He clearly had Emmet confused with someone else, and knew nothing about *Gigantopithecus*.

Still staring at the sketch, Emmet began blindly picking out the crate's packing material and its contents. He didn't even register what he was doing until the third item. He stopped, scrutinizing the tooth resting like a petrified fig in his palm. It was different. Smoother. Whiter. Fresher. The mystery of the crate returned to him; that it appeared to have been both sent to and from Samantha, had been sent originally *from* Seattle.

He glanced inside. More teeth. And jawbones. Jawbones. Only three had ever been found to date. And here there were two in this one crate. He snatched one up, surprised by its easy heft. And then it hit like lightning. Bone. He wasn't holding rock but bone. Young bone.

His pulse tingled, his heart fluttered with a twist of disbelief and acceptance.

He swapped the tooth for the enclosed notes, skimming them, then looking up at the lower jaw he held and the crate that originated out of Seattle. Out of North America.

Endangered species. Samantha's delayed arrival. Secretary Mason coming here in search of her.

The business card glared up at him from his desktop. Emmet glanced at the open doorway into the workshop. He dropped everything but the notes and sprinted around the corner of his desk.

Mason walked through the silence of the hallway, taking his time, enjoying the solitude. True solitude. Not the false impression of it that was always tainted by the lurking of shadows.

The offices he passed were all closed and dark. The sterile white walls and polished tile floor were a refreshing flavor compared to the decadence of Washington. If only the public knew the comforts they provided for their politicians. But he pushed such thoughts away. This morning was not one for discouragement but for victory.

Mason angled his path to the left and across the hall, toward the stairs leading down to the garage levels. He took the first stair, running a hand lightly along the old, maple rail.

The Endangered Species Act. The most powerful tool for conservation ever passed by Congress. And the one law with a bite that far exceeded its bark. The spotted owl, the grizzly, the Pacific salmon, all paled in comparison to what he just witnessed. An ape, a giant ape as cuddly as a teddy bear. And more than that, a branch from our own family tree. The protection of a key threatened species under the ESA was so broad and encompassing that an entire ecosystem could be saved simply by the listing of one name. *Ursus arctos horribilis* was a prime example, and was why Mason was under so much heat to take the bruin off the list. But protecting a helpless, defenseless animal was one thing. Imagine if the name added to the list was a relative of ours and lived in our own backyard. How much more would be preserved beyond a single ecosystem. Humans would do anything to save their own flesh and blood, perhaps even weaning themselves off their addiction for more land, leaving enough untouched that should Lewis and Clark be alive today they might recognize the landscape they once explored.

Certainly Mason had had his reservations and doubts, the notion itself was admittedly fodder for fiction, but all concerns had vanished the instant he had laid eyes on old George. If an animal such as he had existed at one time somewhere on earth, even if on a different continent, then why not two hundred years ago along the Lewis and Clark trail? And if so, then why not today? There simply was no good reason why not. So all he had to do now was wait for his plan to come together, for the pieces that had already been set in motion to fall into place. There was no stopping it now.

He came to the first landing, continued past the door to Level A, and descended two more steps before he saw the tall figure in black overcoat at the next lower landing.

Mason froze, foot half off the end of the step. There was no need to question. He recognized his shadow by the beating of his heart.

Hand clutching the rail, he spun around to see another shadow at the top of the stairs. He moved for his only escape even as the door to Level A opened, revealing a third man in overcoat. This one brandishing a wicked taser, crackling with electricity.

As the gloved hand raised the sparking taser, he thought for a way out, but it was too late, his error complete. He had crossed the line without seeing it, still couldn't see it. Though he could hear someone calling his name.

"Secretary Mason. Hold up. Secretary Mason."

The notes flapped through the air, and his flat feet slapped against the tiled floor as Emmet dashed down the hall. There was still a chance. He'd come into the hall as the secretary began down the stairs. He could catch him, had to. There was too much here that made no sense, yet connected too neatly. The weight in his chest that made him believe Samantha was in danger, that her tardiness wasn't the futile actions of a daughter too afraid to accept her father's dying, and the impossibility of yesterday that suddenly this morning seemed obviously possible. He pushed his aging legs and lungs to their limit.

He slid to a stop at the top of the stairs, leaning over the banister to see down the stairwell in hopes he could catch which level the secretary was parked on. Luck was with him. The door to Level A, the one he'd parked on, was only now clicking closed.

"Secretary Mason." Emmet took the steps two at a time, moving like he had not in twenty years. He hit the landing, his free hand reaching for the door handle. His voice echoed. "Secretary Mason. Hold on."

Specimen A's signal gained pace. It was closing on them, attracted to them like a bee to honey. But how had it found them? Sam could hardly find herself in this netherworld with her goggles on, let alone without. And now she couldn't even see ten feet as the infernal things were missing, dispatched by the immortal gunman. His body lay in the ferns on the other side of Jon's. So maybe not that immortal.

Ian was arguing with Sixen as he gathered up their gear, which essentially was nothing more than a small cache of firearms. The scene played out in slow motion behind her. Ian commanding Sixen he keep his word and get them to the cabin, that Sixen could hunt the bloody beast all he wanted after that. And Sixen countering that he agreed before only because Jon was alive. Now that Jon wasn't, he was free to continue after his Tsadja'tko. They were nearly to the point of drawing weapons on each other.

All the while the signal grew stronger in the background and Sam sat staring at the lone gunman's dead body in the weakening moonlight. He was clad from head to toe in black military gear, wore a specialized mask and a sleek black semi-automatic rifle strapped to his back. He was not a random, independent force of one acting out his own agenda. He was too well-funded, trained, organized, and committed. He surely represented many more like him, men with the brains and influence to set him in motion. Men who must have a great deal at stake to go to such desperate measures. Murder was a messy business that any intelligent man, regardless of conscience, would avoid at all costs. And that was why this gunman was acting out his orders under the radar. Therein lied her hope. They were either afraid of the consequences of having their deeds brought under the scrutiny of daylight, or there was an equal and opposite force also at play, one with the power to shut them down for good. If the latter were true then her task was not as difficult as Jon's had been. She only need seek out the enemies of this lone gunman to find her allies. Then the truth could be set free, whatever it may be.

She was missing some minor detail here though, something about the mercenary demanded her attention. But she couldn't focus with Jon's lifeless body lying so close to her, the arguing behind her, and the steadily increasing pace of the signal.

And the question the signal begged soon stole her thoughts away from the dead gunman.

Ian and Sixen didn't see her at first, not until she nearly stood between them, repeating the question to them again. "How did it find us?"

Stunned out of their arguing, they both held their tongues as they turned to her.

She held up the chirping GPS device. The reading put Specimen A at a thousand meters and moving at a steady clip in their direction. "If it is hunting us, for mutual reasons as you say, Sixen, then shouldn't we figure out *how* it found us? Wouldn't it be important to know, seeing as we had no clue where it was even with this thing?" She shoved the device right up to Sixen's nose. "And it wasn't the gunshot. It knew we were here before that."

The dark hid most of their expressions, but she sensed enough of Sixen's to know she had his attention. In fact, his sudden stare made her uncomfortable, yet there was no warning for the response she got.

"Are you bleeding?"

He knew she had a few scrapes and abrasions, nothing serious. So his meaning escaped her until she glanced at Ian and felt his darkening expression. Then it clicked. A rash of baby goose bumps spread down her arms as the possibility sunk in.

"The smell of sex, and the smell of a woman menstruating, both are very alluring to the devil."

Her knees nearly buckled. She had no strength left for a blow such as this. The notion that this animal was honing in on their location by her scent alone sat like a ton of ice on her back, chilling her to the quick. She flashed her eyes at Ian. He was speechless at first, then slowly the words came. Words that left Ian as visibly disturbed as Sam felt hearing them.

"I dunno know, Sam. I have seen it happen with gorillas and orangutans. And I know it happens with bears."

Beep. Beep.

She stared at the read-out screen, felt their eyes follow hers. Nine hundred thirty meters. Nine hundred twenty.

That was it then. There was no escape, no eluding it. The night would end, and the sun would rise, but either they or it would not be alive to see the new day. She brought her eyes up to Ian's, the night unable to completely defeat their radiance. She wanted to say she was sorry, for the lost time between them and for the odds they now faced. But the resolute defiance that glared back at her froze her tongue. He was far from giving up.

He grabbed her hand, and it was like he was reaching down and plucking her from a ledge, pulling her out of despair. Then he turned on Sixen to restate his demands. But there was no need. Sixen raised a hand in defense.

"You have my word. I'll get you two to the cabin."

Unified by the same goal, the two men swept up the arms and gear, two soldiers preparing for battle. Yet Sam saw clearly their different agendas. Ian was bent on getting to the cabin to survive, to make his last stand, while Sixen was still the hunter, playing the bait. Like chum to a shark, Sam had become that bait.

The image threatened to paralyze her, to lock her knees and overpower her. But the sight of Jon's body in the ferns and moss jolted her into motion. As long as someone needed her, there was reason to fight on. And until she made it home, she would fight.

Sixen and Ian stepped into stride, aiming back down the narrow wisp of a path. Sam broke Ian's grip on her hand and went instead to Jon.

"Sam. Samantha." His hand grabbed hers again and pulled. "We can't. We just can't."

She resisted, looking from Jon's pale, lifeless face to Ian's flushed and battered.

"I'll come back for him. I swear, Sam. But the living come before the dead."

Her strength gave in and she watched Jon's body vanish into the forest as Ian raced her along the trail like the desperate prey that they now were. The same old guilt of selfishly guarding her own life at the expense of others echoed again in her heart even as their predator's beacon sounded in her ears. But Ian was right. Living was the only way to truly honor the dead.

The night and forest rushed past her. Branches and roots were nearly as good at stealing her balance and footing as the dark and mist were at stealing her sight. She could do nothing but stumble through and follow Ian's lead. In that panicked blur that shrouded her mind, she pictured the bodies of Jon and the gunman being dragged away into the trees, taken to join those of the campers and the devil's mourned companion.

As unnerving as the thought was, it was made worse by what it jostled loose. And suddenly Sam was concerned with more than keeping her footing and the diminishing reading on the device. She saw a second man in black military fatigues behind each tree and within each shadow. If one had survived the mines, then why not the other, the one she knew as Stephen Thatcher.

Emmet yanked on the door so hard it slammed against the wall as he rushed through to the garage. Level A stretched out before him, as empty as when he'd arrived. Except for that dark sedan.

The rear door on his side was open. Two men in black overcoats were assisting the secretary's limp form inside. He opened his mouth to call out again, and heard instead a voice from behind him, deep and smooth as castor oil.

"Good morning, Dr. Strauss."

Emmet spun around, thinking this morning had long since become anything but, and saw a third man step from the shadow behind a cement pillar. His face was weathered and tight, stretched over bone, the eyes set back in their sockets. The taut skin around the stranger's mouth coiled into the smile of one who had just bagged two birds with one stone. The air turned cold and thin in the near silence of the garage. And as the man raised what could only be an electric taser, Emmet had perfect clarity of thought. Samantha's forgotten warning came back to him with an added chill. He should not have opened the Seattle crate. That was why they were here, for the bones. The bones now left alone in his office until discovered by Ms. Kingston.

"You smell that?"

Sixen's whisper arrested them in their tracks. Ian panned his mini Maglite—their only light—through the trees crowding the trail like an unwieldy hedge.

The Indian sniffed the air. "The stink." Sniff. "Smell that stink?"

Sam did. The foul, pungent odor was unmistakable, and the most terrifying sensation she'd ever had. Since losing the signal—the damn GPS being as reliable as a dime-store watch—there had been no sign of Specimen A. Nothing. Until the naked, five-toed footprints appeared on the trail in front of them. It had circled them. Had navigated the dense forest without a single snapping of a branch. Even Sixen had been surprised. Very surprised.

The air was still, the night unmoving. And Sam's heart was nearly beating through her shirt. They had no choice but to continue, to walk overtop the deep line of impressions in the mud. It was now between them and their destination, their only hope for survival.

The mist had thickened into spotty curtains of fog, and overhead the canopy refused all light from the heavens, what little there might be as the thunder was quickly gaining on them. Now and again the occasional gap in the branches allowed a peek into the forest's dank underbelly, where wicked-shaped shadows danced beyond Ian's light. With each step she became more convinced it was out there among them, looking back at her through the limbs and moss. But each time she thought she saw it, it was gone.

She was revved so tightly, her nerves so thin, she could feel the pressure of the wet air on her skin, felt the mist pass across her face. She kept her finger well off the trigger, afraid she would empty the revolver on the next menacing shadow.

No one spoke. There was nothing to say, nothing to do but walk, watch, and wait. Watching for the next five-toed footprint to show itself in the soft trail, and waiting for the moment when the footprints stopped. And though they were the ones armed, with each new print she felt more and more like just another link in the food chain, the feeling of invincible dominion over nature a forgotten memory.

Ian aimed the light and the barrel of the rifle he stole from the dead gunman at another track, this one too having fallen right in the center of the trail, where the dirt was wettest. He looked back to her, shook his head, and continued. She understood his concern. The repeated coincidences were disturbing. This animal was going out if its way to leave a deep, intimidating track.

Sam checked over her shoulder, confirming Sixen was keeping pace behind her. Though without a light, she saw only his dark figure moving through an even darker background.

Ian stopped again, his right hand held up as if he were making a left turn on a bicycle. She nearly slammed into his back. He crouched without a word. She thought she heard the swish of pine needles and searched the trail ahead before curiosity forced her to look down over Ian's shoulder.

Centered in the trail and in his light was a pile of jet-black feces, still steaming in the air. The scent wafted up, stinging her eyes.

"Smells like gorilla, only twice the volume."

"Smells more like bear." Sixen stood at her side, facing the forest and glancing over his shoulder at the load of crap.

Ian ran his light up ahead on the trail. "Something's not right here. There aren't any more tracks." A neatly undisturbed patch of mud stretched into the dark.

She grabbed Ian's wrist as the cold panic ran down her. "Ian."

"I know."

He stepped in front of her, his rifle trained down the path. A single branch swayed in his light. The panic had reached her feet, freezing them to the trail.

Ian reached back with one arm, pulling her. "Stand back to back with me. Keep your weapon on the trees to the right. Sixen, you watch the left. Move slowly, but move."

"But Ian—"

"Do it."

Branches rustled to her right. She whipped the gun over, locking her elbows as she held it two-handed. She took another step, and another, as Ian kept them on the move. His light panned to her right, and she caught a glimpse of two yellow eyes. Two yellow eyes. Then a blur of gray crossed the path. Her gun jerked back toward her. A *crack* shot through the night, then a second. Ian's light came over her shoulder. The trail lit up, and a set of antlers and a white fluffy tail disappeared back into the forest.

"Ian. Ian. Oh my God, Ian." She shook all the way down to her boots.

"I'm right here, Sam. Ease up. Ease up." His hand was on hers, pointing the gun at the ground. "It was a deer, only a deer."

He gave her hands a strong squeeze then placed his light in one of them before turning around with his back against hers again. The trail stood stark and empty, though the echoes of the shots still rang in her mind. Two wasted shots. Now she was down to four.

Through fog that hung around them like cheap webbing at a Halloween party, they moved as one, joined at the back. Every sound and every movement was scrutinized and avoided. They traveled without speaking. Sound was a luxury they didn't have.

Eventually the easy road came to an end. They were free of the trees, staring down at the steep descent at their boots. From the west and up the valley floor, a wall of solid, black thunderheads were closing in on them and the moon. Yet enough moonlight came through the mounting cloud cover that Sam could see the obscured field of stumps and logging debris that littered the slope like some mad obstacle course. Clear-cutting on National Park land? The question plagued her mind like a splinter she couldn't ignore yet also couldn't stop to pull. They were now out in the open, exposed to whatever may be watching their descent.

She glimpsed behind her the forest and fog they had come through, wondering how they'd made it out and if they would ever make it all the way out, all the way back to her career, her life, her family. Her father. The forest blurred through swelling tears. All those chances to go to him, to tell him she loved him, to hold his hand. One last chance. Just give her one last chance.

She blinked her eyes dry and watched Ian and Sixen take their first steps into the chaos.

Their progress was tediously slow, and painful. They crawled under as many downed logs as they did over, her hands and knees cutting and bruising, quickly becoming tender to the touch. Time faded away into the night, as if she lived an entire lifetime within the slashing, struggling to the bottom while she watched their backs. Farther down the valley, thunder strikes rumbled, echoes from a gigantic bowling alley. Brilliant blue fingers raced across the sky. Things were going to get wet again, very wet.

She followed Ian up and over an old spruce. Hoisting herself by clutching a broken joint from a lost branch, she came to her feet on top. Ian and Sixen dropped down the other side. The end of the slashing was right there, just below them. From there the forest stood black and impenetrable. She inhaled to ease the pain in her lungs and muscles and scanned back up the cut, as she'd done atop every log. Expecting to see the same dark, chaotic field of discarded timber, she knelt to drop down after Ian, and then she saw the movement.

The GPS receiver squawked to life. *Beep. Beep.*

Near the top, something moved over the logs, a dark shape cutting through the night. It came down at an angle, heading in a straight line for them. It moved fast, too fast, as if on open and level ground. Sam watched unbreathing as the tall, erect figure gained on them. Nothing could traverse this hellish landscape with such grace and speed. Nothing. And yet she sat there witnessing it, terrified to the bone. It would be on top of them in only a few minutes. A few minutes.

She leapt off the log, landing in a sprint. "Move. Move."

But Ian and Sixen already were. The return of the signal was all they needed to hear.

Hands a bloody mess, her feet on fire, she cleared the last few yards and, in unison with Ian and Sixen, pulled the .357 from her belt and aimed behind them. With the chatter of the signal in her ear, she fully expected to see it bearing down on them, was ready to empty her last four rounds into it. She instead saw nothing. Not a thing moved in the waning moonlight, not even a shadow.

New York

Ms. Kingston pushed the squeaking, bone-laden cart down the long, dimly lit hall of the storage basement of the Physical Anthropology Department. The sound of her skirt swishing back and forth over her hips joined the squish of her soft-soled shoes. She avoided any place below the department's offices and labs, but none as much as this floor. This early in the day and after hours the museum felt more like a morgue. Death everywhere and from every time. She already had the creepies from the first trips down this morning, and they were waiting for her right where she left them. At the elevator doors.

Lord knows she wouldn't be down here at all, but she wasn't about to leave Emmet alone to be jacked around by those stiff, white collars upstairs. He'd been building this exhibit for months now, staying late, crafting George like a work of art. And now in their infinite wisdom they were pulling the plug on the exhibit's feature attraction.

Morons.

If she didn't take care of this mess for him, she knew sure as hell that little miss goldilocks, Emmet's new assistant, wouldn't have a clue.

She stopped at the single door at the end of the hall that read: Primate Storage. The floor-to-ceiling shelving sat just beyond, through the inset window in the door. Pulling it open, thankful she had left it unlocked and the light on, she contorted her frame to keep the door open while wheeling the cart inside. Sleepy fluorescent bulbs buzzed overhead like bats on the ceiling of a lost cavern. As she let the door swing closed, she thought she heard another door open and close, and glanced back over her glasses through the window to the elevator way at the other end. The up and down arrows glowed red in the distant gray, and all the hall's doors were closed. She was still alone down here. Even so, it was best to unload the last of the bones and get her sweet-tart patooty back up among the living. And find out where the blazes Emmet slunk off to.

Rows of boxes stacked to the ceiling on metal shelving ran off into the far corners. She headed for the aisle labeled Old World Apes.

Turning into the aisle, her shoes squished along as she passed boxes labeled *Pan* (CHIMPANZEES) and then those labeled *Pongo* (ORANGUTANS). She stopped at those labeled *Gorilla* (GORILLAS) and parked the cart such that she could easily bend down to the shelf below where she had been adding Dr. Russell's latest specimens to the handful of small boxes making up the meager *Gigantopithecus* collection.

Taking the box of fossilized teeth from the cart, the last of the shipment, she slid it in next to the others waiting to be catalogued and examined. If and when that ever happened. The museum obviously didn't place this ape too high on its priority list. As she tucked the box in under the shadow of the above gorilla shelf, the teeth of rock clattered to rest with an eerie echo. She hurried to unload the last bunch.

She pulled the final crate over to the edge of the cart, the one that had been setting open on Emmet's desk. She had tried to find him, to check to be sure these were also to be archived with the others. When she couldn't, she made an executive decision and slapped the crate onto the cart and headed to the elevators for the last time of her career. If he needed them, he knew where to find them.

She reached in and pulled out one of the lower jaws. But now she wasn't so sure. These were all bone, not fossils. They couldn't be Giganto, and they seemed awfully large for gorilla. She looked the jaw over again, the chains on her glasses dangling low and tickling her cheeks.

The elevator doors rang. Or did they? And footsteps too?

She looked up, the sounds ringing about in her head, nearly scaring the bejesus out of her. She checked up and down the aisle. No one.

The jaw was still in her hand, the other bones in the crate. She glanced from the lower Giganto boxes to the ones labeled *Gorilla*. She pulled out the nearest of the latter and dumped the jaw into it, then poured in the rest from Emmet's mysterious crate. She shivered at the hollow sound of the bones clanking together as she hastily made her way out of the aisle.

Proper identification wasn't her problem. She'd tell Emmet and have him come down here and correct them if need be. They were close enough for her.

She came to the door and reached to open it, catching a glimpse of movement through the glass. She checked again, thinking she'd seen a flap of a black overcoat going into one of the other rooms. The hall was empty.

Goose bumps tingled her arms. God bless retirement.

She hit the lights, hustled into the glow of the hall before the dark could touch her, and turned to lock the door. Fumbling with nervous fingers for the right key among those hanging around her wrist, she heard the soft *clud* of a door closing against its jamb. This time for sure.

Her eyes flashed to the tiny inset window and the reflection of the hall behind her. Her fingers stopped their fumbling with the keys, and her breath held in her lungs. Barely more than shadows on the glass, two men in long, black overcoats strode her way.

Olympic National Park
3:57 AM

The promise of morning hung only three hours distant on the eastern horizon. And a cold, wet dawn it would be, because the worst of the storm's fury had caught them.

Rain fell in torrent sheets whipped by the wind, liquefying the ground underfoot. Thunder rolled up and down the valley as jagged blue forks of light cut the black soup of sky. The resulting illumination flashed like a thousand flood lamps, painting long, short-lived shadows across the empty field of windswept grass. Then the entire field and the humble wooden structure at the far side blinked back into the night. But she had seen it. The summer ranger cabin, at last. Sixen had kept his word.

Rain streaming down her face, the chill of it soaking into her already numb bones, Sam met Ian's glance and nodded. He trotted out of the trees first, stamping through the mush of what used to be the trail. Head down, she fought the wind, keeping pace behind him. Tromping through the muck with hell raging overhead, the moment hung over them with all the surrealness of the worst of nightmares. The long-awaited shelter hauntingly close, yet too distant. The weary pain throughout her body nearly too much to bare.

Her light finally fell on the simple log cabin, the yellow lance passing over an empty porch and windows black as mirrors. The structure sat as silent and deserted as had the lab upon her arrival. The memory stabbed her with a shiver.

Ian held the gunman's snub-nosed rifle at his shoulder as he crept up to the porch's four plank steps. His eyes, though, were on the trees. Sam too swept the light along the nearest stand of cedars, feeling Ian's wariness deeper than he ever could. They were naked now, blind, left to their own senses, as feeble as they might be. The GPS unit no longer warned them of other company the forest was keeping. Yet they both knew it was out there. Drawn to them, to Sam, by its all-too-human blood lust.

Rain fell through the sweeping beam, the laden cedar boughs bounced in the breeze. Somewhere within the clutch of the forest the GPS device was surely singing away. She prayed it provided the edge Sixen needed to end the nightmare, yet feared in her heart it would only warn him of his own demise.

Sixen hugged the edge of the gorge, reducing the approaches to defend in half. He navigated by only the hint of dawn and the random cracks of lightning, as did his prey. And that was why the white man always failed in his pursuit of the devil. You had to see the forest the same way the devil did, had to smell it the same way, had to be in the forest as he was. Sixen read the display on Mr. Rettig's device—eighty-one meters—then turned it off and slipped it away into a sticky, wet pocket. Most of all, you had to move through the forest with the silence of a sleeping spruce.

He carried his rifle balanced in two hands as he came to the concrete and iron anchor of the hand-operated, one-man gondola. The thick cable spanned the gorge to the opposite anchor. It meant he was close to the cabin. And so was his Tsadja'tko. The devil in his cunning knew their destination, had beaten them to it. But cunning was a two-edged sword.

A flash of lightning lit the sky, the black drop-off to his right, and the skeleton of the gondola carriage suspended from the cable. In the instant of illumination, he noticed the muddy track on the floor in the carriage and two in the ground beneath it. The gondola had only recently come to rest on this side.

His eyes darted among the trees, up and down the ledge. Rain fell, tree limbs swayed. There was no one.

He inspected the gondola closer, estimating the last passenger had arrived before this latest heavy rain began, but not long before. He also noticed the heads of the bolts where the cable was fastened into the anchor were sheared off. The bare metal core of the remaining threads glinted with a fresh sharpness in the glow of distant lightning. Only the stubborn bond of rust and age kept the narrow cage of the gondola from plummeting into the abyss. Someone had wanted to be sure the next passenger would be the last.

From his left, not far, came a deep, breathy grunt. Deeper even than a bear. Closer to that of a man.

His pulse only mildly affected, Sixen brought finger to trigger and stepped clear of the anchor, searching the drapes of moss and tree limbs. He would be sure to warn Mr. Rettig from the gondola just as soon as his business here was done.

Ian's boots *thunked* off the steps, hers followed. The warped boards of the porch creaked and popped as they came under the roof. She cringed at the revealing sound within the suddenly muffled banter of the storm. The rain now beat a tattoo on the rooftop instead of their heads. She could breathe, could hear, the air a touch warmer, even if only imagined. Her grip on the revolver loosened, her shoulders released their squeeze on her neck. They had made it.

The glow of her light revealed a large, four-paned window, a rustic, weather-beaten door, and a pair of elk antlers hanging inverted above it. The reflection of the glass kept the interior hidden. She imagined it to be far less than home sweet home, but it would be warm, dry and safe. Ian reached for the doorknob, giving it a testing turn, and surprised them both when the door floated open on its hinges, uttering the faintest of a squeak. It wasn't locked. They exchanged curious looks but didn't speak. As if encroaching on a cursed tomb, they shared a sense that until they knew what lay inside they would be wise to hold their tongues.

Not having the energy to contemplate how a seasonal ranger cabin could be left unlocked, Sam stepped inside after Ian, grateful they had not had to tear the door down to do so. A quick pan of her light revealed a wooden floor, a plain table and chairs, and a narrow staircase leading up to a loft. The place bore all the signs of neglect one would expect. The air tasted of it.

A muddy pool collected at their feet as they inhaled the dry warmth and confirmed the obvious. They were alone.

Ian closed the door and moved to the cupboards lining the far wall adjacent to the tiny excuse for a kitchen: no stove, no faucet, no running water, but plenty of shifting shadows. He set the rifle down and opened them all in turn. Glancing back at her, his eyes held her with concern. "Have a seat, take a rest bit. We're safe here. I'll check upstairs for some blankets and maybe even dry clothes."

Having no more reason to argue, to keep her guard up, she pulled a chair from the table to her and slumped into it like wet laundry. She laid the revolver on the table with a *clud* and stood the flashlight on its end next to it. It was over. She felt it in her muscles as they released one at a time from her eyebrows to her pinky toes. She even granted herself the pleasure of imagining herself floating in her oversized tub, its bubbly bliss seeping into every pore, massaging her from the inside out. But there was no sense of victory, no elation. They were survivors only, not victors. There were none this night, just those blessed enough to be alive.

"There's not much here," Ian was saying as he pilfered the shelves. "Some canned food, plates, other junk."

Meaning there was no radio. Sam couldn't respond. She sat there, drifting, savoring the peace.

"I'll check up top for those blankets." And the radio. The thump of his boots up the staircase faded away as her eyes slipped closed.

Her body tingled with a lazy warmth that spread up from her toes and back down again. The dark behind her eyelids beckoned her, pulled her deeper into its warm embrace. She resisted at first, but was beyond fighting it. Ian's voice drifted through the dark, announcing he had found a radio, one that worked. He was asking about a frequency. She couldn't think what he meant, couldn't think of anything except the slack of her muscles, the tingle in her toes, and the weight lifting from her eyes.

But then they snapped open. She was on the edge of the chair, the tingle gone, replaced by a sick, empty rush in her belly. She had heard a noise. Or had she?

The beam from the light ascended to the ceiling, leaking up into the loft. The room's warmth had been sucked away, leaving a cold vacuum that pressed against her temples. Ian's boots thumped about overhead. But that was not what she had heard.

Light flashed in the distance through the window. Thunder clapped its applause. And in the thunder's backwash she heard it again. *Waahhiit.* A whistle blown by the wind. The same whistle from the campsite, just before the attack.

She was on her feet, reaching for the light. It knew they were here. They weren't safe, only trapped.

Her hand closed around the flashlight as she noticed it stood alone on the table.

Her revolver was gone.

Behind her. Something was behind her. She spun. The light caught a face. Blue eyes gleaming. Wet hair. Polished white-toothed grin.

Stephen Thatcher.

Sixen recognized the odor drifting through the air.

Fronds brushed his legs with silence as Sixen eased himself deeper into the forest's heart. His own no longer beat a steady rhythm. The devil was near. He felt him, felt his breath, his stink, and his mutual lust for the kill, the blood. Sixen wanted more than that, though. He wanted the devil's heart and the devil's power over death.

Lightning penetrated the canopy, causing the night to shimmer among the hairy limbs of cedar, the capes of moss, and the spines of spruce. Even so, Sixen moved not by sight but by feel. He felt the forest, let it guide him. Just as it did for the devil.

Waahiit. The whistle came again, floating through the air like a cold breath.

Sixen held his stride, his one boot still in the air. He eased it down into the mush of the forest floor. From his left, his ears were certain this time the sound came from his left. But his gut and generations of inherited wisdom disagreed, telling him it came from his right. He thought of the attack at the campsite, of how Mr. Ostman had been correct about them coordinating in pairs. Sixen smiled. This one was no longer working with a companion. They were out here one on one. Man to demon.

He raised his rifle and moved off to his left, trusting his ears and wondering for an instant how it was then that his ancestors had ever confused the issue about the devil being able to throw its voice.

Like the near silent rubbing of two sticks, motion came at his back.

He turned, raising his weapon, only to have it ripped from his grasp. He heard the crack of bone before he felt it, and had time for one lingering thought. Only a fool ignored generations of knowledge.

He watched her rise up from her chair, reach for the flashlight even as his hand pulled the .357 back to himself. She had no idea he stood so close behind her that he smelled her wet hair and sweet musky fragrance. He could do anything to her right now. She would be as defenseless as a little girl. But there was no pleasure in that. And after the many days spent as intimately close to her as her shadow, he could no longer settle for anything less than pleasure. Loyalty. Duty. Self-restraint. Time had dulled their command of his wants. He glanced again at the sexy, black, snub-nosed semiautomatic rifle atop the kitchen shelves to his left. And the fact that they had made it to the cabin with Locke's Krinkov meant he was now the ranking CO. He would finish the mission, but his wants would be satisfied just the same. He deserved no less.

His blood surged with joy when she finally spun around, aware now that she was no longer alone. Her eyes swelled like the dark crescents on her shirt as she inhaled. Beads of rain and sweat rolled down her long sleek neck, disappearing into the V of her cleavage left exposed by several missing buttons. Strands of hair clung to her smooth forehead and flushed cheeks. Her lips parted as air rushed into her panicked lungs. He raised a finger to his lips. Motioned upstairs by the silent glance of his eyes to the clumsy fumbling of her hapless hero.

Light flashed in from the front window and the small one at his back. Shadows sprouted up from the dusty, neglected floor only to be snuffed by the greedy darkness. In that instant, he saw her trembling, her indecision, her stubborn need to fight back. He welcomed it, begged for it, needed it. So much so he was nearly blind to the one shadow that stretched the length of the floor and across the table. The one that came through the glass from the front porch. Thunder shuddered though the cabin, muting the hum of the storm and startling his senses to the presence outside. The silverback had joined the party. His finger on the trigger of the .357 twitched. His pulse purred. And in the wash of the thunder, the *clump* of boots descending wooden stairs filled his ears.

*   *   *   *

His eyes held her tighter than his gloved hands ever could, gripping her with his obvious intention, his desire, his animal want. Her every muscle locked with icy fear, as if a single twitch would set him in motion. Every muscle except those in her hand holding the flashlight. Her fingers wrapped around the thin cylinder until her nails cut into her palm. The thunder faded. She heard her breathing again. Then the sound of Ian's boots on the stairs. Hope danced up her spine. Foolish, vain hope.

For Ian had no warning. Neither did she.

Stephen Thatcher struck like a viper. His arm snapped up at shoulder height, aiming her stolen revolver dead straight at Ian, while his other hand delivered a painful strike to her free hand with the speed of two venomous fangs. Her wrist crumpled under his grip, rendering her hostage to the pain and pressure. Her new hunched-over position gave her an angle on Ian. He stood on the last step, hugging an armful of blankets and a tiny, black, handheld two-way radio. The unbelieving shock, fear, and rage swirling across his face mimicked her own heart. She screamed out inside with frustration and want to relieve his torment in seeing her this way, in the clutch of eager evil, and to prevent him from doing something stupid. But it was too late. He'd already dropped the blankets and raised his pistol from his belt to an equal aim on Stephen Thatcher.

A sick, confident hiss escaped Stephen's lips. He glanced toward the window at her back. His dry whisper disturbed the air even less than the glow of her light. "We have company."

Two soft thuds vibrated along the floor, emanating from the porch outside.

It was here. She pictured its bulk hunched over, under the roof, watching them, biding its time. She smelled it too, or imagined she did, that sour rank that turned her stomach and softened her knees.

United in their fear, in their hard-wired need for preservation, the three of them eyed each other, listened, breathed, and waited. The guns remained at full arm's lengths. The interior of the cabin went tight as an oil drum, as did Sam's chest.

Silence, unnatural and impossible silence amid a pestering storm.

The glass shattered behind Stephen, at the rear of the kitchen. Shards of it sparkled on the floor around his boots. Rain whipped inside along with a knotted, flailing, tree limb draped in moss. Only it was no branch, but an arm. Thick as her waist and ending in a hand as wide as her chest. Five grasping fingers tore at the window frame and wall. Making the hole bigger. So it could fit.

There was the flash of a face in the light, of an expression. One that struck her cold with its humanity. Its blood-lust hunger.

Stephen was turning to confront the new threat, pulling her along, keeping Ian frozen by the aim of her carelessly placed weapon. Anger burned out from her soul on flames of guilt. Guilt of her hand in their sure deaths. Ian would die because of her selfishness. He would die because she had led the silverback to them, led the shark to the chum. They would all die.

The rage burned through her limbs, thawing them, until they acted on their own.

Her hand fisted around the flashlight flew up at Stephen's face, powered by her full weight shifting into his chest. The bulb shattered on impact with his cheekbone, the crunch of lens and bone grinding together in the veil of darkness that instantly fell.

His grip on her other hand fell away like unlocked shackles. She was running for the door, her feet lightened by Ian's yelling for her to do exactly that. To get out. To get away.

The splintering crash of the demolition of the cabin's rear wall chased her, grabbed at her shoulders as she twisted the knob and sprinted onto the porch. The first crack of gunfire stunned her ears nearly deaf. The second came in quick succession before she even landed on the grass in full stride.

An evil cry of contempt raced after her. She didn't look back, but threw herself into the assailing rain and wind. She aimed for the trees, for their security. The only security left. Entering with lungs heaving and legs churning, she could refrain from glancing back no longer. Ian. She had to know.

Through torrents of billowing rain she saw someone dive out the front window, blowing out the glass, rolling on his shoulder, and coming up in a mad sprint. He held a pistol. And was amazingly headed straight for her.

But the night was too thick. Too thick to know if it was Ian.

He ran for the trees where he'd thought he had seen her enter, a stabbing pain in his hand and forehead catching up to him. What was left of the window shattered behind him. The porch complained under immense weight. There was no time for looking over his shoulder, and there was no need. Ian had seen enough inside. If the rear wall and the two rounds he had sent into the silverback were not enough to slow the bloke down, the last two in his 9mm would only be wasted.

The clip-clip of sprinting legs kept pace alongside him through the trees at a distance. He would need at least one of those last two bullets, for man not beast. He was not alone in his escape.

The 9mm in one hand, two-way radio in the other, he crossed his arms in front of his face as he plunged after Sam like mad through the mesh of moss and tree limbs. The forest's resistance whipped his forearms, tore at his clothes, and tripped his feet. He had to get to her first. Had to find her alive. He would not let her die alone and certainly not at the hands of the man clipping through the trees nearly faster than himself.

Cracking branches and soft, heavy breathing guided him. He was gaining on her. They both were. The night's dull gray light offered only glimpses of his surroundings, the pitfalls and snares awaiting his one misstep. Until a flash from the storm snapped a shot of her back, her hair flowing behind her. He was so close.

As he heard Sam ahead of him, he heard the forest parting behind him, the raspy breathing that hung in the air just short of his collar, the sounds of small trees snapping off at their bases, and the forest's debris being crushed underfoot.

Clip, clip, clip. The man abreast of him was gaining, closing the gap, beating through the trees like they weren't there. The fury behind him was so close Ian squeezed his shoulders and ducked his head, preparing for the attack that hadn't yet come. He had to get there first. He dug deeper, pushed his legs, ignored the mire of the forest. They would go together if that was the way it went down.

Frequent flashes of lightning burned images of her desperate weaving between trees in his mind and on his heart. She sensed the pursuers too. Whenever she banked to the left or right, the bloody rogue would accelerate around, causing her, and them all, to flee back in the other direction.

They were cattle being herded to the slaughter. But herded where was the question.

In the next flash Sam was gone. So too was the shadowy figure that had been matching him stride for stride. A dense wall of tangled bush raced toward him. He saw the uprooted fir to his right, but not the one to his left. His boot caught solid, upending him, sending him face first into the muck.

He tucked, rolled, losing the grip on the radio. It spun off into the night. In anticipation of the attack, the temptation of his exposed, defenseless backside, he came up with a squeeze of the 9mm's trigger. His second-to-last round ripped into the forest, snapping branches as it shot through the canopy.

But there was no attack. Nothing.

The approaching dawn leached through the treetops, painting the shaggy trunks in alabaster gray. Shadows shimmied up and down, hopped from one to another. His frantic breathing was nearly suffocating as he brought a hand off the grip of the pistol and felt for the radio as he watched the unmoving forest. His fingers bumped across the solid, smooth texture of plastic. The radio. He ran his hand back that way and hit something new. He picked it up. And more from touch than sight he knew it to be his GPS tracking receiver.

Sixen.

Then the forest moved. Motion blurred with desperate frenzy directly ahead. Branches tore off tree trunks. A looming shadow darker than the night came at him, barreling between firs that gave ground as it passed among them.

Fat fingers of light split the sky, illuminating in terrific detail the narrow chasm at her feet. Rain cascaded down on her in huge drops while the howl of the storm whipped at her face and bent the boughs of the trees lining the gorge. The sour flutter in her belly beat faster, rising up her throat. Her boots stuck to the granite ledge on this side as she stared across the black void to the forest creeping over the opposite edge. Between, the bottom was lost in the night and depth, but it was there, somewhere far below. A corkscrew wind blew up the cut, twisting the rain into swirling, sideways sheets.

The rusty, bowed cable spanned across her vision to the other side. On this side, the creak and groan of the swaying hand gondola taunted her with an escape she knew she hadn't the courage to use. She inhaled, dropping the flutter down out of her throat if only for an instant. This was it. There was nowhere else to run.

The crack of a gunshot. The rustle of carefully parted tree limbs.

She turned her back on the yawning depths, desperate with hope to see Ian step from the trees. Alone.

The uniformed figure of Stephen Thatcher joined her on the ledge instead. He glanced about with a dirty smile. "Oh, that's right. You have a thing for heights. I understand. I have a thing for women."

Her hope, faith, will to live all sunk into the wet, filthy toes of her boots. She had nothing to defend herself, only her bare, trembling hands. But if she had, if she had the heft of the full-chambered .357 in her hand right now, she would use it. Without thought, she would raise it, take aim without warning, and send all six hot balls of lead into his advancing chest as fast as her finger could work the trigger. She had no question in her mind, and that struck her cold with fear as much as his probing eyes and closing presence. He and the night had driven her to the point of welcomed violence, and it made her hate and despise them both as much as she feared them.

He came slowly to the left, then right. She danced in the opposite, matching his stare, giving him no satisfaction of seeing the terror roiling within. With every step she took a half step back, closer to the ledge. She would jump before his hands ever touched her. Or at least she prayed for the strength to do so.

Even so, he advanced on her without a word. Coming within a breath of her. His eyes gleamed with fearless confidence and desire. She couldn't retreat any farther. Her strength lost, oh God it was lost. She couldn't jump, couldn't move. And then his hand ever-so-slowly reached out and took hers. Its smooth warmth sent sick chills up her arm. The grip tightened until she was his.

He leaned in closer, his lips brushing her cheek. His right eye and cheek were purple and swollen like a plum. A hot whisper crept into her ear. "Now then, where were we?"

The tiniest of a prick stuck her throat. She glanced down at a three-inch blade tucked in under her jaw.

She dared not even swallow.

Beep, beep, beep.

Their eyes locked, then he spun around to face the trees. Thunder clapped across the valley. Rain beat against the granite. *Beepbeepbeep...*

Sixen. Hope. She had to hope.

He spun them left to right—the knife cutting into her—watching the whole forest at once, trying to guess the exit point, and who it was that was coming. For someone surely was. And fast. And not alone.

The signal was singing with the rapid pace of a quickly closing gap. But there was another element to the signal, as if the signal itself were on the move. Growing steadily, frantically nearer. The chaotic, mixed chirping rang through the trees and rain, promising the two of them company any moment.

Her hope took anchor as she too studied the fir limbs and spruce boughs.

He was becoming panicked, though he hid it well. He yelled into the night. "I thought the silverback had finished you back there. I'm impressed." He moved them to the left, her feet catching. "Always send a man to do a monkey's job. The beautiful Dr. Russell is waiting to watch me—"

Two saplings parted, shoved aside by a figure at a dead sprint. Ian. His face. His face was a mask she had never seen him wear before, or any man. He was set to kill or die in the act.

Beep...

His hand came up, aiming a short, square pistol barrel.

Beep...

Stephen spun, throwing her in front.

A flash of explosion. *CRACK.* She was falling back, toward the edge, into the night. Being pulled by a weight latched to her arm. A dead weight.

The abyss rose up to greet her, smiling with open maw, sucking her into its gullet. Then she was being pulled back, back from the dead. Something had her. She looked, her feet still miraculously on firm ground, and saw Ian. He had her arm. He had her. Had her for the rest of her life.

With his one hand keeping its warm grip on her forearm, Ian glanced at the still hot pistol in his other and then over the ledge. With a flick of the wrist he sent it over, plummeting after Stephen.

"No more ammo."

His shadowed expression of lost innocence and his tone made her wonder if he would have discarded the weapon even if it carried a full clip, wanting nothing more to do with the evil tool.

Rain dripped down her back, pooled in the folds of her shirt, the fabric soaked clean through. Another flash lit the ledge, placing center stage the only other thing sharing the narrow space between pine and gravity. The gondola.

Beep, beep...

Their time was running ice thin, giving her only opportunity for a deep breath and a tight squeeze of Ian's own forearm. She prayed there would be time later for more, far more.

Ian appraised the gondola and the spanning cable bobbing in the wind. Then his eyes searched hers, seeking strength she didn't know if she had but that she desperately wanted. "If you can't. I'll stand with you—"

"I can." She had to, or else they were both dead. Ian would not leave her alone to face it. And no one had ever had a better reason to live than that.

Those two little words shocked them both into mad action, and she was at the gondola before she could think. For death was coming. She saw the taller trees rustling, the contagious motion spreading through the smaller ones closer to the ledge.

Their movements were clumsy, frantic. Desperate. It took what felt like minutes to get her up and inside the slick, wet skeleton of the gondola. Ian was nearly in when he paused, staring at the cement and granite anchor the cable was bolted into.

Trees were bristling right up to the ledge. The GPS was singing like never before. "Ian," she yelled. But he turned back from the anchor, his eyes cold and dark even in this hellish night and pushed the gondola over the edge.

"You first."

Ten thousand frozen razor blades wouldn't have cut her as deeply. There wasn't time for seconds. He knew that. And must have somehow known too that his extra weight would have doomed them both. The unsaid prayer and good-bye were all too clear in his voice.

Yet she resisted and reached for him, sending the carriage wobbling on the cable. Her belly flipped three times over, her chest sucked hollow. The black nothingness of the gorge came under her, the hungry maw opening again. She was forced to grab the aged, iron rope to right the carriage and keep from tipping out. Rain swirled in her face. Wind hit her from below and every other way. Ian stood motionless beneath the cable helplessly watching her slide away to safety on the pull of gravity.

Lightning forked out of the clouds, slamming into a tree upstream. It exploded like a drum of gasoline into a blazing torch of sparks and flames that lit this corner of the night. Thunder barreled through the gorge, echoing into the heavens. She saw Ian clear as day, his arms at his sides, his face set in resignation. And she saw too the pair of green reflections to his right. Eye shine.

It stood comfortably on two legs, towering many feet over Ian. A massive crested head sat atop, not between, its shoulders. Thick, muscled arms drooped down to mid-thigh. A long, scraggly mane collected the rain in dozens of grimy, knotted strands giving the eerie impression of dreadlocks. In its face was simple madness. Suicidal rage. The orange off-glow of the enflamed spruce hid none of its expression. An expression as rich with emotion as any human's. And in its eyes burned a depth of soul she had only witnessed in her own fellow man. A soul! The image and realization struck her ice cold in that fleeting instant. Inside, in its heart, it was the same as herself, the same as Ian, terrified by the ripeness of its own mortality, yet willing to sacrifice its own life for those it held dear.

"Ian! Behind you!" The words burned like bitter acid from her tongue. She squeezed her palms around the cable, arresting her crossing with every ounce of energy in every muscle and tendon from her fingers to her ankles.

From her words or his own senses, he turned to confront a beast as old as time, a fossil in flesh and blood. *Gigantopithecus.* Sasquatch. The ape of a thousand names.

It reared back, searing the night with a cry that tore the very fabric of reality, reverberating off the granite cliffs with all the malevolence of a demon from another dimension. Then in an instant it was on Ian, carrying them both over the edge.

Horror rippled through Sam as fast as the wave that came at her through the cable. She saw or imagined Ian's eyes go wide as it hit him and then the cable. Enveloped in its clutch, Ian disappeared as they fell, then caught. The cable held them fast as Sam watched with breathless terror, helpless to do anything else. Then a twang rang across the gorge, followed by grinding metal, and they were all falling.

Weightlessness overwhelmed her. The cable went slack, whipping in the empty expanse. The ape and Ian dropped out of sight. A silent rush filled her ears, her mind. She thought of nothing, felt nothing but the air gushing up past her. Falling. Falling.

Then she lurched to a bone-crashing stop into the metal frame of the carriage. Tingling pain lit through her ribs as the whole wreckage slammed into the cliff. Sparks jumped off the granite as the carriage and cable scraped and swung back across the rock face. The runners had caught, were twisted in the cable, holding her hostage above the abyss.

Above, from her twisted position within the mangled metal bars, she made out the faint horizon of the cliff's ledge. Her heart in her throat, choking off her air, she managed a look below, into the dark soul of the night.

A sore ache, deep and spreading, came over her. Ian was gone. She was alone. Alive only for the moment, suspended by fate to prolong the anguish.

Rain ran down her face. The carriage ground to a tenuous hold on the granite. She felt its cold presence against her back. She looked again to the ledge and the wickedness stirring in the sky. The brief and fleeting temptation to let go of the bars, to take the easy way out, taunted her. But she banished the thought before it took root, as she knew her father had done every day since his diagnosis.

Instead, she grabbed hold of the cable, reached up, and took her first pull for the top.

Somewhere in the fog of his mind, the click of a door closing shut echoed like steel pots in a cave.

Mason knew enough that the sound meant he was alone. Brought here and left to die alone in his office. Suicide. To the world it would look like suicide, yet another in a long line of well-disguised murders.

His empty prescription bottle lay uncapped alongside his face on his desk. Twenty times the daily dose was working its way through his veins, shutting down the muscles as it passed. He felt the kiss of the cool, hard wood on his cheek, the drool pooling from his lips, and the ache in his jaw from their hands. The rest of his body didn't exist, was adrift on the same plane of bliss as his mind. He stared at the orange plastic bottle and the label detailing his doctor's dosage orders. It was gibberish to him now. He saw it only with one eye. The other wouldn't open.

Suicide.

No one would question it. An autopsy probably wouldn't even be performed. He had no family to request it. Mercy. He had taken mercy on his soul. That's how everyone would see it. He had finally opted out of the pain. His shadows. He had underestimated them by a great margin. And that made his lip twitch with anger. Not at being outwitted, but anger at not being able to warn those he left behind. The nation he so truly loved. It knew not of the beast that walked in its shadow.

His lips quivered with strain as he willed his head off the desk, believing somehow he might yet destroy the illusion of suicide.

The bottle mocked him, laughed through its open mouth. He was dead. There was no changing that. His mind was only too stubborn to accept it. But soon the lack of blood supply would convince even that great keeper of arrogant confidence. Thomas Jefferson Mason. Dead. Suicide. Murder. It made no difference.

His lips curled at the corners in smile, or so he imagined. He may be dead, but he died in victory, not defeat. He had bested his shadows at their own game. It may have taken two hundred years, but Thomas Jefferson's dying wish was about to be granted. The dots would finally be connected. The legendary American's unconstitutional sins would soon be forgiven. Redemption granted. The shadows knew not what was about to hit them. The cleansing, searing blaze of truth unveiled.

The gibberish on the bottle's label transformed, writhing like snakes until he saw his great ancestor's handwriting and the final lines of his confession.

> I tremble for my country when I reflect that God is just. For this reason I break my own Oath to those who have sinned with me. I have spared the skull, the journals and Lewis's letter from the damning heat of fire and destruction hoping one day they might right some of the wrongs I have bestowed upon this great Empire. For if nothing else I am guilty of setting the ends above the means, and as such I pray history and God may forgive me, and that a time may one day come when we will have the distance to overcome the weaknesses of our fathers.

Mason blinked his one eye and the gibberish returned. His cheek and jaw had drifted away with the rest of him, on their way to meet Jefferson, to report back and tell him that he was indeed forgiven, at least by Mason.

Breathing. He could not tell if he was breathing. His lips. They began to drift too. He was completely afloat. The bottle was gone, replaced by an everlasting horizon of light that carried into the eternities.

He left behind no sadness or pain. Only a plan. And those few who knew him best would be grateful, for a slow death had never been for him.

Olympic National Park
2:41 PM

Her heart pounded against her harness as seconds stretched by. The chatter of the rotating blades whipped the damp air through the open belly of the helicopter. Despite the search and rescue crew's heavy jacket, shivers shimmied up her spine, and not only from the chill. Sam glanced away from the short man in helmet and headphones leaning out the other side of the chopper, working the winch and basket. The wait was killing her.

The Hoh sat perfectly framed through the open bay. A wide mouth of rocky sand bars curved out of sight. The forest crept down to the water's milky surface to drink. Mist hung like smoke in the air. Somewhere up valley, Jon's body could still be lying in the ferns, his clothes soaked, his skin stiff and cold. He had given his life for what he believed to be true, for his own integrity. And the world would never know. The anonymous martyr. He could have set the field of paleoanthropology on its head. All of science for that matter. He would have had the career her father had been so driven to create.

The helicopter lurched, nudged by another crosswind. The winch whined, chugged.

Her father. Her mother. She had taken them for granted her entire life, had been too afraid to embrace them for fear of one day having to let go. And now she would take one last smile, one last open-armed hug and kiss. One last moment in their presence. That would be worth an eternity without them.

And to think there might have been hope of a cure one day, that millions like her father, suffering in their own beds, might have had time with their loved ones extended, the march of death delayed if even for a season. But all the evidence of that hope was gone, destroyed by an evil hand she as yet could not understand, just as she could not understand the charred remains of the lab she had found, other than to know greed was at its core. Ian and she were the only evidence left, and witnesses were proof of nothing. Only a type specimen could convince, that was if you survived the encounter. The overpowering burden of their failure was one she would have to carry for the rest of her life. She had come so close and yet victory had been snatched from her grasp. To top it off, she had nothing to show for her absence from her father's side. And there would be no victory in the future so long as whatever infinite power was at work against them went unchallenged. A challenge that would require a helping hand from the inside, someone who could do battle within the shadows of the government, someone she had not a clue as how to approach. And that was what sealed their failure. The public could not fight them on their own, and yet they knew not where to turn in their search for help.

The whining of the winch slowed. She looked back to the man in the helmet and headphones. He was guiding the cable, pulling it closer to the helicopter. She turned in her seat, pushed the harness to its limit. Her hands were damp, her mind a rush of static. Two hands soiled nearly black and wrapped around the cable rose into view, then a head of long blonde hair and rounded shoulders. The basket stopped even with the floor, rotating around. Ian's battered and stained face turned her way, his eyes searching her out, finding her and holding her. She looked straight back into his, as deep as she could, and saw all of him. There was nothing left to hide between them. Certainly not the tears that leaked down her cheeks. He was being pulled inside, out of his harness and the basket, and set in the seat next to her. His left leg, its pant leg torn and soaked a deep purple, was kept straight. He ran his hands through his tangled hair, his eyes still on her, and only her. He was being strapped into a seat harness by the man in the helmet. His eyes sparkled in the waning light as he smiled, dimples sinking into his curved cheeks. "Miss me?"

Miss him, she wanted to rip off their harnesses and squeeze her body against him so tightly their heartbeats became one. He was supposed to be dead, not sitting here next to her, grinning like a sixteen-year-old on his first date. She had once been afraid to embrace him too, as she had with her parents, afraid of the pain that might come. But no longer. She'd take every second that came, cherishing each and every one. Instead of tearing through the harnesses, she simply smiled back, her tears hot on her cheeks, and squeezed his hand. He squeezed back, his clear blue eyes telegraphing the same deep need, and the relief at having time, all the time in the world.

The man in the helmet began checking Ian, tending his wounds.

"If you two are done saying hello, perhaps, Mr. Rettig, you could fill me in on what the hell happened!" Director Simonsen leaned around the front seat next to the pilot's. He yelled through his earphones, giving her a nasty eye. "Dr. Russell here appears to have amnesia. I hope it's not contagious."

Sam ignored him, having gotten what she needed from his and Prescott's command of resources. She savored instead the beautiful sight of Ian, alive, his hand in hers.

Ian gave her a wink, then released her hand and pulled the two-way radio from his shirt and handed it to Simonsen with a shrug. "Sorry, mate. We got lost, that's all."

"Lost? Don't mess with me Rettig." Simonsen spit as he spoke, his words laced with venom he had apparently inherited from Prescott. "You hold out on me and your careers are over, finished. You understand? Samantha?"

She placed her hand on Ian's thigh, his wet pants cool on her skin, and gazed out her side of the chopper as it banked and headed back down the valley. What career? Hers was already finished. She certainly couldn't go back to studying and professing a lie.

Simonsen's ranting threats droned on in the background. Her hand was in Ian's again. No amount of threats could change the facts. Thatcher and company had been too thorough. Nothing Simonsen wanted had been left behind. Not even so much as a tooth.

The chopper banked again, following the riverbed. Sam let go of Ian's hand, slapping her shirt pockets, then pant pockets. The tooth. Jon had given her his tooth.

Her palm slapped down on a lump in her pants pocket. She shoved her hand in, feeling the satisfying crown of a molar, and the shredded mush of the lab notes. She pulled them free, the digested paper falling through her fingers to the steel floor of the chopper, useless. But the tooth she held up, rotating it in her fingers. She shared a glance with Ian, thinking then of the other teeth and jawbones sent to Emmet in New York. For Emmet's sake she hoped there was at least one loose end not yet tied up by whatever hand was behind the actions of Thatcher and company. A tight knot in her chest gave her doubt, because she had witnessed their thoroughness. They left no loose ends.

A sound, a vengeful voice, rose over the cut of rotors and the wind. It stretched on into a whistle, then a defiant scream. Instead of a wracking stab of terror, a calm surprise settled over her. Her nerves were too calloused, fried. There was no surprise in Ian's eyes. He knew it too had survived. And whatever had happened in those hours after the cable snapped sending them down into the Hoh was surely playing out again in his head. She saw it in his face, the twitch of small muscles around his mouth. Then the scream faded into the rotors, and Ian blinked the nightmare from his eyes.

Simonsen was staring at them both from the front seat, looking more unsettled by the moment. The man in helmet and headphones was leaning out his side of the chopper, staring out on the fresh carpet of endless evergreen and thickening mist.

"What in heaven's name was that?"

Sam massaged the tooth between her fingers, feeling the bone, the weight, the truth. He wouldn't believe her if she told him.

Never doubt that a small group of thoughtful citizens can change the world. Indeed, it is the only thing that ever has.
—Margaret Mead

Monticello
May 7
9:28 AM

Aidan Thwaite checked his watch. Twenty-eight minutes late. Secretary Mason was not coming. And no matter how much he wished the secretary were just being rude, the appointment having slipped his mind and that he would barrel through the front doors any minute panting with excuses on his breath, the truth appeared to be far worse. Secretary Mason was dead of a suicide.

At least that's what Thwaite had gleaned from eavesdropping on the two senators' frantic cell phone conversations over the past five minutes. They seemed to have also learned of a very recent and mysterious death involving a Dr. Emmet Strauss. Though the connection between the two had eluded him.

Across the table, inside the small conference room adjacent to the parlor, the two senators paced in opposing directions, phones still at their ears, making call after call. The opened FedEx package lay in the center of the oak table handcrafted from a sketch by Jefferson himself. And spread out atop the often-polished surface were the package's contents: a handwritten note from the secretary, a typed proposal, a letter of obvious date sheathed inside the finest archiving material available, and three leather-bound field journals—one of them still lying open to its last few pages.

The senators had been wary upon arrival, skittish fawns among a pack of wolves, itching with impatience as the minutes came and went without a sign of the host. Only to then change into the curious political weasels they were when the FedEx driver delivered a package addressed to the secretary himself. Thwaite had hoped they would have waited longer for the secretary to arrive before opening it, but he was well over his head. This, he realized with the opening of the package, was far beyond the issue of who had claim on these items, Monticello and thus himself, or some higher power. For a higher power and higher purpose were surely at work inside this humble room on this fine morning, a power cured over centuries of patience and brooding. The stuffy, Pinesol-tainted air was ripe with prophetic fulfillment. Thwaite glanced from the hump draped in white cloth at his feet and then at the senators pacing the carpet thin. This was big, and he was a fortunate witness to history in the present, unlike from his usual spectator's seat watching only the echoed ghosts of history come and gone. He was more than content to wait and watch.

Finally one and then the other stopped their pacing and hung up their phones. They stared at each other for a moment like hawks. The one senator, the one he believed to be Pratt, spoke first. "A suicide and a car accident on the same day, coincidence?"

The other, Smith, shook his head. "Not likely. And it's not a coincidence that so many of these names in here," he tapped a finger on the pages of the opened journals, "match those on our own list."

"Like Keyes."

"Exactly."

The look they shared confirmed all that Thwaite conjectured. These two men had been given a mandate from the past, a presidential order that spanned the centuries. They had just been given the keys to golden careers and reserved suites in the penthouse of American history. Their eyes danced with possibility, with full understanding of both the gift given and the responsibility it demanded.

"Then we better find this Dr. Russell. And fast. Before they do." The two senators weren't wasting any time.

Unlike Thwaite. He had been stalling for as long as he could. But the moment had come. It was time to part with the greatest discovery of his career. He cleared the nervous excitement from his throat as he reached down for the final surprise. "Excuse me, but I believe the secretary also wanted you to have this. It goes with the journals, specifically the one you're still missing. The one sent to Dr. Russell."

He set it on the oak with a solid *thunk*, and slowly removed the cloth with all the flair of a museum director unveiling its latest exhibit. The breathless gasp of the two senators was sudden but no less expected. Thwaite had done the very same when he had finally laid eyes on the skull. Incomprehensible in its size, commanding in its presence, the skull now sat center stage on the table, its years of slumber finally brought to rest. The facial structure, eerily familiar and yet otherworldly foreign, was certainly not that of a gorilla, or any primate Thwaite knew of. Jefferson couldn't have been more right to keep it from the American people. There would have been no understanding, no preservation then, only fear. Thwaite wondered if things would prove all that different now.

Chicago
May 9
9:10 AM

Honeymooning Hikers Missing in Olympics

FORKS—Searchers combed the area of the Hoh valley where the missing newly married couple of Cotton and Cheryl Jones were last believed to have camped. Their vehicle was found at the trailhead, and two backpacks were recovered from a logjam on the river. Authorities believe the two fell from a bridge that collapsed during a storm. The search for their bodies will continue for another forty-eight hours.

A chemical fire in a nearby National Park laboratory, killing all resident zoologists, is believed to be an accident and unrelated to the missing honeymooners.

Sam tossed the back section of yesterday's *Seattle Times* onto her crowded desk. Simmering, blistering beneath her skin, she could hardly restrain her anger. How easily the truth could be tainted, reworded, revised, until there was nothing left of it but a hollow husk that bore no resemblance to itself. She glanced at the precarious stack of mail on the corner of her desk. She looked away and stood, finding herself striding over to her window overlooking the campus. Folding her arms for comfort, she leaned against the glass and watched a dark sedan with tinted windows pull into her building's parking lot.

It had only been three days, so a wave of panic and paranoia washed over her in reflex. But she forced it down, breathing deeply and evenly. She was no longer a threat to them. All she had was a story, one that would surely not be deemed more credible than the fine journalism being reported in the *Times*, and of course Jon's tooth, to which they were ignorant. She slid a hand into a pocket in the front of her slacks and played the tooth through her fingers as two men in black suits stepped from the sedan and headed up the stairs leading to her building's entrance.

If only she'd arrived in New York sooner, then maybe she would still have a cause to be paranoid, and maybe Emmet would still be alive. Instead she had arrived only to find Emmet's workshop and office being packed up and hauled away, to find wires sticking out of the walls, twisted back on themselves for keeping, dust balls cowering and exposed in the corners, and his old tattered chair and chipped desk standing alone as testimony to the truth. That Emmet had received Jon's crate, had opened it, and that he and the bones had been swept away like every other bit of evidence that fell like crumbs to the floor. The lie she had been told, though she was sure the museum had believed it to be the truth, was that

Emmet had fallen asleep at the wheel and driven into the sound—and the bones, she presumed, had gone with him, because they were nowhere to be found. "Coincidentally," Ms. Kingston had suffered some equally tragic fate the very same day.

Needless to say their exhibit had been canceled, and by now George had no doubt been carted off into a dark, corner basement somewhere to be forgotten, which was probably for the best. He may have been a work of art, but he was all wrong.

Watching the students mill about the campus, frantic in their efforts to squeeze more time into the day, Sam felt again her father's cool, frail hand in hers. Saw again his shadowed gaze. Smelled the death stealing him away even as she had sat at his side two days past, alone in the room with only her mother as silent company. He had been beyond speech, beyond anything more than keeping his rasping breath moving in and out. A tear escaped her eyelashes, rolled down her cheek. At least she had said good-bye, had been there to reaffirm their love before he passed. He died knowing she was his daughter, heart and soul, and there was nothing more she could have hoped for. When she saw him next, at his funeral, she would see his body that had been left behind, but she would know he was standing there with her, full-faced with a dark head of hair. He would always be with her now, as much a part of her as her own beating heart. No distance or span of time could ever separate them again.

Standing silent another moment at the window, mourning the loss of her father, Jon, and too many others, she finally straightened with resolve, wiped her eyes, and committed to getting on with it. The business of her life.

She stepped back to her desk, eyeing the stack of mail with acceptance. The time had come.

She began sorting through the junk and had gone through half the stack before she came to it. A business-size envelope from her doctor's office. Resting beneath it, though, was a FedEx package with a return address of Washington, D.C. Her curiosity too strong and her habit of avoiding bad news not yet fully broken, she set the business envelope aside and instead opened the package.

Out slid a book, apparently sent anonymously. There was no accompanying letter. Not being a history professor, it took a moment or two to grasp what she held in her hands, even despite the title on the weathered leather cover. It was a journal. Meriwether Lewis's journal.

She glanced up at the anonymous FedEx envelope and thought of the last time she had received such a mystery in the mail. "Oh, not again."

But there was nothing to lose, so she opened the journal and quickly noticed a separate sheet of paper peeking out near the back. She flipped to that page and pulled out the sheet. Handwritten on it was a date and time that had already come and gone, and a place—Monticello. Below that was written two names and a single phone number. The names bore the title of senator. Shrugging, she glanced down at the opened page in the journal—and nearly fell from her chair.

There, staring up at her from the page, was a brilliantly hand-sketched image of a primate skull that was nearly identical to those Emmet had crafted in the development of George. Her heart skipped a beat as she jumped to the one of many available conclusions that most answered her hopes and prayers, that this was a message, a means of establishing contact, by someone on the inside. Someone ready to do battle.

A knock came from her open office door, startling her from her trance. In the instant it took for her to look up in reply, her paranoia had flared in all its intensity reminding her of the government-issue sedan and two black suits.

Agent Barnett rapped his knuckle solidly on Dr. Russell's open office door to politely get her attention without giving her a start. Judging by the expression on her face as she looked up from her desk, he had instead done just that, if not more. She looked ready to pounce or even leap from the window in flight. Rushing to calm her, he extended his badge and introduced themselves with a smile. "Dr. Russell, I presume. We're Agents Barnett and Terhar of the FBI."

Her expression softened slightly into confusion and then almost into that of understanding. She was holding a leather-bound book and an opened FedEx envelope lay on her desk. It appeared their operation was off to a good start.

Her cell phone rang as she was about to speak. She picked it up from her desk, no doubt checking the caller ID. She gave them both a smile of her own. "Excuse me for a minute."

The speaker on the phone was strong enough for Agent Barnett to catch both sides of the conversation.

"Ian, thank God it's you."

"The search is being called off, Sam. They didn't find Jon's body."

"I know. I read the paper."

The man's voice became muffled, something urgent, something about getting a signal.

Dr. Russell pressed a finger into her other ear. "Ian, what was that?"

"I said, I located Specimen A. I got a fix on its signal. And it's moved outside the park. How soon can you catch a flight?"

She looked up at them both, then specifically at him.

Agent Barnett smiled again. "Plane's fueled and awaiting your arrival."

Science is to be used as a tool not a dogma, to distinguish for us what is possible from what is not so that we may not fall prey to the conspiracy within our own minds.
—Samantha Russell

View Top Development
May 10
2:46 AM

The wipers slapped back and forth over the windshield of his cruiser, rain blurring the glass faster than the view into the night could be reclaimed. The yellow glow from the vehicle's caution lights revealed only a hint of the freshly poured blacktop and skeleton-framed homes. The beating on the roof of the car and that of his own heart nearly prevented Officer Fairfax from hearing Dr. Russell's voice through his cell phone.

"Are you sure about the tracks?"

Water dripped from the wet hair clinging to his forehead as he watched the night for the first sign of approach, picturing the hourglass-shaped, five-toed impressions in the mud. The cold drops on his forehead sent a shiver across his back. "They're just like you described, and like nothing I've ever seen. And there are no witnesses, at least none that were alive when I arrived."

The tension in her voice was crystal clear, even if her words were not. "A body count? How many?"

A shadow stirred off to his left, near the trees. He squinted through the driver-side glass, bringing his weapon up, pressing the barrel to the window. Twenty years on the beat, and the dark had never played tricks with him. But then he had never seen bodies like these. Every instinct earned over those years told him to forget all this and just call for backup. "Three, maybe more. I hustled back to the cruiser to call as soon as I found the tracks."

"Good. Then stay put. And remember, do not contact anyone else until we get there."

Against every ingrained and trained bone in his body, he complied. "Understood. I'll wait for you at my patrol car." He pressed the END button and tossed the phone onto the passenger seat, then grabbed his flashlight from his lap, keeping his thumb ready on the switch.

Rain pounded the metal overhead. The wipers swished back and forth. His rapid breath fogged the glass.

He couldn't hear or see a thing.

The agents moved as one down the hall within the Department of Interior building. They slowed and finally came to a silent stop outside the door to the office of the Director of the National Park Service, Frank H. Keyes. Dressed in black combat gear, Kevlar vests, and armed with a search warrant, they didn't bother knocking. The lock resisted for a split second and then they were rushing inside, keeping their disciplined formation while calling out, "FBI. We have a warrant."

But there was no one to resist their unwelcome entrance, no one to challenge their aggressive stances with weapons held in firing position.

They turned on the lights at the switch, the sputter of the bulbs sounding like the tiny, frantic legs of roaches scurrying into the shadows. The office was empty, save for a letter of resignation on the bare floor.

Turning to leave, they filed through the open door, the last pausing with his black-gloved finger on the switch. And then he, too, filed out, leaving the light on in warning to the roaches not to return.

The beams from the Tahoe's headlights cut the dark and rain, flashing over the thick walls of trees and ferns lining the winding road. If Sam didn't know better, she could easily believe they were on a backcountry road climbing a remote mountain pass rather than driving through a new residential development that, like so many in the West, had sprouted like a weed on the landscape.

The Tahoe tilted hard to the left as Ian took the next bend without touching the brakes. Cloaked from the weather and night, the vehicle raced them between the spectral trees looming overhead, carrying them ever closer to their destination and back into the nightmare. Equipment shifted in the rear cargo bay, impatient in its wait to be put into action. The FBI had been more than generous, providing the best the taxpayers' money could buy, even throwing in Agents Barnett and Terhar, sitting in the back seats holding onto the vehicle's safety handles as Ian took yet another turn without braking. The best part had been obtaining access to local law enforcement, such as good old Officer Fairfax.

Lights blinked ahead, skimming through the cedars, blinding her when a truck burst around the corner. The Tahoe shook as Ian swerved onto the shoulder. Stacks of naked, fresh lumber flashed in their headlights. A sign on the rear of the truck's trailer read: SUTHERLAND LUMBER—STEWARDS OF AMERICA'S FORESTS

The truck rumbled into the night, leaving them once again alone with the banter of the rain and the hum of the Tahoe's engine. This close to the park's borders and Sam couldn't help but connect the logging truck with the clear-cut scar in the trees they had crossed three nights ago.

Connecting the dots. It was what no one had yet done, and what the public had proved incapable of doing. That is until now. The news had reported FBI raids on many governmental agencies and private corporations. The purpose of the raids had not been reported, but Sam was certain they were connected in some way with whoever had anonymously sent her Lewis's journal, and she didn't believe it a coincidence that two of the firms named in the news were Prescott's and Sutherland's. The final dot yet to be connected, though, was that of a type specimen. A flesh and bone body. Without it the cure and the species that carried it would be lost with the permanence of extinction. Man was not and never would be a creative force within nature. Humans were merely an end, not a means. This new species was proof of that. Man had failed to create a cure to cancer, but they might find one already in existence within its genes.

The jagged edges of the opened envelope from her doctor's office peeked up at her from the pocket in the passenger-side door. The fate of her family tree had finally caught up with her, had been forced to travel by way of the U.S. Postal Service. The news had not come as a surprise. She was, after all, her father's daughter, in life and now in disease. But her fate need not be the same as his and all the others who came before him. As long as humans didn't completely sever their umbilical cord with Mother Nature there would always be hope.

She looked at Ian, his eyes reading the road as he careened the Tahoe ever higher and closer. The wounds of three nights past were evident in his posture. The tight lift of his shoulder. The one leg kept as straight as possible beneath the wheel. The raw scabs on his cheeks and forehead lit by the faint illumination of the console. But he was alive, and would be her strength in fighting the disease, once she told him. Tonight, though, they both needed clear heads, uncluttered by selfish emotions and personal fears.

Unknowingly, she had slipped the tooth, Jon's tooth, from a pocket in her black flak jacket. It rolled smoothly in her fingers. She felt the ridges, knew them now by memory. She checked the luminescent face of her watch. Eight minutes since the call from Officer Fairfax. The wipers swept across the glass on high, vainly fighting the relentless rain. She estimated how long before the trail was too cold, how long before they were too late. The molar rolled over her fingertips to her thumb and back to her pinky. If there were in fact a body count, then indeed they were already too late.

Ian swung the Tahoe off the two-lane road and through a well-manicured entrance into a brand new housing development. Large, brass letters fastened into a granite boulder situated among the rhododendrons and blossoming hydrangeas welcomed them to View Top. The unpainted blacktop led them down row after row of freshly poured foundations, unfinished frame walls, and unlandscaped bare yards. The once-virgin forest stood haunting beyond the range of headlights, the ground from the road to the trees raw and uneven from the recent clearing. Mounds of stumps, roots, and forest debris hunkered in the dark as they passed, hiding any beast of evil or good that might be out this night. The weight of her sidearm comforted her, as best as anything could.

The faint yellow caution lights of a parked car seeped through the rain. Sam stopped fingering the tooth, pressing the ridges into her palm. Ian rolled the Tahoe to a slow, quiet stop behind the black and white State Trooper's cruiser. Exhaust from the cruiser's tailpipe faded in the breeze, and the caution lights went out. This was it. She was back in harm's way. The sick and almost familiar warmth spread beneath her clothes.

The driver-side door opened and a lanky frame she took to be that of Officer Fairfax stepped into the night's fury. He waved a light at them over the cruiser's roof. Ian killed the headlights, washing the view through the windshield in an inky, silent black. He reached over, gave her hand a squeeze. "You don't have to leave the car, you know."

She returned his squeeze. "Yes I do." She backed it up with a smile and then slipped the tooth into a thigh pocket of her black cargo pants and opened the door. She heard Agent Barnett make on offhand remark to his partner as they opened their doors. Something about no one giving him the option to stay in the car.

Rain swooped down on her as she stepped into a cold puddle that rose to the ankle of her boot. She tugged the bill of her cap lower, eased the door closed and strode to the rear of the Tahoe. Her hands were anxious with adrenaline as she opened the rear bay doors and began gearing up. She shoved her goggles inside her pack, slipped it over her shoulder, then grabbed a light and closed the doors with the barest of a click. The agents were staring at her with big grins. "What?"

Ian slapped them both on the shoulder. "Easy, mates. She's taken."

Officer Fairfax waited next to his car, his pistol in hand and his face far too white. Sam sucked in a breath.

"I've been here about eighteen minutes, but the report of gunshots came in closer to thirty." He swung the lance of his light behind him, beyond the naked, framed walls of an unfinished middle-class mansion. "The tracks and the bodies are up there."

Ian limped beside her as they followed the officer up and around the home. Ian wore his goggles on his forehead, his rifle strapped over his shoulder, his light playing the dark ahead of them. Sam gripped the cool iron of her sidearm tighter, her finger reluctantly tapping the trigger guard.

She scanned the remnant trees with her light as they came behind the home. Two saplings nearest the foundation had been snapped at their tops like twigs.

She glanced at Ian, the anxious adrenaline advancing from her hands to every corner of her being. Ian nodded that he saw them too.

Officer Fairfax had stopped, was shining his light on the ground. Sam kept her light from his face, letting him maintain his private struggle with his fear.

Lying in the mud was a body, face up, or was it face down? A sourness squirmed up her throat from her stomach. The man's eyes were open, his face smeared with mud, yet Sam also saw his back, the pools of rain collecting on the shoulders of his black combat jacket. His neck had been snapped, his head twisted one hundred eighty degrees. A high-caliber rifle kept him company in the mud. He was no innocent bystander. He was one of *them*. She gave him not another second's thought as she roamed her light about the soon-to-be yard.

Officer Fairfax motioned to the nearest stud wall of the home. "And there's this one, and then one at the back of the yard by the trees."

Agent Terhar panned his light over the studs. Fifteen feet up, a second body dangled from a stained and splintered two-by-four inside the home. Darker stains ran down the adjacent lumber. A hole had been torn through the outside wall as the body had been thrown up and through. Agent Barnett let out a soft whistle of amazement.

Ian mourned this man for as long as she had the first. "Where are the tracks?"

"Everywhere, it seems, but the clearest are back by the third body."

She turned from the house, swallowing down another reflexive mouthful of bile, and followed the officer. The wind shifted, bringing the stench of the area full in her face. She swallowed it down, too.

Officer Fairfax stopped after only a few strides and pointed with his light. His message was received loud and clear: this was as far as he went. Sam continued past, Ian and the two agents following behind her. Her light soon caught the third body lying near the forest's edge. Then she saw the pig, gutted and chained to a tree stump. Not the usual bait, but it must have worked. The face and hair of the dead man were Native American. Like Sixen, this Indian guide never received his due pay either.

She quickly noted the three, maybe four, clear, deep tracks, but the rain was doing its best to wash them clean. There were probably dozens more that had already been lost.

Two of the tracks headed into the brush, along a thin game trail. She followed them, pushing into the wet needles, the rain plummeting down through the trees around her. Bumps rose and hairs tingled on the back of her neck when she didn't hear Ian follow. He was caught behind by a question from Officer Fairfax.

Her .357 out, her flashlight crossed beneath it, she cleared through the blinding green in front of her until she came to stand on a ledge overlooking the mass of lights of the lower and older phase of the development that spread up the hillside into the forest like an urban cancer. She thought of her father. One thought led to the other, and always would.

Connect the dots.

She stepped to the lip of the ledge, aiming her light and .357 into the ferns and brush covering the descent back into the trees. Dropping into a crouch, she studied the ground at the bottom of the ten-foot drop. Two long, deep gashes in the ground confirmed she was still on his trail. Specimen A. The wounded rogue.

Connect the dots. Make the public believe. Was it even possible? She didn't even believe, and she had lived it.

The swish of Ian and the agents coming down the trail to join her soothed her pulse and tender nerves. *Beep…beep…*Ian had turned on his GPS receiver.

She took a long breath as if it might be her last. Then she stood to pull her goggles from her pack and lower them over her eyes, blotting out the view of the black stretch of unbroken forest that led straight to the beckoning bedroom and kitchen lights of the unsuspecting homes below.

About the Author

Eric Penz is a partner in an insurance and financial services agency. He earned his bachelor of science degree in environmental biology from Eastern Washington University in 1995. His postgraduate work was done at the University of Washington where he completed a two-year literary program in commercial fiction. Between managing his clients' portfolios and writing, he spends his spare time as an amateur adventure athlete. He and his wife and their two boys make their home in Issaquah, Wash.

To continue the hunt for the mythic Sasquatch, visit www.cryptid.com.

978-0-595-67305-6
0-595-67305-8

Printed in the United States
42981LVS00007B/13

9 780595 673056